I0576587

Thomas Erskine

Letters of Thomas Erskine of Linlathen

Thomas Erskine

Letters of Thomas Erskine of Linlathen

ISBN/EAN: 9783337133955

Printed in Europe, USA, Canada, Australia, Japan

Cover: Foto ©Raphael Reischuk / pixelio.de

More available books at **www.hansebooks.com**

LETTERS OF

THOMAS ERSKINE

OF LINLATHEN

Edinburgh: Printed by Thomas and Archibald Constable,

FOR

DAVID DOUGLAS.

LONDON . .	HAMILTON, ADAMS, AND CO.
CAMBRIDGE .	MACMILLAN AND CO.
GLASGOW	JAMES MACLEHOSE.

Letters of

THOMAS ERSKINE

OF LINLATHEN

FROM 1800 TILL 1840

Edited by

WILLIAM HANNA, D.D.

AUTHOR OF ' MEMOIRS OF DR. CHALMERS,' ETC.

G. P. PUTNAM'S SONS

FOURTH AVENUE AND TWENTY-THIRD STREET

NEW YORK

1877

PREFACE.

The late Bishop Ewing, who knew Mr. Erskine intimately, has said, "Should any one attempt to write the life of Mr. Erskine, the difficulty must ever present itself to him that what he has to depict is spirit and not matter, that he has to convey light, to represent sound—an almost insuperable difficulty. Perhaps it can only in a measure be overcome by giving his very words, his thoughts, as they came fresh from his heart, in letters, memoranda, and such like materials."[1] This is what the Editor of these volumes has attempted; confining himself to the task of arranging Mr. Erskine's letters in such order, giving such information, when necessary, as to the persons addressed, and interlacing them occasionally with such illustrative narrative, that by its setting the mirror may be made to reflect, as clearly and fully as possible, the pure bright image of one who moved so lovingly and attractively among his fellow-men, who walked so closely and constantly with God.

[1] *Present Day Papers,* Third Series, p. 11.

As the letters from 1840 downwards are already in the press, to be presented to the public in a separate volume, the Editor takes this opportunity of requesting those who may have any letters from Mr. Erskine, or any information which it may seem desirable he should possess, to communicate with him as soon as convenient.

16 Magdala Crescent,
    Edinburgh, 1*st March* 1877.

CONTENTS.

APPENDIX.

LETTERS OF THOMAS ERSKINE.

CHAPTER I.

Ancestry and Earlier Years.

THE great-grandfather of Thomas Erskine was the Honourable Colonel John Erskine of Carnock, great-great-grandson of the distinguished Earl of Mar, the wise Regent of Scotland, and the faithful counsellor of King James VI. Driven, like his elder brother, the third Lord Cardross,[1] into exile under the reign of the last of the Stuarts, Colonel Erskine repaired to The Hague, took part in the expedition of the Prince of Orange into England, and largely contributed to the settlement of the new government in Scotland. One thing however interfered with the public recognition of his services. Imagining that he would thereby be held as approving of the constitution of the Church of England and the manner of its connection with the State, he could not be persuaded to take the oaths of allegiance and abjuration. Surprised at not finding Colonel Erskine's name in a list which he had asked his confidential advisers to present to him of those friends in Scotland entitled to recognition and reward, King William inquired, and was told the reason of the omission. "It may be so," was the King's reply, "but I know

---

[1] See Appendix, No. I. p. 363.

A

Lieutenant-Colonel Erskine to be a firmer friend to the
Government than many of those who have taken that
oath." Fifty years' faithful discharge of all the duties of
a good and loyal subject proved that the King's judgment
was correct. In the last Scottish Parliament he represented the town of Stirling; in 1707 had a seat in
the United Parliament of Great Britain; and, at the
general election in the following year, was chosen as
member for the Stirling district of burghs. There was,
however, another assembly in which he found a more
congenial sphere of public usefulness. For the long
period of upwards of forty years he was returned annually
by the Presbytery of Dunfermline, within whose bounds
his estate of Carnock lay, as one of their representatives to
the General Assembly of the Church of Scotland.

Throughout this period he was on terms of close and
affectionate friendship with Wodrow the historian, and the
published correspondence of that indefatigable collector
and narrator fully informs us of the influential part taken
by him in all the affairs of the Church. Writing to one
of his correspondents, Dr. Coleman of Boston, Wodrow
says, "In one of mine to Dr. Mather, I said somewhat of
worthy Colonel Erskine, but very far below what I might
and ought to have said of that excellent gentleman. You
are pleased to make so much of the little that I dropt,
that there is no room for me to add anything. I shall
only do him the justice to say that the care of all the
churches is upon him, if upon any since the apostles'
days."[1] It was one of the many tokens of the confidence
which the Church of Scotland reposed in him, that when,
in 1735, three special Commissioners were despatched to
London to urge upon the Crown and Government the
rescinding of the Act of 1712, which restored the rights of

[1] Wodrow Correspondence, vol. ii. p. 286.

Patrons, he was one of the three—the single layman—selected to take part in this important mission.

Universally respected as he was, the Black Colonel (so called from his complexion, and to distinguish him from his nephew, the White Colonel) had his own peculiarities. In those days the road from Edinburgh to Queensferry—the one always taken by the Colonel on his way to and from the capital—ran through the estate of Barnton. Without regard either to the rights or convenience of the public, the proprietor of that estate got the road diverted from its old course, and he enclosed by a wall the park through a part of which it had passed. Whenever in coming and going they came up to this wall, the Colonel and his servant regularly dismounted, made a gap through it at either end, and kept to the old road. Without remonstrance or resistance the proprietor wisely and quietly had the gaps built up again.

During the last ten years of his life [1] Colonel Erskine was afflicted with asthma. One day, when he was suffering from an attack which put a fresh edge upon a temper naturally somewhat inclined to irritability, fires for burning kelp had been kindled under authority of the magistrates upon the beach of the Firth of Forth, which lay immediately below his house at Culross. Imagining that the smoke aggravated his asthma, the Colonel sent down peremptory orders that the fires should be put out. They were not obeyed. Unable to walk, he at once called for his horse, drew his sword, and handed it to his grandson, a youth of fourteen, then living with him. Down through the steep street of the village they went, determined with their own hands to extinguish the fires. The magistrates were too quick and too many for them.

---

[1] He died at Edinburgh on the 13th of January 1743, in the eighty-second year of his age.

Gathering their retainers, they surrounded the Colonel and his grandson, and took them prisoners. The falseness and awkwardness of the position revealed themselves to him in a moment. Another fire, that of his own quick passion, was at once extinguished. "This is all nonsense," he said to the magistrates; "we are all in the wrong; come along to the inn, and let us dine together and forget this folly." The invitation was as promptly accepted as it had been given, the best dinner the innkeeper could produce was supplied, and the evening spent in perfect good-humour. The youth who upon this occasion filled the somewhat ludicrous position of sword-bearer, marching before his grandfather, was no other than Dr. John Erskine, who afterwards became the eminent divine, and whose father, the Colonel's eldest son,[1] was then practising at the bar in Edinburgh.

This son in his character and life was a singular contrast to his father. Thoughtful, retiring, diffident, taking little interest in public matters, whether of Church or State, he gave himself to the study of law, and was called to the Scottish bar in 1719, in his twenty-third year. For eighteen years he practised in his profession without particularly distinguishing himself, the feebleness of his voice and his constitutional modesty keeping him from pleading much in open Court. He was however laying deep the foundations of that knowledge which led to his appointment in 1737 as Professor of Scottish Law in the University of Edinburgh. For twenty-eight years he taught with pre-eminent ability and success, drawing around him a larger number of students than had ever previously attended such a class. In 1754 he published

---

[1] Colonel Erskine was four times married: first, to a daughter of Mure of Caldwell, without issue; second, to a daughter of Dundas of Kincavel, by whom he had four sons and a daughter; third, to a daughter of Stirling of Keir, without issue; and fourth, to a daughter of Stuart of Dunearn, by whom he had one son.

his *Principles of the Law of Scotland*, intended chiefly as a text-book for the use of his students. In 1765 he resigned his Professorship and retired to Cardross, an estate lying near the Lake of Menteith, originally belonging to his ancestors, the Lords Cardross (from which indeed they had taken the title), that for a generation or two had been alienated from the family, which he had purchased and restored to it. Here for the last three years of his life he occupied himself in perfecting *The Institutes of the Law of Scotland*, a work which for a hundred years has kept its place of eminence and authority as one of the ablest expositions in theory and practice of the Law of Scotland, and has earned for its author the well-merited title of the "Blackstone of Scottish Jurisprudence."[1]

The Professor's only child by his first wife,—a daughter of the Hon. James Melville of Balgarvie,[2] was Dr. John Erskine, of whose life and writings so full an account has been given by Sir Henry Moncreiff. For fifty years Dr. Erskine was the centre of a very large religious circle— having among his correspondents Bishops Warburton and Hurd in England, Jonathan Edwards and Dr. Cotton Mather in America, and many distinguished divines of the Continent, in whose labours and their results he took so lively an interest, that in his sixtieth year he acquired the Dutch and German languages, then little known in Scotland. More, perhaps, than any other individual, he contributed to whatever progress theological literature made in Scotland during the last half of the eighteenth century. But it was chiefly as a devout Christian, a devoted pastor, and a zealous ecclesiastic, that he was known. In the latter character he acted for many years as the leader of the popular or

---

[1] John Erskine died at Cardross on the 1st of March 1768, in the seventy-third year of his age.

[2] Brother of the second Earl of Leven and third of Melville.

Evangelical party in the Church of Scotland. The friendly
and affectionate intercourse which he through life main-
tained with the leader of the opposite party, Dr. Robertson
the historian, tells what the spirit was in which that leader-
ship was conducted. For twenty-three years they were
associated as colleagues in the pastoral charge of the church
and parish of the Greyfriars in Edinburgh. They were
men of opposite principles, sentiments, and pursuits, yet
they lived in unbroken harmony. Of Dr. Erskine's sermon
on the death of Dr. Robertson, Dugald Stewart has said
that "it would be difficult to say whether it reflected
greater honour on the character of the writer or of him
whom it commemorates." Sir Harry's full-length portrait
of Dr. Erskine is now looked at by few—its colours are
fading away; but so long as *Guy Mannering* survives, that
other picture, which Sir Walter has drawn of the form and
attitude and action of the aged minister in the pulpit of
Greyfriars, will be hanging in the world's galleries before
all eyes, and Pleydell's truthful testimony to Dr. Erskine's
character and worth be listened to.

The eldest son of the author of the *Institutes* by his
second marriage, with a daughter of Mr. Stirling of Keir,
was James, who succeeded to the estate of Cardross, and
who married a daughter of the Earl of Elgin. The second
son was David, who practised as a Writer to the Signet in
Edinburgh,—"allowed," says Sir Henry Moncreiff,[1] "by all
competent judges, to have been one of the ablest and most
honourable men whom his profession has ever produced."
His success corresponded with his ability and integrity,
one fruit of which was the purchase of the estate of
Linlathen, in the neighbourhood of Dundee, possessed now
by his grandson. From the family record the following
abstract is taken :—

[1] *Life and Writings of John Erskine, D.D.*, p. 11.

DAVID ERSKINE and ANN GRAHAM, married 29th April 1781.

JOHN, born 22d February   1782 ; died 3d August   1789.
WILLIAM, born 1st October   1783 ; died 30th May   1784.
ANN, born 4th September   1786 ; died 5th May   1804.
JAMES, born 2d November   1787 ; died 26th August 1816.
THOMAS, born 13th October   1788 ; died 20th March   1870.
CHRISTIAN, born 19th October 1789 ; died 1st December 1866.
DAVID, born 1st October   1791 ; died 23d March   1867.

Accompanied by his wife and his cousin, Miss Ann Erskine of Cardross—leaving his children in charge of their grandmother at Airth—the father of this family went to Italy in search of health, and died at Naples on the 5th April 1791. On her return from laying her husband in the grave there, Mrs. Erskine remained with her children for about a year at Airth, and it was there that a few months after her father's death her youngest daughter was born, to whom in consequence his name—David—was given, rather an unusual one for a female to bear. On leaving Airth, Linlathen was of course open for their residence, but Mrs. Erskine, for the children's education, preferred remaining in Edinburgh.

The first glimpse we get of Thomas is one given by himself. "I remember," he once said to the Dean of Westminster, "in 1793—I was then five years old—the immense impression produced by the death of Louis XVI. Bruce the traveller came in a snow-storm to call at the house where I was staying. Mrs. Henderson, the housekeeper, being asked who it was that had arrived—'Wha is it?' she exclaimed; 'why, wha should it be but Kinnaird, greetin' as if there werena a saunt on earth but himsel' and the King of France.'"

The place where Thomas was at this time living was Airth Castle, near to which Kinnaird House lay. Mrs. Graham of Airth was the only grandmother that he ever knew; and deep indeed must have been the impression which one in every way so remarkable made upon his childhood. He saw in her a striking variation from that type of strict Presbyterian piety which a long line of his paternal ancestry had exhibited, and of which a living and most attractive specimen had been before his eyes in that venerable uncle around whose knees from infancy he had played. His grandmother, Mrs. Graham of Airth (a Stirling of Ardoch), was an Episcopalian, and a Jacobite of the highest and purest type. For the Georges she never prayed. Every Sunday, at the hour when the bell of the parish church summoned her neighbours to the Presbyterian worship, she had the Episcopal Service read in her own dwelling, the windows of which looked into the churchyard. But there was no austerity either in her politics or her religion, and the spirit of a deep and gentle piety, in varying forms, appears to have spread among her daughters, of whom Mrs. David Erskine, Thomas's mother, was the eldest.

Mrs. Graham's second daughter, Mary, married John Stirling, Esq. of Kippendavie and Kippenross, whose home supplied no less than thirteen cousins to Thomas Erskine; one daughter of the family, Katherine, becoming the wife of his brother James, and another, the youngest daughter, Jane,[1] his own peculiar friend, whom he was accustomed in after life to associate with the Duchesse de Broglie as the two most remarkable women he had ever met. The only one of this family who survived Mr. Erskine was Captain James Stirling of Glentyan; who was not only his much loved friend through life, but was closely associated with him

---

[1] In her later life she lived much in Paris, and counted among her many friends there Ary Scheffer. In his "Christus Consolator," this eminent artist had presented in one of the figures his ideal of female beauty, and was greatly struck, on being first introduced to Miss Stirling, to find in her the almost exact embodiment of that ideal. She was introduced afterwards in many of his pictures.

in his religious history and love of art. In the days
of his boyhood, Thomas was often at Kippenross. One
can easily imagine how warm the welcome was that
greeted him—sympathy with his widowed mother giving
tenderness to his uncle's and aunt's embrace; bright and
happy groups of winning cousinhood gathering around
him, carrying him off to sport under the shadows of
Kippendavie's own noble trees, or perhaps to wander to
the old Cathedral of Dunblane, which lay quite near, and
to tread along the good Bishop's walk. Thirty years afterwards he writes, "I live at Albano, on the road to Rome.
The whole district is beautiful to the utmost wish, and full
of delicious shade from immense trees, chiefly evergreen
oaks, of which there is one as large as the Kippenross tree,
indeed much larger—thirty feet round at four feet from
the ground."

Other and stronger links than those of its loveliness bound
his heart to Kippenross. "I am at dear Kippenross," he
writes to his cousin Rachel on his return from Italy in 1828.
"It is a profound enjoyment to me, for its loveliness has
been mixed up with many of my earliest and most enduring impressions, with many joys and many sorrows, with
things of earth and things of heaven, and the sight of it
recalls them all and gives a freshness to memory, and
surrounds me anew with those who are dead or distant . . .
I need not speak to you about it, but there is a spell in it
on my spirit beyond what I have experienced from any
other spot on earth."

Our next glimpse of Thomas is in his seventh year.
Ann, his eldest sister, had a spinal affection. Her mother,
hearing that there was a person in Hinckley in Leicestershire who had effected many wonderful cures of that
disease, took her daughter there, and finding that in order
to accomplish her purpose she would have to remain in

England for some months, sent for James and Thomas.
Mr. and Mrs. Hay of Dunse Castle brought the boys up to
Leicestershire, taking with them a daughter of their own,
whom they left at Hinckley. This daughter, Miss Hay of
Kingston Grange, who is still living, writes to a friend
on 17th October 1876: "I lived a year in the family of
Mr. Erskine's dear mother, and was treated like one of her
own children. I was between seven and eight years old
when I went, and Mr. Erskine six months younger, and to
us that year seemed an age, and laid the foundation of a
life-long friendship." Miss Hay's mother was one of an
older group of cousins than those of Kippenross; the
children of that uncle of Cardross and Lady Christian his
wife, spoken of with so much veneration in the following
letters. Their eldest daughter (Janet) married Mr. Hay
of Dunse Castle, and their fourth daughter (Matilda) Mr.
Graham of Gartur, a place in the neighbourhood of Stirling.
Marion (Manie) and Rachel were two unmarried daughters;
the latter, the "dear dear cousin Rachel," to whom the
longest, and in some respects most interesting series, of
letters in these volumes was addressed.

Writing from Gartur in 1825, Mr. Erskine says, "I am
going to Cardross to-day; I have not been there for
nearly twenty years, but I passed some part of my childhood there, and it looks beautiful and venerable to my
memory. "I remember," he says twelve years later, in
1837, "the last vacation that James and I spent at Cardross with our little dog Jemmy. I had not been well, and
we came out before the regular time; they were cutting
the lawn for hay, and I remember my uncle and aunt
walking among the hay-makers, looking so kind and so
venerable, and so much loved and so much honoured."
"What are you doing?" he writes from Paris to dear
cousin Rachel in 1838. "Enjoying lovely Cardross, fair

and noble Cardross, with its grave square tower, and its trees, under which our fathers' fathers have played, and its beautiful extent of grass, and its seclusion, and its simple peasantry." Death had removed Mrs. Hay, and Rachel writes to him that her sister Mrs. Graham was dying at Gartur, when in 1839 he writes from Geneva to his sister : " Our three cousins have a place to themselves in my mind, quite apart from all other people ; they are connected with my early remembrance of their father and mother, and of Cardross, which is the purest remembrance that I have."

From Hinckley the following letter, the earliest existing specimen of Thomas's writing, was sent to his grandmother at Airth :—

MY DEAR GRANDMAMMA,—I hope you and aunt Jane are well. Mamma has heard from aunt M'Dowall of my dear sister. I never can forget Airth and all the large gardens, and our little gardens which you were so good as to give us. I hope old Body[1] is well, and Mrs. Henderson, and John Campbell,[2] and I hope old nurse is better. I had almost forgotten to mention the good wife of the whole, and her little girl. Have you good luck with the horses, cows, sheep, and poultry ? I read a great many entertaining and instructive books, of which I am very fond.[3] I get Latin with brother James. In my accounts I am gotten into division, and I hope I shall soon write better. Mamma informs me that my sisters are gone to Airth. I beg my love to them. I likewise beg my duty and love to aunt Jane.—I am, my dear Grandmamma, your dutiful and affectionate grandson, THOS. ERSKINE.

On returning from Hinckley to Edinburgh, Thomas and his brother were sent to the High School, then under the

---

[1] The henwife.

[2] The butler—an old eccentric domestic,—the hero of the story give Dean Ramsay, in his *Reminiscences*, p. 85, 20th Edition.

[3] A special favourite was Knolles' *History of the Turks*.

Rectorship of Dr. Adam. Of their course and progress there nothing is now known. Two memories of his school-boy days Thomas carried with him, vivid to the close of life—one of profound regard for, and tender sympathy with, the Rector; the other of recoil and indignation at the sufferings he had seen inflicted by one of the Masters —the Willie of " the peck o' maut "—who, as Sir Walter tells us, was "inhumanly cruel to the boys under his charge."

In 1802 the boys were sent to a school at Durham. The two following letters written by Thomas at this time have been preserved :—

DURHAM, *Sept.* 25, 1802.

MY DEAR SISTER CHRISTIAN,—I am ashamed of having been so long of answering your kind letter. I shall begin by thanking you sincerely. I was extremely sorry for poor Marion Dalrymple's death. I expect to see Mr. Sandilands soon now. I was very happy to see he had so many passengers in his ship. I hope all your friends at Walkinshaw are well, particularly my dear uncle and aunt M'Dowall. Do you know, Christian, Davie never sent her love or compliments to me in her letter to James, and only mentions my name once, and then it is squeezed up in a small hole between two lines, and then she says that all sent love to Tom, but never herself. Tell her that I am prodigiously angry at her, and that I cannot be appeased unless she write me a letter on her birthday. I'll write one to her on that day perhaps, but don't tell her so, for she would think it no great matter; now remember and scold her as she deserves. We have had excellent weather here for a good time, and all the crops are in almost. Mr. Britton has gotten a little white pony, which is constantly going about the doors. The little girl Isabella is an extraordinary sort of animal. The country about Durham is the most beautiful place almost I ever saw, the river is so fine, and the steep banks are so splendidly fringed over with trees. The Cathedral, or, as it is here always called, the Abbey, is indeed a remarkably fine building; there are eight bells in it, of which the largest, which is called Bow Bell, contains three when turned up. The town is a dirty hole in general. Tell Bess that James sends his love to his dear Bess in answer to her affectionate address; so do I. We both join in love to all our friends at Walkinshaw, viz., uncle and aunt, Davie, Anny, Dowly, and all the rest of our cousins. Remember us both kindly to Miss Porteous.[1] If ever you see any of our friends, though not mentioned in the above list, remember us kindly to them. And now, my dear sister, farewell. May God keep you in his fear, and preserve you from all perils both of body and soul, and I remain your affectionate brother,

THOMAS ERSKINE.

N.B.—The above epistle was written in darkness, so you will excuse all defects.

DURHAM, 19*th October* 1802.

MY DEAREST CHRISTIAN,—I wish you many happy returns of the 19th. I beg your pardon for not having one ready for you (one signifies letter), but you know that there are such things as forgets and delays in this world, and I must own that I forgot to do it till your letter reminded me of my duty; but I hope that when you remember that you yourself delayed a little you will forgive it. When I saw the direction I thought it was from Ann; but I think differently in one point from you. You say that I need not care what my companions are since James is with me, for you know that it is necessary for me to be a great part of the day with them. Tell Annie that I am much obliged to her for her five lines, though I might think they were

---

[1] The governess.

from Jemmy the coachman, or the dog Flora, as well as
from her, as her name is not there, and theirs are. She
stops with " We have gotten a new garden, and it is coming
on "—, here she breaks off on a sudden. Tell her that I am
sorry for her fall, as well as for Willie's. You don't mention any of the rest of my cousins, so I suppose they are
well. Has George arrived the length of breeches yet?
You neither mention Mr. Kemp nor Miss Porteous in your
letter, which I think you might have done. 21st.—I had
not time to finish my letter before, so now I am going to
put the completing hand to it. I wish the next time you
write that you would inform me of your different studies
and employments, how you are coming on with your music,
and everything else, and how Davie is coming on in everything. I like the drawing very much ; I am to begin with
Indian ink next Saturday. I have only been doing horses,
cows, asses, goats, dogs, and such like, and faces, etc. How
are you coming on in your figures? 23d.—Christian, I
daresay you may have heard of my excellent aunt Lady
Hamilton's death,[1] but, however, we may be comforted
that she was for some time before this melancholy event
so weak and complaining that her death might rather be
looked upon as a blessing. We are taught in a certain
place that we should not mourn for our friends as those
without hope ; we should rather endeavour, by imitating
her many good qualities, to fit ourselves for that blessed
place where every tear is wiped from every eye ; where we
meet our friends never to part again. I know that Davie
will be very much affected. Tell her to dry her tears, and
to prepare herself for that place where we are assured all

---

[1] Margaret, sixth daughter of James Stirling of Keir, born 1720,
married 1750 Sir Hugh Hamilton of Rosehall, died 1802. An admirable
picture of this lady, taken by Sir Henry Raeburn near the close of her
life, was exhibited in Edinburgh in 1876 in the collection of Sir Henry's
portraits.

the faithful followers of Christ will live for ever and ever.
I have written to cousin Christy Lauriston, so I suppose
when she writes she will tell me particulars. I was prepared for this, for the last time I saw her, though I could
not positively foresee that it would be the very last time,
yet I thought it might. I hope I may have the great
pleasure of seeing my dear uncle Doctor Erskine again.[1] I
wonder how Miss Johnston (I mean Miss Sophy)[2] will bear
my aunt's death ; she will feel a great [*torn*] by this. Now
my dear Christy, farewell. May God bless you both, and
I remain, your very affectionate brother,

THOMAS ERSKINE.

P.S.—Give my kindest love to all my friends at Walkinshaw.

His mother's youngest sister had married D. H. Macdowall, Esq., and was residing with her family at Walkinshaw, near Paisley. Christian and Davie, Thomas's
younger sisters, were at the time living with them. Walkinshaw was indeed a cherished retreat for all the Erskines
in the days of their childhood ; their aunt there, one whose
bright and winning ways bound them lovingly to her.

Returning from Durham, Thomas entered as a student in
the University of Edinburgh. Of his life at College as little
can now be known as of his life at school. We know more
of his daily recreations than of his daily studies, it having
been his practice to walk every day to and from the top of
Arthur's Seat, a distance which he made it a point of accom-
plishing always within an hour. Having attended the
Law classes, and passed the necessary trials, he was admitted

---

[1] It is uncertain whether this hope was fulfilled. Dr. Erskine died at
his house in Lauriston Lane, Edinburgh, on the 19th January 1803 ; having
been born in 1721.

[2] Sophia, or, as she was called, Suff Johnston, one of the old-school
ladies described by Lord Cockburn. See *Memorials*, pp. 52-54, 3d edition,
1872.

a member of the Faculty of Advocates in 1810, and remained in Edinburghfor the next six years.

His mother's sister, Elizabeth, third daughter of Mr. Graham of Airth, had married James Dundas, Esq. of Ochtertyre. Throughout Mr. Erskine's life at college, and his attendance at the Parliament House, the two families lived within a few doors of each other, the Erskines in St. David Street, the Dundases in St. Andrew Square. Their intercourse was as affectionate as it was close and constant. His uncle's hospitality and his aunt's sparkling wit brought to the supper parties in St. Andrew Square many distinguished and agreeable visitors, among whom the young advocate found himself at home. With one of the younger sons of the family, George, Lord Manor, the daily intercourse of earlier years was in later life renewed, to Mr. Erskine's special gratification. Two only of the large family of the Dundases now survive, Sir David Dundas of Ochtertyre and Mrs. J. Stirling of Glentyan, of whom Mr. Erskine was wont to say that he could not remember the time when he did not love her.

The years during which he attended the Parliament House formed one of the most brilliant periods in the history of the Scottish Bar. Walter Scott was then daily to be seen sitting at the table as one of the Clerks of the Court of Session, wondering eyes fixed on him, as *Waverley, Guy Mannering, The Antiquary, The Tales of My Landlord*, appeared in quick succession, the mystery of their authorship gradually unfolding itself. The *Edinburgh Review*, established a few years before, was at the height of its popularity and power : Jeffrey, Cockburn, Fullerton, with all of whom our young advocate was on terms of closest friendship, now at the height of their fame as pleaders. His brother's marriage in 1811, and residence at Linlathen, removing from his side the influence hitherto the most potent, threw Thomas Erskine in his twenty-third year into the very heart of a society as peculiarly fitted to impress as he was open to the impression. One of the effects he has himself recorded. " I was brought up from my childhood," he says in the latest of his writings, " in the belief of the supernatural and miraculous in connection with religion, especially in connection · with the person and life and teaching of Jesus Christ, and like many in the present day, I came, in after life, to have misgivings as to the credibility of this wonderful history. But the patient study of the narrative and of its place in the history of the world, and the perception of a light in it which entirely satisfied my reason and my conscience, finally overcame these misgivings, and forced on me the conviction of its truth."[1]

Those misgivings came to him at the time of his close association with men, few of whom made any profession of a faith in Christianity. Other things beside patient study conspired to re-establish him in the faith of his childhood. His cousin, Patrick Stirling of Kippenross,[2] to whom he was much attached, was a few years his senior. After serving for a short time in the Peninsula as captain of the 14th Light Dragoons, he had married, the same year that Thomas Erskine was called to the Bar. When but thirty-three years of age a mortal malady fell upon him. He went to the south of England in vain. Death drew near, and he longed to see before he died, his youngest child, an only daughter, little more than a year old. Thomas

---

[1] *The Spiritual Order*, etc., pp. 82-3.

[2] In Dunblane Cathedral there is a marble tablet with the following inscription :—"Sacred to the memory of John Stirling of Kippendavie, and Patrick Stirling, his eldest son, who, ' with a lively hope of an inheritance incorruptible,' departed this life, A.D. 1816. Patrick at Hastings, 30th March, aged 33 ; John at Kippenross, 17th June, aged 73, and are interred in one grave in the family burying-place."

Erskine willingly undertook the task of conveying her. They reached Hastings in time for the dying father's wish to be gratified, and for such singular manifestations of trust and peace, and lively hope on his part, as carried home to his cousin's heart a profound impression at once of the power and preciousness of Christian faith. Not only was his own faith so fixed thereby as not again to falter,—for the first time a zeal to awaken a like faith in others was kindled. A short time afterwards another dear friend was on his death-bed, to whom he ventured to speak of that faith. His doing so was so promptly and keenly resented that he was instantly turned out of the room. But the word spoken had not been in vain. His dying friend relented, sent for him, and begged him to remain with him to the last, which he did. Then followed the death of his only brother James, of typhus fever, at Broadstairs. They had been close companions from infancy till 1805, when James joined the 41st Regiment, with which he served in Canada till 1808. He served afterwards as captain of the 87th Regiment, in the Walcheren Expedition, and retired in 1810. In 1811 he married his cousin Katherine Stirling of Kippenross, and went to reside at Linlathen. Five happy years were spent there. During those years Thomas was often with them. Four children were born, all of whom died within four days after birth. Looking back over fifty intervening years Thomas wrote afterwards to his friend Dr. Wylie of Carluke :—

There are few now living who knew Linlathen when *he* and she lived there ; but no one who was ever privileged to see it could forget it. I think my brother was the most remarkable man I ever knew. On looking back through a long vista of years, during which I have come in contact with many remarkable, unforgetable persons, he stands out

by himself, as one in whom worth of moral character,
manliness, truth, and perfect regard for the rights, interests,
and feelings of every human being, accomplished more in
producing the sentiment of veneration (I would even say)
than I have known produced by all the talents in the
world, accompanied even by the average amount of moral
endowment. I never knew a young man venerated except
himself.[1] He was only a year older than myself, and I
venerated him from my infancy; and dear Mrs. Erskine
was a most fitting wife for him. That upper world must
be a wonderful meeting-place—meeting in God.—Yours
ever truly,   T. ERSKINE.

Sir Harry Moncreiff, who must have known him well,
says of James Erskine, that " he died in the prime of life,
equally regretted for the good sense and affectionate
manners, and for the genuine piety and purity of mind,
which eminently distinguished him."[2]

It were vain now to attempt to estimate the kind and
extent of that moulding power which such an elder brother
must have exerted, and equally vain to estimate the depth
of the impression his death must have made. The only
letters connected with that event which have been preserved
are the following :—

Sept. 2d, 1816.

MY DEAR COUSIN,[3]—God's thoughts are not as our
thoughts, nor His ways as our ways. May He by His
Holy Spirit conform our wills unto His holy will.

---

[1] "This young man must have made a strong impression on others than
his own family, for, many years after his death, General Elphinston, our
Commander-in-chief in the Afghan war, on hearing Mr. Erskine's name,
asked if he were brother to Captain Erskine of such-and-such a regiment,
and, on being answered in the affirmative, said, ' He was the best soldier
and the best man I ever knew.' I shall never forget the voice in which
Mr. Erskine repeated these words."—*Contemporary Review,* May 1870.

[2] *Life of Dr. Erskine,* p. 11.

[3] Mrs. Burnett of Kemnay, daughter of Dr. Charles Stuart of Dunearn.

Katherine is wonderfully supported, but it is an awful blow. Pray for us, that this dispensation may be sanctified to us, that we may look more to Christ, that we may look wholly to Christ. Oh! there is nothing else of any consequence. We live in the midst of shadows, and we think them realities. Lord, open Thou our eyes that we may see the truth, and that we may be assured that Thy love is better than life. We hardly know yet what has happened to us,—it seems a troubled dream; but we know that it is the Lord, and that He doeth all things well. K. is quite resigned, quite peaceful. How good is God! I need not write any more. Let us pray.—Yours most affection·ately,   T. ERSKINE.

DUNDEE, Sept. 17th.

THE remains of my brother are to be interred on Saturday at one o'clock. . . . I left our mourners really well, and resting on the Rock of Ages.

Sept. 22d.

YOUR letter grieved my soul. If I had such another brother to lose, I would willingly give up my earthly joy in him to cure such a sorrow as yours. But it cost more to redeem a soul. . . . I have only returned from paying the last duties to the kindest of friends and brothers merely mortal; my heart is stunned; I have lost a Christian friend, a spiritual guide. But thanks be to God, I can look to the Good Shepherd, and can trust him for the supply of all my wants, for remission of sins, and for renewal of heart, and for faith that I may see His wise love in all His dispensations towards me. Many new duties are indeed imposed on me, and I beg the prayers of my friends for grace to discharge them to the glory of the Imposer. I have just written to my poor sister, from whom I received a letter yesterday. She is well.—Farewell,

T. ERSKINE.

The new duties imposed on him by his succession to the estate of Linlathen, induced Thomas Erskine to leave Edinburgh and bid farewell to the Bar.   He did not like to do so without some expression of his own deep and ardent faith.   He drew up a paper, which he thought of putting into the hands of his companions at the Bar when he parted from them.   Though fully and carefully written, this paper was never used as originally intended.   It lay bye unthought of, till he became so well known and so highly esteemed as a writer, that he was asked to furnish Introductory Essays to some of Chalmers and Collins' Series of Select Christian Authors.   He bethought him then of the paper—headed "Salvation"—which he had drawn up some years before, and handed it to the publishers.   It appeared in 1825 as an Introductory Essay to the Letters of the Rev. Samuel Rutherford.   It merits special regard at once from the date and the object of its composition.   The reader not only will find in it the same purity, ease, and gracefulness of style, and the same felicity of illustration, by which his after writings were characterised, but that key-note of doctrinal theology struck which ran through them all. "It follows," he says, " that a restoration to spiritual health, or conformity to the Divine character, is the *ultimate object* of God in His dealings with the children of men.   Whatever else God hath done with regard to men, has been subsidiary, and with a view to this ; even the unspeakable work of Christ, and pardon freely offered through His cross, have been but means to a further end ; and that end is, that the adopted children of the family of God might be conformed to the likeness of their elder brother,—that they might resemble Him in character, and thus enter into His joy. . . . The sole object of Christian belief is to produce the Christian character, and unless this is done nothing is done."[1]

[1] *Letters of the Rev. Samuel Rutherford.*   Introd. Essay, pp. xiii., xxv.

CHAPTER II.

Letters to Dr. Chalmers, and publication of "Remarks on the Internal Evidence for the Truth of Revealed Religion."

THE first incident of the new life at Linlathen was the marriage there on the 14th October 1817, of Mr. Erskine's sister Christian, to Charles Stirling, Esq., fourth son of William Stirling, Esq. of Keir. Cadder House, in which the newly married couple took up their abode, and in which they continued to reside during the remainder of their lives, lay in the immediate vicinity of Glasgow. The house of a sister to whom he was so tenderly attached was as a second home to Mr. Erskine, and his earliest visits to it brought him to the neighbourhood of Glasgow at the very time when Dr. Chalmers was at the height of his fame there as a preacher. Acquaintance quickly ripened into friendship, and it so happens that the only letters of Mr. Erskine written during the years 1818 and 1819, which have been preserved, are those addressed to his new friend. It was after a first visit to Dr. Chalmers, in the autumn of 1818, that the following letters were written :—

1. TO DR. CHALMERS.

MY DEAR FRIEND,—I am under the government of others at present, so you must excuse the fluctuation of my plans.

I am afraid that I cannot have the pleasure of seeing you again at this time. I am sorry for it, but I hope soon to meet you here or elsewhere. I hope that I have benefited by my visit to you. Certainly I was much struck with some circumstances in your conduct, and I will tell you what these are. You have been much followed, by great and small, by learned and ignorant, and yet you listened, with the meek candour of a learner, to one whom you could not but consider as your inferior by far. If you had opened to me all mysteries and all knowledge, you could not have brought to my conscience the strong conviction of the necessity and the reality of Christianity with half the force that this deportment of yours impressed upon me.

As I cannot converse with you, I must write a little upon the *justification* of James. From the 14th verse of the second chapter, substitute *exercise* or *action* instead of *work*, wherever the word occurs, and read the 21st and 22d verses thus: " Was it not by the exercise of his faith that Abraham our father became a righteous character, seeing (we read) that he offered up his son Isaac on the altar? Seest thou how faith manifested itself (in action) in exercise, and by this exercise faith became perfect or confirmed, *i.e.* became a permanent and predominating principle of action?" And then I think that in the next verse it is only the latter part, viz., " And he was called, or became the friend of God," that directly applies to the apostle's argument,—the first part of the verse describes the forensic effect of the principle, the latter its practical and moral effect.

I need not say how delighted I should be were you to favour me with a visit at Linlathen. I never expect an answer to my letters from you, so anything in that way will be only an unlooked-for pleasure, as I know the scantiness of your time.—Yours, with much affection and respect, T. ERSKINE.

2. TO DR. CHALMERS.

LINLATHEN, *5th Sept.* 1818.

MY DEAR SIR,—I am much gratified with the prospect which your letter holds out to me of hearing from you occasionally. To those whose hearts are apt to get slack and cold amidst the difficulties of the narrow way, everything which acts as a stimulus is most desirable, and the sympathy of our fellow-travellers does stimulate ; although I know also by experience, that there are few things which require to be connected with a sterner guard over our own hearts, because there are few things which tend more to self-deception, as we easily imagine ourselves to be in the right way while we are talking about it.

I shall send you by my sister a paraphrase translation of James, which will explain to you the view which I take of it. I do not think that faith and works are ever directly opposed to each other in the Bible, except when the method of justification before God is treated of. In other cases a *work* seems to be considered just as a modification of the principle which produced it. In this way an act proceeding from deceit, self-righteousness, indolence, etc., although perhaps beneficial to the interest of mankind at large, would be called deceit, self-righteousness, etc.,—and as faith is the only legitimate source of Christian conduct, walking by faith is the generic name for Christian action. For this reason I am inclined to think that work in James means merely exercise. Thus in a physical case, a man's lifting a hundredweight means his capacity of lifting this weight carried into effect,—if he produces the same effect by steam or otherwise, the same result ensues, but the principle is different ; if he does it by his own strength, and practises it, the principle of bodily vigour will be exercised and so increased ; in the other case, his skill in dynamics only is exercised and increased. So a Christian action means simply the Christian principle carried into effect in a particular instance, and the practice of this strengthens the principle; but if the same result is produced by a different cause, the action morally takes its name from that cause, and the exercise of it will only strengthen the principle which produced it. This of itself may not seem much to the point, but when you compare it with the translation you may see the bearing of it. It seems to me of great consequence to remember that the connection between the Christian faith and character is not arbitrary but necessary,—that it is not the connection which subsists between the fir and the ship in which it is inserted as a mast, but the connection which subsists between the fir and its root before it is cut down. And this constitutes the closeness of the union which subsists between Christ and His people; His work of love received by faith becomes the principle and root of spiritual life within them. This principle is not subject to the influence or condemnation of sin, it is the immortal tie which binds the Father of spirits to all His family throughout the universe. It is sweet to think of those who having by mercy been made partakers of this new and interminable life, have departed from this scene of death to a nearer and fuller enjoyment of the fountain of their spiritual being. They are like Him, for they see Him as He is. The veil being removed, like mirrors they reflect back His own character, and thus partake His joy.

On this day three years ago I witnessed the departure of a friend who I hope is now with the Lord. What a comfort it is to think that your father according to the flesh is a branch of the true vine![1]

The manuscript is much scored and much dirtied. When you have read it be so good as to return it to my sister, and to give me your opinion.—Yours with much regard,

T. ERSKINE.

---

[1] Dr. Chalmers's father died 26th July 1818.

3. TO DR. CHALMERS.

LINLATHEN, 21*st Nov.* 1818.

My DEAR SIR,—I am afraid that you will begin to think my correspondence rather troublesome, especially if occasionally interlarded by such packages as that which has I hope already reached you by the Perth coach. It is a considerable tax upon your kindness and patience to ask you to read that paper, but yet I entertain hopes that you will do it. It contains views of divine truth which have of late very much commended themselves to my understanding—solving many apparent difficulties, and exhibiting a beautiful consistency through the whole scheme. With those views also I think the internal evidence of religion is intimately connected. In this manner :—The Christian character, however much it may be despised or hated in practice, yet in theory commands the approbation even of the natural reason. Supposing it to be perfected, it is *necessarily* accompanied by perfect happiness. But then the formation of this character is opposed by the strongest and most active principles of our constitution. Pride, the passions, and the appetites, are in constant operation, and are in direct opposition to the formation of this character ; and even the perception of the evil of sin, which is the first element of holiness, drives us from it by producing despair. Now the gospel presents us with a history of facts, the belief of which must by the nature of things produce this character, bringing our thoughts and wills into union with the Supreme Will, and increasing our sense of the evil of sin whilst it annihilates despair. In short, the gospel is most precisely suited to the wants and the diseases of the human soul.

My soul is diseased—I see to a demonstration that the gospel is every way calculated to remove this disease, that, if accepted, it *must* remove it. I can discover no other cure. The gospel is then the true remedy, and nothing but a refutation of what now seems to me an axiom can tear me from it.   I must be shown some other remedy superior to this, or I must be shown that this is no remedy —all other argument is irrelevant.   I may be told about difficulties attending the facts, but I still insist that it is true in morals; it is true in nature, it is true in the constitution of man, it is true in the character of God.   " Whether he be a sinner, I know not; one thing I know, that whereas I was blind, now I can see."   And it is not only after the cure that I see this; it was the sight of this suitableness which attracted me.   I saw that it was a pearl of great price; its value was stamped upon it by Him whose image it is.   It is this suitableness which converts the infidel, as well as confirms and advances the believer.

My dear sir, I should like much to see two or three sermons by you on the views contained in my package.   It appears to me that much evil both in *orthodoxy* and *heterodoxy* arises from inattention to these views, and also much cavil and much scepticism.   I am sensible that I am taking a great liberty with you, but the kindness with which you have always treated me, and the importance of the cause, must be my excuse.

I entreat your prayers for me, that my heart may be broken and contrite, deeply impressed with a sense of sin, and with the view of the freeness of Divine grace.   May your Master direct and prosper your labours for others, and at the same time keep your own heart and mind in the knowledge and love of Him.—Farewell.   Yours affectionately,   T. ERSKINE.

When you have done with my packet you may send it to my sister.

The package which accompanied this letter was the first draft of the " Remarks on the Internal Evidence for the Truth of Revealed Religion."   It thus appears that the first use to which Mr. Erskine turned the leisure and quiet of his residence at Linlathen, was to exhibit as lucidly and impressively as he could, and for the benefit of others, that proof of the Divine origin of Christianity by which he had himself been so peculiarly and powerfully attracted, convinced, impressed. The personal interest thus attaching to the earliest of his publications is enhanced by what is told us in the latest of them.

"When I ask myself," he says, "what reason or right I have to believe that a man who lived in Palestine 1865 years ago was the Son of God, in order to be certain that in this belief I have hold of a substance and not of a mere shadow, I must discern in the history itself a light and truth which will meet the demands both of my reason and conscience. In fact, however true the history may be, it cannot be of any moral or spiritual benefit to me until I apprehend its truth and meaning. This, and nothing less than this, is what I require, not only in this great concern, but in all others; for the only real instruction is that which helps us to perceive the truth and meaning of things, not that which merely asserts that such and such things are true, and insists on our accepting them as such.

"It has been the chief aim of my life to possess such an apprehension of the truth of Christianity as this; and it is now forty-five years since I ventured to give through the press an utterance to this desire, and to accompany it with a sketch of the meagre progress I had then made in realising it."

The "Remarks on the Internal Evidence," etc., was published in 1820, forty-five years before this passage was written. It met with an immediate and universal welcome —nine editions having been called for within nine succeeding years.[1] Its peculiar charms of method, style, and illustrations, were new to the public. There was much

[1] For some remarkable testimonies as to this volume, see Appendix, No. II. p. 364.

in the volume to attract interest and kindle admiration, nothing that awakened any suspicion or distrust. The Edinburgh "Christian Instructor,"[1] prompt as that organ of the Evangelical party in Scotland was to detect the slightest deviation from Calvinistic Theology, found nothing to find fault with, had nothing but lavish and unlimited praise to bestow. And yet many of those views which, when more fully expressed afterwards, met with so severe a condemnation, are to be found here in more than their germ. It was in his happiest manner that this new writer indicated what the kind of evidence in favour of Christianity was which he intended to unfold.

"I shall suppose that the steam-engine, and the application of it to the movement of vessels, was known in China in the days of Archimedes; and that a foolish lying traveller had found his way from Sicily to China, and had there seen an exhibition of a steam-boat, and had been admitted to examine the mechanical apparatus of it,—and upon his return home, had, amongst many palpable fables, related the true particulars of this exhibition,—what feeling would this relation have probably excited in his audience. . . . Some of the rabble might probably give a stupid and wondering kind of credit to the whole; whilst the judicious but unscientific hearers would reject the whole. Now, supposing that the relation had come to the ears of Archimedes, and that he had sent for the man, and interrogated him; and, from his unorderly and unscientific, but accurate specification of boilers, and cylinders, and pipes, and furnaces, and wheels, had drawn out the mechanical theory of the steam-boat,—he might have told his friends, 'The traveller may be a liar; but this is a truth. I have a stronger evidence for it than his testimony, or the testimony of any man: It is a truth in the nature of things.

[1] See an elaborate review.

The effect which the man has described is the legitimate and certain result of the apparatus which he has described. If he has fabricated this account, he must be a great philosopher.   At all events, his narration is founded on an unquestionable general truth.' . . . We reason precisely in the same way with regard to men and their actions. . . . If an intimate and judicious friend of Julius Cæsar had retired to some distant corner of the world, before the commencement of the political career of that wonderful man, and had there received an accurate history of every circumstance of his conduct, how would he have received it ?   He would certainly have believed it ; and not merely because he knew that Cæsar was ambitious, but also because he could discern that every step of his progress, as recorded in the history, was adapted with admirable intelligence to accomplish the object of his ambition.   His belief of the history, therefore, would rest on two considerations,—first, that the object attributed by it to Cæsar corresponded with the general principle under which he had classed the moral character of Cæsar ; and, secondly, that there was evident, through the course of the history, a perfect adaptation of means to an end.   He would have believed just on the same principle that compelled Archimedes to believe the history of the steam-boat.

" In all these processes of reasoning, we have examples of conviction, upon an evidence which is, most strictly speaking, internal,—an evidence altogether independent of our confidence in the veracity of the narrator of the facts. . .

" The first faint outline of Christianity presents to us a view of God operating on the characters of men through a manifestation of his own character, in order that, by leading them to participate, in some measure, of his moral likeness, they may also in some measure participate of his happiness. . . .

"The object of this Dissertation is to analyse the component parts of the Christian scheme of doctrine, with reference to its bearings both on the character of God and on the character of man; and to demonstrate, that its facts not only present an expressive exhibition of all the moral qualities which can be conceived to reside in the Divine mind, but also contain all those objects which have a natural tendency to excite and suggest in the human mind that combination of moral feelings which has been termed moral perfection. We shall thus arrive at a conclusion with regard to the facts of revelation, analogous to that at which Archimedes arrived with regard to the narrative of the traveller,—viz., a conviction that they contain a general truth in relation to the characters both of God and of man; and that therefore the Apostles must either have witnessed them, as they assert, or they must have been the most marvellous philosophers that the world ever saw. Their system is true in the nature of things, even were they proved to be impostors.

"This theory of internal evidence, though founded on analogy, is yet essentially different in almost all respects from that view of the subject which Bishop Butler has given, in his most valuable and philosophical work on the Analogy of natural and revealed religion. His design was to answer objections against revealed religion, arising out of the difficulties connected with many of its doctrines, by showing that precisely the same difficulties occur in natural religion and in the ordinary course of providence. This argument converts even the difficulties of revelation into evidences of its genuineness; because it employs them to establish the identity of the Author of Revelation and the Author of Nature. My object is quite different. I mean to show that there is an intelligible and necessary connection between the doctrinal facts of revelation and the character of

God (as deduced from natural religion), in the same way
as there is an intelligible and necessary connection between
the character of a man and his most characteristic actions;
and further, that the belief of these doctrinal facts has an
intelligible and necessary tendency to produce the Christian character, in the same way that the belief of danger
has an intelligible and necessary tendency to produce fear."

Coming in the execution of this design to speak specifi-
cally of the truths and facts of Christianity, he says :—

"The doctrine of the atonement is the great subject of
revelation.   God is represented as delighting in it, as being
glorified by it, and as being most fully manifested by it.
All the other doctrines radiate from this as their centre. ..
The design of the atonement was to make mercy towards this offcast race consistent with the honour and the
holiness of the Divine government.   To accomplish this
gracious purpose, the Eternal Word, who was God, took on
himself the nature of man, and as the elder brother and
representative and champion of the guilty family, he so-
lemnly acknowledged the justice of the sentence pronounced
against sin, and submitted himself to its full weight of
woe, in the stead of his adopted kindred.   God's justice
found rest here; his law was magnified and made honourable. . . .   The doctrine of the atonement through Jesus
Christ, which is the corner-stone of Christianity, and to
which all the other doctrines of revelation are subservient,
has had to encounter the misapprehension of the understanding as well as the pride of the heart. . . .   It has
been sometimes so incautiously stated, as to give ground to
cavillers for the charge that the Christian scheme repre-
sents God's attribute of justice as utterly at variance with
every moral principle.   The allegation has assumed a form
somewhat resembling this, 'that according to Christianity,
God indeed apportions to every instance and degree of

transgression its proper punishment; but that, while he rigidly exacts this punishment, he is not much concerned whether the person who pays it be the real criminal or an innocent being, provided only that it is a full equivalent; nay, that he is under a strange necessity to cancel guilt whenever this equivalent of punishment is tendered to him by whatever hand.' This perversion has arisen from the habit amongst some writers on religion of pressing too far the analogy between a crime and a pecuniary debt. It is not surprising that any one who entertains such a view of the subject should reject Christianity as a revelation of the God of holiness and goodness. But this is not the view given in the Bible."

Soon after the publication of the "Remarks," Mr. J. Haldane, in a letter to his friend, Dr. Charles Stuart, took exception generally to the character of the evidence relied on, as having nothing in it amounting to positive proof, and particularly to that statement relative to the atonement which has been quoted. The contents of this letter were communicated by Dr. Stuart to Mr. Erskine, who had gone with his sister to spend the winter of 1820-21 in the south of England. Mr. Erskine instantly replied :—

4. TO DR. CHARLES STUART.

HASTINGS, 19*th January* 1821.

MY DEAR FRIEND,—I shall, God willing, send you a long letter before a week is over, on the subject of Mr. J. Haldane's letter. I return both you and him my thanks for it, although it makes me regret that I ever published. I think that he has mistaken me in some things; but if he does, many others may do so too, and I may be the means of mischief. Will you look over the Romans and Galatians with a view to the atonement, and observe whether salva-

C

tion by grace, free undeserved grace, be not the great inference, with love and confidence and humility in its train.   I
do verily believe that the ideas of commutation as often
held are not scriptural.   As Adam's sin covered all his
natural descendants, so Christ's obedience unto death
covers all his spiritual seed.   Christ died under the sentence
pronounced against sin, as the representative of his people :
His death stands for theirs, their life is bound up in Him.
Yours sincerely attached,   T. ERSKINE.

5. TO DR. CHARLES STUART.

HASTINGS, 1*st February* 1821.

MY DEAR FRIEND,—Are not you delighted and edified
by Mr. Russell's Letters ?[1]   I do think that they contain
some of the most striking, and animating, and spiritualising
statements of divine truth that ever I met with in human
compositions.   I hope that they are extensively read, and
I pray that the Divine Spirit may accompany them.   They
are meant for Christians certainly, but there is a sense in
them which I think may recommend them even to others.
I must tell you now what appears to me the error of Mr.
Haldane's criticism.

First.—He has not attended to the object of the Essay.
That object was to demonstrate the reality of the Christian
doctrines, *i.e.* of the facts attributed by Scripture to God's
government, by proving their harmony with the character
of God, and their adaptation to the needs of men.   If this
proof is made out, *the reality of the facts is the inference to be
drawn from it.*   Look at the fifth page, and read over the
example of Cæsar's friend forming a judgment of the truth
of his history.   The suitableness of Cæsar's actions to

---

[1] *Letters, chiefly Practical and Consolatory.* By David Russell, Minister
of the Gospel, Dundee. Mr. Russell was minister of the Independent
Church there.

accomplish his ambitious designs is the evidence of the reality of the history in his friend's judgment.

Second.—Mr. Haldane says that the comparison of the atonement to the payment of a debt is common in Scripture. He gives no reference, and I have in vain looked for it. When sin is compared to a debt, it is said to be *freely* discharged, as in Luke vii. 42 ; and in the parable of the debts of 10,000 talents and 100 pence, etc. I do not believe that the atonement of the Saviour is ever compared to the repayment of a sum of money.

Captain James Paterson[1] was, on the 4th September 1821, married to David, youngest sister of Mr. Erskine.

Captain Paterson on his marriage not only left the army, but consented to take up his residence at Linlathen. This opened the way for Mr. Erskine carrying out a long cherished intention of visiting, and making a prolonged stay on the Continent. He left Linlathen in the summer of 1822. While on his way through England, the following letters were written.

6. TO THE SAME.

HARROGATE, *Wednesday, July* 1822.

MY DEAR FRIEND,—I intend to leave this almost immediately. I take Hinckley on my way, that I may recall past scenes and anticipate future ones. The days of man are as a shadow. How many have been cut down since I was there! Soon must I follow. Soon must the end of all things be. Were it not for the fountain opened for sin and for uncleanness, what a dark prospect we should have! I am occupied with the Romans, but it would excite astonishment in you, if not anger, to see the exceeding slowness of my progress. Ἁμαρτία is a most formidable word as well as thing. It is very difficult to bring unequivocal

---

[1] Youngest son of Mr. Paterson of Castle Huntly.

reasons for its meaning in many places. Sometimes it signifies the evil disposition, sometimes guilt and consciousness of guilt, and sometimes the condemnation which it merits. Law, spirit, flesh, all bristling with difficulties. And then, moreover, the apparent presumption in condemning the long-received views of these passages would make many unwilling to listen, or to receive anything from me. . . . I was hearing Mrs. Stevens last night again. Really I am not acquainted with those who preach better than she does, and I never saw a place where Christianity seemed in more holy and happy exercise than in Mrs. Cheape's house at Knaresboro'. You probably know that Mrs. Cheape and Mrs. Stevens are the sisters of that Mr. Fisher who is stationed at Meerut as one of the Company's chaplains. Mrs. Stevens was the first of the family who knew the Lord. By her instrumentality her sisters and brother, and Mr. Cheape, were impressed; and her labours in Knaresboro' have been blessed and honoured by God in a wonderful manner. . . .

I like Mr. Cheape very much. He is a very amiable man indeed, and all the branches of the family appear to be of the same kindly, and bland, and gentle construction. But above all, they seem to live entirely for eternity,—everything of the world, except its duties, is shut out. The missionary spirit is strong in them. . . . The more I see of the English Christians belonging to the Establishment, the better I like them. They seem to have so much of the spirit of love amongst them. . . .

I think frequently of you and your sorrows, and commend you and them to Him who afflicteth not willingly, nor grieves the children of men; and I think often of your kindness to me, and pray that it may be returned to you an hundredfold into your bosom.

Our paths in this world may not touch again, but my

hope is that the Good Shepherd will keep us from straying out of the path which leads to His heavenly fold. My desire is to consider, and to feel everything to be dross in comparison with His love, and to grow daily in the sense of my exceeding need for His salvation, and of His exceeding and overflowing sufficiency. Farewell. I beg to be remembered at the Throne of Grace by you, and I remain, yours affectionately,　　　　　　　　　　T. Erskine.

7. TO DR. CHARLES STUART.

London, 12th August 1822.

My dear Friend,—I shall probably have left England by the time you receive this letter. . . . In the letter before the last which I received from you, I thought that I perceived a tremulousness of hand, which made me apprehensive, until next day when I received a letter as firm and decided in point of penmanship as any that I ever received from you. Perhaps you may be kind enough to write to me to the Post Office, Berlin, or Dresden. A letter from you would be a great treat to me in a foreign land. . . .

My dear friend, in bidding you farewell it is a comfort to know that the Throne of Grace is a meeting-place for all those who know the Lord, however distant they may be locally; and that yet a few days, and the whole of the members of that family shall be united, never again to be parted. Pray for me that the word may abide in me, accompanied by the Spirit, and that I may be sanctified by it. Remember me before God. . . .

Farewell, I think of you almost as a father.

T. Erskine.

Dr. Charles Stuart of Dunearn had married Mr. Thomas Erskine's cousin Mary, the eldest daughter of the Rev. Dr. John Erskine. Dr. Stuart was a lineal descendant of the Regent Murray, and stood at one time third in succession to

the earldom.   In earlier life he entered the Church of Scotland, and was presented to the parish of Cramond, near Edinburgh.   Having adopted views on Church Establishments
and other subjects which he considered inconsistent with his
position as a clergyman of the Church of Scotland, he
resigned his charge, studied medicine, and took his degree
as a physician.   A lover of all good men, he was a promoter
of every enterprise which had for its object the diffusion
of the gospel.   He co-operated with Mr. James Haldane,
Mr. Christopher Anderson, Dr. M'Crie, and others, in the
formation of the Gaelic School Society.   At the first
annual meeting of that Society after Dr. Stuart's death,
Dr. M'Crie, in moving that a notice of that event should
be entered in the records of the Society, said, " It is well
known that the first idea of a distinct Society for promot-
ing the education of our countrymen in the Highlands and
Islands, originated with Dr. Stuart. . . . I had the honour
and happiness of an intimate acquaintance with him during a considerable number of years,—I always found in
him the honourable feelings of the gentleman, the refined
and liberal thinking of the scholar, and the unaffected and
humble piety of the Christian." [1]   Dr. Chalmers shared
the sentiments so expressed.   " I feel the utmost gratitude,"
he said to Dr. Stuart in 1814, "for the friendly attention
and fatherly care I have ever experienced at your hands."[2]
As the relationships were closer, deeper still were Mr.
Erskine's attachment and gratitude, of which the reader
will find a most touching and beautiful expression in the
letter of this volume dated 14th June 1826.[3]

[1] *Life of Dr. M'Crie,* p. 200.
[2] *Memoirs of Dr. Chalmers,* vol. i. p. 370.
[3] P. 73.

CHAPTER III.

IN August 1822, Mr. Erskine left London and crossed over to the Netherlands. The autumn months were given to North Germany, the mid-winter months to Geneva. The spring of 1823 was spent in Paris,—summer saw him in the south of France. From Bordeaux he passed by the foot of the Pyrenees and the coast of the Mediterranean to Piedmont, and thence to Geneva, for a short second visit. Crossing the Alps in October, and lingering for a few weeks in the north of Italy, he proceeded to Rome, where he passed the winter of 1823-24. After a third and longer visit to Geneva he returned to Linlathen in the summer of 1825.

The following letters belong to this period :—

8. TO HIS SISTER MRS. STIRLING.

BRUSSELS, *September* 9, 1822.

MY DEAR SISTER,—This is a beautiful country, and the towns are monuments of the ancient grandeur and riches of the inhabitants. Our towns in Great Britain are poor things in comparison of them in point of splendour, even Edinburgh. I have great delight in walking about the streets, and surveying the houses which once contained the chief nobility of Spain and Germany, and all that was fortunate in mercantile speculation. The gable-ends are universally towards the street, which has a very imposing

effect. Their modern buildings are fine, certainly in much
better taste, I should say, than at home; but it is the
antique outline which takes my fancy, and occasionally
compensates to me for being from home.

The forest of Ardennes, which lies between the field of
Waterloo (that part of it is called Soignies), is, you remember, the scene of Shakespeare's " As you Like it." I got a
horse yesterday, and rode away at a venture through it. It
contains about one hundred thousand acres. It is a most
wonderful place. I lighted upon an old convent, which
had been evacuated during the French government, and is
now uninhabited. The immense height of the trees would
astonish you. They look like antediluvian patriarchs. I
have seen trees of greater girth often, but they carry up
the same circumference about forty or fifty, or even more
feet. The principal wood now standing is beech, the oak
having been cut down for ship-building during the war.

9. TO CAPTAIN AND MRS. PATERSON.

BERLIN, *9th Oct.* 1822.

MY DEAR FRIENDS,—At Frankfort I was much pleased
with my company. Mr. Bost appears to me a most thorough
Christian—nothing but a Christian—desiring that only.
Mr. Manuel is a Swiss, a very interesting one, afflicted
with the *mal de pays*—an imaginative man who can repeat
a great deal of Shakespeare and *Burns*, but who is, I
believe, a child of God. Mr. Bost is unimaginative. The
family of heaven, though they have the family likeness, are
often very different. The family feature is, "Whom having
not seen, they love." Is not that it, my mother, and sister,
and brother?

From Frankfort we travelled by Marburg to Cassel, a
most remarkable place,—fine collection of paintings, some
beautiful Italian ones of Carlo Dolce, Titian, and Guido

Reni; many fine Rembrandts and Vandycks and Rubenses. The Ducal residence, Wilhelmshöhe, the most striking union of art and nature in forming a princely place. To be sure, the fountains don't play except they are desired; but what of that? The whole country is composed of hills, like the hills at Strowan, covered with beautiful wood, some of it grand oaks, standing open and separate like an immense grove, some of it thick woodland and coppice. We sometimes see great herds of swine eating the acorns under these oaks, herded by a gentleman in a cocked hat and white coat lined with scarlet.

10. TO DR. CHARLES STUART.

HAMBURG, 2d *Nov.* 1822
(*my brother's birthday*).

MY DEAR FRIEND,—Your letter which I received at Berlin was most acceptable to me. I have often during my journey had you upon my mind, and would have given for an hour's conversation with you what a pilgrim through the desert would give for a draught of water. I have, however, met with many green spots through the desert; and springs and palm-trees, and many hours of pleasing and profitable conversation too, though not with you, my dear friend. I am at present very comfortably situated. My friends are Mr. Merle d'Aubigné, of whom Mr. Haldane will tell you. He is an estimable man, a faithful preacher, and, what is rare here, an unprejudiced and unmystical student of the Word of God. Mr. Matthews is the pastor of an Independent church here. At Berlin, I made the acquaintance of a young Professor who lectures in their University on theology, and on the books of the Old and New Testament. He loves the truth, and will, I hope, be more and more enlightened himself, and blessed in his instructions to others. Our ambassador at Berlin, who takes an interest in all these things, introduced me to him. This Professor, whose name is Tholuck, is a self-taught linguist, one of the Murrays and Leydens. I should like well to study the Oriental languages under him. My want of German is a great want, and a great stupidity moreover, which I am endeavouring now to correct as fast as I can.

11. TO HIS SISTER MRS. STIRLING.

DRESDEN, *7th Decr.* 1822.

MY DEAR CHRISTIAN,—At Leipzig we went over the field of battle in which about 900,000 men were engaged in mortal contest for five days. Mr. Campé (a correspondent of Mr. Baumeister) conducted us in his carriage. He was in Leipzig at the time, and saw everything which could be seen. He saw Bonaparte both before and after the action. He says that he bore his fate with exceeding calmness; that there was not the slightest appearance of agitation on his person; and he was standing close to him as he mounted his horse to go away, four hours before the allied monarchs met in the town. To-day we visited the picture-gallery here, which is one of the richest in Europe. One of Raphael's *chefs-d'œuvre*, a Madonna, the most lovely picture I ever saw—several beautiful Titians and Annibal Carraccis and Carlo Dolces.

Oh! what a secure peace we should have were we really resting on the gospel; but it is just taken by the by, and then it produces no fruit either of holiness or happiness. Let us set to it in earnest, my dear sister, for nothing else will last. Read that sermon of Leighton's entitled "The Believer a Hero." The text I think is, "He shall not be afraid of evil tidings, his heart is fixed, trusting in the Lord." I used to read that sermon very often, and always with pleasure. I wish that I had the volume with me.

HERRNHUT, 12th Decr. 1822.

MY DEAR SIR,—I have often thought of you since we parted, and of the promise which I made to you of writing, and this place has recalled both very forcibly to my recollection. We have often conversed about Moravianism, and here I am in the metropolis of Moravianism. Here I am an eye-witness of the order and tranquillity and gentleness and cleanliness of Moravianism, and I feel convinced that the mere date at the top of my page will make this letter acceptable to you. Every person you meet in the street bows, or wishes you good-morning or good-night with the air of a brother or a sister. There is a repose in every face and in every action that you see. The burial-ground, *Gottes acker* (God's acre, or field), is a most interesting spot, close by the town, which seems to give a lesson of silence and peace to the whole district. There may, however, be a mannerism in all this. It is very beautiful no doubt, but surely Christianity was never intended to interfere with the natural relations of life, and to form men into artificial communities, but rather to infuse its own character and life into those relations which already existed. Herrnhut is a Christian Lanark or Sparta—in some measure at least.

I have seen many most valuable people on the Continent. There is a great deal of cordiality in Germany, and I have been received as a brother by many of them, and they are all anxious to furnish me with further introductions. In general I find the Calvinistic points in great disrepute amongst evangelical Germans. They do not seem to understand the distinction between moral and natural necessity, and they imagine that they can distinguish between foreknowledge and predestination in God. For my own part, I do not find predestination directly in the Bible, but I could no more separate the belief of predestination from my idea of God, than I could separate the conviction of moral responsibility from my own consciousness. I do not, to be sure, see how these two things coincide, but I am prepared for my own ignorance on these points. We know things, not absolutely as they are in themselves, but relatively as they are to us and to our practical necessities. I understand both these things as they relate to me, but I don't see their relation to each other, because I don't see them as they are absolutely. Arminians have no right to attribute reprobation to Calvinists, and Calvinists have no right to attribute self-righteousness to Arminians. Both inductions may be just in metaphysics, but religion is not a piece of metaphysics.

I find the distinction of objective and subjective religion very important. Some of the Christians whom I have seen here make their religion entirely an interior thing, *i.e.* entirely *subjective.* In the Bible it is objective, *i.e.* it consists of the history of God's dealings chiefly—but objective for the purpose of producing subjective religion. The Moravians are objective—they don't talk of faith, but of the cross and the glory of Christ.

I see also the great importance of stating the facts of revelation rather than the dogmas which are educible from these forms. This also the Moravians attend to. I desire to be a little child. I have seen many very infantine characters, not affected simplicity, but genuine unintentionalness and humility, with excellent understandings. They are not so practical as the English, but they are cleverer in thought. I have formed some friendships, which I hope will last for ever. There is a Heubner at Wittenberg, a most delightful man—he lives close by the place where Luther studied, and where the Spirit of God came mightily upon him; a Leonhardi at Dresden, with whom, however, I am obliged to speak in Latin; a Merle d'Aubigné at Hamburg, the descendant of the friend of Henry IV. of France.   I need not tell you names, but I wish you knew the persons.   My dear sir, I recommend myself and my friend Mr. Stirling to your prayers.   Mr. S. met me at Hamburg.—Yours most truly,   T. ERSKINE.

I feel afraid of Baxter's Saints' Rest.[1]   You could do it well.   I cannot command my time at present.   A letter to Geneva, *poste restante*, will be acceptable.

13. TO DR. CHARLES STUART.

PARIS, 10*th March* 1823.

MY DEAR, DEAR FRIEND,—I fear that you think me forgetful, but I have had cause.   My companion has been very unwell, and this has kept me in such a state of anxiety for some months, I may say, that I have been able to do little in any way.   Never a day passes in which I do not think of you; and in which I do not commend you and your concerns to the Keeper of Israel.

I am sorry to find by the appearance of the second edition of my Essay,[2] that a letter which I wrote to Mr. Innes from Hamburg has miscarried.   It contained a division into sections, which is very much wanting, and many additions, and some subtractions.   I shall set about it again, but it is not so fresh to me as it was then.   Will you tell Mr. Waugh to remit to Mr. Ewing, for his academy, any share of the profit of the work which falls to me, and that soon?   I have met here with Mr. Noel,[3] and my dear friends the Moneys,[4] of whom I have spoken to you.   Their Christian

---

[1] The reference here is to the Introductory Essay to Baxter's "Saints' Rest," which he supplied for Collins' "Series of Select Christian Authors."

[2] The "Essay on Faith."   See Appendix, No. III. p. 369.

[3] The Honourable and Rev. Gerard Noel.

[4] W. Money, Esq., was consul at Venice.

intercourse has been a great comfort to me, and I stood much in need of it. Mrs. Money is one of the most amiable Christians I have ever seen. Every look, and word, and action, savours of the gospel. There is a Mr. Wilder here, of whom you may have heard. It was he who found out the Christian people in the mountains near Lyons, and who wrote the letters about them which appeared in many of the magazines. He is very useful here. Not long ago he made a very bold, and yet wise attack on the superstitions which, contrary to the feelings of the people, have been re-introduced by the Jesuits here. There was a procession of pilgrims up Calvary, a hill in the neighbourhood of Paris. This had existed before the Revolution, but had been abolished by Bonaparte, along with all useless public ceremonies. At the foot of this hill Mr. W. took his stand with 1500 tracts, which he gave to the pilgrims as they went up, and which they received with great readiness; and next day these pilgrims recommended him to give some of these little books to the Jesuit missionaries who were preaching there, for that they required them at least as much as anybody else. The police came to stop his proceedings. They asked, "By what authority doest thou these things?" He answered, "By the authority of my Lord Jesus Christ," and forced a New Testament on the acceptance of the officer, who was so taken by the ready and intrepid manner of Mr. W., that he could not refuse it. He has meetings at his house every Sunday evening for prayer and reading the Scriptures.[1] I have made the ac-

[1] Mr. Wilder writes from New York to Mr. Erskine in 1851, twenty-eight years after they had met in Paris :—"I need not say that I shall ever retain the liveliest recollection of the happy hours my family and myself have been privileged to pass in your agreeable company, nor of the edification which we have so often, with numerous Christian friends, derived from your able expositions of the Scriptures under our roof at Paris. Never shall I forget the manifestation of your friendship and courtesy towards

quaintance of a few French.   Certainly there is a readiness in this country to receive the gospel, but the political circumstances are very unfavourable.   Additional Bible Societies are prohibited.   How little do the Governments of this world perceive their own interests in relation to the gospel !   They know not that whoever falls on that stone shall be broken.   Mr. Money tells me that Wilberforce thought the Essay on Faith very obscure.   I think that its undivided state gives it that character.   But if he finds it obscure, how many must there be who will find it so too !

The people of this country are much cleverer than our people, but they seem to want sense very much.   The proceedings of their Chambers are quite absurd.

I regret the loss of the letter to Mr. Waugh, because I feel persuaded that the Essay in its present state can do little good.   People are so little accustomed to exercise their understandings on religious subjects, that it becomes a very important duty in a writer to make himself thoroughly intelligible.

There is at least the praise of consistency due to this Government.   They are precipitating themselves into a war, which threatens the Bourbons more than Spain ; and, at the same time, they are putting their prohibition on the extension of the Bible Society.   " And the Lord hardened Pharaoh's heart, and he would not let Israel go."   I think we have reason to expect great and striking events soon.   Principles on all subjects are becoming more defined and decided, and more sensibly opposed to their opposites.   There will be fewer neutrals soon.   A side must be taken

me in coming expressly from Brussels to Paris to bid me and my family an affectionate farewell at the period of our departure for this country, nor of the delightful whole night we passed together conversing of the things which pertain to our present, future, and eternal peace.

in the politics both of heaven and earth. Liberal principles doubtless prepare the way for Christianity, but it
seldom happens that the active supporters of these principles have any religion at all. Hitherto liberalism and
infidelity have been confederates, but I hope that this
league will not last long. I think that I shall return to
Geneva again, and stay some time, and wait the event of
present elements. There is a shaking in the nations, and
I trust that the Desire of all nations will soon establish
His kingdom everywhere. This city of Paris is a wonderful world in itself,—it is almost more wonderful than
London; its population is so dense and so various. But
I must finish. Write to me soon.—Yours affectionately,

                                                T. ERSKINE.

14. TO DR. CHARLES STUART.

PARIS, 31*st March* 1823.

MY DEAR FRIEND,—. . . You ask me on what ground
Malan charged me with Arminianism. I maintain that
guilt in man always supposed *power*—that there could be
no guilt unless there existed the power of doing or abstain-
ing. I admit that no man ever believes or obeys except
by divine teaching and divine support. But I affirm that
no man in the ordinary exercise of his faculties lies under
any natural incapacity of believing truth, or obeying what
is just and reasonable, or, if he does lie under any such
natural incapacity, that it is impossible to suppose that any
guilt can attach to him in consequence of unbelief or
disobedience. This doctrine Malan condemns, that is to
say, he condemns it in words; for I am persuaded that
neither he nor any one else can differ from me in reality
on this point. I love Malan; there is something most
apostolical in his whole deportment, and his mode of
instruction I think in general very scriptural. His minis-

try has been much honoured by God. Wherever he goes an impression is made. I think his fault as a theologian is that he is too fond of dialectical language. He was quite frank and most affectionate; but our conversation was not of that kind which could be very profitable to either of us, for we were arguing. My chief society here has been the Money family, who are most amiable. They grow upon my affections very much. Yesterday Mr. Noel gave us two excellent discourses on the resurrection: "If ye then be risen with Christ," etc. We had a meeting of seventy-five English in the Hotel, and a most attentive audience they were. In case there should be a demand for a new edition of the essay on *Faith*, I wish you would send me any hints that you may think important. I admire Mr. Russell's Letters[1] very much. I am getting some of them translated for France and Switzerland. Farewell, my dear friend. May the blessed Spirit of peace dwell in you, and bestow on you largely the earnest of future glory.—Yours affectionately,   T. ERSKINE.

15. TO HIS SISTER MRS. PATERSON.

PARIS, *19th April* 1823.

MY DEAR DAVIE,—I trust in God that your child is now quite restored, and that you have been by this dispensation led both to prayer and to thanksgiving. I am persuaded that there is nothing in the world or in the universe, in time or in eternity, worth our thoughts but God and his will. I desire that this persuasion may be at the very bottom of my heart, planted there and watered there by the Spirit of holiness. We have great things to transact with him, my dear Davie, and they ought to occupy our whole

[1] These letters had this additional interest to Mr. Erskine, that a number of them were originally addressed, with the happiest effect, to one of his sisters.

hearts, and to employ our whole strength. What a happiness and security there is in abiding ever in the sense of the divine presence; and what a strange thing it is, that having once enjoyed, we should ever consent to be without it for a moment. We have enjoyed the Moneys much. They are really amongst the excellent and the kind of the earth. They are returned home. . . . The Wilders, an American family here that has been the centre of Christianity in Paris, I may say, are going away soon. Paris had begun to be a home, and it is now unhomed by these dispersions. I have had much love and kindness from the Wilders. They are going back to America. The husband has been here twenty years, a firm and dauntless champion of the truth in every way. He has been the originator of most of the religious Societies here.

Archibald for some time amused himself in the purchase of bronzes; and partly to please him and partly to please myself, I have also bought some. I have bought two beautiful vases, which I hope my mother won't grudge to Airth. I never gave uncle Tom[1] anything; and I thought they would suit his room, and be a kindly memorial of my regard. I have bought a repeater, to let my mother know what o'clock it is at night, and it goes very accurately besides, and she has not a good watch. Moreover, I have a gladiator, and a bull, and a Cicero. The bull is admirable. Ask uncle Tom to come and look at it and the rest. . . . I have attended the anniversaries of the Tract Society, the Bible Society, and what they call here *La Société de la Morale Chrétienne*, which takes cognisance and superintendence of all benevolent objects, such as the abolition of the slave-trade, prisons, education, etc. I was much gratified. Noel spoke at the Bible Society, *i.e.* he read a speech which

---

[1] Thomas Graham, Esq. of Airth, his mother's brother.

had been translated for him by our excellent and kind friend the Baron de .Staël, who is a zealous and most able supporter of all religious and benevolent objects. I have received much kindness both from him and his sister, the Duchesse de Broglie.[1]—Yours affectionately,   T. E.

16. TO HIS SISTER MRS. PATERSON.

Nice, 24th July 1823.

MY DEAR DAVIE,—I have been a great defaulter in the way of correspondence lately. This has been partly owing to the effect which this southern sun has had upon my eyes, and partly to the moving life which I have been leading for the last month. There are two ways of going to Geneva from Bordeaux, one direct and short, by Lyons right across the country; the other by the foot of the Pyrenees and the coast of the Mediterranean, through Montauban, Toulouse, Montpellier, Nismes, Marseilles, and Piedmont. I chose this latter chiefly because the Protestantism of France is strongest and most Christian in this direction; and I feel myself repaid for my journey, although my idea of the sum of real religion among the French Protestants has been considerably narrowed by personal inspection. What I saw of Chabrant (at Toulouse) I liked well; but the most really active minister that I have met with in the French Church is Lissignol, at Montpellier— he is a true labourer, in season and out of season. Would you believe it?—there is scarcely such a thing as a second service on Sundays throughout their churches; and as there are often two ministers in each of their churches, each man contents himself with making one sermon in a fortnight. Lissignol has a colleague, who is an enemy to the truth, and who, in fact, preaches against him; but he has prevailed to have two services, and he has one in the week also, besides a

---

[1] Daughter of the celebrated Madame de Staël.

catechising in the church, which is the same thing, and
prayer-meetings and private instructions in abundance.
He prints and distributes tracts, and does what he can in
every way.   He accompanied me to Nismes, where he held
a meeting, at which none of the ministers of the place
(though some of them apparently good men) attended; so
jealous are Established Churches in general of having religion made the property of individuals, and of having it
considered as a thing independent of their fixed hours, and
places, and officers.   At Nismes I also met with an English Methodist, who preaches and labours much—a Mr.
Cook.   He has four parishes, besides prayer-meetings.   He
seems to have the prospect of usefulness in stirring up the
clergy about him to a zeal for the souls of their flocks.   I
gave Lissignol Mr. Russell's catechism, with which he was
exceedingly delighted.   He is to translate it and circulate
it (though I hope that it is already translated at Geneva).
I have been passing over mountains covered to the top with
myrtles in full flower, and every variety of odorous plant.
The air was filled with fragrance, the incense of nature to
her God.   The sun went down, the moon rose on these
gigantic, and fantastic, and lovely scenes.   I had many
thoughts of distant friends.   Oh for a lively sense of the
constant presence of that Friend whose love was and is
stronger than death, who dies not any more, and who
makes the death of His people an inlet to His nearer
presence and perfect enjoyment.   I stand much in need
of this, and yet I seek it but faintly, and therefore I have
little of it.   Pray for me.   T. E.

17. TO HIS SISTER MRS. STIRLING.

GENEVA, *9th September* 1823.

MY DEAR CHRISTIAN,—. . . This day had been fixed
by Mr. Noel and me for an expedition to Chamouni,

Mont Blanc, and the glaciers; but Mrs. Noel is very delicate, and the day was not very promising. I hope to
make it out to-morrow, either with them or alone. The
Jeffreys, and Cockburn, and Richardson are here. Harry[1]
looked so like home, that I could scarce help thinking myself
in Charlotte Square. He is much fatigued, however, and
has got a little cold in crossing the Alps; but don't mention this, for it might give needless uneasiness to his wife.
Jeffrey is like a game-cock;—you know that his wife is a
great favourite of mine. Her father, Mr. Wilkes, was here
with them, but has left them. He was much attached to our
James. I never knew anybody who was acquainted with
James without loving him. There was a mixture of gentleness, and melancholy, and sensitiveness, and manliness, and
modesty, and intelligence, and truth in his composition,
that I never saw except in himself.

You may suppose that Mr. Noel is a great comfort here
to me. Mrs. Noel is certainly much better than she has
been for years. My host and hostess, Mr. and Mme. Cramer,
are two excellent kind people, who make their house quite
a home to me.

This is a lovely land,—oh, most lovely! My dear
sister, I hope you are finding happiness and strength in
Christianity, and that you know what it is to be sensible
of the presence of God. Religion seems to me to consist
in that. Give my love to your husband, and to Archibald,
and our friends at Keir, and Linlathen (write them, for

---

[1] "My dear Tom,—I was much gratified by your letter. It breathed the
affection which I have ever received from you, and which I can truly say
I have always been delighted to return. We have been more separated
throughout life, both by distance and by pursuits, than at earlier periods
I thought likely. But this has never cooled my regard, nor yours. I do
not think that we ever had a word of personal difference, and I am unconscious of one moment's alienation, throughout an acquaintance not far
short of forty years. God bless you, my dear Tom."—*Extract of letter
from Lord Cockburn to Mr. Erskine,* dated 19th October 1830.

I have not written for some time, waiting for letters), and Airth. Is the bonny Spat looking bonny? and the canal, and the Lago Kelvino,[1] and the pheasants, and what not?

18. TO HIS SISTER MRS. PATERSON.

MILAN, 10*th November* 1823.

MY DEAR ITALY,[2]—How does that northern climate suit your sunny constitution; and how does the stunted vegetation on the Tay supply the want of the luxuriant life which exults and wantons in every leaf and every flower in this fair land? I left Geneva and its much-loved contents three weeks ago. I coasted the lake, and ascended the Upper Rhone, and arrived at the Simplon in splendid weather. I slept on the top, and admired, I cannot tell you how much, the magnificence of the descent. Different small streams have chosen or found out the most convenient way of getting down the mountain, and the road is guided by those streams; but our small scale of mountain scenery can give you no idea of the tremendous chasms, and overhanging precipices, and desolate ravines, and everlasting snows; and all this mixed with sweet woodland scenery, which, when I passed, showed every tint that nature owns.

I have since visited the lakes, Maggiore and Como, both lovely—how lovely! You know the beauty of the foliage of the sweet chestnuts; but you cannot so easily conceive the effect of a continued grove of them of every fantastic and venerable shape, upon the side of a hill—intermediate spots clothed with vines trained on trees in the Italian mode, and the ground strewed with the leaves and fruit

---

[1] Cadder stood on the banks of the Kelvin, which supplied this garden-lake with water.

[2] A name given to her among the family, in allusion to her sunny temperament.

of the chestnut.   The Maggiore is softer in its character
than Como; but the magnificent range of the Alps behind
perhaps gives it more variety.   The Lake of Como is
bounded by its two sides as by two walls, in some cases
almost perpendicular.   There is not even a mule road on
either side !   And on one side the steepness of the rocks
does not admit even of a footpath the whole way, or even
for a considerable way.   But you see olives, and vines, and
laurels, and chestnuts, etc., in overflowing and rich redund-
ance.   The gentlemen who inhabit the numerous villas on
its banks keep each a boat instead of horses and carriages,
which could not come there, and would be of no use if they
could.   Some of these villas are most superb, and belong
to the first and richest nobility of the north of Italy.   I
saw some of Canova's finest pieces of sculpture in one of
them ; and I saw myrtles in blossom at the same time
[*November*] in a hedge before the house !   Write, Christian,
that, after the Lago Kelvino, I do not believe there is anything more enchanting than Como.

I am writing over anew my essay on *Faith* for a French
translation.   I hope to improve it much, particularly in its
arrangement.

I have been in absolute solitude for three weeks.   I don't
know even the name of a creature in Milan.   But I am
very comfortable and happy when I can keep near God ;
and solitude is not adverse to that, though, and at the
same time, it will not produce it.   We are as much led
away by our own imaginations as by those of others.   The
constant sense of the divine presence is the important
thing and the delightful thing, and, at the same time, wonderful to say, it is the great difficulty. . . . There are some
very fine pictures here of Guercino, and Carracci, and Guido
Reni, and Salvator, and one Raphael, and Leonardo da
Vinci's great piece of the Supper much defaced (fresco) :

his colours are oil, and it appears that water-colours stand
best in these frescos. The Cathedral is immense—all
white marble—it is really unutterable. I go soon to Genoa,
where the Noels are for the winter. I shall stay there a
week or two, and then Florence. You may write to Florence.
. . . Farewell. The Lord's blessing be with you all.

19. TO HIS SISTER MRS. STIRLING.

FLORENCE, *Feb.* 1824.

MY DEAR CHRISTIAN,—My dear sister, what a strange
world it is! It seems most extraordinary to myself that
I can, in the midst of such a world of death, and sin, and
sorrow, find enjoyment in marble cut into certain forms,
and colours laid on canvas; and yet I really find immense
enjoyment in it—I feel almost as if I had gotten a new sense.

There must have been a most surpassing genius in these
old Greek sculptors. It is not merely perfect beauty and
perfect grace which they have drawn out from the secret
treasures of nature, but they have transmitted to us their
highest thoughts and their loveliest sentiments, all fresh,
and living, and breathing as when they first appeared to
their own inspired souls, in a form that cannot be mistaken,
and infinitely more eloquent and imposing than any language. No words can describe the Niobe, that union of
all that is desolate and all that is noble—the desperation
proceeding from the knowledge that her enemies were
deities, and yet that heroism which never even glances at
her own personal danger. The Venus is very beautiful,
though I prefer the Niobe infinitely. The perfect modesty
of the Venus is at least equal to her beauty; you could
really scarcely imagine it possible that an unclothed figure
could be so naturally and unaffectedly modest. There are
many most delightful pictures too, several very fine Raphaels
and Titians, which last rise daily in my judgment in spite

of Sir Joshua Reynolds.   I cannot sympathise with Sir
Joshua either, in his admiration for Michael Angelo. . . .
I have just been interrupted by a visit from a descendant
of Michael Angelo, who has asked me to his house to see
some of the remains of his illustrious ancestor.   Cumming
Bruce is here, whom I like much; and young Mure, Caldwell, a fine young man.—Yours affectionately,   T. E.

20. TO THE SAME.

ROME, 25*th February* 1824.

MY DEAR CHRISTIAN,—It is never from forgetfulness,
and far less from indifference, that my letters to you are
unfrequent; for there is no person in the world that I like
better, or think oftener of, than yourself; but really the
business of seeing sights is a full occupation of time, and a
most fatiguing occupation too. . . .

This place from which I write is just a mighty monument of the uncertainty of human things—it is a home for
the afflicted and ruined and disappointed; for here they
will see the traces of a heavier affliction, and a deeper and
more widely extended ruin, and a more unlooked-for blight
than their own.   Here they do not see the tombs of individuals, but of empires—they walk over the ashes of all
that this world has produced of mighty, and glorious, and
enduring, of cheerful and prosperous; and they may thus
have the consolation of thinking that, when they suffer,
they only share the common inheritance of man.   Thank
God, we have better and more solid consolation than the
mere knowledge that we have the whole of our race, past
and present, as our companions in sorrow.   We have
learned that according to the plans of Divine wisdom, sorrow
is the seed of joy, and that out of the fragments of this
life a higher life is to be formed. . . .

The Noels have gone this morning for Naples.   They

pressed me very hard to go with them, but I want to see more of this place, and to get more into its spirit. Rome is not a place to see in company with others. It is too solemn and overwhelming in its principle to admit ever of being felt by a number of people together. Ten people can admire a column or a statue together; but ten people cannot look together into the abyss of past time, and glory and genius. It is like looking into a grave, or conversing with a departed spirit. I cannot tell you anything which you do not find better in books; only that the half of the truth can never be told you of the general interest of the scene, or of the magnificence of St. Peter's, or of the magic of the Apollo. . . . My dear Christian, I hope Charles is not feeling his arm troublesome; if he does, come away, and I shall be your cicerone. It would be an immense delight to me to see you, and I know that both you and Charles would delight in it. Take a lesson in Italian now and then, by way of preparation. Give my best love to all friends, especially the *Laird himsel'.*—Yours affectionately,   T. E.

21. TO DR. CHARLES STUART.

Rome, 19*th April* 1824.

My dear Friend,— . . . This city on the seven hills is really a wonderful place. It is full of history and prophecy—full both of the past and the future; and the religious system which has been concocted here fills up the sum of its marvels. Yesterday was Easter Day, and the way of celebrating the resurrection of our Lord which has been adopted here, is to illuminate St. Peter's from the ground to the Cross on the cupola, and to set off artificial fireworks from St. Angelo! This was the work of the evening, and in the forenoon the Pope gave his benediction from a balcony in the Quirinal, which was announced to those who

were not present by the firing of cannon! My astonishment is, that the thing goes on, for all the people seem to
regard it with perfect levity; they like it merely as a
spectacle, and surely they could easily have the same
spectacle without the expense and load of the system to
which it is attached. Assuredly there is not a place on
the earth which is better fitted to be considered as the
representative of human nature in all its efforts, and especially in its rebellion against heaven; and as such it stands
forth in Scripture. There we see it set up as the mark of
the denunciations of God. It is the great theatre on which
man has exhibited his powers, and his weakness, and his
corruption; he has endeavoured to do everything without
God, and the ruins of the Forum and the Palatine tell the
success; he has endeavoured even to be religious without
God, and that experiment I should think is drawing to its
conclusion. I suppose that you have heard by this time of
the measures which have been taken by the Government
of the Canton de Vaud against the Momiers as they are
called, *i.e.* against real religion. The common people are
against it, *i.e.* serious religion in Switzerland, which is not
a usual thing (although the Wesleys found the same thing,
to be sure, in England), and the Government, leaning upon
this feeling, has forbidden all meetings for religious purposes amongst the Momiers, under severe penalties. I
have a great mind to send the narrative which Empeytaz
(a friend of Lady Carnegie) has written to me of the trans-
actions, to Mr. F. Gordon, in case any statement on the subject should be required. But it is not wise nor safe to raise
much cry in England about these matters,—it only exas-
perates the Continental Governments, without effecting any
change. So if I send, there must be no use of that sort
made of it. . . .

I have just heard this morning also from my good kind

mother, who is my most constant and faithful correspondent. She tells me she is going to Harrogate this summer, along with a party of our relations, who go more for the sake of Mrs. Cheape and Mrs. Stevens than for the waters. She tells me very agreeable things of the —— family. It is good news indeed to hear that the bounds of the Saviour's kingdom are extending.—Yours affectionately,   T. E.

22. TO HIS BROTHER-IN-LAW, CAPTAIN PATERSON.

Rome, 17*th May* 1824.

MY DEAR JAMES,—I have just received the intelligence of dear Ralph's death.[1] I desire to return thanks for the mercy of God towards him, in giving him a clear sense of the necessity and the sufficiency of the great atonement. I don't think that there was one of my relations to whom I felt so much brotherliness as to Ralph; he had a noble heart and a gentle heart, and self seemed to have little to do in his composition. It is a heart-breaking blow to his family. Oh may it be blessed to them, and, if their hearts are broken, may they have new hearts given them from above! It is a purpose of love, however, we know—Ralph and Jeannie, the eldest and the youngest. The root must shake, whilst the branches fall. Mr. Dundas will feel it strongly.

I am going to Naples to-morrow : I wish to see the place where my father died. There is a poor Swiss here who is dying. I leave my servant here to look after him when I am at Naples, and if he is alive when I return, I must stay with him. He has no earthly friend here but me. I shall write to my mother at Harrogate from Naples. Give my love to Davie and the children, and to the Dundas family most particularly and affectionately. I wish we were all

His cousin, Ralph Dundas, second son of James Dundas, Esq. of Ochtertyre.

fairly grafted into the true Vine, and then, come life or come death, all would be well.   Farewell, my dear brother. The sight of your hand from Paris gave me a start; it is a hand I should like well to clasp again.

By the by, a few days ago I sent some corrections for a fourth edition of the Essay on Faith[1] to Waugh and Innes. They relate chiefly to the arrangement.   I should like well that Mr. Russell's eye and mind glanced over them.   If he has any business in Edinburgh for a day, he might do it. There is no judgment that I have the same confidence in.

I intend to be back at Geneva by the end of June; but that will depend on the life of the Swiss.   He is a thorough Christian.—Yours, etc.,   T. ERSKINE.

23. TO DR. CHARLES STUART.

ROME, *27th June* 1824.

MY DEAR FRIEND,—. . . I am preparing to leave this capital of the world now, and to return to Geneva.   This is a place for collecting the materials of future thought and feeling; and I do not think that in this respect I have altogether lost my time here.   Providence has called me to be the witness of a most interesting scene lately—the death of a poor Swiss artist, a peaceful and faithful follower of Christ.   His lungs had been attacked some years ago. In this situation it pleased God to make him acquainted with that truth which comforts the mourner and strengthens the faint, through the instrumentality of a very worthy man, a Mr. Perrot, whom I know.   Since that time he has been sustained, and enabled to walk on in the narrow path. Last autumn, when Mr. Noel left Geneva for Italy, he was requested by Mr. Perrot to take this poor sick artist along with him, which he did as far as Florence, from whence he proceeded alone to Rome.   The winter was very severe,

[1] This edition was issued in 1825.

and the health of this poor man (I should not say *poor*, for
he is rich), evidently declined apace. He was without
friends, without comforts, without sleep, for whenever he
lay down the cough seized him, and in a country whose
language was strange to him ; but he was not without God,
and God was to him friends, and comfort, and rest, and
home. I arrived here about the middle of February, and
got acquainted with him, and saw him occasionally. He
could go about and walk a little then, and he used to come
and sit with Mr. Noel and me from time to time ; and we
always found him most edifying, as far as his extreme
modesty would permit him to communicate to us his
Christian experience. For long he had been in the habit
of living much alone, and of speaking more to God than to
man ; and this high intercourse had left its traces on him
—its blessed traces of holiness and peace. As the spring
advanced he got worse and weaker, and in April he became
unable to leave his room. I saw a great deal of him then.
I was particularly struck with the exceeding seriousness
of his mind. He was much afraid of thinking or speaking
of religion in an unfit or unawakened state of mind, or
rather, I should say, without intense feeling. His conscience
went so far on this matter that he would not allow me to
read to him, unless his mind could come to the stretch.
He was afraid of dishonouring God by not giving Him the
whole effort and exertion of his spirit. He used to tell
me that his sleepless nights were delightful opportunities
of communion with God. The joy which filled his heart
received very little abatement from his disease. On the
day before his death he told me that he had " had moments
that day which he could not express—*des moments inex-
primables.*" You who are in health, he said, can scarcely
conceive the manifestations which God makes to His people
as they stand on the brink of the grave. He has finished

his course, and kept the faith, and received the crown.[1]
My dear R. D. has also, I rejoice to hear, been made a
bright monument of the grace of God.   Let us then be of
good courage and follow the pillar of cloud and of fire, as it
conducts us into the promised land.   My dear friend, I
long to see you again.   I have many friends, but few fathers.
When Mr. W. Erskine[2] from Bombay arrives, I hope that
you will see him.   I am sure that he must be a very amiable
and a very able man.—Yours affectionately,   T. E.

24. TO DR. CHARLES STUART.

BASLE, 18*th August* 1824.

MY DEAR FRIEND,—I am very sorry to find that you
have had some painful family trials[3] lately.   May the gracious
Sender sanctify them to you and to all interested!   You
certainly have not your good things in this life.   They
are, I confidently trust, awaiting you in that mansion which
the blessed Redeemer has gone before to prepare for sinners
who have found it good to be afflicted, and who have been
driven out of every other refuge, and forced to seek shelter
only under the shadow of His grace.   There is peace with
Him, and in vain do we expect it out of His presence.
We must live continually under the sense of His presence—
of His near presence.   I am persuaded that this is the very
secret and heart of religion.   The great use of the Christian doctrines is just to make us acquainted with the character of the great Being in whose hand we live, and with
our relation to Him.   We are short-sighted, and often

[1] For two interesting and affecting notices of this Swiss artist, see
Appendix, No. IV. p. 371.

[2] Sir James Mackintosh's son-in-law, author of the "History of India
under the two first Sovereigns of the House of Taimur."

[3] One of the most painful—the fatal duel in which Sir Alexander
Boswell was shot by the eldest son of Dr. Stuart, James Stuart, Esq. of
Dunearn.

mistake good for evil; but the light of his presence makes
us see plainly. Let us live in prayer for this great blessing
of seeing, and loving, and reposing in God, as manifested
in the cross of Christ.

I arrived at this interesting place last night. The
atmosphere of the place is peaceful and holy. . . .

25. TO HIS SISTER MRS. STIRLING.

GENEVA, *22d Sept.* 1824.

MY DEAR CHRISTIAN,—. . . . You were well off for
weather in crossing the Simplon, and I am sure that you
have enjoyed it much, and that you are satisfied that even
Switzerland cannot show anything superior to it in sublimity. You were also delighted with Baveno; I am sure you
could not be otherwise. And [I am sure] that you have
been struck with the appearance of rich production through
Lombardy. Virgil calls Italy "the bounteous mother of
men and fruits." You are at present surrounded by the
purple vintage. I delight in that exuberance of nature
that pours itself almost unasked over these sunny hills,
and vales, and plains. I shall direct this to Florence.
You must go to the Gallery about twelve, when one of the
custodes, who are gentlemen, and do not receive money,
commences the round of all the *camere* or chambers. The
tribune, in which the chiefest specimens, both of sculpture
and painting, are assembled, is generally open. There is
the Venus de Medici and a beautiful Apollo. There are
several Raphaels. Now, just begin and study Raphael.
Remark the goodness, and the worth, and the piety of his
faces, separate altogether from the fine art and execution.
There are two little Madonnas, or rather Holy Families, on
the left hand as you enter, in his early style, with blue
landscape behind them. Observe the face of the young

Saviour in one of these. The St. John in the Desert is very striking. Observe Domenichino's portrait of a Cardinal, very like Dr. Chalmers, I think, when he appears gruff, in which predicament you perhaps have never seen him. In the Pitti, hunt Raphael without remorse or shame. There are several in all his manners. Observe Ezekiel's Vision; what a colossal and imposing strength he has contrived to represent in that small compass! Madonna della Seggiola—the loveliest head I ever saw, except the one at Dresden. The St. Mark by *Fra Bartolomeo*. That was a great painter; attend to him. A portrait of Hippolito de' Medici, by Titian, in one of the back rooms, over the door—a splendid thing, look for it. Ask for the room where two Salvator Rosas hang. It is not usually shown, but ask. There are also beautiful Poussins there. Go to the church of Santa Croce, where the great men of Florence are buried—most interesting. Go to the Annunciata Vestibule to see the frescoes of Andrea del Sarto and his scholars; he was a great painter too. Go also to the Santa Maria Novella—curious old frescoes. There is an Irish padre named Padre Tomaso (Father Thomas), who likes to show the English the sights there. You may ask for him if you are curious to see the oldest frescoes. Go to the chapel of the Medici. Observe the statues of that family by Michael Angelo. There is something very imposing and solemn in those two statues—very unlike the antique, but fully giving the idea of the baronial character and chivalry of the middle ages. The Church of the Medici itself is much more rich than beautiful. Admire the baptistery, especially the door towards the Cathedral. Admire also the bridge of Santa Trinità, which is most beautiful in its form. Farewell, my dear sister. In the midst of all that, keep near God. Draw nigh unto Him, and He says that He will draw nigh unto us. . . .

E

26. TO HIS SISTER MRS. STIRLING.

GENÈVE, *27th Oct.* 1824.

MY DEARLY BELOVED CHRISTIAN,—. . . Do you find
yourselves at home now in Rome? Have you got the
camere of Raphael by heart? Have you drunk the spirit of
the Apollo and the Mercury (falsely and foully degraded
into Antinous), and the Laocoon? There is an eternity
in all these things—a vivacious principle of beauty and of
nobleness—which knows no age. And the Grand Juno,
and the Minerva in the Braccio Nuovo, and Thorwald-
sen's John the Baptist and his hearers, and Christ and the
Apostles. But I always haver when I commence on these
things, and they'll trot me at home if I don't take care of
myself. There is no trotting on the Continent. I hope
you go to the Vatican as often as you can, and that you
expand your spirit in St. Peter's. There also, there is an
eternity—and a different world from that which is without,
and a different climate. And the splendid mosaics, and the
tall beckoning silent figures of the saints and martyrs, and
the light and the air which play so freely through it.
And observe how beautifully the dome rests upon the
four arches! There is a Prophet Isaiah, by Raphael, in St.
Augustine. Go often to St. Andrea della Valle, and taste
Domenichino, the St. John especially. I hope that you will
enjoy all these things, for your own sake, and for my sake
in the way of companionship when you come home—*mais
le déjeûner est servi.* The Cramers and Vernets inquire
most kindly always after you.

Try, Christian, and connect these works of art with the
religious sentiment. That seems to me the great secret of
taste as well as of enjoyment. God is the source of beauty
—in Him you find the spring and fountain-head. My
dear sister, may He bless you, etc.

27. TO THE SAME.

Genève, 29th Oct. 1824.

(The day of the month with me is entirely
a piece of guess-work.)

MY DEAREST CHRISTIAN,— . . . Cultivate the high friendship and acquaintanceship of God. Be looking to Him hourly for that rich gift which He has promised to bestow—His Holy Spirit, His own blessed presence in the heart. It may indeed well be called an unspeakable gift; no tongue can speak it, no heart adequately conceive it. I am looking for it, my sister, and I am confident that one day it will be given. Although He seem to tarry, He yet really tarrieth not. As I said before, endeavour to see God in the arts. Everything of sublime or beautiful touches the infinite. You can put no limit to the sublime or the beautiful; the finest exhibitions of them only point you farther on, and farther and farther until you reach that Source whence all things flow. You may see power, and love, and purity or holiness in every fine work; where these are wanting, really beauty and sublimity are wanting.—Farewell. T. E.

CHAPTER IV.

Letters at Home, 1825-26.

In the spring of 1825 Mr. Erskine returned to Scotland, taking up his headquarters at Linlathen, where his " mother and sister and household " were—in the summer months making a round of the cousinhood, the Dundases, the Grahams, the Stirlings, etc.; in autumn exchanging visits with Dr. Chalmers, now resident at St. Andrews; giving a large part of the winter to his sister, Mrs. Stirling, at Cadder; and in August 1826 leaving Linlathen again for another visit to the Continent.

The following letters were written during this period :—

28. TO DR. CHALMERS.

LINLATHEN, *6th May* 1825.

MY DEAR FRIEND,—I am happy to think that I am so near you once more. There are many subjects on which I wish to speak to you, beyond the reach and the extent of a letter, which I have been treasuring up for you during my peregrinations. Will you give me the geographical plan of your life for the next month, that I may see where I can cross you? I have spent this last week in renewing my acquaintance with my mother and sister and household, and I purpose to set off on Monday first, to make a circuit of friendships, beginning with Edinburgh, and then taking the Stirling environs, and then Glasgow and Ren-

frewshire.   If you remain another month at St. Andrews,
I shall take you on my return.   I have a most cordial wish
to see you, for, though I have not given you much epistolary evidence of my remembrance, yet there are few whom
I hold so dear.   I shall send you the speech of the Duke
de Broglie in the French House of Peers, on the question
of the law of Sacrilege, which his wife, the daughter of
Madame de Staël, desired me to give to you, with her compliments.

Give my kindest regards to Mrs. Chalmers and your
children.   You had better address your answer to the care
of James Dundas, Esq., St. Andrew Square, Edinburgh.

T. ERSKINE.

29. TO MR. MONTAGU.

GARTUR, 11th *August* 1825.

MY DEAR FRIEND,—How is Mrs. Montagu?   I have
been blaming myself for not making inquiries about her,
and for not thanking you for your letter and for Gurney's
book.   There is one thing that I feel assured of in her
case, and it is, that she is one of those for whom all things
work together for good—she is a pilgrim in her Lord's
service, either acting or suffering.   And where I am, says
He, there shall My servants be   I had a letter from Mr.
Noel the other day, giving tolerable accounts of Mrs. N.'s
health.   His plans are yet entirely unsettled.   I should
like to see him fixed in a good-sized chapel in London, or
in Mr. Way's chapel in Paris, perhaps.   What do you
think of that?   I heard from the General at Vevey lately.
I like these voices that come from a distance, reminding
us of kindness which is never past, and of pleasant scenes,
and of that union which no distance can destroy, and of
that family who are travelling all of them to the same
home.   I hope you see the Waldegraves occasionally.

I like Mrs. Waldegrave very much. She has a delightful natural disposition, and I am sure that Mrs. Montagu's society would be of great service to her. I hope that you are neither at London nor at Brighton in this weather, but in some place where there are shady trees and green fields. Tell Mrs. M. that I have just met a friend of hers who has been uttering much kindness of her—Mrs. Erskine of Cardross, the sister of Miss Elphinstone. I am going to Cardross to-day. I have not been there for nearly twenty years, but I passed some part of my childhood there, and it looks beautiful and venerable to my memory, like the mountains of Neuchatel to you. Are you going away to these mountains again, do you think? I hope you cultivate George Wigram's affection for you, excellent fellow that he is.

Have you formed any plan yet for yourselves : where you are to live, and what you are to do? I sometimes regret that I have not some fixed necessary employment. There is much time lost when one has to consider every day how the day is to be spent. And when we have learned to offer up every duty connected with our situation in life as a sacrifice to God, a settled employment becomes just a settled habit of prayer. I would not choose a town life if I had my choice; at the same time there is really little difference :—

> Whilst place we seek, or place we shun,
> The soul finds happiness in none ;
> But with our God to guide our way,
> 'Tis equal joy to go or stay.

I am on the world at present, paying visits to my friends. It will soon be all over. He that shall come will come, and will not tarry. Give my affectionate regards to Mrs. Montagu, and believe me, my dear Sir, to be most truly yours,   T. ERSKINE.

30. TO DR. CHALMERS.

MY DEAR FRIEND,—I thank you for your kind invitation, which I feel anxious enough to accept. I am quite sure that I could work better in your house than I can in my own. My secular business is really nothing at present, but I live in terror of it whilst I am in my own house. I am going to pay a visit at Keir and some other places in that neighbourhood, and then I intend to return by Edinburgh. If you are at home about that time, I might profit by your invitation. I shall leave this on Wednesday, if nothing comes in the way. I have had a letter within these few days from Madame de Broglie, who tells me that she has been reading your Civic Economy with much satisfaction. I wish you would enable me to say to her that you have read her husband's speech on the law of Sacrilege. She has much of high and free mind, and her thoughts are all feelings. I wish you knew her; there are very few people that I prize like her. Perhaps you would be so good as to send me a line to Keir, Dunblane, giving me an idea of your movements for three weeks or a month. I beg to be kindly remembered to Mrs. Chalmers and to Grace. Farewell.—Yours affectionately,   T. ERSKINE.

LINLATHEN, 23d *July* 1825.

It was not till some weeks later that the visit to St. Andrews was made out, and of it the sole remembrance now is in this short note :—

TO THE SAME.

MY DEAR SIR,—I have left my coloured spectacles behind me at St. Andrews; they are of a greyish-blue, in a red case. I should not have troubled you about such a trifle, had it not been that I received them from *a De Staël* as a memorial, and I should be sorry to lose them on that account. When you find them, keep them till I come for them.—Farewell. Yours most affectionately,   T. E.

EDINBURGH, 22*d Nov.*

31. TO MISS C. ERSKINE.[1]

LINLATHEN, 2*d April* 1826.

MY DEAR COUSIN,—I often wonder at the very little intercourse that sometimes passes between persons who feel very closely knit together. I feel very near to you, and yet what is the amount of our intercourse through the year? This world is a place for making acquaintances rather than for cultivating friendships. We cannot cultivate friendship here—we must just stop a little; and, in the meantime, let us cultivate that only friendship which we can cultivate here, a friendship with that Friend who sticketh closer than any created friend, even with Him who loved us and gave Himself for us, and hath made us unto our God kings and priests. Ay, this is the friendship that is worth having, and it is the root of all other friendships. We shall be good friends of each other in that city of God if we are here friends to its King. Many of our friends are gone to that city, and are joined to the cloud of witnesses who bore their testimony that the reproach of Christ is greater riches than the treasures of this world, and His cross greater happiness than its ease. They now know both parts of the inheritance, both the suffering and the glory; and they see that suffering is the thing out of which God makes glory—it is the raw material of glory. Have you got the Pilgrim's Progress? Read the account of Mr. Standfast's passing over the river near the end of Christian's

---

[1] The Rev. Dr. John Erskine had nine sons and five daughters, of whom only one son and three daughters survived him. The eldest daughter, Mary, was Mrs. Stuart of Dunearn—the youngest, Christian, was the cousin to whom this letter was addressed.

pilgrimage. There are two young sufferers that I wish to hear about and whom you care and know about,—Ly. L. B. and J. E.[1] For I think of her as one on whom I trust that the new name is written, and though I have never seen her to my knowledge, yet my expectation of her society through eternity gives me the feeling of tried acquaintanceship.

32. TO MISS STUART.[2]

CADDER, *14th June* 1826.

MY DEAR MISS STUART,—I wish to let you understand that my love and reverence for your father have not died with him, but that he still holds his place in my affection and in my gratitude. I have to bless God for my acquaintance with him. I found in him a friend, and a father, and a guide. The intercourse which I had with him was a continual incitement to me in the search after God, and I regard it as one of the talents of which I have to give in an account; and I now feel how negligent I was in the use of it. I did not know a human being on this earth on whose faithful and affectionate friendship I more confidently relied, and he is now in glory—in the second part of the inheritance. He suffered with Christ I believe here, and now I feel a joyful assurance that he reigns with Him. His soul had the mark of God upon it. The desire of his soul was after God, and his business was to understand the will and word of God. I think that it was on the Monday after he was taken ill that he said to me, as I was pressing his hand on taking leave, "*I hope to spend an eternity with you.*" Amen.

[1] Lady Lucy Bruce, afterwards Lady Lucy Grant of Kilgraston, and Miss Jane Erskine, daughter of Mr. E. Erskine of Bombay.

[2] Daughter of Dr. Charles Stuart.

33. TO M. MERLE D'AUBIGNÉ.

LINLATHEN, DUNDEE, 26*th June* 1826.

MY DEAR FRIEND AND BROTHER,—Grace, mercy, and peace be unto you! Perhaps you think that I have been ungrateful and forgetful of the claims of friendship with regard to you, but there is not a man breathing on the earth whom I love more than you, or think of more frequently. Take this assurance in place of a regularly sustained epistolary correspondence. Well, how are you getting on in the pilgrimage? Oh, what I wish is, that spiritual eye, and ear, and heart, that might see, and hear, and feel God in everything—in every object of nature, in every event of time, in every duty, every difficulty, every sorrow, every joy. Enoch walked with God, and God took him. What a history of a life below and a removal to a life above! Such a life below let us try to lead, my friend, and let us daily learn to count all things but loss for the excellency of the knowledge of Christ Jesus. I should like well to be with you for a little while; it is a pleasure to me to feel with you, and to think with you, and to know also that you have a pleasure in letting your spirit walk with mine. It is possible that I may be on the Continent soon again, and you will be one of my attracting points, but I shall let you know before, and arrange with you our times of meeting. I know not what may have been your lot since I parted with you, whether sorrowful or joyful, but I trust that it has been accompanied with a Father's blessing to your soul. As I look upon you as one of God's children, I may presume that you have had sorrow, for the promise is, " In the world ye shall have tribulation; *in Me* ye shall have peace." How sweet the promise is! How consoling to receive tribulation as the fulfilment of a Father's promise —as the private cipher agreed on between the Saviour and the saved! I have been seeing a good deal of sorrow lately, and I have myself drunk a little of that salutary cup—Ye shall drink of the cup that *I* drink of. Is it not a high privilege to partake with the King of Righteousness and the King of Peace—the friend of the friendless, my refuge, my portion? You will have felt with the poor Moneys, both in their sorrow and in their consolation with which our gracious Lord has visited their wounded hearts. Remember me kindly to the M— family. My sister, whom you saw at Brussels, and Mr. Stirling, are in the same house with me at present, and they send you their kindest regards. You gained their affections very much, and I liked them the better for liking you so well. Farewell, my dear friend. Remember me before the throne where the answerer of prayer sits, and ask for me what you feel that you need for yourself—a heart devoted singly to God, breathing after communion with Him, and consecrating all its movements to His service. When you write to your mother, give her my affectionate regards.—Yours, in the bond which endures, T. ERSKINE.

34. TO MRS. MONTAGU.

LINLATHEN, *Thursday,* 13*th July* 1826.

MY DEAR MRS. MONTAGU,— . . . Malan has been a good deal in Scotland. I daresay he has been a good deal disappointed with many things and persons that he has seen here. Religion in Scotland is too much a thing of science, and too little a thing of personal application and interest. His reality pleases me very much; but I cannot go along with his continual demand of assurance of salvation from every person that he meets. I think that he confounds two things which are distinct—*pardon* and *salvation*. Pardon is a free gift without respect of character in those who receive it; salvation respects the character, and is in fact only another name for sanctification; it arises from the spiritual understanding and belief of the pardon revealed to the soul by the Spirit of God. I believe that I have the first, viz., pardon, for I read that the blood of Christ cleanseth from all sin; but I cannot believe that I have salvation when I feel the evil heart of unbelief opposing the will of God within me.

Prayer is our business in this world—prayer for that all-efficient Spirit, who can make, and who alone can make, all things new. I need that operation. I feel that I can do nothing.—Yours affectionately,   T. ERSKINE.

35. TO MISS C. ERSKINE.

LINLATHEN, *9th August* 1826.

MY DEAR COUSIN,—I hope you don't think that I have forgotten you because I have never inquired after you since I left you. I can assure you that it is not with me, "out of sight out of mind." But my heart has been sore occupied with many things—with parting from my friends and from my duties. I sometimes question whether I am right, and that is a heavy question when the answer is not perfectly clear. I think I am right, but yet I desert a post which cannot be otherwise filled. I trust that the Good Shepherd will lead me, and make me to hear His voice, and follow it. My heart often wanders down your lane, and enters your quiet dwelling, and sits down with you, and escapes into the past and the future, the two great eternities between which the *present* stands as an agitated point. The past is with God, and the future is with God, and so also is the present, but we don't feel this so much. There is too much emotion connected with the present to allow us to see it as it really is. Eternity is to my mind just the same thing as God, and when I lose myself in eternity, I feel that I lose myself in God. That is a good

way of losing ourselves, is it not?   That loss is great gain.
I remember you at least twice a day—in connection with
eternity, and in connection with some earthly friends whom
you love.   I have given you Dr. Stuart's place.   No, I cannot say that; he shall keep his own place in my heart,
though he wants not the prayers of his friends.   I hope
that you are getting on pretty well, in spirit, and, if it be
God's will, in body also.   Do you hear from Rachel occasionally?   She is a faithful correspondent and a faithful
friend.   I like to say that of her to one who knows how
true it is.   How is Miss Stuart?   I trust that she is reaping the precious fruits of affliction, and that she drinks
more of the Fountain now that her chief cistern is broken.
I expect to be in town in about a week, when I hope to
see you a little before I go hence, and to take another *tack
of my key*, and another turn in Heriot's green.   Farewell.
Believe me, with love and affection, to be yours,   T. E.
1 Peter v. 10.

36. TO HIS SISTER MRS. STIRLING.

Sept. 1826.

My Kitty,— . . . I saw Warwick Castle and Kenil-
worth, and a very beautiful country about Wellsbourne.
The day that we arrived from Hinckley there was a shower
of hail that broke a great deal of the glass of the neighbourhood, killed partridges and poultry, and cut cucumbers
in two.   William is a devoted fox-hunter.   Lord Mackenzie
says that a man might as well be hanged as be a fox-hunter,
for he is utterly lost to the use of life.   Lord M. may have
a right to speak, for he is useful ; but I think an idle traveller is as much lost, and might be taken up and hanged
on equally good grounds.   Write to me to Paris, chez
Lafitte ; I shall send also to Poste Restante, of course ; and
let me know your plans for the winter.   If we lived nearer,

we would be mutual helps.   I hope to improve my absence
at present by cultivating the opportunity of intercourse
with God, uninterrupted by the creature; I desire to know
what that life is which is hid with Christ in God—to know
it experimentally as my own life, to feel Christ as the
fountain-head of my life, a fountain out of the reach of
danger.   That is the only safe life, is it not, my dear
sister?   Oh, let us not be half Christians; I have been
that.   Kitty, I hope it may please God to give you and
me to know what flesh and blood cannot reveal to us.
The thought of you is to me always a cheering, pleasing
thought; you are a part of all my expectations of worldly
happiness.   Oh, may we be conducted to one of those
mansions.   Love to Charles; I love him.   T. E.

37. TO MISS C. ERSKINE.

LONDON, *7th September* 1826.

MY DEAR COUSIN,—I must pay you one more little
visit before I leave the country.   I sleep, or more properly
spend, this night on board the steam-packet for Boulogne,
and then the sea will separate between me and you, and
much of what is dear to me on this earth.   I have been
detained beyond my purposed time by different circumstances.   Indeed, I expected to have been in Geneva before
now; but it is always soon enough to leave one's country.
London is to me at present a desert.   I have hardly a
friend in town.   Mrs. Rich,[1] and Christy, and Maria, make
up my account, with a few stragglers.   I am just going to
try Mrs. Oliphant.   I expect to meet on the other side of
the water with the Torphichens[2] and dear Katherine and

[1] Daughter of Sir James Mackintosh.

[2] Mr. Erskine's cousin Margaret, second daughter of John Stirling, Esq.
of Kippendavie and Kippenross, married James Sandilands, tenth Lord
Torphichen.

Jane.[1] The Continent has something of the home feeling
about it as long as they remained there, and now I have
friends there—real friends—friends for eternity. But the
home feeling is wanting, the charm of blood-relation-
ships grows upon me very much. I love my kindred, and
much reason have I to thank God that so many of my
kindred according to the flesh belong to the family of
heaven. Christy and Maria, I am glad to find, like Edinburgh, and will probably return there soon to reside. You
are one of their chief points of attraction. There is something very interesting to me in their silent unexpressed
affection. They are true people, but their loss is that they
have never had anything either to do or to think of. They
seem to be without excitement. Would you prefer having
too little or too much excitability?

Hold me in your memory as I do you, near and dear.
Give my kind regards to Miss Stuart, whom I often think
of as her dear father's representative. When and where
shall we meet again? In the Lord, and in the Lord's
time. Remember me kindly to your brother and any
friends. I could send friendly words to your garden, and
your sun-dial, and your elder-bush, and your quiet Lane.[2]

[1] His sister-in-law and cousin Mrs. James Erskine, and her sister Miss
Jane Stirling.

[2] Dr. Erskine's family lived in Lauriston Lane.

CHAPTER V.

38. TO HIS SISTER MRS. PATERSON.

PARIS, 2d *October* 1826.

MY DEAR DAVIE,—Yesterday was your birthday, and it was also Sunday, and I thought much of you and yours during its services. For the first time in my life, I received the sacrament twice on one day : first, according to the Church of England, at Mr. Way's ; and again in the evening, at a small reunion of French Protestants, under Mr. Olivier, one of the exiles from the Canton de Vaud. This last service was very simple and very sweet. It was between 8 and 9 o'clock at night. It was a supper; the meeting was assembled just to break bread and pray. Olivier's address was on the duty of purging out the old leaven when we keep this feast. The characteristic of all these persecuted Christians is reality, and oh reality is everything ! They have found religion to be a thing worth suffering for, they have found it a support under suffering ; and they speak of it to others, not as of a logical system, but as of a new life, a heavenly strength, a very present help in trouble, and a medicine and a remedy for every evil under the sun. My dear Davie, I knew that you would be thinking of me, and thus we met together. May the Lord unite us in the bond of Christian love, and faith, and hope. . . . I read the 53d Psalm this morning, and I thought how many fools this vain world holds. I felt my heart condemn me as one of them. . . .

I have been walking in the Tuileries with Merle, and talking with him about many things. You remember he had written to me about a proposal that he should be the tutor of the Prince of Orange's family. He has been hesitating about accepting it, from conscientious motives; for there is another governor, and he fears that he may not have full liberty in giving such religious instruction as he may think proper, in consequence of the interference and opposition of this man. As we came home, we met Mr. Lewis Way, who was coming on horseback to call on me. He was looking up at the Column in the centre of the Place Vendôme, and he repeated a tirade of thirty or forty blank verses on the subject, composed on the occasion; very good indeed. He told me that the colossal statue of Napoleon, which was made to stand on the top of it, was now at the foot of the Duke of Wellington's staircase. . . . Farewell. I am going to my table-d'hôte. Yours affectionately.

Oct. 4th.—I intend to set out for Geneva to-morrow.

39. TO MISS RACHEL ERSKINE.

COPPET, 1*st November* 1826.

DEAR COUSIN RACHEL,—It is near midnight, and I set off to-morrow morning early for the Simplon. It is not therefore with the idea of writing a long letter at present that I sit down now, but with the view of beginning one, which may bear some marks of my journey from this to Venice, and which may bear testimony to you of my love for you, whether I am in England, or Switzerland, or Italy. I leave several real friends here—most interesting, affectionate, confidential friends; and there are in fact as many of them as might satisfy any moderate appetite for friendship. I certainly could not have thought it possible for a stranger to have furnished himself with such an assortment of that article in so short a time. This house, for one, has been a home to me, and the family have been my brothers and my sister. There has been sorrow here also amongst my friends; indeed, my friends have a sort of luck for sorrow; but good-night, you shall have a little more from the Simplon.

Friday night, Brigue.—I left Coppet on Thursday morning. There are very few people in the world, at home or abroad, that I like half as well as I like Madame de Broglie, there is such a truth about her, such a superiority to everything that is little and low in character, such an activity of occupation with the thoughts and interests of eternity, such an expansion of fine and high mind dedicated to Him from whom it comes, and such a depth, and, at the same time, a *naïveté* of sentiment. And I have received from her the kindness of sisterly friendship. She, and her husband, and her brother were up to bid me adieu at 7 in the morning. . . . You have often heard me speak of Madame Vernet,[1] whom I like second best here. I wish you knew her. She has all the warmth and energy of heart that cousin Annie had—a continual spring-tide of strong and generous feeling. She always puts me in mind of the well of waters springing up unto everlasting life. I have conversed many hours with her, and I never felt her feeling flag for an instant,—it is an unfailing stream from the fountain above. Her intellect is far from being of the first order, naturally, and it has not been much cultivated; but her heart, impregnated by religion, is full of genius. I have said that I liked her second best, and yet were I permitted and required to change altogether with any other human being—character, hopes, feelings, for time and eternity—I

---

[1] One of the Pictet family, mother-in-law of Diodati and of the Baron de Staël.

think that I should name Madame Vernet. You will think
it curious that I should make any comparison between her
and cousin Annie when I tell you that she has not a single
particle of merriment in her composition. She is essentially
serious. You remember what Bishop Burnet says of Leighton, that he had known him twenty years, and that he had
never all that time known him to say a word or do an action that he would not wish to have been the last word or
action of his life. I have not known Madame Vernet
twenty years, but in other respects, I could say the same
thing of her. I arrived here this morning and made an
attempt to get up the mountain, but there has been and is
a heavy fall of snow, and I was forced back again. Sir N.
and Lady Mildmay are fellow-prisoners with me here.
We dined together as fellow-sufferers. Oh! it is a land of
beauty this—of beauty that thrills the heart. I can weep
at will whilst I look at it. There is a deep melancholy in
the highest order of natural beauty, and a holiness. It
seems to recall the original state of man, and to reproach
him, and yet to compassionate him for having lost it. I
don't wonder at your remaining unseduced by Sully's
château, but if you came here, I would not answer for
your nationality. No, nor yet for Mrs. Graham's, which
I conceive is still stronger than yours. But I must say
good-night. Here is a text for you, " And now, little children, abide in Him, that when He shall appear we may have
confidence, and not be ashamed before Him at His coming."

Saturday, 4th November.—Still at Brigue. The mountain is still inaccessible, but the snow has ceased to fall,
and the sun has shown himself. I have been walking and
wandering at this place in the midst of the Alps. I went
into a churchyard, and was attracted by a lighted candle
at the end of a low long vault. I found that the candle,
as usual, was standing before a crucifix; but the walls of

the vault on each side were lined with human skulls, piled one above another, from the ground to the roof. It is a shocking sight. The eyeless holes have such a fixed stare, and the jaws grin so ghastly,—the palace of the soul, without its tenant. My friend Gaussen, at Geneva, holds that the spirit is in a state of total insensibility from the instant of death until the instant of the general resurrection. The interval between death and judgment is in this way absolutely annihilated for them. Their last thought in this world will be instantaneously followed by the sound of the last trumpet. Their eye has just before death rested on the face of a friend on earth. The eye is closed, and instantaneously opened to behold the Saviour descend from heaven with clouds and great glory. If this be the case (which, however, I cannot make up my mind to entirely) when we look on the spectacle of death, it is striking to reflect that our accountable existence is passing during a period which is to the dead absolutely nothing, and that the first thought which will stir the beings to whom these trappings once belonged, and still belong perhaps, is to be a thought excited by the sight of Christ coming in power.

Sunday, 5th.—Still at Brigue. I have spent this day among the sanctities of nature—amongst glens, and green glades, and water-falls, and towering rocks, and autumnal colours, and fallen leaves, and gushing springs. There is something delightful in coming upon a fine water-fall by surprise, as it were, unconducted to it even by a footpath, so that you may almost consider yourself as the discoverer of it. Many such I saw to-day living in their own loveliness, unseen and unadmired. God made them and He pronounced them good, and the smile of His approbation seems still to dwell upon them, unpolluted and unmixed with the stupid gaze of man. The Rhone (before entering the Lake of Geneva) passes by this place, soon after issuing from the glacier; and as he hurries along, he receives supplies from the mountains which line his route. Each of these supplies forms a beautiful glen, branching off, higher up, into smaller ones, and exhibiting every variety of beauty; and then the vegetation, though vastly inferior to the south side of the mountain, is still very rich, fine sweet chestnuts and walnuts, and every kind of bush and shrub. I read several psalms in these little sanctuaries. Forty-second psalm, " deep calleth unto deep," water-fall calleth to water-fall. His afflictions followed so hard one upon another, that they seemed to call to each other. Do you ask for a heart which pants after God, which thirsts after Him, which renounces every other dependence, which chooses Him for its portion? I have been reading to-day a new little work of Malan's. It is called *la Mort du Fils Ainé.* It is the history of a death-bed conversion. It is very delightful to think of the inexhaustible riches of the love of God in Christ Jesus. I have seen a death-bed lately. Robert Melville, Lord Leven's brother, died at Geneva a few days ago. I have a particular destiny for witnessing such scenes. May He whose providence leads me into them, bless them to my soul. Oh that He would teach me Himself the import of eternity! I bless his name for what he has revealed to me, and am confounded before Him when I think how unfaithful and how negligent I have been under all His communications and invitations. I wrote to cousin C. before his death. I ought to have kept the letter till the history was finished; but I wrote Christian immediately afterwards, and requested her to write the accounts to Lauriston. Your last letter was a great treat to me, but all your letters are treats indeed. I hope to be on the top of the mountain to-morrow. " Lead us to the Rock that is higher than we." Good-night.

This day was a festival. The people are Roman Catholics,

and whilst I was out on my travels, and in the very midst of all the adorations of nature, I came across a procession, consisting of the greater part of the population of this neighbourhood (as I should imagine), clergy and laity, in cowls, and gowns, and coats of divers colours, carrying the host and banners, and flags of every description. Sometimes they sung, and sometimes they knelt; and ever and anon there was a discharge of musketry, and then a peal of church bells. It is a woful business. Their picturesque appearance amongst these rocks and thickets is a very poor compensation to the heart for the delusion out of which such scenes proceed, and which is strengthened by them. These mummeries are so little like intercourse with the God of holy love, and that is our God and our Father. I wonder how Mary Graham is to-day, and our other invalids, Jane Erskine, George Mac, Lady Lucy. I left a poor friend in Geneva, with a child in a fever, and this day was to be the critical day, the doctors told her. Her husband was at Berne, so ill that she dare not write the whole truth to him for fear of killing him. Their only surviving child. They had lost another five months ago; but the father, and the mother, and the child (though only nine) are all Christians. They are in possession of the only remedy for every evil under the sun. I like them well. What a privilege to be permitted to commend our friends to God, to know that they, as well as we, are in the hands of a Father, who afflicteth not willingly, but for our profit, that we might be partakers of His holiness!

Tuesday 7th, Simplon.—I remained Monday at Brigue, and had a delightful walk. I thought cousin Manie would have been enchanted with it, but it requires strength to have the full enjoyment of that country—muscles fit for climbing, and practised in it. The roads by which we must penetrate into its beauty and its mystery are more like chamois-paths than man-paths. The character of adventure and enterprise that belongs to these walks adds much to their interest in my estimation. If I had had paper and ability, I should have liked to have taken a sketch of a most curious scene which I came upon—a branch of the Rhone coming out of an immense hole, that recalled to me both the crater of Vesuvius and the Coliseum. I need not attempt to describe it, but it is worth going a good way to see. And now I am on the top of the Simplon, surrounded by eternal snows. The ascent was very diffi-cult. The road was very poorly cut through the snow, rather trodden indeed than cut ; and even that barely wide enough for one carriage, so that it was a prodigious *embar-ras* the meeting with other carriages coming down. I don't believe that more than two feet of snow had fallen, but the road was in many places covered with avalanches to the depth of several feet. The views were very magnificent, as you may suppose. Our wheels were taken off, and we were placed on traineaux or sledges, which slide more easily along the snow, and have the advantage of not sinking. The ——— are still my fellow-travellers. They are remark-ably civil, but I have been accustomed to such a different style of society, that I don't find them at all satisfactory, —they know nothing of God or eternity. What an extra-ordinary, and what an awful thing to say of any one born and educated in England, the land of Bibles—of any one born to die, and whose happiness through eternity depends entirely on the nature of his relation with God. Blessed is the man whom Thou choosest, O Lord, and causest to approach unto Thee. Grant to us that we may approach near unto Thee, that we may dwell in the secret of the Most High, and abide under the shadow of the Almighty. Good-night, my dear, dear Rachel. May God bless you and repay your kindness to me a hundred-fold in the blessings of eternity.

8th, Wednesday.—I hail you from Italy. I am now at Baveno, on the Lago Maggiore. I have been here twice before, and I have always stopped a day or two. The scenery is enchanting, the sky without a cloud, and the moon reflected by the lake and the distant Alpine snows. The descent from the Simplon, on the Italian side, is much more striking than on the Swiss side. The immense masses of rock, thrown together and piled one above another, give the idea of the ruins of a world. Nothing of man is to be seen, except the road on which we travel, which is, to be sure, a wonderful work. The snow lay thick till near the foot of the mountain. The road follows the course of a torrent which bursts its way through a narrow ravine, in many places scarcely wide enough to admit of the road. The precipitous rocks on each side are the very image of irresistible strength. Sometimes they rise like a wall, perpendicularly for many hundred feet, and sometimes they assume the varied shapes of ancient battlements and bartisans. As the torrent seldom runs many hundred yards perfectly straight, the road which coasts it is just a succession of glens shut in at both ends. The dashing of the torrent is the only sound which interrupts the silence of nature, if, indeed, it can be said at all to interrupt it. Well, I am on the south side of the Alps once more. As I look at them, I feel that they rise between me and my native land, and all the friends that I have in the world. Their immense forms, covered with snow, seem to forbid all intercourse; but that they cannot do, nothing but God can do that. I am perhaps at this moment thinking of the same thing with you, and is there not a perpetual spiritual intercourse between those who trust in the same Saviour, who love the same Father? Yes, the day is near when these " mountains shall depart, and these hills be removed ; but my kindness shall not depart, neither shall the covenant of my peace be removed, saith the Lord, who hath mercy on thee." Good-night. I saw the star of evening set to-night, and I thought of Holywell, where last I looked at it with you. Do you remember?

9th, Thursday, Baveno.—I have passed the greater part of this day in walking about this beautiful place. The —— have gone on to Milan, with all the Brigue party except myself. One of the party was a young Bolognese officer, who had been with Bonaparte at Moscow. I admired the perfect simplicity with which he answered any questions that were put to him on the subject. It is a great deal for a man not to be a coxcomb in such circumstances. My dear cousin, do you remember how to find out the north polar star by the indication of the two stars in the Great Bear called the Pointers? I told you once, and I have just now been looking at it, and thinking of you and other friends in the north. I like to associate my friends with particular stars, there is something so sweet, and intimate, and confidential in a star. The sun and the moon, but especially the sun, are too universal and general for particular friendship; but you may consider a star as your own. The moon is shining, and the white Alps, by her pale light, look like the ghosts of past ages as they mark their wild and livid tracery upon the deep blue of heaven. I would call them "their high mightinesses" were they not so unlike the beau-ideal of a Dutchman. How is Lady Mary?[1] I wish she were acquainted with the Noels. I have a great mind to tell him to try to make her acquaintance. I don't think that she could do anything but like him, for he is so likeable. I have just been reading the 118th Psalm, "I called upon the Lord in my distress, the Lord answered me and set me in a large place." This is written for our learning. It is written to the end that we

---

[1] Lady Mary Bruce.

also may call upon the Lord in distress, in the assurance
that we shall be answered.   I wish —— and all of us knew
that secret a little better, then the Lord would be our
strength and our song, He would become our salvation.
Give my kind regards to Henrietta.[1]   I am glad, both for
the honour of the inn-keeper and post-boy, and also for the
sake of Mrs. Graham's pocket, that she got back her money.
I lived a fortnight once at Keswick, and am well versed in
the beauties of the lake.

Baveno, 10*th*, *Friday*.—I know it must be a great bore to
get pages filled with phrases about lakes, and mountains,
and blue skies, especially if one's good-nature makes it a
matter of conscience to read them.   What a blessing it is
that there are things so good and so delightful, that no re-
petition of them can convert them into bores.   Were there
not some such things, eternity would be but a melancholy
prospect for us.   The song of heaven is called a new song,
although I suppose its elements must always be the same
to express its unwearying nature.   The affections are always
new, and to say the truth, whatever weariness my descriptions of the aforesaid mountains may produce in you, the
mountains themselves, and the blue sky into which they
push their pointed tops, and the rising sun, and the setting
sun, and the shining hosts of heaven, and the lake in whose
glassy surface all these reflect themselves, never tire me.
Their silence, and their simplicity, and their beauty are
ever new to me, there is no over-excitement in them.   I
went to-day to see a little lake a few miles from this—il
Lago d'Orta.   It is very beautiful, as everything is here.
I enjoy the solitude of these expeditions very much.   I am
thoroughly free.   As I rowed past a large chateau in a delicious situation, I had the curiosity to ask whose it was.
The boatman told me, and then added, *la contessa è morta
sta notte*,—the countess died this very night!   Yes, the

great spoiler is on the earth following the steps of sin. It
is a lovely place, but death entered it last night and carried
away his prey. It was a solemn night for her. How was
she prepared? Did she know Him, whom to know is everlasting life? He that believeth on me, though he were
dead, yet shall he live, and he that liveth and believeth on
me shall never die. This is just the reality after which
Poussin painted his Arcadian tomb (of which I have sent
you the engraving by Catherine). My heart often returns
to the Ochil hills, and your grand western boundary lighted
up by the setting sun, and the view from the Castle, and the
Links, and the Meadows, and the Pentlands from Heriot's
Green. And oh! how memory delights to revive the
various feelings of earthly or heavenly origin which have
been associated with these sweet scenes. But the night is
coming, on which some one will say of us what the boatman said of the countess, "he—she died last night." My
dear friends, may our God grant unto us that we may find
mercy of the Lord on that day.

Como, Sunday, 12*th.*—I came here yesterday. Though the
mountain boundary is fine through the whole of this Alpine
country, yet there are points and stretches superior to the
rest, and certainly I saw one of the finest yesterday, in
passing by Varese, between the Lago Maggiore and the
Lake of Como. "Thy faithfulness standeth like the great
mountains." I should like to think that you are at Mrs.
Greig's to-day and hearing (as I did once there), "In me
ye shall have peace;" but wherever you are, I hope that
your spirit may be touched from on high, and that your
soul may be fed by words from the mouth of God.

Milan, Thursday, 16*th.*—Milan is not a place that interests me. The cathedral is fine, and there are a few good
pictures—Leonardo da Vinci's Last Supper, Raphael's car-
toon of the School of Athens, and his Marriage of Joseph
and the Virgin, of which there is a beautiful engraving by

Longhi. It is worth your while to go to Linlathen to see that engraving. Oh, there is something there better than paintings or engravings—there is Christian worth and Christian love. At this distance I may venture to say, that I am acquainted with no person whose heart I believe to be more sincerely devoted to God than Davie. What you say is very true. I never can take pleasure in that place or in that country. But what have I to do with pleasure? If I were satisfied that my duty did not call me there, I should not hesitate. But I do not think that I shall be home before next November. . . . My dear, dear cousin, how I should like to see you beside me now! There are very few persons that I could tolerate as travelling companions, but you are one: I could tolerate you.

40. TO MISS RACHEL ERSKINE.

VENICE, 2d *January* 1827.

MY DEAR FRIEND,—It is a real pleasure to me to write to you. . . . —— is dead. Oh! do you not feel how true that word is, "Blessed are the dead that die in the Lord." I don't know what the state of his mind was, but I have a hope (which I would not willingly think contrary to the revelation of mercy) of the ultimate salvation of all.[1] I trust that He who came to bruise the serpent's head will not cease his work of compassion until he has expelled the fatal poison from every individual of our race. I humbly think that the promise bears this wide interpretation. You think not, I know. Well, the Judge of all the earth will do right. The Lord reigneth. —— has entered the invisible world. Oh that the living could realise the estimate which the dead form of things—things temporal and things eternal. My mother has given me the particulars of ——'s last days. We know not what the Spirit of the Creator

---

[1] One of the earliest expressions of a hope which he had cherished for some years.

says to the spirit of the creature at that awful time. I
hope for the departed (I hope in that unmeasured love
which gave the Saviour; in fact, my soul refuses to believe
in final ruin, when it contemplates the blood of Christ), and
I rejoice for the weeping friends that the last scene had so
much of peace and promise in it. I have been reading
over your letters again, and I cannot express to you what
I feel for your affection. May God's love dwell in your
heart and give you peace eternal. . . . When I pray for
my friends, I always pray that their prayers for me may be
heard. . . . What is the honest language of your heart?
Not of the conscience, but of the heart? I know no book
of man's composition that goes more to the quick than
Adam's *Private Thoughts.* He received the testimony of
the Bible concerning the depravity and deceitfulness of his
own heart, and he took part with God against himself.
That is what I should like to do truly and decidedly, to
take part with God against myself. I have been detained
here by the hospitality of my kind Christian friends, the
Moneys, much longer than I had intended. They have
great reason for thankfulness in the matter of their family,
who are all amiable, and almost all already pious, though
very young, yet they have great sorrows and anxieties !
Oh, "who shall deliver me from this body of death?"
Blessed be God, there is an answer to this most critical
question in the last verse of the 7th chapter of the Romans.

I leave this in the course of a few days for Rome, by
Mantua and Parma (where I have never yet been, and
where Correggio's finest pictures are) to Bologna, and then
by the way of Ancona. . . . You know that this is a very
singular place; it rises out of the water. Its streets are
canals, and its conveyances gondolas. Its oldest and most
characteristic palaces are of an architecture quite peculiar,
unconformed to any order, forming the link between

eastern and western architecture, or Christian and Maho-
metan, if it is not too absurd to designate material struc-
tures by such names. St. Mark's, the great cathedral, is
a good deal in the Mosque style. It is surmounted by
several domes or cupolas, of no great size. The famous
bronze horses are over the chief entrance. It is loaded
both inside and out with pillars of every kind of marble,
brought from every quarter of the world. It was built
evidently by the spoilers and the merchants of the East,
and this is the grand trophy of their exploits. They have
dedicated to God what they have robbed from men.

4th January.—I like to put several days into my letters
to you, that you may better understand how often and
how dearly I think of you. I hope my friends are all
well. I had a heavy, superstitious apprehension darkening
my mind yesterday. All things are in my Father's hand.
Oh for a right childlike dependence on His love! I have
been picture-hunting to-day. Almost all the good pictures
which were in the hands of individuals are sold out of
Venice. And at this very time there is a negotiation
going forward for the sale of the Barberigo collection, the
last good collection of genuine Titians. I saw to-day the
son of the last Doge, the same who abdicated passively,
and thus basely terminated a high career of fourteen
centuries. I don't like the character of the old Venetian
state. It was a dark, bloody, selfish aristocracy. It was
a government of spies and informers. It had neither
virtue nor generosity. It had not even the chivalry that
belonged to almost all other aristocracies. The Doge was
nothing, and the people were nothing, the council of *ten*
was all in all. They were the state inquisitors, they spied
upon the Doge, they spied upon the people, they had their
midnight examinations and consultations, they had the
bocca di Leone, the lion's mouth, for receiving calumnies,

and suspicions, and lies of every sort, and woe to those who
fell under their jealousy! The torture was always ready
to force confession from weakness, and agony from the
brave. And then there was the Bridge of Sighs, and the
deep dungeons, unvisited by a single ray from heaven,
under the level of the canals. I am not sorry that they
are gone; but were I a Venetian, I should prefer a native
despotism to a stranger's. Happy those who are citizens
of that city which has no need of the sun, nor of the moon,
for the Lord God and the Lamb are the light thereof. All
human governments must be bad, more or less, until men
cease to be bad. But you know that I am a lover of liberty
in its largest meaning.

January 5.—There are many fine pictures in the public
buildings and churches. There are four or five magnificent
Titians, and a splendid Paul Veronese in the Pisani Palace,
in which the portraits of the family of the Pisani are introduced in the characters of Darius's family, presented to
Alexander the Great. But to my mind the Venetian
school is generally uninteresting, in consequence of the want
of ideality and delicacy; they are too like nature in its
coarseness. I can forgive an aberration from nature when
the wanderer strays into a higher country and a purer
atmosphere. The expression of Domenichino's St. Cecilia
at Cadder is more a feeling in my heart at this moment,
than all the magic of this school of colourists. Titian has
mind too, undoubtedly immense mind, but not a beautiful
or poetical mind.

January 6 (1827).—This is the Epiphany, you know, or
the feast of the three kings, who have been substituted by
the Catholics in the place of the Magi or wise men from
the East, who brought gifts to the new-born Saviour. They
were conducted by a star. He himself calls himself the
bright and the morning star. I love the stars. I wish

they conducted me to Christ. Sometimes they do. Oh where is that eternal fountain of light from which their lovely lamps are filled! Even as the hart panteth after the water-brooks, so would my soul pant after that Fountain of life, and light, and joy. I saw one of their ceremonies in St. Mark's, and heard some of their music. The church itself is most imposing with its many arches and its gilded mosaics, representing all the saints, and martyrs, and hermits that ever lived; but their ceremonies are disgusting to common sense, and their music is not to my taste. The patriarch is a very good sort of man. I have dined with him twice. There is a kindness in his manner which is very attractive. He is most unbigoted, and I have caught myself often speaking to him about the foolish idolatries of his Church, as if he had been a Protestant. He answered me to such observations by saying that it was more difficult to build up than to pull down, and that, in the present state of ignorance in Italy, the discontinuance of these ceremonies would probably lead to entire irreligion amongst the people,—that he did what he could towards erecting schools and extending the advantage of education. He is reported to be the natural brother of the Emperor. He certainly has considerable influence, which he uses humbly and beneficently. He is going away to another archbishopric in Hungary, much to the regret of the people of Venice. He comes to Mr. Money's occasionally, and seems to enjoy the quiet domestic society that he finds there. . . . I have bought two or three pictures here, but no great things. I am quite nauseated, in fact, with the Venetian school at present. . . .

This is indeed a very remarkable place, the narrowest wynd leading from the High Street to the Cowgate is much broader than the generality of the streets here. In some of them two persons have difficulty in passing, and then

they don't run straight, so that it is extremely difficult to
know the way.   When the inhabitants of the better class
go from one place to another, they generally go in gondolas,
so that they have no occasion to get acquainted with the
streets (or *calli* as they are called), and hence, in fact, many
persons who have lived all their lives in Venice are as little
acquainted with it as you are, with the exception of the
Piazza di San Marco, the Ponti di Rialto, and the Riva leading to the public garden.   They go to bed about three in the
morning or so, and get up pretty early too ; but they sleep
a little during the day, and in truth their life is a long sleep,
or at least a dream.   They have nothing to do but to pass
the time, which they do by drinking coffee a dozen of times
in the day, by attending the theatres, walking on the Piazza
or Piazzetta, and evening parties.   Good-night, my dear,
dear friend.

7th January.—This is the Lord's Day, and I have just
now partaken of the symbols of his body and blood, the
emblems of our spiritual food whilst we pass through the
wilderness.   His holy love is our bread and our wine, our
strength and our rejoicing.   Our food must be suited to
our labour.   Well, our labour is, "Thou shalt love the Lord
thy God with all thy heart," etc.   And is not our food
suited to this labour, the dying love of Christ ?   The manna
strengthened the Israelites for their journey through the
wilderness, and they were refreshed by the water which
flowed from the rock which followed them.   But this is the
true bread that our Father has provided for us, and the
true wine of gladness too.   Whom have we in heaven but
thee, and there is none upon earth to be desired beside
thee ?   My thoughts on this occasion travelled homewards
(if any place on earth is worthy of the name), and rested
on those whom I most dearly love, and whom I hope to
meet in peace at the marriage supper of the Lamb.   Oh let

us be serious and diligent, and seek to be near to Him, and
to have much and constant communion with Him. Are
you not surprised when you think how little of your soul
is really occupied with this divine love and hope? The
sixth chapter of St. John is the best illustration of the
institution of the Supper. I don't much approve of the
rarity of the occurrence of this ordinance in most churches,
it gives the idea of a greater and lesser degree of holiness;
for if we are to be more devout or religious on sacrament
Sundays, of course we may be less devout on others. We
ought to be continually partaking of the true bread.

January 9.—This morning a young man, Mr. Long (the
Miss Elphinstones are acquainted with his family), who has
been residing with us here ever since my arrival at Venice,
left us for Florence and Rome. He has been lately awakened to the importance of eternal things. Eternal things,
how paltry all other things look in the presence of that
word eternal! I see sometimes that it is not worth while
being happy in this world. God is more than happiness,—
I would seek Him. I have heard lately from my friends
in Switzerland, from Coppet, and from Carra, the Vernets'
place. The Baron de Staël is just about to be married to
a daughter of Madame Vernet. The friends on both sides
are much pleased. I am a friend of both sides, and I am
much satisfied (forsooth). She is an amiable, well-minded,
and well-hearted girl. She is pious, and I really believe
that that is the reason of their marriage. I used to think
that he would have liked to form some high political connection by his marriage, and I regard this fact as an evidence, and a tolerably strong evidence, that he has chosen
for himself a portion which is not temporal. Dear Madame
Vernet is well pleased, and Madame de Broglie is delighted.
I like that absolute freedom from ambition that I see in
these people. I have got a portrait of the blind old Dan-

dolo, the Venetian Doge, who at the age of eighty scaled
the walls of Constantinople, or at least was the first to dis-
embark for the attack of that place, painted in 1500 or so,
by the brother of Titian's master, taken from an older portrait. You don't care for that. Well, my heart is with
you. May the God of peace be with you ! Write to Rome.
I go in two days.

41. TO HIS SISTER MRS. STIRLING.

BOLOGNA, *Feb.* 1827.

MY DEAREST KITTY,— . . . When I was at Venice I
bought many things out of sheer idleness—some not much
worth, but there are two portraits in my gallery which are
rarities. They are by Gentil Bellini, but their interest does
not arise from that circumstance ; one is the portrait of
old Dandolo, the eighty-year-old Doge who took Constantinople : this portrait was painted in 1480, copied from
another, probably the original. Dandolo lived about 1220.
This portrait has been in the Dandolo family till lately,
and I have got their attestation of its genuineness. The
other portrait is still more curious; its history is this.
Soon after Mahomet the Great had taken Constantinople,
he took a fancy to have a picture of himself, and as he
knew that his allies, the Venetians, had skilful painters,
he desired that one might be sent who could do him justice.
The Venetian ambassador at Constantinople then was a
patrician of the family of Zen ; he was the patron of Gentil
Bellini, and in return for this good office Bellini gave Zen
a present of the original draught which he made of the
Sultan, and from which he afterwards copied the portrait
which remained in Constantinople. The Zen family, like
almost all the other Venetian families, is at present in great
poverty, and I bought from them this most curious and living
painting for sixty base sequins. It is very thin and sketchy,

but life itself—and such grand life. I have been at Bologna for some days, and have been enjoying the Academy
very much ; these Domenichinos, especially the martyrdom
of Sta. Agnese, are the works of a fine heart and a high
genius. I would not give the Sta. Agnese for the two best
Correggios in Parma, though I know that I am speaking
treason against the established authorities in the kingdom of
the fine arts. The lights of Correggio are indeed wonderful,
but Domenichino seems to me to speak a fuller language to
the heart. Correggio is too fondling, I think. After I had
been here three or four days, my *domestico di piazza* took
me to see a Sta. Cecilia. When I came out, I told him
that a friend of mine, about eighteen months ago, had
bought what I was sure was the original of this picture ;
he immediately asked me, with great keenness, if it was
not Signor Carlo Stirling that I meant. I told him yes,
when he informed me that he had also been your cicerone.
I said to him that I had often heard you speak of him
with great approbation. He spoke of you most warmly,
always calling Charles Signor Carlo, whose rapid manner
of settling with the picture-dealers he could not sufficiently
admire—*era furiosa*, he repeated. I have been endeavouring to do a little myself here ; I have been probing for a
very fine Titian ; I don't think I shall get it; the man asks
1200 louis, and I have offered 1200 scudi, according to
that good lesson which you gave me, and which I wish
that I had always followed. Whilst this great negotiation
is going on, I have been lying on my oars—till this day,
when I could not resist making a little purchase, which is
now perched on a chair before me, or rather, I should say,
two purchases, a very fine sketch, which I hope is *original-
issimo*, of Ludovico Carracci, for his great picture of the
Transfiguration, in the gallery, and a beautiful abbozzo of
Paolo, with a sky and architecture worth thrice what I

paid for it.   Venice is not so good a place for buying pictures as Bologna.   I think that I rather threw away my
money there upon Barbini.   Do you know, my dear Kitty,
just two or three days before I left Venice the thin Barbini
died suddenly from the rupture of a blood-vessel—carried
away from the pictures, and shows, and shadows of things,
to look on the great realities.   I find that the solitude and
tranquillity of my evenings are very necessary to repair the
distractions of the day.   I hope that you and dear Signor
Carlo have quiet wherever you are, and that you are ad-
vancing in the race set before us. . . . I have an acquaintance here, a Marchese di Grudotti, who is a handsome gay
young man, very fond of England; he wonders why I don't
take advantage of his acquaintance to get into society here.
I told him that my business was to keep quiet.   He was
with Bonaparte at Moscow.   I met him crossing the Simplon, when he gave me his address, and requested me to
call on him when I came to Bologna.   He took me to-day
to the public library, and introduced me to Mezzofanti, the
great linguist, who was very conversable and modest, with
all his fame; I shall see more of him, I hope.

42. TO MISS RACHEL ERSKINE.

ROME, 13*th March* 1827.

MY DEAR COUSIN,— . . . I have been here a month
nearly.   Rome is a home to me, so vast, so desolate, so
beautiful, so full of the past and the future, and so cut off
from the present.   It is an image of eternity. . . . I live
next door to my old residence, on the Monte Pincio, which
commands a view of the whole city, *i.e.* the modern city,
for the situation of the ancient city is different, 180 steps
of stairs above the level of the ordinary habitations.   This
is a tolerable security for solitude.   My visiting friends
would need to be strong in body and willing in mind.

My occupations here are quite different from what they
were when I was here last. I go rarely to see any of the
galleries. I remain a good deal in the house, where I read
and write; and when I go out it is on horseback, which
enables me to traverse the wilderness of the ancient city
without fatigue or consumption of time. Oh! it is a place
full of instruction and inspiration. The handwriting which
Belshazzar saw is to be seen here on many a wall, and
ruined arch, and broken column. Man was here taken in
all his pride and all his glory, and weighed in the balance,
and found wanting; and this mighty queen of cities is now
the sepulchre of past fame. I went the other day to the
burying-ground of the Protestants to see Mrs. Erskine's
tomb. There her body lies, beside that of Miss Bathurst,
who was drowned whilst I was here. I had often spoken
to Mrs. Erskine about her. Miss B.'s death, so suddenly
torn from the society of time and hurried into the society
of eternity in a moment, without the slightest previous
warning. Mrs. E. was extremely kind to me, and she liked
to hear of heavenly things. The monument and the
inscription are very proper. Not far from her is the body
of my poor Swiss friend, Baillod. My dear friend, every
hour is bringing on that solemn conclusion, when the mighty
angel, with one foot on the land and one on the sea, shall
swear by Him who liveth for ever, that time shall be no
longer. I know not what bodies may yet be buried here,
but I know that the dead who die in the Lord are blessed
—blessed not for a day, but for eternity—pronounced
blessed not by the weak and ignorant voice of man, but
by Him who cannot lie. Oh! how blessed. I was struck
this morning by a passage in Adam's *Private Thoughts.*
He says, "I never look upon a dead corpse, and yet my
soul perhaps must one day behold my own. What an
awful moment! how happy will be the sight, if soul and

body have lived together for eternity! how dreadful if they have not! and what a call is there in this thought to make sure of rejoicing then!"

I left Venice about the middle of January, in weather as wintry as Scotland could have furnished, bitter frost and deep snow. I went by Parma to Bologna. At Parma they have got the finest work of Correggio. It is a Holy Family, with St. Jerome standing beside them. There is something very absurd in that entire disregard of dates, of which all these great painters were guilty. St. Jerome lived, I believe, in the fourth century, but there he is with his lion, which is his symbol as well as St. Mark's. So far for its nonsense, but it might have been ten times as much nonsense with perfect impunity, for there is a loveliness in it which enchants and subdues. Mary Magdalene, who, according to the established custom of those gentlemen, almost always makes a part of the holy family, is kissing the foot of the infant Saviour with an expression of holy and gentle love unutterable. . . . I have been reading Doddridge. I am much struck with the deep seriousness of his expostulations and entreaties. I have never read him through before. I believe that there are few books of modern times that have been so signally blessed to the conviction and conversion of sinners. It was composed by a praying man, and his prayer has been answered ever since. . . .

God seems in this world to bring things out of their opposites—life out of death, joy out of sorrow, holiness out of pollution, glory out of shame. The cross is the King's highway to His kingdom. He went Himself that way, and amidst all the darkness of nature, the light of His countenance still shines on that way, and on those who walk there. . . .

43. TO MISS RACHEL ERSKINE.

ROME, *5th April* 1827.

MY DEAREST COUSIN RACHEL,—So Lady Oswald has been called away from her important post, to give an account of her stewardship. I never saw her, but from what I have heard of her, I cannot but consider her removal as a most solemn and dark dispensation. The mother of a young and numerous family, a supporter of the name and character of Christianity, a wife, a friend,—a friend too of some who have few friends to lose. Well, the Lord hath done it, and He doeth all things well. He does not need instruments in His work, and sometimes He seems to intend to make His own fatherly love, and care, and power more manifest and more felt by removing intermediate instruments. When the disciples heard that their Lord was about to leave them, they gave themselves up for lost, but he told them that it was for their advantage that he should go away, as otherwise the Comforter would not come unto them. Even so now God can make darkness light before these mourners, and crooked things straight. He may speak through this event to the widowed husband's heart, and He may draw the eyes of the orphans to himself. He took little children in his arms and blessed them when he was upon earth, and he changeth not. He yet takes them in his arms. May it please Him to do so now, and to attract every friend she had to himself, to fill the void in their affections. The Bruces will feel this deeply.

I have just returned from a funeral. I think I mentioned to you a young Irish clergyman who had come abroad for his health ; but the disease was beyond the reach of climate. He continued to sink during the whole winter. When I came to Rome, Dr. Peebles introduced me to his room. I feel it always a great privilege to be with the dying, and

I have enjoyed this privilege. I have conversed with him upon the things of God, and the riches of divine grace treasured up in the Saviour. I have heard him express his hope in that love which brought that Saviour from heaven to save us, and he has now, I trust, entered into peace. He had a narrow range of ideas, and had no imagination to assist or mislead his religious feelings. His spirit had never strained itself to apprehend the things of infinity, but he was conscientious and faithful to his light, and he never shook. He saw death approaching with the most perfect calmness, and he retained his self-possession to the very last moment. I don't believe that the thought of death ever quickened his pulse a single beat. Death lets in the light of eternity on life, and passes a true judgment on it. Happiness is not to be sought, but holiness; unhappiness is not to be shunned, but sin. What does Lady Oswald, or my poor friend Gresson, think of earthly joy or sorrow now? Oh! how they will despise and wonder at that folly which puts a value upon anything but the favour of God. His love might have been sought and enjoyed in every event, in every duty, at every moment; and what paltry things drew us from Him! Thus the highest saint in heaven will think on the review of life.

6th April.—My dearest, I have just received your letter, full of sorrow, alas, alas! His sisters will feel it deeply,[1] but my sympathy follows the dead more than the living. You know the universality of my hopes for sinners. I hope that He who came to bruise the serpent's head and to destroy the works of the devil, will not cease his labours of love till every particle of evil introduced into this world

---

[1] Charles Hay died at Paris. He was the youngest brother of the late William Hay, Esq. of Dunse Castle, and grandson of James Erskine, Esq. of Cardross, who was Thomas Erskine's uncle.

has been converted into good. When I was in Paris our common walk together was a burial-ground at the top of his street; and I had sometimes the hope that God would speak to his heart out of these graves. I loved him well, and I ought to have written more to him. He wrote to me, and he received kindly at least anything that was said to him, however contrary to his own notions or feelings. There was much true-heartedness in him. I trust that in the records of eternity there is an hour fixed when his spirit shall look on the Sun of Righteousness, and be converted into his likeness; and even I should wish to hope that the God of all grace had, before He called him hence, given him a preparation for it. Every person who knew him must know that his feelings were always far above his expressions, and he talked lightly sometimes of things which he did not feel lightly. . . . The churchyard (burying-ground, I mean) is increasing its associations for me. Mrs. Erskine, Baillod the Swiss artist, Scholl, another Swiss, whose family I know, Mrs. Colquit's daughter, and now Gresson. The situation is most beautiful, and the weather lovely. The sun and the blue sky so pure, and beautiful, and melancholy, and the young leaves coming out : the mystery of nature's yearly resurrection spreading its charm over the earth. I have not yet lost my delight in nature. I don't go to see pictures and statues now ; but I can look at the blue of heaven, and at the clear deep shadows of the mountains, and at the sun which sets just before my windows, and I can mourn with the ruined walls. Well, " the mountains shall depart and the hills be removed, but my kindness shall not depart, neither shall the covenant of my peace be removed, saith the Lord that hath mercy on thee." That is something worth repeating. It is from the mouth of God, and it is said to you and me. It is something for a living hour or a dying hour, or an hour beyond time. I have talked with Gresson about these things, and I have often repeated to him those words, and now he knows all about it. Perhaps he remembers our conversations, and wonders at the deadness and darkness of them. I had a little copy of the Psalms with me at the funeral, which I opened, and read the concluding verses of the 73d Psalm, from the 23d verse, and I pulled some leaves of which I send you two. My darling cousin, God bless you ! You are probably retired to your room just now. I hope you do not allow your mind to feed uselessly upon sorrow, not that I expect you are ever to be free of sorrow, but that you ask the knowledge of that blessed secret which is contained in that word, "as sorrowful, yet always rejoicing." . . . I would join your prayers, that God would comfort the mourners, and sanctify unto them their afflictions, and that he would give us to know his holy love in Christ Jesus. That is life eternal, whether in this world or in another. That is the only portion. It is about midnight here, and time is little more than an hour earlier at Gartur. It is about eleven now with you. I like to think of you. I know the shape of your room, and the chair. I know some that you pray for, and many that you think of. What are you thinking of now ? The sorrows of the living, or the blessedness of the dead who die in the Lord, or that blessed remedy which heals all evils, the blood of Christ ? Good-night. . .

7th April.—And is it possible that Charles Hay is dead ? How near it brings death when one dies whom we have seen so young, and with whom we have never associated the idea of death. Oh ! the blessed refuge described in the 57th Psalm, first verse. That is the remedy for every evil under the sun.

44. TO MISS C. ERSKINE.

ROME, 12*th April* 1827.

MY DEAR COUSIN,—I am away far from you in body, but I have confidence in you that your affection does not depend altogether on your eye. I know that you love many whom you do not see, and whom you will never see until the resurrection day. The spiritual world is just near or distant, according to our own thoughts of it. It is always near and close to those whose hearts are upon it. That ladder which Jacob saw in his dream at Bethel is Jesus Christ. On Him, as on a ladder, the soul can mount to God, and to the place where God dwells, surrounded by the love and praise of blessed angels and redeemed sinners, and down the ladder the blessing of God, the gifts of the Spirit, and the intimations of His loving-kindness, descend to us. It is good exercise to run up and down that ladder, and, my dear cousin, thank God we may do this though confined to a bed or a sofa, and there we may meet our friends out of the body or in the body. I hope you sometimes think of me when you are upon the ladder, and that you look about for me. Ah! there is a time coming, I hope, when we shall go up and come no more down, but be pillars in the temple of our God, and go no more out. There is one thought that I am sure connects you and me very much together, a thought partly of earth and partly of heaven, and that is the thought of Dr. Stuart. I often feel a wish to write to him, to ask what he thinks of certain things, for I have no friend now of the same kind on earth. I have excellent friends, but none who take the same vivid interest that he did in some subjects that occupy me. I have this instant received a letter from Christian and her husband, mentioning the death of Mary Graham.[1] Alas! alas! my poor uncle and aunts. She was a sweet and beautiful

---

[1] Only daughter of his uncle, Thomas Graham, Esq. of Airth.

flower, and I hope now transplanted into the paradise of God. And Charles Hay too! Dear Mary's removal had been long expected. She had herself for long had it from time to time presented to her mind by faithful friends who counselled her, and prayed with her, and kept her from deluding herself. Katherine[1] was there, and were I dying, I should like to have Katherine at my deathbed. But there was no Katherine at Charles's bedside. I saw a great deal of him when I passed through Paris in the end of last September. He was full of kind-heartedness and true-heartedness. And Robert[2] so far off! His sisters must feel very severely. They have not been permitted to receive the last words and looks of any of their brothers. May God bless these wounds to the spiritual good of those who suffer from them! Young spirits: how many are now dead whose births I remember, gone to be added to the generations of past time! I have been reading lately Irving's book on the Prophecies, and a very striking book it is. He writes evidently with the fullest conviction that his interpretation is right. If he is right, we are on the eve of a tremendous catastrophe, in comparison with which all the calamities of the French Revolution are as nothing. Infidelity is to destroy Popery, and to break up the very foundations of all the civil and political institutions of Europe, and then infidelity itself is to be destroyed with a fearful destruction. I have only got one volume yet, but really I think he marks the coincidence of the prophecies and the events of the last forty years very fairly. According to his view, our blessed Lord is himself to appear on earth in forty years. Our eyes shall be opened from the dust of death to behold Him. Miss Trail,[3] who took Dr. Stuart's miniature for me, lent me the book. Give my kindest regards to Miss Stuart, and to any friends who

[1] His sister-in-law and cousin, Mrs. James Erskine.
[2] Robert Hay.   [3] Daughter of the minister of Panbride.

inquire about me. I think often of your Lane, and your garden, and your gum-cistus plant, and the key of Heriot's Green, and of the venerable forms that I remember moving there, but are now no longer seen by the mortal eye. I wonder whether we are ever to see each other in this world. I should like it; but let us meet on the ladder, and meet in the upper sanctuary. God grant it, for Christ's sake. Remember me kindly to your brother and to the Burnetts, through Miss Stuart. There are three young friends of mine, four I should say, gone hence since I left home—George Macdowall, Mary Graham, Jane Erskine, Charles Hay; and I have attended two death-beds, Robert Melville's, and a young Irish clergyman here at Rome. Arise, depart, this is not your rest. Is not that the interpretation of it all? And then, " Come unto me and I will give you rest." That is sweet.—Yours affectionately, T. E.

45. TO DR. CHALMERS.

Rome, 19*th April* 1827.

My dear Sir,—This letter will probably find you in the midst of the business of the General Assembly, harassed considerably both by friends and foes. In the meantime I am quietly looking upon the seat of the Beast, and wondering at him, at the manner of his existence, and at his duration. I have met here with Irving's book upon the Prophecies. I don't suppose that any mere interpreter of prophecy has ever before assumed such a tone of confidence and authority. I am a little surprised that the fate of former interpreters has not warned him. He is scarcely meek enough. He seems to intend to brave and insult such of his readers as hesitate about yielding their entire consent; but it is a magnificent book, full of honest zeal. There is a Romish priest here, who, in the reign of the last Pope, wrote a book on the Prophecies, in which the year 1830 is fixed as the termination of all the wrath; he car-

ried his MS. to the regular licenser, who showed it to the
Pope before granting leave to publish : the Pope desired
that licence should be given him to publish it in the year
1831. I have an Italian master, who is a true, honest,
believing Catholic, and who cordially pities the souls of the
Protestants. He tells me that the study of the Prophecies
here is becoming much more general than formerly, and
that there are many expecting a great crisis.

I am almost a believer in the nearness of the end, and I
like to encourage in myself any idea which leads to watchfulness and prayer, and which gives a greater prominency
to spiritual and eternal objects. I desire to look and wait
for the coming of the Lord, and to long for his appearing.
I wish you were here for a month now, instead of making
your usual tour. The Niobé of nations is a happy name
for Rome. She is full of beauty and interest and sorrow,
but there is a lie in her right hand. I have met with
some good specimens of Christianity from our own country
here at Rome. I have never yet seen a Catholic who was
deeply spiritually-minded. I have not found any in the
style of à Kempis ; they are formalists even when they are
honest believers, which is not a very usual thing amongst
the tolerably educated classes, and never at all in France.
The functions of the Holy Week are just over, and such
mummery to be sure ! and then the celebration of Easter
by an illumination ! The existence of such a system,
ecclesiastical and political, is a fact as unaccountable, or
more so, than the continued separate preservation of the
Jews,—the government of a corporation of priests submitted to during the military turbulency of the middle
ages, and the enlightened revolutionary scepticism of the
present day, and a system of imposition, and which imposes
upon no one, and is yet opposed by no one. It is a very
strange thing. I was out at Tivoli the other day ; though
the cascades are ruined, yet it has beauty enough, and to

spare. They are trying to repair them. There are olive trees there above a thousand years old—five would reach to the flood. The time since Adam's creation looks very short when measured in this way—a succession of six olive-trees. The obelisks (Egyptian), of which there are many here, bring us still nearer. My eye at this moment rests on the Pantheon, the most beautiful thing in Rome.

Give my best regards to Mrs. Chalmers and your children. Farewell. Many thanks for your letter.—Yours most truly,   T. Erskine.

46. TO MISS RACHEL ERSKINE.

Rome, *May* 2, 1827.

My DEAR COUSIN,—I know that I cannot hear from you now for some time, so I must even write to you instead of it, as the next best thing. I have been now nearly three months in this place, and I don't tire of it, but I have a strong presentiment that its judgment is drawing very near. I know not whether to impute it to the restlessness of my own mind, but my impression is that turbulent times are approaching, that the world's rest is again to be broken in upon, and that destruction is again to sweep the kingdom of the Beast. Our own country seems fermenting, and in all the other countries of Europe there is a deep though silent preparation going forward for political eruptions. Is it not a strange thing that so little good fruit has been produced by God's revelations to man? Is it not dreadful and yet true, that any light which has ever shone from heaven upon this earth, has rather served as a testimony against man, than as a guide and a joy to him? Is this not melancholy, and enough to make any one melancholy who thinks of it? It is indeed a great mystery. The Word has become flesh and has dwelt among us, and yet not one in a thousand has heard of it, and not one in a hundred thousand has been sanctified by it. Surely there is some great

thing coming.   But we are of yesterday and know nothing.
What does Mary Graham know now? or Charles Hay?
I should like to have you sitting by me just now.   I have
received your letter, your kind letter—it could not be yours
if it were not kind and generous.   I will not speak now of
its contents.   I like your little codicil which you always
pack up in it so adroitly that no postmaster has hitherto
suspected its existence.   I am ashamed of my paltry letters
in answer to your histories.   I met yesterday with Sir
William Gell, one of our unfortunate Queen's attendants; he
is a man of great antiquarian lore, and delights in communicating it to any who will take interest in it.   He is a
reader of hieroglyphics : he says that the oldest obelisk in
Rome, that at St. John Lateran, is contemporary with
Abraham.   What do you think of that?—a few hundred
years later than the deluge.   The human race is a very
recent creation.   It was only the other day that Adam and
Eve were in Eden walking with God, and I hope we shall all
be walking with God again soon, for oh it is a dull thing as
well as a wicked thing to walk without Him.   I have got a
very beautiful little drawing of the first appearance of our
parents before God after their offence, by a German artist
here.   It is one of a series intended to be engraved for a
Bible.   The Deity is represented in the human form, which
perhaps you will be a little shocked by, but in that form
there is a compassion, and a regret, and a holy dignity, which
will soon reconcile you to the apparent impropriety.   If I
had a good opportunity, I daresay that I should send it
home to you to keep for me till I came to claim it.   Good
night, my dear cousin.   The weather is lovely, and the
acacia trees in fullest blow and beauty, the Campagna clad
in the richest green, all the vegetable world in the beauty
of its youth, and the sun and the sky in glory.   I saw a fire-
fly to-night as I was coming home.   Good-night again.

H

3d May.—I rode to Gabii to-day,—one of the earliest conquests of the Republic, and the great quarry of their earliest buildings.   You know that most of their massy stone buildings, and especially in that early time, were made without cement of any kind—one immense block was laid above another—well fitted in surface to receive it, and so they remain some of them in spite of time, and earthquakes, and fires, and floods, and wars, and Pagans and Christians. You know that Miss F. Mackenzie is here now.   I don't see nearly so much of her as I ought to do, or as I wish to do, for she has the attraction of unhappiness as well as many other good qualities.   This night I have been taking leave of friends who are going off to-morrow morning for Naples.   You tell me not to go to Naples, but just to come home, but I have engaged to go : however I intend to make but a short stay there ; I wish to see the islands, I did not visit them when I was there last, and they have the fame of exceeding beauty.   Also my courier is engaged to be married to the daughter of the innkeeper at Mola di Gaeta, and as he has made me his confidant through the whole affair, I must go to Naples that he may see her in passing. He is an excellent servant, and very much attached—to his master I mean,—for as to the *ragazza de Mola*, as he calls her, though I have no doubt that he will be a good husband, yet I don't think that he would lose a night's rest by the engagement being broken off.   Good-night.   This is very incoherent gossip to send to such a distance.   My dear cousin, there is more worth in ——, she is most conscientious, and she has real friendship in her as well as real piety, that I can answer for.   Is the Limekilns man in this earthly prison yet?   Blessed are the dead who die in the Lord.   I have been reading a very curious book lately by Law, the author of the "Serious Call ;" it is entitled the *Spirit of Prayer*, most mystical it is, but most beautiful.   It

is not the gospel, but I think it may be profitably read by
those who know the gospel. Those passages which I admired so much in the translator's preface to à Kempis are
taken from it. Perhaps I mentioned this to you before.

6th, Albano.—I came here yesterday on my way to
Naples, and have passed my Sunday here. Albano is a
fairy land, and the season is enchanting. The air is full
of fragrance from the flowers, and of music from the birds.
The nightingale is the chief minstrel. All the other birds
seem to be listeners and learners for the time ; occasionally
the cuckoo is heard. Ariccia is close to Albano, you know.
I went there and found the house in which Mrs. Erskine
died. I went into her room. Oh for readiness !—and
Charles Hay too now—who next ? I wrote to the girls
some time ago. Law in his latter days took to reading
the works of Jacob Böhme, a German divine, and from him
he learned much. I should like to read him too, but I
must re-learn German in order to fit myself for it. I like
the German mind better than the mind of any other nation,
our own not excepted. We are very meagre in comparison
of them. I like the Prussian *chargé d'affaires* at Rome.[1]
The last time I saw him, he was telling me of cases of som-
nambulism, or animal magnetism as it is called. He says
that many extraordinary instances have been quite authen-
ticated. They are as extraordinary as the most remarkable
cases of second sight in the Highlands. Good-night.

7th, Mola di Gaeta.—The Mediterranean is spread beneath
my eye. The shore is covered with the remains of ancient
villas. The lemon-trees are loaded with fruit, and the
orange-trees with blossom. The productions of the southern climates are becoming more frequent. I have seen
several palm-trees to-day, beautiful things they are, children of the sun, and associated in my mind with Abraham

[1] Chevalier Bunsen.

and the patriarchs who sat under palm-trees, and Deborah who judged Israel under a palm-tree. Did not I mention Irving's book on the Prophecies to you? It is worth your reading. Do the Keir ladies take interest in the signs of the times? Give them my best love—I love them well, and I do not wonder at any degree of friendship between Jeannie and Lady M., for friendship is a thing of the heart, and it may exist amidst many dissimilarities when there is so strong an agreement, as there is between them, in love to God.

8th, Mola.—It is a lovely morning. The bay so sweetly curved—the ripple of the clear water on the shore. The islands, which have not yet thrown off their morning veil of mist, if anything so light can be called mist, and then Vesuvius stretching to the west and south, and the promontory and town of Gaeta, and many an olive-clad hill, to the north. It is not six o'clock yet in your country. How fresh everything is, and these warblers that fill the air with music. For a moment one might forget that solemn word, "Cursed be the ground for thy sake," but the appearance of the people recalls it. The earth was cursed not for its own sake, and no curse can be severe which is not deserved—it is the evil desert itself which is the curse —except in one instance, where the righteous suffered for the wicked; and blessed be His name, the day is coming when that sacrifice of His shall have its perfect work, when sin shall be no more, when the waters of human bitterness shall be healed, when there shall be no more curse.

9th, Naples.—I arrived here yesterday, and I am now sitting in the house where my father died, the Crocelle, in the 1791. I have often wished that I had the slightest trace of him in my memory, but I was just two years old when he left home. I know nothing of my father's mind, except very general traits. I don't know how he felt when he

knew that he was on the borders of the invisible world.
There is something very striking in the relation between a
father and a child when death prevents any personal acquaintance between them.   When he parted from me, he
knew as little of me as I did of him, and yet no doubt he
felt an interest in me ; but when he looked at me he could
no more conjecture what was within me, or what my destiny might probably be, than he could conjecture what was
going on in the moon.   What a strange interest that is
which we can thus take in beings that we are absolutely
ignorant of!   I feel a love for my father, and a deep interest in him.   Are these earthly connections to extend beyond this world in any shape?   When I was last here the
Hays were constantly with me.   Many of the jokes which
amused Charles recur to my mind at present.   Oh let us
be very scrupulous in abiding closely and constantly in
Christ, and in avoiding the serpent's meat, the dust of this
world, and in eating the bread which came down from
heaven.   Good-night, God bless all my dear cousins.—
Yours ever,   T. E.

47. TO MISS RACHEL ERSKINE.

Island of Ischia, *4th June* 1827.

My dear Cousin,—. . . This is a beautiful place.   The
view from the house where I am living is, I think, the very
finest that I ever saw.   I have found here a poor man who
took the fever of the country in Sicily about a year ago,
and he has been in a state of constant suffering ever since.
Bodily pain is a great trial.   It interferes with the mind's
power of thought, that power on which we pride ourselves,
and which we convert into an idol, although it is a gift
from God.   He tells me that he is seeking God, but cannot
find Him ; and that he reads the Bible, but cannot get
satisfaction from it.   Alas! alas!   I was at Capri the other

day, the island where the Emperor Tiberius had a palace,
where he spent much of his time in profligacy, and in
cruelty, and in misery.   Jesus was in Judea when that
building was erected.   It is a very singular island, divided
into two parts by a range of rocks, so lofty and so steep
that there is no communication, except by means of a stair
cut in the rock (of immense antiquity it must be) of 535
steep steps, and there is no landing-place on the upper part
from the sea either.   Every foot of the island which is not
under cultivation is covered with myrtles, which were just
coming into flower.   Good-night.—I have been tempted to
stay two or three days more here.   I enter into the spirit of
its beauty—it is not like anything else I have ever seen.   La
Sentinella is the name of my inn ; and it received its name
from its being the post of an outlook who gave notice of
the approach of Saracen corsairs, who used to ravage this
country some centuries ago, and carry off the inhabitants
as slaves.   It commands the whole view of the Neapolitan
coast, from Vesuvius northward to Terracina—a coast of
most picturesque, and bold and various form, and then the
island of Procida, dividing that part of the sea into lakes,
and then the unbounded ocean to the west—and the home
scenery of the island, which is rich and wild beyond fancy.
The house is situated on the point of a narrow ridge of very
elevated ground, and overlooks the sea ; on each side of the
ridge, about 20 yards on the one side, and not so much
as one yard on the other, the ground sinks down into a
beautiful theatre, covered at present with one mass of
verdure.

Naples, 12*th.*—I am again in the Crocelle, where my
father lived, and suffered, and died, and where cousin Annie
assisted my mother in tending him.   I have been hesitating whether I should not stay out the summer here, being
thereto induced by a report that the mountain is making

noises indicative of an eruption. That is a spectacle which
I should be sorry to lose if I had it in my power to see it.
But I scarcely think that anything of the kind is near. No
fire appears in the crater, nothing but smoke. There has
been a great deal of rain lately, which increases the quantity
of smoke. . . . I have met with two or three persons who
have interested me very much. Prince Leopold is here.
The Prince still feels his wife's death very much. I have
never seen him. . . .

June 1827.

Mola di Gaeta, 16th June 1827.—. . . I left Naples on
the 14th. That morning I saw the sun rise from the top
of Vesuvius. It was very glorious, and the fresh, sweet,
wholesome beauty of the Bay of Naples was a striking contrast to the burning, parched, sulphurous breath and look
of the crater. I met Miss Mackenzie here at Mola, on her
way from Naples to Rome. She is, I believe, going on a
work of friendship. There is a poor lady of her acquaintance near Naples, who is in great want of some friend, and
who has pressed her very much to come to her.

Rome, 23d. . . .—Within the last six weeks I have seen
much misery in different forms. I wonder now how life ever
could have appeared to me a sunny thing. There is a
heavy cloud over it. I really wish to be home now, but I
know not when I may be permitted. Farewell, my dear
cousin. May the Father of our Lord Jesus Christ bless
you with the spirit of holy unworldly peace, extinguishing
in you the life of the old nature, and giving you a new life,
yea, becoming Himself your life. Will you ask Mr. Greig, as
a particular favour, that he would conscientiously, as unto
the Lord, and not as unto man, assist my friends in finding
some proper person for the Ferry Chapel ?[1] Farewell.

[1] A chapel in the village of Broughty-Ferry, which lay near Linlathen.

48. TO HIS SISTER MRS. PATERSON.

ALBANO, *4th July* 1827.

MY DEAR DAVIE,—I am sorry to say that I am still here. I had hoped to have been on the other side of the Alps before this time; but I have had various businesses given me to do by Him who appoints all things. At Naples I felt that I had a mission for three or four persons; and since I have come back to Rome, I have found a case of distress waiting for me, which has perplexed me a good deal as to plans of moving. . . . When I may get away I know not; but I am very desirous to get once more amongst Christian people. . . . I live at Albano, on the road to Rome. The whole district is beautiful to the utmost wish, and full of delicious shade from immense trees, chiefly ever-green oaks, of which there is one as large as the Kippenross tree, indeed much larger, thirty feet round at four feet from the ground.—Yours affectionately,

T. E.

49. TO THE SAME.

ALBANO, *26th July* 1827.

. . . It is warm here, but I have never yet felt the heat oppressive, not so much so as when I was at Gartur last year. There are woods, and valleys, and lakes, and mountains so near that they maintain a perpetual freshness in the air; but they say that it is dreadful in Rome. I have bought a horse, and make constant use of him in conveying me over this lovely country. The two lakes of Albano and Nemi were, at some period beyond the memory of man, the craters of two immense volcanos, in form very like the crater of Vesuvius. These craters are not above half way up filled with water, and the banks (which are very precipitous from the water edge) are covered with wood of every age, and boldly broken by immense volcanic rocks; and their top ridge is crowned by picturesque villages, and convents with white walls, and lofty pines, and cypresses, and ilexes. At sunset the bells from these villages and convents, as they answer each other from the different points of the ridge, and as they sink or swell on the breeze, produce that effect which Mrs. Radcliffe intended to produce in many of her descriptions. Humboldt, in his descriptions of the South American scenery, compares it with this district from Nemi to Tivoli, which he thinks the finest in the old world. It wants, however, the magic light of Naples. The view from the Sentinella at Ischia is of a higher order in my humble opinion. The Appian Way, the queen of the old Roman roads, passes through Albano. Its course is marked by the massive antique pavement, and by the ruined monuments of the forgotten dead, which line it on both sides. I think that it was a fine idea in the old Romans (and it was the custom also in Greek cities) to erect their tombs by the sides of their principal roads and approaches to their towns. It is far better than Westminster Abbey, especially when you are obliged to pay half-a-crown to see them there. These tombs were magnificent towers, round or square, almost solid through, from twenty to thirty or more feet in diameter. Many of them, Adrian's tomb, now called the Castle of St. Angelo, for instance, and the Cecilia Metella, were employed as military positions in after-times. I am reading German and Dante, who has been very well translated into English lately by—I forget his name just now. I am at present occupied with the Purgatory, in which there is much beautiful poetry. The idea of great present suffering, enlightened by the assurance of future eternal blessedness, is a fine subject for poetry and for thought (which poetry ought to be). In truth this world is purgatory to a spirit that knows God, and the terms which Dante addresses to the spirits with whom he converses in purgatory may properly be addressed to every Christian :—

> O creatura che ti mondi,
> Per tornar bella a colui che ti fece.
> O creature who thyself unsoilest,
> To return beautiful to Him who thee made.

27th.—The Secretary to the French Embassy here, a friend of mine, tells me that he is going to-morrow to Paris with despatches; and as a motive to give him letters, he says that he goes quicker than the post. I should like to go myself, but I cannot leave the poor invalid. I have just returned from a delicious ride, part of the way through a forest of fine old chestnut trees. They look like antediluvian patriarchs. . . . I expect the Prussian *chargé d'affaires* out in this neighbourhood immediately, which I look to with pleasure, for I really like the man. He has a fine, wide, adventurous, metaphysical German capacity, and is, I believe, a Christian. He is married to an English woman, a very good woman. I shall ride with him and learn German philosophy. God bless you.

50. TO HIS SISTER MRS. STIRLING.

ALBANO, *31st July* 1827.

MY DEAREST SISTER,— . . . I am living a very regular life here. I get up early, between four and five in the morning, for the mornings and evenings are the only times for exercise. I ride out till eight, when I breakfast, and then remain in the house till six in the evening, with the exception of an hour in the middle of the day, which I pass in a delicious *bosco* here close to my house, under the shade of oaks and ilexes. I have a great deal of time at my disposal by this division of the day, and I read and study a good deal. I am learning German, which is much to my taste, and this very day M. Bunsen, the Prussian *chargé d'affaires*, is coming out from Rome to reside for the summer at Castello Gandolfo, which is a pleasure to me, for he is an instructive, excellent man, and is very friendly with me.—Yours ever,   T. E.

51. TO MISS RACHEL ERSKINE.

September 1827.—. . . When I was in Paris I visited ——'s tomb. He had so few friends that I feel it to be more particularly incumbent on those few to give many thoughts to his memory. Were I the sole friend of any one, I should consider myself in some sort his monument. . . . I hear that our dear Lauriston cousin is more infirm. She is certainly, as we all are, nearer her journey's end. I am loath to think of the spark of life ever being extinguished in that kind and worthy breast whilst she remains amongst us. Her father, and mother, and sister, still seem to survive in her. What a crowd of recollections she has gathered upon herself! Yes, although we are persuaded that our friends are going to eternal bliss, yet we must mourn their departure. And we ought to do so. The idea of a dear friend departing without being mourned is horrible.

52. TO THE SAME.

LINLATHEN, 10*th November* 1827.

MY DEAR FRIEND,— . . . How reluctant we are that any of our friends should get into the promised land, whilst we are in the wilderness. Ay, and what a hold we take of the wilderness in spite of all its barrenness and fiery serpents. This arises from a want of spirituality. Don't you think so? I wish you would read the "Spirit of Prayer" and the "Spirit of Love," two works by Law, the author of the "Serious Call," and tell me what you think of them.

I have been much struck by them. There is a great spirituality in them. I really like them much better than Mr. Irving's "Prophecies." They are, however, very mystical, and if your taste is much averse to mysticism, you may not like them. But I think that you can scarcely help liking them, such a view they give of the love of our God, and of that intimate, and blessed, and glorious union with Himself, to which He hath called us. But what is the use of recommending books to those who are taught of the Spirit to read the Bible, and to see in it a message from their loving Father to their own souls? Happy the heart that has learned to say *my* God! All religion is contained in that short expression, and all the blessedness that man or angel is capable of.

Dr. Chalmers is appointed to the Divinity Chair in the Edinburgh University. May the Lord bless His work in the hand of His servant.

53. TO DR. CHALMERS.

LINLATHEN, 10*th Nov.* 1827.

MY DEAR SIR,—I cannot express to you how much I have been delighted by your appointment to the Divinity Chair in Edinburgh. I have felt it to be a matter of much thankfulness and much hope. It is the situation to which the wishes of many have long destined you, from the conviction that you have a particular gift for the discharge of its high duties. May the Lord answer the many prayers which have been and will be presented on your behalf on this occasion, and send an awakening spirit to arouse and vivify the torpid Church of Scotland, and employ you as an honoured instrument for exciting and preparing many who may be zealous and wise pleaders for God with the coming generation.

I am loath to miss your preliminary lectures this year, but I must go to the west, to see my friends at Cadder. I hope, however, that you will think seriously of publishing your Moral Philosophy lectures, or at least the views which you have given of the subject, so far as they differ from those which have been prevalent in this country for three quarters of a century back. Moral Philosophy and self-conceited infidelity have long been near neighbours, and may in fact be expected to be so whilst man wishes to form a system in which God can be dispensed with, *i.e.* whilst man continues as he is.

On my return from the west country, I hope to be able to pay you a visit. All here desire to be remembered by you. Give my best regards to Mrs. Chalmers and your children.—Yours most truly,   T. ERSKINE.

I intend to set out for the west on Tuesday or Wednesday first.

CHAPTER VI.

Case of the Rev. J. M'Leod Campbell of Row—Letters of 1828,
1829, and 1830.

THE ten years from 1828 to 1838, from his fortieth
to his fiftieth year—intervening betwixt two lengthened
visits to the Continent,—formed the most memorable
period in Mr. Erskine's life. This period witnessed the
rise and progress of what was commonly called the Row
or Gairloch Heresy; the springing up in alarm and indignation of the Calvinism of the Church of Scotland, to put
its foot upon this movement, and stamp it out; the alleged ·
miraculous manifestations, the healings, the speaking with
tongues, the prophesyings at Port-Glasgow; the shooting
up into the heavens ecclesiastical of that most brilliant
meteor, Edward Irving, and the sad and sudden quenching
of the great light in a great darkness, out of that darkness
the strange form emerging of a Church, in its order and
offices novel, elaborate, ornate, complete. Of all these Mr.
Erskine was not only a highly interested spectator; in most
of them he was deeply and personally concerned. In the
midst of such excitement and activity as he never before
and never afterwards passed through, came death after
death in the family circle at Linlathen, sweeping half of
its whole number into the grave, breaking up for a time the
happy household there, and sending Mr. Erskine to spend
six months of solitary study in his sister's house at Cadder.

The following pages will help the reader to follow his foot-steps throughout this period, so far as they can now be traced.

On returning to Scotland in October 1827, Mr. Erskine lost no time in committing to the press a work the pre-paration of which had engaged his leisure hours on the Continent. "The Unconditional Freeness of the Gospel" was published early in 1828.[1] It excited so immediate and wide an interest, that a second edition was called for before the end of the year. Its author was not prepared for so cordial a reception of this volume by some, still less for so severe a reprobation of it by others. Dr. Chalmers, though dissenting from one of its positions, went cordially in with its leading principles, and said, over and over again to his friends, that it was one of the most delightful books that ever had been written. There was another reader of it, the impression made on whom was destined to have wide effects. Frederick Denison Maurice, in 1852, dedicating the volume on "The Prophets and Kings of the Old Testament" to Mr. Erskine, says, "The pleasure of associating my name with yours, and the kind interest which you expressed in some of these sermons when you heard them preached, might not be a sufficient excuse for the liberty which I take in dedicating them to you. But I have a much stronger reason. I am under obligations to you, which the subject of this volume espe-cially brings to my mind, and which other motives, beside personal gratitude, urge me to acknowledge. . . . Have we a gospel for men, for all men? Is it a gospel that God's will is a will to all good, a will to deliver them from all evil? Is it a gospel that He has reconciled the world unto Himself? Is it this absolutely, or this with a multitude of reservations, explanations, contradictions? It is more

[1] See extracts in Appendix, No. V. p. 379.

than twenty years since a book of yours brought home to
my mind the conviction, that no gospel but this can be of
any use to the world, and that the gospel of Jesus Christ
is such a one. . . . Many of my conclusions may differ
widely from those into which you have been led : I should be
grieved to make you responsible for them.   But if I have
tried in those sermons to show that the story of the
prophets and kings of the Old Testament is as directly
applicable to the modern world as any Covenanter ever
dreamed, but that it is applicable because it is a continual
witness for a God of righteousness, not only against idolatry,
but against that notion of a mere sovereign Baal or Bel,
which underlies all idolatry, all tyranny, all immorality,
I may claim you as their spiritual progenitor."

The following letter was at the same time addressed to
Mr. Erskine :—

MY DEAR FRIEND,—You will see by a book which will
reach you by this post that I have taken a great liberty
with your name.   I was afraid you would refuse me if I
asked you beforehand, or that I should make you responsible for what I said.   I have longed to do what I
have done for many years, when an occasion should offer.
I wished to tell others how much I believe they as well as
I owe to your books, how they seem to me to mark a crisis
in the theological movement of this time.   I would rather
take another, less public, way of saying what I owe to your
personal kindness and your conversation, but you will, I
hope, forgive me and believe that I did think it a duty to
express what I feel towards you, in connection with the
task which God has shown me that I am to perform for
His Church, that of testifying that the grace of God has
appeared to all men.   Accept our best and most cordial

Christmas greetings to you and all your circle. . . .— Ever, my dear friend, yours very affectionately,

F. D. MAURICE.

December 21, 1852.

It was long after its publication before Mr. Erskine knew that this book had rendered such a service in such a quarter. But it was not long till he was surprised and delighted to find that the ideas of the love of God in Jesus Christ as embracing the whole human family, of the incarnation and death of the Redeemer, as having removed all obstacles to the immediate, free, and full forgiveness of every sinner of our race, almost in the very form in which he had himself in this volume expressed them, were already being fervently proclaimed by at least one minister of the Church of Scotland. If not before, it must have been immediately after the publication of the " Unconditional Freeness," that he heard Mr. M'Leod Campbell preach in Edinburgh. Returning from the church Mr. Erskine said with great emphasis to a friend who accompanied him, " I have heard to-day from that pulpit what I believe to be the true gospel."

Hearing his own favourite ideas unfolded and enforced with such intense earnestness, and learning at the same time of the gathering storm which was so soon to burst over the preacher's head, Mr. Erskine in the summer of 1828 made his first pilgrimage to Row, a parish lying on the banks of the beautiful Gairloch, in Dumbartonshire, of which Mr. Campbell had been ordained as the minister in 1825. Personal acquaintance deepened exceedingly the first favourable impressions. One life-lasting friendship began. Here, too, and now, another kindred friendship had its birth.

One Sunday in the preceding summer (1827) "my pulpit," says Mr. Campbell, " was occupied by my young friend

Mr. Scott.[1]   I heard him with very peculiar delight.   His preaching, though his second Sabbath, was with a sober, solemn composure, that would have seemed a delightful attainment in a man of much experience.   The progress he has already made in the divine life, the elevation and clearness of his views, the spirit of love which he breathes in every word, and the single-eyed devotedness to his Master's glory, are to me most delightful illustrations of the power of simple faith."[2]

Mr. Scott was with Mr. Campbell again in the summer of 1828, and there met Mr. Erskine.[3]   It was quite unique the triple friendship which had thus a common birthtime and birthplace; one peculiar feature marking it in each case.   "That historical independence," Dr. Campbell wrote a year or two before his death, "which we mark when two minds, working apart and without any interchange of thought, arrive at the same conclusions, is always an interesting and striking fact when it occurs; and it did occur as to Scott and myself; and also as to Mr. Erskine and me, and I believe too as to Mr. Erskine and Scott."[4]   All through life each of these three friends found

---

[1] Mr. A. J. Scott, son of the Rev. Dr. Scott of Greenock, afterwards Principal of Owens College, Manchester.

[2] *Reminiscences,* p. 22.

Edward Irving met with Scott during the same summer (1828) and arrived as rapidly at the same high estimate of Scott, and invited him to be his assistant in London.   "Sandy Scott," he wrote to Dr. Chalmers a month or two afterwards, "is a most precious youth, the finest and strongest faculty for pure theology I have yet met with."   Nor did his after experience of him in one of the closest of clerical relationships alter this estimate.   "A young man," he wrote of him in 1830, "so learned and accomplished in all kinds of discipline I have never met with, and as pious as he is learned, and of great, very great, discernment in the truth, and faithfulness Godward and manward."—*Irving's Life,* vol. ii. 68, 126.

[3] They met first in 1826 when Scott was attending some classes in the Edinburgh University, and was acting as tutor in the family of one of Mr. Erskine's friends.

[4] *Life of the Rev. Mr. Story,* p. 152.

in the other two what he found in none beside.   Intellectually, socially, spiritually, they moved in separate orbits; each having a path of his own, which with absolute independence he pursued.   But the paths lay very close to one another; and so entirely on the same plane, sloping upwards to the great central Source of light and life and love, as to constitute a separate sphere of religious ideas, aims, and aspirations, apart from and far above that of many with whom their names came afterwards to be associated.

Writing to a common friend in 1870, shortly after Mr. Erskine's death, Dr. Campbell spoke of him, "As one of the two my friendship with whom had its first commencement forty-three years ago, in the joy of seeing eye to eye in the light of the love of God to man, which each of us had known before we met in it; and as with that other (our dear Scott) my original fellow-helper in the gospel, my bond with him was very special, and since one of us three was taken, exclusive."[1]

"Dear cousin Rachel," when first she heard of the visit to Row, and the intimacy with Mr. Campbell, was somewhat alarmed, and ventured with semi-maternal anxiety, as being many years his senior, to remonstrate.   The letters which follow show what pains he took to allay her fears and win her sympathy.   His brother-in-law, Captain Paterson, and his wife, went heartily with Mr. Erskine from the beginning.   For three months in each of the summers of 1829 and 1830 they lived together at Row.   Unsatisfied with all that pen and press[2] could do, Mr. Erskine,

---

[1] _Reminiscences_, p. 44.

[2] In 1830 a little volume was issued from R. B. Lusk's prolific press at Greenock, entitled " Extracts of Letters to a Christian Friend by a Lady, with an Introductory Essay by Thomas Erskine, Esq., Advocate." This Introductory Essay contains the clearest and most condensed statement of all that was peculiar in the teaching of Mr. Campbell and of Mr. Erskine

especially when in the neighbourhood of Row, addressed
meetings and preached to small congregations sometimes
three hours every day, and often more. Mr. Campbell
needed all the support that could be given. His friends
were few, his opponents all-powerful. From almost every
leading pulpit in Scotland he had been denounced. Dr.
Barr of Port-Glasgow, Dr. Hamilton of Strathblane, Dr.
Burns of Paisley, Dr. Smyth of Glasgow, Dr. Thomson of
Edinburgh, vied with one another in expressing through
the press their sense of the depth and dangerous nature
of the errors into which he had fallen.

At first his own people adhered loyally and almost
unanimously to him. At last, on the 30th March 1830, a
few of their number lodged a complaint against him before
the Presbytery of Dumbarton. The General Assembly of
that year instructed the Presbytery to take it up, and, as
it was a matter of so very grave a character, to "carry on
their proceedings till the cause is ripe for a final judgment,
notwithstanding any appeal or complaint on preliminary
points." The first step taken by the Presbytery, in carrying out the instructions of the General Assembly, was to
appoint a Presbyterial visitation of the parish of Row, to
be held on Thursday, the 8th July, and to require the minister of the parish to preach before them. Mr. Erskine
was present on that occasion. Besides expressing its judgment in private upon some of the expressions employed by
the preacher, the Presbytery at this meeting instructed
the complainers against Mr. Campbell to have their charges
regularly framed into a libel (or indictment), and to present
it, with a list of witnesses, at the next ordinary meeting of

at this time, and was frequently referred to as such by those who wrote in
opposition to them. See the "Gairloch Heresy Tried," by Dr. Burns of
Paisley ; "A Vindication of the Religion of the Land, etc., in a Letter to
Thomas Erskine, Esq., by the Rev. A. Robertson, A.M.," etc. etc.

the Court in the first week of September. This was done. The libel was served upon Mr. Campbell, and he was summoned to appear on the 20th of the same month, and give in his answers.

The libel bore, "That albeit the doctrine of universal atonement and pardon through the death of Christ, as also the doctrine that assurance is of the essence of faith, and necessary to salvation, are contrary to the Holy Scriptures and to the Confession, yet true it is that you, the said Mr. John M'Leod Campbell, hold and have repeatedly promulgated and expressed the aforesaid doctrines."

As to his doctrine regarding the extent of the atonement Mr. Campbell in his answers was quite explicit. "I hold and teach," he said, "that Christ died for all men ; that the propitiation which He made for sin was for the sins of all mankind ; that those for whom He gave himself an offering and a sacrifice unto God for a sweet-smelling savour, were the children of men without exception and without distinction."[1] It was as to what he taught regarding universal pardon that Mr. Campbell felt that he was most liable to misapprehension. Many indeed of his best friends, and among them that friend who stood out so valiantly in his defence at every stage of the proceedings against him, the Rev. Mr. Story of Roseneath, regretted that he had ever adopted the expression, and given to it a meaning which he himself admitted was not the one in which it was ordinarily used, nor the one in which it was generally employed in Holy Writ.[2] He gave, however, from the beginning, his own interpretation of the sense that he attached to it. "The pardon of sin," he said in his first answers, " may be understood to mean either an act of indemnity to the sinner, giving him security from all the consequences of having

[1] *The Whole Proceedings*, etc., p. 16.
[2] See *Life of Mr. Story*, p. 190.

sinned against God, irrespective of any condition as to moral character; or as the act of God in receiving back to the bosom of His love the returning sinner; or thirdly, as the removing the judicial barrier which guilt interposes between the sinner and God; so making the fact of being a sinner no hindrance to his coming to God, as to a reconciled Father." In the first of these senses, Mr. Campbell held that pardon was not only " not the portion of all, but, in fact, it is not the portion of any." In the second of these senses, " I do not," he said, " hold pardon to be universal,[1] but limited to those who believe, and to those who repent." It was in the third sense alone that he admitted that he did " hold and teach the doctrine of universal pardon through the death of Christ."

As to the assurance of faith, which with many has been confounded with the faith of assurance,—" I feel more difficulty," Mr. Campbell says, " in arguing the point from the Scriptures than either of the others, because the Scriptures *everywhere assume* that to believe God's expressed love and to be assured of it are the same thing." He admitted that " a regenerate person may for a time be so overcome of Satan as to stand in doubt of that truth which is the anchor of his soul, and in this way lose the consciousness of security."[2]

Mr. Campbell's answers were accounted unsatisfactory, the relevancy of the libel was sustained, and the Presbytery proceeded to an examination of witnesses extending over many days. Among these witnesses, Captain Paterson from Linlathen, and Captain Stirling of Glentyan, appeared in favour of Mr. Campbell. Mr. Erskine's own headquarters were all the while at Row, and he watched the whole proceedings with the liveliest interest. The Presbytery,

---

[1] *The Whole Proceedings*, etc., pp. 32, 34, 36.
[2] *Ibid.* pp. 46, 47.

on the 29th of March 1831, found the libel "proven" by a
majority of eleven to two, and the matter was appealed to
the Synod of Glasgow and Ayr, which on the 14th April
came to a similar finding, remitting the case for final adjudi-
cation to the General Assembly. That Court took up the
case on Tuesday, the 24th of May 1831. Mr. Wylie of
Carluke, Mr. Story of Roseneath, and Mr. Campbell, were
heard at length, and it was not till long after midnight
that the Assembly entered on the consideration of the
evidence given before the Presbytery. That evidence formed
a printed volume of many hundred pages, and had only
been put into the hands of the members in the course of
the forenoon. It was proposed to adjourn the consideration of it till the next day. The proposal was rejected.
There were so many other cases, it was alleged, to be disposed
of, that this one must be concluded before they separated.
The counsel for the accused and the representatives of the
Presbytery and Synod addressed the House. The matter
was now at last in the Assembly's hands. It took little
time to deliberate. A few short speeches, and Dr. Cook
moved, Dr. Patrick Macfarlane seconding him, that Mr.
Campbell should be deposed, the Rev. Lewis Rose of Nigg
that he should be suspended. Before the roll was called,
Mr. Campbell's father, the Rev. Dr. Campbell of Kilninver,
rose, and read a letter and a petition signed by nineteen-
twentieths of the parishioners of Row. " It was stated at
the bar," Dr. Campbell said, "that Mr. Campbell's parish was
against him. I have read these papers that the House
may see this to be untrue. Moderator, I am the oldest
father at present in this house ; I have been forty years a
minister in the Church. It is gratifying to my feelings to
state what I have now done, and it ought to be gratifying
to yours, for you should be glad to hear that any one of
your brethren has been useful in his parish, and is beloved

by his people. A great deal was said, from the other side
of the House, about dealing gently and leniently with
Mr. C. Now, I would just ask, where is the leniency and
gentleness, if you go into the motion on your table, and
cut him off *brevi manu* from the Church? You have not
done Mr. C. justice, in attending to what has this day
been laid before you. You have heard him this day
in his own defence, and he has told you what he teaches.——
That he just teaches that "God so loved the world, that
He gave His only begotten Son, that whosoever believeth
in Him should not perish, but have everlasting life;" and
with regard to universal pardon, he has told you, that he
just means by it, 'That sinners may come to God, through
Jesus Christ, as to a reconciled Father.' Now, I am sure
there is none among us all who has anything to say against
this. And with regard to assurance, Sir, what he says is
no more than this, that a sceptic is no Christian, that
doubting God is not believing Him. And he has told you
that he abhors what are called the Antinomian doctrines
of 'the Marrow;' and I am sure, Sir, I can say that I
never heard any preacher more earnestly and powerfully
recommending holiness of heart and life. It was certainly
what I never expected, that a motion on your table for his
immediate deposition should have come from my old friend
Dr. Cook. But I do not stand here to deprecate your wrath.
I bow to any decision to which you may think it right
to come. Moderator, I am not afraid for my son. Though
his brethren cast him out, the Master whom he serves will
not forsake him; and, while I live, I will never be ashamed
to be the father of so holy and blameless a son."[1]

The roll being called, and the votes marked, it was found
that 119 had voted for the first motion, and only 6 for the
second. Before the sentence of deposition was actually

[1] *The Whole Proceedings*, etc., pp. 176, 177.

pronounced, some slight discussion as to the order of procedure took place. Dr. Macknight of Edinburgh, who held at the time the office of Chief Clerk of the Assembly, on being appealed to, in the height of his emotion, and meaning exactly the reverse of what he said, was heard to declare that " these doctrines of Mr. Campbell would remain and flourish after the Church of Scotland had perished, and was forgotten." Mr. Erskine, who was present, caught the words. Turning to those behind him, he whispered, " This spake he not of himself, but being High Priest—he prophesied."

Two days thereafter, on the evening of the 27th May 1831, the same Assembly that had deposed Mr. M'Leod Campbell from the office of the ministry deprived Mr. A. J. Scott of his licence as a preacher of the gospel. This licence had been granted him in 1827. Not long thereafter he was led to entertain opinions identical as to the universality of atonement with those held by Mr. Campbell, and similar as to the Sabbath question with those afterwards expressed by Dr. Norman M'Leod. Under the impression that this of itself disqualified him from holding office in the Church, he had relinquished the idea of the ministry and was studying medicine in Edinburgh, when Edward Irving's earnest invitation was given to him to become his assistant in London, and to act as missionary in a poor district of the City. Understanding that in this situation he would be left perfectly free and unfettered, he accepted the situation, and discharged its duties with more than satisfaction to Mr. Irving. " Your son," the latter wrote to the Rev. Dr. Scott of Greenock, " has taken up the Cross, and I think he will not lay it down till he receives the crown. He is a very stay to me ; he comforts me greatly." In October 1830 the small Scotch congregation at Woolwich invited Mr. Scott to become their

minister.   Acceptance of this invitation involved ordination by the Presbytery of London, and that again involved
subscription to the Westminster Confession of Faith.   In
these circumstances, and before the call was in his hands,
he thought it right to address the following letter to the
Moderator of the London Presbytery :—

LONDON, October 1830.

REVEREND AND DEAR SIR,—Not having yet received
the call from the congregation at Woolwich, I am unwilling
to delay any longer putting into a permanent form my
determination regarding that call, in order that you may,
at as early a period as possible, communicate it to the
Presbytery.

Not believing that I could, consistently with truth, sign
as a confession of my faith a statement in which it is
asserted that "none are redeemed by Christ but the elect
only," *West. Conf.*, chap. iii. sect. 6 ; or that "to all those
for whom He hath purchased redemption He doth certainly
and effectually communicate the same" (chap. viii. sect. 8),
implying "that He died for their sins only" (chap. xi.
sect. 4) ; seeing I believe that God would have all men
to be saved and come to the knowledge of the truth, in
testimony whereof Christ gave Himself a ransom for all
men ;—having also a firm conviction that the Sabbath and
the Lord's day are not, as stated in the Confession (chap. xxi.
sect. 7), one ordinance, but two, perfectly distinct, the one
Jewish, the other Christian ;—believing that the powers
enumerated (chap. xxx. sect. 2) are greater in kind than
could have been conferred on me by the imposition of the
hands of the Presbytery, while by accepting ordination I
should recognise in them a right and ability to convey
such powers,—I may not accept ordination while my
signing the Westminster Confession is made the condition

of my receiving it, as it would be by the Presbytery in London, and therefore resign again into their hands every claim or right which I might found on the call addressed to me by the Scotch congregation at Woolwich inviting me to become their pastor.

You will oblige me, dear Sir, by communicating this resolution to the Presbytery, etc.   A. J. S.

Believing that by this communication he not only declined the call from Woolwich, but virtually gave up all prospect of ever being a minister of the Scotch Church, Mr. Scott felt himself brought back to the position in which Mr. Irving had found him in Edinburgh, and was preparing to live by classical and mathematical teaching, when Mr. Irving interposed. " He conceived," Mr. Scott tells us, " that I ought not to anticipate the actual decision of the Church—to assume myself cut off from her communion by an act of my own without her express sentence. In compliance with his desire I agreed with the Presbytery of London that a reference should be made to the Scotch Presbytery which had conferred my licence."   The object of this reference to the Presbytery of Paisley, and through it by appeal to the General Assembly, was to test the questions whether continuance in office implied that a faith in every article of the Confession remained unshaken and unchanged, and whether such a measure of disagreement with the articles as Mr. Scott had acknowledged was incompatible with his being a minister of the Church. When the matter came before the General Assembly the discussion was brief. Professing his willingness to sign the old National Confession, Mr. Scott was entering on an argument intended to show that wherein he differed from the Westminster Confession, it differed from Holy Scripture, when he was interrupted. Such a line of argument

was held not only to be incompetent but to be an insult
to the Court.   Without a dissentient voice, the Assembly
found that " Mr. Scott having declared that he did not
believe the whole doctrine of the Confession of Faith,
deprived him of his licence as a preacher of the Gospel,
and prohibited all its ministers from employing him to
preach in their churches."

Scott and Campbell held the same doctrine as to the atonement.   To Scott, however, it appeared that their view of this
doctrine was directly contrary to that affirmed in the Confession.   Campbell thought otherwise, and endeavoured to con-
vince the Assembly that though not in full harmony with what
he taught, the Confession did not absolutely contradict it.
The two friends were present each at the other's trial before
the Assembly.   When Scott's case closed they walked home
together.   " After that dreary night in the Assembly," he
tells us, " the dawn breaking upon us as we returned at
length, alike condemned, to our lodging in the New Town of
Edinburgh, I turned round and looked upon my companion's
face under the pale light, and asked him, Could you sign the
Confession now ?   His answer was No.   The Assembly was
right : our doctrine and the Confession are incompatible."

Rigidly adhering to the whole doctrine of the Westminster Confession, and imperatively demanding a like
adherence on the part of all office-bearers of the Church,
the General Assembly of 1831 had apparently no alterna-
tive but to eject Mr. Campbell and Mr. Scott.   Nearly
half a century has passed since then, and it is believed that
the Church now would eject neither the one nor the other.
If so, there must have come over her some modification
either of her own belief in the whole doctrine of the Confession or of her demand for an entire conformity there-
with.   To many that Confession may not now appear as
full and perfect a representation of Divine truth as it did

to the men of a bygone generation. To many it may appear as setting forth but one side or aspect of that truth. To many it may appear as too wide in its range, too minute in its details, to warrant the requirement of subscription to all its articles. To many these articles may appear to be of such different relative worth and importance that unbelief of some of them ought not to involve forfeiture of office. However in these respects it may be, it is certain that the Church is not standing now on the ground she occupied forty-seven years ago, and the time may come ere long for her to acknowledge and vindicate the change in her position.

54. TO DR. CHALMERS.

CADDER, GLASGOW, 19*th July* 1828.

DEAR SIR,—. . . I am much interested and gratified by what you say of Mrs. Chalmers's opinion of my work. I looked for the opposition of all regular theologians, and for the concurrence of untheological Christians in general —for, whatever the logical system of a Christian may be, I am persuaded that the free, undeserved, and general love of God to the world, to the sinful family of Adam, is the true ground on which each individual of our race must rest. I know no other and see no other in the Bible. The particular love is manifested in revealing to each individual the knowledge of the general love; but it is not on the particular revelation that a man can or ought to rest— it is on the general love thus revealed to him. I have added a few sentences in the second edition on the subject of Justification, which I think make my view of it a little clearer, and I shall desire the bookseller to send you one of them. At the same time, I believe that a man may be very right whilst he thinks my view of it very wrong.

You have had much reason for thankfulness for the

preservation of Mrs. Chalmers and your children at Kirk-caldy.[1] I desire to thank God along with you for His fatherly protection on that occasion.—With best regards to her and all your children, I remain, my dear Sir, with affectionate regard,   T. ERSKINE.

This will be my headquarters until I hear from you.

55. TO MISS RACHEL ERSKINE.

LINLATHEN, *6th September* 1828.

MY DEAR FRIEND,—I have been looking for a letter from you, with considerable impatience, for some time now. I hope you got my letter from Gartur, containing the con-clusion of Habakkuk. It was very hurried, and from that cause it was probably obscure; but I should like to know whether it was understood or not. I feel its importance very much. My dear cousin, do you not feel that the Christianity of the present day is a very low thing, if it is indeed a thing at all, and not a mere set of words and forms? Our systems make God a mere bundle of doctrines, but He is the great One with whom we have to do in every-thing. It seems to me that the great dislike for anything supernatural in religion at present arises just from this circumstance, that religion is for the most part a covert atheism, and there is a general shrinking from anything like an indication that there is a real power and a real Being at work around us, whom we can neither comprehend nor guard against. Who is it that asks things from God and gets them? Yet it is said, " Whatsoever ye shall ask in my name ye shall receive." And God is faithful to His word. Have not you felt the weakness of your faith long? I am sure that I have felt mine to be as nothing. Well,

---

[1] Mrs. Chalmers and one of her daughters were in the church at Kirkcaldy in which Mr. Irving was to preach, when the gallery fell. They both escaped unhurt.

why have we so long laboured under this misery? "Ye have not, because ye ask not." My dear cousin, we are not straitened in God, we are straitened in ourselves. Young Scott, the son of Dr. Scott of Greenock, is with us. He is a highly gifted man. May the mighty God bless him, and strengthen him for the work that he may be called to! He preached last night in Dundee. There was one thing which he said upon the universality of the love of God to sinners which I shall repeat to you. When God was manifested in Christ, in the man Christ Jesus, that man fulfilled the whole law, of which the second great division is, Thou shalt love thy neighbour as thyself. If there had been any single man upon earth whom He did not love as Himself, He would have been a breaker of the law. But He fulfilled the whole law, and loved every man, as He loved Himself—ay and more; and as He thus fulfilled the law, He said, "He that hath seen me, hath seen the Father;" that is to say, My love to men is the very image of my Father's love to them.

There is a sweet blessed death-bed here, which I am privileged to attend. May the Lord bless these opportunities, and deliver me from the deadness of my own corrupt heart! It is the death-bed of a girl of fourteen,[1] who is kept in perfect peace because she trusteth in the strength of the weak, and the help of the helpless. We hear that uncle Tom and my aunts are coming to-day. We are all well here, old and young. Give my best love to my dear cousins. All here send love. Write soon.— Yours affectionately,   T. E.

56. TO THE SAME.

LINLATHEN, *9th October* 1828.

MY DEAR FRIEND,—Our letters crossed again, accord-

---

[1] The niece of Mrs. Machar.

ing to their former habit, but certainly by my fault. Well, your friends have had another call to turn from the creature. Poor Lady Eliza, I can conceive such a trial to be full of bitterness to a mother;—that creature on whom a being has been bestowed through her as a channel, and to whom she has been thus connected by a tie that we cannot suppose can be ever broken or forgotten, that creature has passed into another state, without ever having known her love to her, although it was bone of her bone and flesh of her flesh, and she has loved it, and loves it, without having the slightest knowledge of it; but they are to meet again. How wonderfully God connects man with man! He could make all men by direct acts of separate creation, but He makes one the channel of being to another; and so of the comforts of life, and so also of the higher life. This order in Providence is just a call to love. He makes us fellow-workers with himself. I trust that this may be sanctified to them all. I hope that they are on their guard against an intellectual religion. I think that the present age seems especially exposed to this delusion, and a fearful delusion it is. People quote the examples of Sir Isaac Newton, and Pascal, and such great men, as arguments in favour of religion, whereas a sanctified idiot like poor Joseph is an argument worth a thousand Newtons. "Thou hast hid these things from the wise and prudent, and hast revealed them unto babes." It was not the beautiful arrangement and harmony of God's revelation that supported Habakkuk under the Chaldean invasion, it was the love of God in the revelation. You say that you are jealous about Mr. Campbell of the Row, and that you are afraid. If he is left to himself, I am sure he will go far enough wrong, but I believe that God has given him grace to be faithful. Katherine and Jane have just left us. They had been at Helensburgh and Row lately, and were struck just

as I was by what they saw there. . . . I am thinking of
setting about a fourth essay on the Freeness of the Gospel,
and making Habakkuk the text of it. The whole system
of Providence in this world is just the Chaldean invasion;
and the good news that God hath so loved the world as to
give His Son as a propitiation for the sins of the world, and
that He will yet give unto Him the kingdoms of this world,
and that in Him all the kindreds of the earth shall be
blessed, is the vision which will sustain and vivify all who
believe it, just as it sustained Habakkuk. The Chaldean
scourge was a condemnation on account of sin, and it lay
upon all the Israelites; but to those who believed the
vision, that calamity changed its character. It ceased to
be a condemnation, for they saw love in it, though their
external circumstances continued the same. This is the
meaning of the expression, "the pardon removes no
penalties;" but it changes the character of the penalties,
by showing them to be full of love. And our belief in
Christ will just do this same thing for us, if it does anything at all,—if we do not take a word for a thing, if we
do not receive the grace of God in vain; for the whole
events of time are just one condemnation on account of sin,
and he who does not see the love of God, and the Christ
of God, in them, does not see life, but the condemnation
abideth in him in its own unmitigated character. Yet that
love is in the whole course of events, whether we see it or
shut our eyes against it. In all of them there is a kindness
of God leading men to Himself. If I have not expressed
myself so as to be understood, pray tell me so, and may
the God of love manifest himself fully to our souls, and fill
us with His own love. He that dwelleth in love dwelleth
in God, and God in him. My mother intends to write to
you. Farewell.—Affectionately yours,   T. E.

I expect Mrs. Rich here in a day or two.

K

57. TO MISS STUART.

LINLATHEN, 29*th October* 1828.

MY DEAR FRIEND,—I have felt a desire to communicate with you for some time back, to let you know that I feel with you, and that I wish to hear how you are going on. You know that there is but one Fountain of good in the whole universe, and that you have as free access to it at one time as at another. The water of life that flows from that fountain mixes with every event which befalls us, whatever the appearance of the event may be, and those only are miserable who take the event by itself and leave the water of life which is contained in it untasted; and those only are blessed who drink that water of life in every cup. May the Lord grant unto you, my dear friend, to drink of it continually, and then though sorrowful you will be always rejoicing. I wish to hear about I——. I hope that he is to drink that water in this trial, and that it will be in him a well of water springing up into everlasting life. . . . I would pray for you that you may know by experience the full meaning of Phil. iv. 6, 7. Your own thoughts or cares or anxieties can evidently do no good in this case. Roll your burden on the Lord.—Yours affectionately,   T. ERSKINE.

58. TO MISS RACHEL ERSKINE.

LINLATHEN, 9*th November* 1828.

MY OWN FRIEND WHOM I LOVE,—I am happy to hear of the general well-being and well-doing of B. and M. I wish to hear what the Lord is doing amongst them,—what the Answerer of prayer is doing amongst them. There is much disrespect in asking God for anything, and then not taking the trouble to inquire whether He has done it or not. Is there not something very striking in comparing the apparent quantity of prayer for the King and the Royal Family with their actual state? They are not prayed for, I believe. There are words said about them in church, and God would let men know that He does not hear words. Those only truly pray who know that they have the petitions which they ask. Is this going too far? It excludes me from prayer, but that is no reason against its truth. Our standard is very low in general, and we may like to have it low, in order that it may include ourselves. Many seem to consider prayer only as a wish, and Montgomery's hymn goes on this idea; but prayer is not merely a wish, it supposes confidence. The promise of answer in the Bible is so very unlimited, that the only way of reconciling that promise with what we see and experience, is to raise our standard of prayer. Yes, it is a blessed chapter the 14th of John. I think that the meaning of the first verse is just this: "Let not your heart be troubled, ye believe in a God,—well, know that I am that God." He had been just washing their feet and giving them a charge to love one another as he had loved them, and then he says to them,—Here is comfort for you in all circumstances, you know that there is but one power that orders all things. Well, I who have loved you, and washed your feet, and am about to die for you, I am that one power. Is not this comfort, my dear friend? Is it not rich comfort? Our brother Joseph reigns, and His bowels do yearn upon his brethren, even when He speaks roughly to them: it is then only that He feigns. The day is coming when Joseph will make Himself known to His brethren. Let us hasten unto that day. . . .

59. TO MRS. MONTAGU.

LINLATHEN, *27th November* 1828.

MY DEAR MRS. MONTAGU,—. . . The motive of my writing to you at this moment is to tell you that Mr. Scott, who I believe is acting as assistant to Mr. Irving at present, is a friend very dear to me. I have received something through him. He is a very able minister of the new testament. He does not frustrate the grace of God, and I think you might find him profitable to your soul. In some respects I don't know his equal, and I should like, if it were agreeable to you, to make you acquainted with him, both for your sake and his. He is a very young man, not more than twenty-three I believe. I wish to make him acquainted with you and Mrs. Rich, as some sort of recreation to him in the midst of his labours. If it is in the slightest degree inconvenient for you, don't mind what I have said, except as an expression of my great regard and confidence.

60. TO MISS RACHEL ERSKINE.

LINLATHEN, *26th December* 1828.

MY DEAREST COUSIN,—The feeling that I am unsympathised with by those whose sympathy is dearest to me is not that which pains me most in the communication I have received from you. In general, I feel a great demand for sympathy from those I love, just because I love them, and because that love gives their sympathy a value to me beyond the things themselves in which I ask their sympathy. But it is not so here. The thing in which I ask your sympathy is far dearer to me than any human sympathy; and I long for your sympathy, merely because I think I hold the truth, and I wish you to hold it also. I do not think that you can see the importance or the universality of Christ's atonement, if you can disapprove of the proclamation of it, though by a layman. You have told me that you believe that " Christ is the propitiation for the sins of the whole world," in the obvious sense of these

words. You have told me that you believe that this is
God's message to this world of prodigals, that this is the
message which is the power of God unto salvation to all
who believe it. Well, do you also know that this doctrine
is looked on as a heresy by almost all the teachers of
religion in this country, and that a directly opposite doctrine is preached? If you believe in the universality of
the atonement, you must believe that the limitation of it is
a falsification of the record which God has given concerning
His Son.

I live in the conviction that the record is continually
falsified in the ears of the people of this country by
those whom they are taught to look up to for instruction, to the dishonour of God's grace, and to the injury of
the souls of men. God's message to the world is not
delivered whilst a limited atonement is preached; and so
long as this erroneous interpretation of the message is
preached from our orthodox pulpits, the people may have
the Bible in their hands, but the unfaithful interpretation
will be a veil on their hearts in the reading of it. There
were many Bibles among the Jews when our Lord appeared
amongst them, but the unfaithful interpretation put upon
their contents by the scribes of the time blinded the people
to the truth, and they rejected Him of whom Moses and
the prophets wrote. —— must know that it is most important that even when the people have the Bible in their
hands, there should be some one near to say to them,
" Understandest thou what thou readest?" I have known
people long possessed of the Bible, who never read it, partly
because it was not pressed upon them; and I have known
many who have long read the Bible without ever apprehending, even in theory, its most elementary truths, because they
were accustomed to hear a false interpretation of them
weekly from the pulpit. If ——'s arguments were good,

there need be little anxiety to have a gospel ministry in a place well supplied with Bibles. I see people about me with Bibles in their houses and in their hands (and who think occasionally of religion too, some of them), to whom the message that God loves them is a perfect novelty even in sound. If I can do anything for any of these souls, these immortals, as an instrument in God's hands, am I to hesitate because I am classed in the world's list under one denomination of persons rather than another? I think that Christians are too often popular in the world, just on account of the remaining unchristianity that is in them. As long as Christianity subordinates itself to the world, the world will like it, because the world likes to have its conscience easy as to eternity, and the concurrence of a Christian gives it that ease. My dearly beloved friend, I love you dearly. I know that I am not to expect full sympathy in the creation :—

> " Each in his hidden sphere of joy or woe,
>   Our hermit spirits dwell and range apart."

These are beautiful lines, and most true.

61. TO MISS RACHEL ERSKINE.

CADDER, *Wednesday, 11th March* 1829.

MY DEAR COUSIN,—I was sorry to let the architect leave this for Gartur the other day, without carrying some palpable testimony of my ever grateful and affectionate remembrance of you, and therefore I have begun this letter, that another messenger from us may not go empty-handed to you. I almost wish that I were with you just now, and I wish we could feel the pure sap of the true vine so active within us, and so binding us together by its heavenly sympathy, that we might have an uninterrupted intercourse, and might feel each other's presence in the presence of our

Root, and Head, and Fountain. A friend of mine told me
that he had been at different times sensible of spiritual
blessings bestowed on him through the prayers of particular
persons at a distance. He was conscious of a special
blessing, and he had a most distinct impression that that
blessing came to him through the prayers of a particular
person; and on asking the person afterwards, he learned
that he had been praying for that very blessing on him.
I like such a story exceedingly. I like to think of the
condescension of our God answering such petitioners as
men, to the very letter of their petitions; and I like to
think of His binding souls so close as to make them channels
to each other of the water of life. And thus there is a
great increase of the spirit of thanksgiving, for each blessing is not only a reason of gratitude to the receiver of it,
but also to those whose prayers of love have been answered
in the bestowment of it. I have Keble lying open before
me. The hymns for the holy week are beautiful: Monday
is exquisite. I think that I like it best of them all. The
use made of Andromache's farewell is quite filling to the
heart, and the theology of the fourth stanza, "Thou art as
much his care," etc., is worth, in my mind, the whole Shorter
and Longer Catechisms together. Good-night.

Thursday.— . . . My dear Rachel, "the earnest expectation of the creature waiteth for the manifestation of the
sons of God." None of God's children here are allowed
to have such a lot as would make their expectation of their
heavenly inheritance cease to be an earnest expectation.
I can thank God at present for a quiet mind; but blessed
are those who can really thank Him for an unquiet mind,
who can feel that those agitations which shake their very
soul do not shake the rock on which their souls rest, nor
loosen the bonds which bind them to it. Our Keir friends
sent Christian a letter from Jane Stirling, at Passy, which

gives a most sweet account of Mrs. William Stirling, and
William himself. It is a history of love—the faithful love
of the God of love. She obeys the precept which says,
" Rejoice without ceasing," and she does it naturally without
thinking it obedience. That is what we want. The sap
of a tree requires no laws to instruct it as to the nature of
the fruit which it should produce. It is a law unto itself.
If it were the wrong sap, no law could keep it right. So
the law is just to let us know whether we have got the
right sap or not in us. It describes the fruit of the true
sap. " Rejoice in the Lord always, and again I say rejoice."
That is as much a commandment as " Thou shalt do no
murder." It is as much a description of the fruit of the
true sap. Talk over this matter, will you? God's love
entering into the soul is the true sap. It enters in simply
by the belief of it, as the light enters the eye simply by
seeing it. Write to me again soon. I find that I have
not the faculty of conveying my meaning distinctly. You
say that the laying too much stress on some particular point
suggests in your mind a doubt on it which did not exist
before. But I am apprehensive that this is not the true
explanation of your doubt. I believe that it arises from
discovering that there is indeed a difference in reality,
although the terms employed are somewhat like each
other.—Yours most affectionately,   T. ERSKINE.

Give my best love. Charles and Christian join me.

62. TO MISS RACHEL ERSKINE.

14 ROYAL CRESCENT, *May* 1829.

MY DEAREST COUSIN,—. . . Bishop K. is very amiable,
and sees very well that love is the whole matter; but he
does not show the true way of getting it. He seems to
think that we are to love just by an exertion, a con-

scientious exertion. Now, will you look at the third
chapter of John? In the third verse our Lord says, "Except
a man be born again, he cannot see the kingdom of
heaven." He evidently means by that to inform Nicodemus
that no improvement of his present faculties or principles
could introduce him into the spiritual happiness which
was the perfection of man's being; but that a new life was
wanting in order to this. Well, what is this new life, and
how is it to be had? For, if I don't know how to get it,
my knowledge that it is necessary is of no use to me, but
rather an aggravation of the evil. Look to the sixteenth
verse, "God so loved the world, that he gave his only
begotten Son, that whosoever believeth in Him might not
perish, but have everlasting life." This is the life that is
wanting. And what is it? It can be nothing else than
God's love to the world in the gift of his Son. For what
is it that enters into our hearts when we believe anything?
Is it not the thing that we believe? Thus some friend of
yours does you an unkindness which you know nothing of.
Whilst you are ignorant of it, it does not enter into your
mind, and of course does not affect you in any way. I hear
of it, and tell you. You answer me, "I have known that person all my life, and I don't believe it." Whilst you continue
to disbelieve it, it does not enter into your mind, and gives
you no pain. I bring you irresistible evidence—you believe
it, and it enters and makes you miserable. So when a
history of love is told, what is it that enters, when it is
believed, but the love? It is thus in man's dealings with
man; and though different in degree, and even in kind, yet
in many respects it is thus also in our dealings with God.
"God so loved the world," etc. God's love is the only
spiritual life—the only sap of the universal vine, and it can
only enter, as it cannot but enter, by being believed. I
cannot tell you the delight that I have found in thinking

of God's love to man as a disapproving love. Man confounds love and approbation, or love and interestedness.
Thus a man loves those whom he thinks well of, or who
are necessary to his happiness. But God's love acknowledges and demands nothing either amiable or serviceable
in its objects. The love of my God is not diminished by
his disapprobation of me. There is something remarkable
in Christ's substitution for Barabbas in a way more especial
than for any other individual, that He might be an example
of those for whom He died. I hope dear M. has found God
a "*réfuge très aisé à trouver,*" as the French happily translate, "a habitation whereunto I may alway resort." May
He dwell in her as a strength and a peace, and may she
rejoice in Him with an exceeding joy. May she find Him
in everything, for He is in everything, and then she will
rightly find good in everything. . . .—Yours affectionately,

T. E.

63. To Miss Rachel Erskine.

Row Cottage, Helensburgh, *July* 1829.

My dear Cousin,—I long to speak with you of the
great things of God—of that life which He hath given to
us in His Son, the great Head, and through whom it is
communicated to all the members, as the blood is communicated through the heart to all the members of the
natural body. This is the life hid with Christ in God,
which is brought to light by the gospel; and it is of the
same thing that the disciples were desired by the angel to
testify, when he said to them, "Go and speak to the people
all the words of this life." Death had entered the world
by the belief of a lie: this was the work of the devil, and
He who came to destroy the work of the devil communicated this new life by the belief of a truth. The Word
was with God and was God, and in Him was life, and the

life became light, even the light of men. That is to say,
the invisible life of the Godhead became visible in Jesus
Christ, the Word made flesh. It became intelligible and
palpable in His person and character. And as the light
enters into us by our eyes seeing it, so this life enters into
us by our minds seeing it, *i.e.* by our believing it or knowing it as a truth. Now what does the Spirit testify concerning this light which is life? Look over the first
chapter of the First Epistle of John, and the beginning of
the first chapter of his Gospel. John Baptist was said to
bear witness of that Light, and this is his witness of Him,
" Behold the Lamb of God, who taketh away the sin of the
world," John i. 29. And see also what the Light said of
Himself, John viii. 11 and 12, " Neither do I condemn
thee : go and sin no more. Then spake Jesus again unto
them, saying, I am the light of the world : he that followeth
me shall not walk in darkness, but shall have the light of
life." These two verses ought never to have been severed.
Their meaning consists in their union ; the " Neither do I
condemn thee : go and sin no more," the sanctifying
forgiveness of God manifested in Christ is the light of life,
and he that seeth it hath the life. Precisely the same idea
of the light is given in the first chapter of the First Epistle
of John, 5th verse, " God is light, and in him is no darkness at all, and the blood of Jesus Christ his Son cleanseth
from all sin " (the intervening matter in the sixth and
beginning of the seventh verses is merely a commentary
on the words, God is light). The light consists in the
forgiving holy love. Now mark, the works of light are
works which proceed from seeing the light of this forgiving
love ; as the works of darkness are the works of those who
do not know that they are forgiven. John begins his
Epistle by saying that he was going to declare that which
his own eyes had seen of the Word of life—even that

eternal life which was with the Father, and was manifested unto us. He tells us that by the knowledge of this life, or by having seen this light, he had fellowship with the Father and the Son; and he declares it to others, that they also may partake of this same life, even the life which the Father lives and which the Son lives. And the way which he takes of introducing us into this fellowship is by simply declaring to us the characteristics of that light, which the life had become: "This is the message which we have heard of him and declare unto you, that God is light, and in him is no darkness at all, and the blood of Jesus Christ his Son cleanseth from all sin."

Christ was the New Head of the human nature. Now, my beloved friend, attend. Suppose we were in a church-yard, and saw the earth over the grave, where we had seen a human body interred some time before, begin to move, and at last we saw the head of that human body in perfect life elevating itself above the ground,—if astonishment would allow us to reason, should we not feel assured that the rest of the members would soon follow the head,— should we not know that there was life in the body again because there was life in the head? Christ is the second Adam, the real unfigurative Head of the human body. He had suffered death as a partaker of that tainted life which was under the curse; and then He rose again with a new life infused into Him. In the person of Christ risen then, we see God in fellowship with our nature, even with us; and we also see a life which is communicated to all those who see—" Neither do I condemn thee: go and sin no more;" for this is the life made light, and those who see it have the life. In religious books we find the death of Jesus chiefly, almost exclusively pressed, whereas in the Bible we find that the apostles were ordained to be wit-nesses of His resurrection, Acts i. 22. See also Acts ii.

32, 33 ; also Acts iii. 15-26 ; Acts iv. 33 ; Acts v. 31, 32 ;
x. 40, 41 ; xiii. 32, 33. Is it not clear that the resurrection is pressed on us by the apostles in a way quite different from what it is by ordinary religionists since their
time ?—Yours most affectionately,   T. E.

In the death of Christ the old life was exhausted, and
in the resurrection the new life was infused.

64. TO A CLERICAL FRIEND.

Row Cottage, Helensburgh, 1829.

My dear Brother in the Lord Jesus Christ,—It has
been the subject of much thankful rejoicing on our part,
that it has pleased God to declare the Word of Life through
your mouth to the many souls around you who are perishing through lack of knowledge. It is indeed a high privilege conferred upon a poor sinful worm, to be permitted to
testify to his fellow-sinners that God—the God against
whom we have sinned—loves them, and that He hath
given His Son for them to be the propitiation for their
sins, and that in the knowledge of this there is life eternal.
May the Lord our Righteousness pour down upon you, and
upon the truth spoken by you, and upon the hearts of the
hearers, quickening and refreshing showers of the Holy
Spirit. And may He give testimony to the Word of His
grace, by causing great signs and wonders to be performed
by it on the souls of men. Surely the time is not now
distant, when He who hath so long holden His peace shall
cause the earth to hear His voice ; but as yet there is little
interruption of the deadly sleep in which our race lies
buried. O my friend, is it not a subject of awful wonder
that the Jehovah of Hosts hath come into this earth in the
form of a man, that He might taste death for every man,
and that with the message of His love in His hand, He is
still knocking at the door of every heart, entreating to be

let in, that He may make them partakers of the Divine
nature,—and yet that the earth remains almost as it was
before the birth of Jesus? What is the cause of this? The
truth seemed to prevail mightily and to spread rapidly in
the first age of Christianity. Why has it come to a stand?
Is that Word, which in the days of the apostles was mighty
through God to the pulling down of the strongholds of the
carnal mind and of the enemy of souls, become weak? The
same Word has still the same power, and must produce the
same effects wherever it is proclaimed; that is to say, it will
either draw men to God or it will excite the hatred of the
natural man. But that which is generally preached in this
country as the gospel neither gives life nor excites hatred;
on the contrary, it gives men a vague and deadening hope
of safety, which is quite agreeable to the carnal mind. The
gospel of the present day substitutes the seriousness of man
for the grace of God. If a man has serious thoughts
about God and his own soul, he is both by himself and his
friends thought to be in a safe state, although he knows
nothing of that record which God hath sent to every man,
viz., that God hath given to him eternal life in His Son.
Until men know that their sins are forgiven them, they are
not Christians—they have no life in them—" for except
ye eat the flesh of the Son of Man, and drink his blood, ye
have no life in you,"—and yet now-a-days a man is thought
presumptuous if he believes that God says true when He
says that the blood of Jesus cleanseth from all sin, that is,
if he believes that his own sins are pardoned.

My dear brother, the object of this letter is to pray you
to come here. The preaching here is the application of
our Lord's word, " It is finished," to the hearts and the
consciences of men, and God gives life through the Word.
There is either life or hatred. It is not man's word that I
ask you to listen to. I ask you to come, that you may hear

a word from God which you may speak again to others.
How little is Paul's creed understood : " I live by the faith
of the Son of God." And what faith is that ? " Who loved
me, and gave Himself for me." Paul did not learn this
after he was a Christian ; he became a Christian by believing
it, and no man becomes a Christian in any other way. You
know this truth for yourself. Blessed be God, it is a truth
for every man, and every man who believes it finds life
in it, and every man who rejects it is condemned for rejecting it, and shuts out life from his soul, for it is the Word
of life. Christ is the propitiation for the sins of the whole
world, and He is God's gift of love to the world. He that
believeth hath life, he that believeth not hath not life. But
the gift remains a gift : the love remains, the forgiveness
is a real, fast thing. I pray you come.—Yours most
truly,   T. Erskine.

65. TO MADAME DE STAËL.[1]

25 St. Andrew Square, Edinburgh,
4th Sept. 1829.

Gaussen is quite right in telling you that I do not forget
you before God. But I am much ashamed of my negligence
as a correspondent, especially when I consider what God
has given us to correspond about. My dear friend, we may
speak to each other about God's love—God's forgiving love
in giving us His Son to be the propitiation for our sins.
He has given His Son to you and to me, and in Him He has
given us all things. When the Bible says, " Acquaint
thyself with God and be at peace," it means to say that
there is something in God which necessarily gives peace
to every one that knows it. If a soul is not at peace, the
only reason is because it does not know God. If Joseph's

---

[1] Daughter of Madame Vernet, and daughter-in-law to the celebrated
Madame de Staël.

brethren, as they stood before him, and not knowing who
he was, but hearing him speak roughly to them, had been
told, "This is your brother Joseph," they would immediately
have been filled with terror, thinking that he would now
take vengeance on them for their treatment of him ; but if
they could have looked into his heart, and had seen there
a forgiving love, which yearned over them, and which was
not in the smallest degree affected by their unkindness to
him, it is evident that although they would have reproached
themselves far more than ever they had done before, yet
they would have had a perfect deliverance from all personal
fears on their own account, they would have seen a ground
of confidence in their brother's character which must at once
have given them peace.   If Joseph had loved all of them
except one, then it could not have been said to that one,
" Acquaint thyself with Joseph and be at peace," for the
knowledge that he was really excluded from Joseph's love
would have given him terror and not peace.   And so if
there were a single being whom God did not love, then it
could not have been said to that being, " Acquaint thyself
with God and be at peace."   But as it is said generally to
all, it must also be true to all that God loves them, and
that it is only necessary for them to know God's feelings
towards them, and to look into God's heart, in order to
have perfect peace.   This is the meaning of being saved by
faith.   If God did not love, and had not forgiven us, our
salvation could only be produced by our doing something
which might make a change in God's feelings towards us ;
that would be salvation by works, or by our doing something.   But since God does love us and has forgiven us,
we need not do anything to change God's feelings, and all
that is necessary for our peace and confidence is to know
what the actual state of God's feelings are toward us, and
this is salvation by faith, *c'est à dire*, salvation by knowing

our real circumstances. All human religions are founded on the principle that man must do something, or feel something, or believe something, in order to make God love him and forgive him ; whereas God's religion just contains a declaration that nothing of the kind is necessary on our part in order to make God forgive us, for that He hath *déjà*, already, loved us and forgiven us, and given us His Son, and in Him all things. He hath declared this to the whole race without any exception, as a truth to each individual ; so that the difference between the most miserable hater of God and the happiest child of God does not consist in this, that God loves the one and does not love the other ; but in this, that the one knows God's love to himself and the other does not. It is the same difference as there is between two men standing with their faces to the sun, the one with his eyes shut and the other with his eyes open.

Election does not consist in God's making the light of His love to shine upon one and not upon another, for He loves all, and gave Christ as a ransom for all. It consists in this, that when all refused to open their eyes God forces open the eyes of some, and leaves others to their own obstinacy.[1] Unless all were loved the world could not be charged with the sin of unbelief, for if there existed a man for whom Christ did not die, there could be no sin in that man disbelieving it. If he did believe that Christ died for him, when He did not, he would be believing a lie.

And why has God taken such pains to satisfy us that He has indeed loved and forgiven all men ? Just in order that every individual might see in God a perfect ground of confidence. Unless you know that God has forgiven you, and that He loves you, you cannot

---

[1] Different from the doctrine taught in his volume on "Election," published eight years afterwards.

L

have any confidence in Him; and unless you have
full confidence in Him, you cannot have peace with
Him, you cannot open your heart to Him, you cannot love
Him. It is the belief of His forgiving love to yourself
which can alone open your heart to Him. This is the true
meaning of the doctrine of personal assurance. It is not
that God saves a man because he has an assurance of his
own personal salvation, but that our hearts cannot open to
God until we are satisfied that He loves ourselves with a
forgiving love. Until we are satisfied of His love to us, we
cannot love Him; and therefore we cannot obey Him, for
there is no obedience without love. This is the meaning of
John vi. 28, 29. When the multitude that were following
Jesus asked Him, What shall we do that we may work the
works of God? He answered them, "This is the work of
God, that ye believe on Him whom He hath sent." Their
question was, "How are we to obey the commandments of
God?" and His answer was, "You must begin by believing
in God's forgiving love to you in sending His Son to be the
propitiation for your sins." For until you believe this, it
is impossible for you to obey the least of God's commandments, because the least of His commandments requires
love, and you cannot love Him until you are assured that
He loves you. The knowledge of our own personal forgiveness and of our being personally embraced in the love
of God is the first step in Christianity. No one is a Christian until he knows this. And how may every one know
this? See John i. 29, 2 Cor. v. 19, 1 Tim. ii. 1-6, 1 John
ii. 2. The personal assurance rises out of the general
declaration of forgiveness to all, and peace and joy and
love rise out of the personal assurance.

I long much to see both Madame de Broglie and yourself, but it seems to me that God has called me to be a
witness for the truth at home. I am continually engaged

in preaching to small congregations at present—three hours every day, and often much more.[1] If God lets me see it to be my duty to cross the Channel this autumn to see you, it will be a great delight to me. Give my most brotherly love in Christ Jesus to Madame de Broglie and to your dear mother. Give your child a kiss and a blessing from me, as from one who loved his father. Talk over this letter with Madame de B., and let me know how you feel about it.

66. TO MISS RACHEL ERSKINE.

15th September 1829.

MY DEAR COUSIN,—I have delayed longer than I wished and than I ought, answering your most interesting letter. But besides the entire occupation of my time in objects from which I do not feel myself warranted to withdraw, I have been expecting daily to receive a communication which I was sure would be much valued by you. It is an extract from the journal of young Mr. Buchanan, who belonged to the Turkish Embassy, and who was with —— Bruce during his illness. I find that it will be probably too long to send in a letter. I shall probably send it under cover to Lord Elgin.

I should be very sorry indeed to be the means of depriving —— of such a friend as ——. I doubt not that God will make them channels of good to each other, although they may seem to injure each other at present. Both of them misapprehend altogether the nature and object of personal assurance. —— talks of it as an asserting of one's confidence of an interest in God's forgiveness in spite of doubts and misgivings. I don't quote her words, but the

---

[1] For a notice of Mr. Erskine's evangelistic labours at this period, see Appendix, No. VI. p. 381.

idea is hers. She evidently regards it either as a self-satisfied conclusion to which one is led by a discovery of some supposed good in one's-self, or a wordy boldness of expression belied by an internal apprehension. And she supposes that the person who arrives at it imagines that he has arrived at something which may be approved of by God, and on which he may rest a further confidence. Now, there is nothing of all this in the doctrine. No man has a right to believe anything about his relation to God, except on God's own authority. If God has not told a man that his sins are forgiven him, it would be presumptuous in him to believe that they were forgiven; but if God has told him that they are forgiven, then the presumption consists in disbelieving or doubting it. You would not think it presumptuous in a man to believe that God loves and forgives him, unless you thought that God's forgiving love was limited to a particular class of characters, for instance, to those who believe, or who repent, or who amend; and therefore, when you hear a person say, "that he knows that God loves and forgives him," you immediately suppose that he assumes to himself to belong to one of these classes, and you are inclined to question him. "Are you sure now that your belief, or repentance, or amendment is real?" He might answer you, "God's forgiving love is declared not to any class, not to any character, but just to sin, and to the world, and to all men; and God says that those who don't believe in God's forgiving love to them make God a liar." Read that account on the proclaiming of God's name to Moses given in the 33d and 34th chapters of Exodus, "The Lord, the Lord God, forgiving iniquity, transgression, and sin, without clearing the guilty" (which last expression refers to the sacrifice of Christ, and just means through an atonement). As soon as Moses heard it, he thought, This is just the God that we want, for the people

are continually committing sin, and this is a sin-forgiving
God; and Moses made haste and said, Go with us; for
this is a stiff-necked people. That *for* is an extraordinary
word. Read also the 14th of Numbers, where this name is
repeated.

But what is the use of faith in Christ at all? Is it that
God forgives or loves a man for believing that Jesus Christ
died for him to take away his sins? No one can believe
such an absurdity who exercises his reason at all. No, the
use of faith is just that a man, by knowing that the actual
state of God's feelings towards him, by knowing the reality
and intensity of His forgiving love to him, may have perfect
confidence in God, and thus that his heart may open and let
God's living Spirit enter. Now, what is it that makes man
distrust God? What is it that makes a man start at the
idea of "this night thy soul shall be required of thee"?
What is it but the witness of conscience telling him that he
has deserved and incurred God's anger and condemnation?
And what is it that can do away this distrust? Nothing
but the authentic information that God has forgiven him.
The belief of this information as written in the death
and resurrection of Christ is the faith of the gospel;
and the use of it is, that it makes the character of God
the ground of confidence. If the confidence is not produced, nothing at all is gained for the man, and the information of God is evidently rejected; for the belief of that
would have given confidence, and was intended just for
that end.

My distrust of God arises not from the belief that another
person is under condemnation, but from the apprehension
of my own condemnation, and therefore my confidence is
restored, not by the belief of the pardon of another person,
but from the belief of my own pardon. Any faith short
of this is a faith below man's need, as it is a faith below

God's testimony.	Any faith which is not personal con-
fidence appears to me a mere fallacy.	I have precisely the
same authority and obligation for believing that Christ died
because I had sinned, and rose again because I was pardoned,
that I have for believing that he died and rose at all.	The
Bible goes upon this ground, that no man ever did, or ever
could perform one act of obedience to God until he believed
that his sins were forgiven him.	Till a man knows himself
pardoned, he will work for his pardon, he cannot help
doing it.	And so when God calls on him to work for God,
to love God, to glorify God, He tells him at the same time,
" You need not work for pardon any more, for I have
pardoned you.	Now you may work for God."	It is thus
that self is destroyed.	A man who is working for pardon
appears religious, and is thought religious by the world ;
but it is just the religion of self as much as if he were
working for £1000.	Will you compare the 32d Psalm
with 2 Cor. v. 19 ?	To every man the word of reconcilia-
tion declares the same thing, viz., that God is not imputing
sin unto him ; but it is only the man who believes it who
tastes the blessedness of it.	It is only he who knows
God as his hiding-place.	It is only he whose ear is
opened to hear God's voice saying, " I will teach thee,"
etc.	My beloved Rachel, I feel this most deeply in-
teresting. . . . May the Spirit of holiness and of power
accompany it.

Jesus is called the Light of the world, because He was
the Lamb of God that hath taken away the sin of the world.
For to a world lying under a condemnation everything
must necessarily be dark.	A man knowing himself to be
under a condemnation must either turn away his eyes from
God altogether, or he must have the feeling that he is continually meeting an angry Judge in every circumstance of
his being.	He cannot tell at what moment this Judge may

come upon him and execute the sentence. Every step in life, and the great step especially out of life, must to such a man be a step in the dark, a step in uncertainty, in apprehension. And the more truly conscience performs its duty, the more will this darkness be felt. To such a man, and to a world lying whole and entire in such a state, what could be called light, except the good news that their sin was forgiven? Nothing short of this could take away uncertainty and suspense. Nothing short of this could make death a step in the light. The man, therefore, who does not know himself forgiven is still in darkness, both in the sense that he is walking in uncertainty, and because in such a condition he cannot possibly obey the least of God's commandments. Read 1 John i. 5, 6, 7. If any man say that he has fellowship with God, and yet walks in darkness, in uncertainty, in doubt as to the forgiveness of his sins, he lies and does not the truth. Good-night, my dear, dear friend. I hope that you will see that personal assurance is merely not making God a liar, and that the want of personal assurance is charged with that guilt by the Spirit. See 1 John v. 9, 10, 11. May the Holy Spirit enlighten us! I know that I know nothing; and I feel it to be a hateful sin that we know so little of God, and enjoy Him so little, when His will is that we should know Him and enjoy Him much.

67. TO DR. CHALMERS.

LINLATHEN, *20th October* 1829.

MY DEAR SIR,—You know that I consider the proclamation of pardon through the blood of Christ, as an act already past in favour of every human being, to be essentially the gospel. I consider this to be the only gospel, because this is the only intelligence the belief of which will immediately give peace to creatures under condemnation, when they know their true condition.   When it is supposed that the pardon is not passed into an act in favour of any individual until he believes it, no one can have peace from the gospel until he is confident that he is a believer; and further, his attention is entirely or chiefly directed to that quality of belief in himself which entitles him to appropriate the pardon to himself, so that his joy is not in God's character but in his own.   You object to all this by asking me, "Where is the pardon if the man continues an unbeliever to the end?"   Now, my dear and much respected friend, I think that I distinctly see the answer to this in the Word of God, and I pray God that He may cause you to see it also.   It is this.   The penalty pronounced against Adam's race at the fall was death, or the separation of the soul and body.   There is no more said of it in the Bible.   The death temporal, spiritual, and eternal is an invention of man; death spiritual is just sin, for it is the shutting out of God from the heart, who is the only true life, and therefore it is as improper to say that death spiritual is the punishment of sin, as to say that sin is the punishment of sin.   Under the Adamic dispensation there is no other punishment mentioned in the Bible than death.   Whilst therefore this penalty of the broken law lay upon man, no human being could rise again—that penalty must have lain upon him like a weight keeping him in his grave, and the rising of any human being is a proof of the removal of the penalty in regard to him.   But we are informed that every human being is to rise again, unbelievers as well as believers; that is to say, all men are to be delivered from this penalty or curse of the broken law.   How is this?   "Christ hath redeemed us from the curse of the law, having been made a curse for us," Gal. iii. 13.   "For as in Adam all die, so in Christ shall all be made alive," 1 Cor. xv. 22.   "Therefore as by the offence of one, judgment came upon all men to condemnation, even so by the righteousness of one, the free gift came upon all men to justification of life," Rom. v. 18. "And for this cause He is the mediator of the new testament, that by means of death, for the redemption of the transgressions that were under the first testament, they which are called might receive the promise of eternal inheritance," Heb. ix. 15. All are redeemed from the penalty of the law, and the act by which they have been redeemed is an act in which God's character is so manifested, that the soul which sees it lives by it, *i.e.* receives the eternal life which was in the Father and was manifested in the Son, even that eternal life which consists in knowing the only true God and Jesus Christ whom He hath sent. The soul which believes not in this act which manifests God's holy love is guilty of refusing the testimony of God concerning His Son, and shuts out the eternal life, and falls under the sentence of the second death—second, because the first death is done away.—Yours most affectionately,

T. ERSKINE.

68. TO MISS RACHEL ERSKINE.

CADDER, 1st February 1830.

MY DEAR FRIEND AND COUSIN,—It has pleased God to take our beloved friend and brother Charles Stirling to Himself. And it pleased God also of His abundant grace to make this scene of death a glorious victory. From the beginning of his illness he anticipated the result, and he welcomed it as his Father's summons calling him home. God did great things for him, and during the last days of his life, whilst the struggle was going on, the Good Shepherd never left him for a moment. I was with him the last two days, and heard him say many sweet things, which are now like balm to poor Christian's heart. He said often, " Beloved and glorious Redeemer." " No perplexity, no alarm." "I see the splendour before me." "Oh that He should have done this for such a worm as I am!" Once he said, " This is a sweet dispensation, is not it?" But it is impossible to convey by words any idea of the peace and willingness and childlike confidence which every look and every tone of his voice expressed. This is the Lord's doing, and He is very gracious to Christian also. He has given her songs in this affliction. He has constrained her heart to give Him thanks and praise for the wonderful works which He hath wrought for lost sinners. She is much exhausted, however, for she never left his bed for a minute. My dear friend, we have a God in whom we may well rejoice; a just God, and yet a Saviour. Blessed be His glorious name for ever and ever. Charles said once, " You see in me what sin has done, and what the Saviour has done." It is right that a world of sin should be a world of sorrow, and God is glorified by bringing light out of the creature's darkness, and holiness out of the creature's pollution.

Let our dear friend Miss Stuart share in this letter. I am sure that she will enter both into the sorrow and the joy of it; but oh, the joy is far, very far, above the sorrow. A dear brother delivered from this vile body, and made partaker of the joy of his Lord. She will communicate the intelligence to Mrs. Burnett and John. May the Lord cause you to rejoice in Him as your exceeding joy!—Yours affectionately,   T. Erskine.

69. TO CAPTAIN JAMES STIRLING.

CADDER, 1st *February* 1830.

MY DEAR JAMES,—You have before this heard of the death of beloved Charles. He died the death of the righteous, giving glory to God—not of constraint, but willingly. He saw the whole truth fully and distinctly, and rejoiced in it. Davie and I arrived here at four o'clock on Friday morning, and he survived till Saturday night, between nine and ten. He gave us a loving and cheerful welcome; he told us that his soul was full of peace and joy in the Lord, that God was all light, and no darkness at all; he then said to me, " It has just come to me like a flash of light that you were right about these things;"[1] and then, turning to Christian, he said, " And James and Mary spoke a great deal about it to us also." God thus put a testimony into His servant's heart and mouth at that solemn moment; and I trust that dear Christian has it fully in her heart too. She told me just now, when I was up with her by her bedside (where she is lying very weak), that her eye never lost sight of Christ, and that her peace and even rejoicing had never failed. Blessed be God who giveth the victory, and who always maketh those who trust in Him to triumph. It was most edifying to see how his sense of the evil of sin grew upon him, without ever shaking his perfect confidence in the redeeming work of Christ. It was indeed a scene most glorifying to God. You will rejoice Eliza's heart by telling her these things.

Behold what manner of love the Father hath showed us. I have had some sweet views of the Creator manifested in the Redeemer; and I have tasted the grace of God in that " God has so loved the world," etc.—Farewell, my dear brother in Jesus; give my Christian love to Eliza.

T. ERSKINE.

[1] The Universality of the Atonement, etc.

70. TO HIS SISTER MRS. STIRLING.

BROUGHTY-FERRY, 21*st March* 1830.

MY BELOVED SISTER,—This is the night seven weeks since Charles has been absent from the body and present with the Lord. It was in the anticipation of what he now fully experiences that he said, "And the sinful part adieu." He has bid an eternal adieu to sin and sinful flesh, and he is waiting, in joyful hope, the day when the kingdom of Christ shall be manifested in glory on this earth. Although we remain on earth, we are called to the same high calling, to rejoice in God and to wait for His Son from heaven, even Jesus, who hath saved us from the wrath to come.

My darling Kitty, how are you? How is the spirit, and how is the frail tabernacle? He hath said, "I will never leave thee nor forsake thee." Oh may He grant to you to live very near to Him—in the secret of His presence, under the shadow of His wings—and to feed on the hidden manna, even Jesus our Lord and our Life—flesh of our flesh—bone of our bone.

We passed a very pleasant time in Edinburgh with dear Margaret Paterson, who is a delightful example of the grace of God. She and Ann both speak of what God has done for their souls, with a fulness that would astonish you. . . . —— spoke very warmly of Charles and of you, but alas, very ignorantly attributing Charles's peace at that hour to the remembrance of his well-spent life. Oh what a delusion that is! I have just been thinking of it in this way—as if a child, which had offended against his parent, should afterwards come and recount his various actions, as reasons why he might claim his father's love and forgiveness; and then the father just tells him, You have forgotten your best claim—I am your father—that is your true claim. That

is our claim, my dearest sister. Doubtless Thou art our
Father, though Abraham be ignorant of us, and Jacob
acknowledge us not. . . .—Yours affectionately,   T. E.

71. TO MRS. MACHAR.[1]

EDINBURGH, 7*th July* 1830.

I AM going to Helensburgh to-morrow, with the view of
being present when Mr. Campbell preaches before the
Presbytery on Thursday.   May he be given a mouth and
wisdom by the Holy Ghost ! I have been seeing much more
into the character of our present dispensation, our supply as
the groundwork of future judgment.   The supply is God's
forgiving love and favour.   This belongs to each one of us.
In this time, which is the accepted time and day of salvation, we are dealt with not according to what we are, but
according to what Christ our Head, the Head of every man,
is.   But when the judgment comes we shall be dealt with
according to what we shall then be in ourselves.   And thus
that favour which is upon every man now, if not received
into him so as to become his life, will be his condemnation.—Yours, etc.,   T. ERSKINE.

72. TO MISS RACHEL ERSKINE.

14 ROYAL CRESCENT, 16*th July* 1830.

DEAREST COUSIN RACHEL,—I know that Davie has
written to tell you how the Lord ordered things, and permitted things on the occasion of Mr. Campbell's preaching
before the Presbytery.   You would be much struck with

---

[1] The daughter of a minister of an adjoining parish, who, in 1829, came
to reside in the immediate vicinity of Linlathen.   Mr. Erskine had
ministered great comfort to her in a season of great distress. A mutual
and strong attachment was formed which lasted for life, unbroken by the
circumstance that in 1832 Miss Sim married the Rev. John Machar, D.D.,
Minister of Kingston, and removed with him to Canada, where she has
ever since resided.

this thing in particular, that they had left all general charges against Mr. Campbell, and fixed on one point, and that point the love of God in Christ to every man. The expressions which they animadverted on were, "That the agony of Christ expressed the measure of the love of God to every man," and "that no man could act as a peace-maker between God and man, who could not tell man that God had made peace with him." They have entered it into their record that they regard these statements with abhorrence and detestation.[1] Jehovah is God and not man, therefore are we not consumed. He loves these men with a love that seeks to enter into them, and to make them the habitation of God through the Spirit. He loves them with a love that has brought Him into the flesh to taste death for them, that He might destroy in them the works of him who had the power of death, even the devil. . . .

---

[1] "We have learned that the Presbytery, by a great majority, re-corded their detestation and abhorrence of the doctrine contained in two sentences in the sermon, which we believe are to the following purport : ' God loves every child of Adam with a love the measure of which is to be seen in the agonies of Christ,' and that ' the person who knows that Christ died for every child of Adam is the person who is in the condition to say to every human being, Let there be peace with you, peace between you and your God.'"—*The Whole Proceedings in the case of the Rev. John M'Leod Campbell*, pp. xix., xx. The two sentences are given in almost exactly the same words in the "Notes of a Sermon preached in the Parish Church of Row on Thursday, being the day of the Visitation of that Parish by the Presbytery of Dumbarton, by the Rev. J. M. Campbell. Taken in short-hand. Greenock, 1830." Pp. 23 and 25. These two sentences formed one of the counts in the libel.

CHAPTER VII.

The Spiritual Gifts—Letters from 1830 till 1835.

For five years consecutively, from 1826 till 1830, about fifty individuals, clergy and laity, distinguished for their learning and piety, met in Mr. Drummond's house at Albury for the special study of the prophetic books of the Bible. Widely over England and Scotland a faith in the coming and kingdom of Jesus Christ upon this earth had spread, and with it the expectation that those wonderful gifts by which His first advent had been attended would usher in and accompany the second. But why had those gifts ever been withdrawn? It appeared to many that they had been originally bestowed without limitation as to time, that they formed part of the permanent endowment of the Church, lost through her unfaithfulness. If so, what but want of faith hindered their being restored? Into this faith and expectation Mr. Erskine entered; and now it was reported to him that in that very neighbourhood where he was spending so much of his time (though disconnected with Mr. Campbell's ministry) one of the looked-for gifts had been bestowed. In a cottage at the head of the Garcloch, Isabella Campbell had lived that saintly life told with such beauty and pathos by her devoted pastor, the late Mr. Story of Roseneath. Her death had made her home at Fernicarry a shrine of resort to which the pilgrim steps of many were directed, who gathered round her sister Mary, upon whom the mantle of the departed seemed to have fallen. One Sunday evening in the end of March 1830, as Mary lay in weakness upon a sofa, suffering apparently under the same disease which had carried her sister to the grave, whilst those around her were praying for the restoration of the gifts, suddenly, as if possessed by a superhuman strength, she broke forth, speaking in an unknown tongue, in loud ecstatic utterances, for more than an hour. On the other side of the Clyde, opposite the Gareloch, lay the town of Port-Glasgow. A family of the name of Macdonald was living there at this time ; two twin brothers, James and George, with their sisters. The brothers, shipbuilders, staid and orderly men, two years before had become exceedingly devout. Their religion was of a quiet and unobtrusive type. "Their doctrinal knowledge was at first very limited. They procured no religious books, for years they scarcely read one ; the ministry under which they sat was unimpressive, and if they did adopt peculiar views of divine truth, it was from no heretical writings or preaching, but from the Bible alone that they derived them. For instance, although they soon became classed among the disciples of Mr. Irving, who at that time was beginning to be stigmatised as heretical, the fact was that, so far as I can ascertain, they never read a single volume of his, or at least not for years after their own views were established. And although after a time they began to attend the preaching of the Rev. Mr. Campbell of Row, it was because they had previously been taught of God the same truths, and were attracted to Row by their love of them. . . . Until the eve of the miraculous manifestations in them, the subject of spiritual gifts did not at all occupy their attention, much less their expectations and desires ; nor did it even when their prayers, in

common with those of other Christians, for an outpouring
of the Spirit, began to be answered by the pouring out of
a very extraordinary if not marvellous spirit of prayer
upon themselves."[1] In March 1830 an event occurred in
this family which one of the sisters thus describes : "For
several days Margaret had been so unusually ill that I
quite thought her dying, and on appealing to the doctor he
held out no hope of her recovery unless she were able to go
through a course of powerful medicine, which he acknowledged to be in her then case impossible. She had scarcely
been able to have her bed made for a week. Mrs. ——
and myself had been sitting quietly at her bedside, when
the power of the Spirit came upon her. She said, 'There
will be a mighty baptism of the Spirit this day,' and then
broke forth in a most marvellous setting forth of the
wonderful work of God ; and as if her own weakness had
been altogether lost in the strength of the Holy Ghost, continued with little or no intermission for two or three hours
in mingled praise, prayer, and exhortation. At dinner-
time James and George came home as usual, whom she
addressed at great length, concluding with a solemn prayer
for James, that he might *at that time* be endowed with the
power of the Holy Ghost. Almost instantly, James calmly
said, 'I have got it!' He walked to the window, and
stood silent for a minute or two. I looked at him, and
almost trembled, there was such a change upon his whole
countenance. He then, with a step and manner of the most
indescribable majesty, walked up to Margaret's bedside, and
addressed her in these words, 'Arise and stand upright.'
He repeated the words, took her by the hand, and she
arose."[2]

The same evening James wrote to Mary Campbell

[1] *Memoirs of James and George Macdonald of Port-Glasgow,* by Robert
Norton, M.D., pp. 58, 59, 78.   [2] *Ibid.* pp. 107, 108.

at Fernicarry, "My dear Sister,—Lift up your voice with us; let us exalt His name, for He hath done great things for us, and Holy is His name. There is still power in the name of Jesus—yea, all power in heaven and on earth. Our beloved Margaret hath been made to hear His voice, and to rise up, leap, and walk. Faith in His name has given her soundness in the presence of us all. Mary, my love, lay aside unbelief, it is of the devil; hear God's voice to you also, 'Rise up and walk, what hindereth?'"

Let Mary Campbell herself tell us of wh rt-happened on the receipt of this letter: "Two ' ' living there at me about four hours before my and George, with their never would be strong, that " staid and orderly r.. a miracle being wrought upon me, .'.ly dev...was quite foolish in one who was in such a poor state of health ever to think of going to the heathen. I told them they would see and hear of miracles very soon, and no sooner had the last of the above-mentioned individuals left me, than I was constrained of the Spirit to go and ask the Father, in the name of Jesus, to stretch forth His hand to heal, and that signs and wonders might again be done in the name of His Holy Child Jesus. One thing I was enabled to ask in faith, nothing doubting, which was, that by the next morning I might have some miracle to inform them of. It was not long after this that I received our dear brother James Macdonald's letter, giving me an account of his sister's having been raised, and commanding me to rise and walk. I had scarcely read the first page when I became quite overpowered, and laid it aside for a few minutes; but I had no rest in my spirit until I took it up again and began to read. As I read, every word came with power, but when I came to the command to arise, it came home with a power which no words can describe; it was felt to be indeed the voice of Christ; it was such a voice of power as could not be resisted. A mighty power was instantaneously exerted upon me. I first felt as if I had been lifted up from off the earth, and all my diseases taken off me. At the voice of Jesus I was surely made in a moment to stand upon my feet, leap and walk, sing and rejoice. O that men would praise the Lord for His goodness, for His wonderful works to the children of men."[1]

After her recovery Mary Campbell lived during the summer of ... at Helensburgh. There meetings innumer- ...and myself had ... ...festations extraordinary were made. the power of the Sp... ...w added writing in the unknown ...I be a mighty baptism tongue... ...th in a... ...ent of inspiration came Mary seized the pen, and with a rapidity "like lightning" covered sheets of paper with characters believed to be letters and words. The gift of prophecy too was largely exercised, a gift not to be confounded with foretelling of future events or ordinary Christian teaching, but consisting in inspired exalted utterances, opening up some obscure passage of Scripture, or enforcing some neglected duty, or breaking forth ecstatically into prayer and praise. Crowds gathered round the young attractive rapt enthusiast. "Among their number," says one who wrote in the midst of the excitement, "they can reckon merchants, divinity students, writers to the Signet, advocates. . . . I have known gentlemen who rank high in society come from Edinburgh, join in all the exercises, declare their implicit faith in all Mary Campbell's pretensions, ask her concerning the times and seasons, inquire the meaning of certain passages of Scripture, and bow to her decisions with the utmost deference as one inspired by Heaven."[2]

[1] *A Vindication of the Religion of the Land,* etc., by the Rev. A. Robertson of Greenock, pp. 251, 254.   [2] *Ibid.* p. 311.

From Edinburgh, Dr. Chalmers wrote to his friend Mr. Story of Roseneath, eagerly asking information, desiring especially to have a copy of some of the writing in the alleged unknown tongue. Mr. Story, in order to supply himself with the required information, paid a special visit to Mary Campbell. "I had just taken her by the hand," he writes to Dr. Chalmers, "to bid her adieu, when, obviously possessed by some irresistible power, she uttered for, I should suppose, nearly an hour, sounds altogether new to my ear, but which seemed certainly to be language. . . . I recognise in none (of the written characters) the signs of any language I know, but many have seen her note them down, and it is with inconceivable rapidity, and as if she herself were unconscious of the exertion. Both in speaking and in writing she describes her words and movements as in every respect independent of her own volition. . . . The greater jealousy manifested by you and others the more will you serve the interests of truth, and the more I am persuaded you will be prepared to conclude that these things are of God and not of men."[1]

In Port-Glasgow the area of manifestation was enlarged. The gift of interpretation was added to that of the tongues. By both brothers these two gifts were in constant exercise. They were bestowed also upon others. Prophetic utterances abounded. The excitement grew, the visitors from a distance increased. "Ever since Margaret was raised and the gift of tongues given," writes one of the sisters (May 18th, 1830), "the house has been filled every day with people from all parts of England, Scotland, and Ireland." Special interest was awakened where special hopes in this direction had for some time been cherished.

<hr>

[1] *Memoir of the Life of the Rev. Robert Story*, pp. 209-211. Two years afterward Mr. Story, like Mr. Erskine, saw reason to think differently; see pp. 213-224.

Five delegates came down from London, who stayed three weeks at Port-Glasgow, and had every opportunity of seeing all that was going on, and of becoming personally acquainted with those engaged in it. One of these, a solicitor, recognised and quoted as an entirely competent witness by the writer of an article in the *Edinburgh Review*,[1] closes his description of what he witnessed thus :—

"These persons, while uttering the unknown sounds, as also while speaking in the Spirit in their own language, have every appearance of being under supernatural direction. The manner and voice are (speaking generally) different from what they are at other times, and on ordinary occasions. This difference does not consist merely in the peculiar solemnity and fervour of manner (which they possess), but their whole deportment gives an impression, not to be conveyed in words, that their organs are made use of by supernatural power. In addition to the outward appearances, their own declarations, as the declarations of honest, pious, and sober individuals, may with propriety be taken in evidence. They declare that their organs of speech are made use of by the Spirit of God ; and that they utter that which is given to them, and not the expressions of their own conceptions, or their own intention. I had numerous opportunities of observing a variety of facts fully confirmatory of this.

"In addition to what I have already stated, I have only to add my most decided testimony, that, so far as three weeks' constant communication, and the information of those in the neighbourhood, can enable me to judge (and I conceive that the opportunities I enjoyed enabled me to form a correct judgment), the individuals thus gifted are persons living in

[1] "Pretended Miracles—Irving, Scott, and Erskine." First article in No. 106 of the *Edinburgh Review*, June 1831.

close communion with God, and in love towards Him and
towards all men; abounding in faith and joy and peace;
having an abhorrence of sin, and a thirst for holiness, with an
abasement of self, and yet with a hope full of immortality
such as I never witnessed elsewhere, and which I find no-
where recorded but in the history of the early church:
and just as they are fervent in spirit, so are they diligent in
the performance of all the relative duties of life.   They are
totally devoid of anything like fanaticism or enthusiasm,
but on the contrary are persons of great simplicity of character and of sound common sense.   They have no fanciful
theology of their own: they make no pretensions to deep
knowledge: they are the very opposite of sectarians, both
in conduct and principle: they do not assume to be teachers:
they are not deeply read, but they seek to be taught of God
in the perusal of and meditation on his revealed Word, and
to 'live quiet and peaceable lives in all godliness and
honesty.'"[1]

Mr. Erskine followed in the track of these delegates from
London, staying no less than six weeks in the house of the
Macdonalds, witnessing the manifestations and taking part
in the daily prayer-meetings.   His immediate convictions
and impressions are embodied in a tract, "On the Gifts of
the Spirit," published at Greenock at the close of 1830.
"Whilst I see nothing in Scripture against the reappear-
ance, or rather the continuance, of miraculous gifts in the
Church, but a great deal for it, I must further say that I
see a great deal of internal evidence in the west country
to prove their genuine miraculous character, especially in
the speaking with tongues. . . . After witnessing what I
have witnessed among those people, I cannot think of any
person decidedly condemning them as impostors, without
a feeling of great alarm.   It certainly is not a thing to

[1] Norton's *Memoirs*, pp. 146-148.

be lightly or rashly believed, but neither is it a thing to be lightly or rashly rejected. I believe that it is of God."

Still more fully did Mr. Erskine deal with the whole topic of the gifts of the Spirit in the volume published in the same year (1830), entitled "The Brazen Serpent, or Life coming through Death," not the most popular of his writings, yet the one which goes most fully and deeply into doctrinal theology. It was to this book, even more than to the one on "The Unconditional Freeness of the Gospel," that Mr. Maurice was in the habit of expressing his indebtedness. In its second chapter will be found the seeds of many of those ideas as to the moral character of the atonement, and the manner of its operation in the formation of Christian character, which, transplanted to other soil and subject to other treatment, germinated after fashions not altogether such as the first sower relished. In this volume, after stating at length the scriptural grounds on which it might be concluded that the miraculous gifts were "the permanent endowment of the Church," and that "had the faith of the Church continued pure and full these gifts of the Spirit would never have disappeared," he says, "The world dislikes the recurrence of miracles. And yet it is true that miracles have recurred. I cannot but tell what I have seen and heard. I have heard persons, both men and women, speak with tongues and prophesy, that is, speak in the spirit to edification, exhortation, and comfort."[1]

In the course of a year the chief theatre of the miraculous manifestations had shifted from the west of Scotland to London. With the change of place there came a change of their phase and office. They were no longer regarded, as at the first, simply or mainly as supernatural exhibitions of the Divine presence, expressions of the Divine will, intended to

---

[1] *The Brazen Serpent,* p. 203. See Appendix, No. VII. p. 385.

infuse fresh life and fervour into the faith and worship of
the Church.   To quote from a book of much ability, held
in high repute among the members of the Holy Catholic
Apostolic Church :—" By repeated words it was gradually
made clear that what the Lord meant to show was that the
only remedy for the evil condition of the Church universal,
which we had so much lamented, was the restoration of the
form and order of the Christian Church as one body, as
originally constituted, with the ordinances of that body,—
the long-lost means of unity and channels of truth, viz.,
apostles, prophets, evangelists, and pastors."[1]   Slowly, out
of that strange confusion which disturbed at first the
worship of the church in Regent Square, at command of
those strange voices before and beneath which the grand
humble heroic spirit of Edward Irving bowed and was
broken, the form and order of the Holy Catholic
Apostolic Church arose—a Church eclectic in doctrine,
charitable in spirit, devout in worship, utterly refusing to
be called a new branch or sect, yet claiming to be the one and
only existing Christian society fashioned in all respects after
that perfect model said to be set up in the Jewish
Tabernacle and the Apostolic Constitutions.   This was not
"the healing of the hurt" which Mr. Erskine had been
looking for with such intense anxiety and eager hope.
And the more that this new remedy revealed of its character
and the manner of its working, the more inclined was he
to doubt and distrust its efficacy.

It is evident from the following letters to Lady Elgin,
who became a member of the new society, that already in
the spring of 1833 he had detected what appeared to
him a fatal flaw in that society.   At the same time his
confidence in the heavenly origin of the gifts was otherwise shaken, so that before the end of that year he had to

[1] *The Purpose of God in Creation and Redemption,* p. 163.

announce to his dear cousin Rachel a change of belief regarding them.

This narrative has been prefixed to the letters which follow, as serving to make them more intelligible, and the letters themselves have been given as serving to throw some light on a still obscure passage in the religious history of our country, and as throwing a very clear light upon many features in the character of the writer.[1]

73. TO CAPTAIN PATERSON.

9 BRANDON STREET, 15*th October* 1830.

THE account given by Mr. C. of the prayer-meeting at Port-Glasgow during which the words *disco capito* were used and interpreted is very incorrect.

The facts, as far as I can recollect, are these :—I had been present along with you at one of these meetings before, and we had been both much impressed with the supernatural character of the prayers as well as of the speaking with tongues. In conversing on the subject next day, you remarked to me that there had been, on the preceding evening, a neglect of the Scripture directions for the exercise of the gift of tongues, and in proof of it you pointed out the rule, 1 Cor. xiv. 28, "If there be no interpreter, let him keep silence in the church."

When I returned to Port-Glasgow I mentioned this to them, and their answer was that as interpretation had in some cases been given, they considered themselves permitted to use the tongue when the Spirit gave them utterance, on the faith that interpretation would also be given. They said also that they felt it to be their duty to pray

---

[1] For additional descriptions of the gifts, as well as specimens both of the spoken and written tongues, see Appendix, No. VIII. p. 392.

much for interpretation, according to that word, " Let him that speaketh in a tongue pray that he may interpret." Just before the meeting commenced we were conversing on this subject, so that it was impressed on the minds of those persons who spoke in prayer.

It was a very remarkable meeting. There was a manifestation of the presence and supernatural working of the Spirit of God beyond anything that I had witnessed. The voices struck me also very much, perhaps more than the tongues. It was not their loudness, although they were very loud, but they did not sound to me as if they were the voices of the persons speaking ; they seemed to be uttered through them by another power.

After J. Macdonald had prayed a considerable time, first in English and then in a tongue, the command to pray for interpretation was brought to his mind, and he repeated— " It is written, ' Let him that speaketh in a tongue pray that he may interpret.'" He then prayed for interpretation with great urgency, until he felt that he had secured the answer, and when repeating over the concluding words of what he had spoken in the tongue, which were "*disco capito,*" he said, " And this is the interpretation : the shout of a King is amongst them." The impression which I received from this was, that the passage spoken in the tongue had concluded with the prophecy of Balaam, in which these words occur. I conceived that the words *disco capito* meant simply the shout of a King, and that they, along with their interpretation, had been given to us as words of reference, directing us to the beautiful passage of which they form a part, Numbers xxiii. 19, 20, 21.

I am quite sensible, as you must be after what you have witnessed, that it is impossible to convey in words any idea of what took place that evening. Though there had been no new tongue spoken, the supernatural character of the meeting would have been just the same; the tongues scarcely added to it at all.

Some time after, in conversing over the proceedings of the evening with one of the Macdonalds, I remarked to him that I had observed after the conclusion of the meeting two of the females apparently in great joy embracing each other, and I asked him if he knew any particular cause for it. He told me that for some days back their meetings had been remarkably dead, and thus there had been a great deal of prayer on the subject, and that these two persons had, especially in the forenoon, been much engaged in prayer together about it, and that the outpouring which had taken place that night bore to them a more decided character of being an answer to prayer, inasmuch as they had particularly asked of God "that the shout of a King might once more be amongst them." One of these females was his own sister.

He did not tell me this of himself. I asked him the explanation of the circumstance I have mentioned, which was of the most unobtrusive nature possible, and which indeed was done in a corner, and he answered me most simply; and I felt my own astonishment not a little rebuked by his quiet reception of this direct and literal answer to prayer, as a thing to be at all times confidently looked for.

I gave this history in Mr. C.'s hearing, explaining at the same time my reason for doing so, viz., I thought that those who recognised the moral integrity of the parties would in this remarkable coincidence recognise something supernatural, and that those who had formed no opinion as to their integrity, either on one side or another, would from this case feel that the charge of imposture against them involved in it the charge of such a multiplication of fraud and of blasphemous lying against the Holy Ghost that it was really difficult to believe that any creatures could be so abandoned as to be guilty of it.

There are some things so bad that one would require tolerably strong evidence for their authenticity before believing them. And surely this is one.

74. TO HIS SISTER MRS. STIRLING.

May 1832.

I HAVE just read over the short-hand report of Mr. Irving's trial before the Presbytery. His defence is a very solemn appeal to the church and the world, as well as to his judges, and combining his ejection with what is going on in our Church Courts, and in the sphere of politics, there is a fearful character of judgment and desolateness, both in present things and in prospect. I have called on Dr. Chalmers. His feelings have been roused and excited a good deal on the subject of the gifts, and he seems to think, moreover, that when he says that holiness is a stronger demonstration to his mind of the power of God in the soul of man than any miraculous manifestations whatever, he brings an argument against the existence of the gifts and the propriety of expecting them. Whereas the question truly is, "How or by what means has God said that He would edify His church?" If He has said that He will edify it in holiness and love by means of the gifts, we need not reason about it. . . .

Dear, dear Christian, I hope you can sometimes pray our Father to keep me from the way of evil, whatever that evil may be. Evil in the form of good is what we have to fear. But the carrying about in the body the dying of the Lord Jesus is the strength and the defence. This is to abide in Christ. He is a sure helper, a very present help in every time of trouble.—Farewell, dear sister.

24 DRUMMOND PLACE, *May* 1832.

DEAR SIR,—I have just received the enclosed note for you, in a letter from Madame de Broglie.

Feeling as I do the vast importance of the subject of our conversation the other evening, I cannot go through the common form of forwarding you this note without referring you to some of the passages of Scripture at least which belong to that subject.

Our Lord is especially designated by all the Evangelists as "He who baptiseth with the Holy Ghost." Compare this title with Acts i. 4-8, that you may be convinced that the gift of the Holy Ghost does not mean regeneration, but that which was manifested on the day of Pentecost— for the disciples were already regenerate persons. Compare it also with Ephesians iv. 8-16, where the purpose of the gifts is declared to be—not to give a miraculous attestation to the doctrines, but—to edify the body and preserve unity, and the duration of them is declared to be "until we all come in the unity of the faith and of the knowledge of the Son of God, unto a perfect man, unto the measure of the stature of the fulness of Christ." You yourself remarked that evening that the promise of the Spirit was prominently held forth through the New Testament as the great characteristic and privilege of our dispensation, as in Mark xvi. 17, and that this promise is never recalled, nor, I may add, is any cessation of it hinted at, except in 1 Cor. xiii. 8-10, where these gifts are promised to endure until that which is perfect is come.

You said that the sanctification of the heart is a greater manifestation of the power of the Spirit in man than any miracles. To this I cordially agree. "The greatest of these is charity,—the more excellent way;" but the gifts are not reckoned of as substitutes for that chief end, but as means to it. And if the Lord gives these things as means, surely it is not a genuine humility which says, "I am satisfied without them." When the Lord desired Ahaz to ask a sign, he answered, "I will not ask, neither will I tempt the Lord," but he is severely rebuked for this apparent humility, Isaiah vii. 12, 13.

The 14th and 15th verses of the fourth chapter of Ephesians are very remarkable. One of the objects to be answered by the setting of the gifts in the Church is there said to be, "that we henceforth be no more children tossed to and fro, and carried about with every wind of doctrine, by the sleight of men, and cunning craftiness, whereby they lie in wait to deceive; but, speaking the truth in love, may grow up into Him in all things, which is the Head, even Christ." There must be some principle of unity in a church, in order to the existence of a church. God's scheme for this unity is the manifestation of the gifts; man's scheme in the absence of the gifts is a Confession of Faith. We must either have the one or the other in order to keep the Church together. Now, is it the sin of the Church, or only her misfortune, that she is without the gifts, and therefore obliged to have recourse to a Confession for the purpose of unity? Surely the Westminster divines did not exhaust the Bible; and if they had the Spirit, surely the divines of our day are not excluded from the Spirit, and if so, they ought to thank God for what light was seen before, and press on to farther light in the strength of the Spirit. If it be the sin of the Church to be without the gifts, then the necessity of the Confession is a sinful necessity, and ought not to be pleaded against any man who appeals to the Word and the interpretation of the Spirit.

I pray you to forgive this letter, if you think that it

needs forgiveness. It is the principle in the Scripture that I press, not the particular instances, though I have the fullest conviction of the reality of several of them.

Again I say, forgive what seems to you to need forgiveness in this letter, and believe me to be with true respect and affection, yours sincerely,　　　　T. ERSKINE.

76. TO HIS SISTER MRS. STIRLING.

Saturday night, [*May* 1832].

YOU will, before this reaches you, have learned through the newspapers that Mr. William Dow[1] has been deposed from being a minister in the Church of Scotland. It was very painful to hear them distinctly and avowedly refuse any appeal to the Scriptures, affirming that the interpretation given by the standards was to be regarded as the limit of all preaching and teaching within the Church. I believe that their sentence was according to their consciences, for unless they understand the oneness of the body preserved by the oneness of the Spirit, as set forth in Eph. iv. chapter, they are necessitated to cling to their standards for unity. They were restrained from casting out David Dow. What William Dow said was wise and meek. I was very sorry for Dr. Chalmers, who was Moderator ; he was the mouth of the Assembly in pronouncing the sentence of deposition, which is an awful sentence, being pronounced in the name of Christ, although all of them believed him to be really a faithful servant of Christ. They were very rapid in their proceedings against him ; when a little delay was proposed, for the sake of conferring with him, one man said —" That thou doest, do quickly." The same thing had been said, I believe, at Mr. Campbell's trial, on a similar proposal being made. And the Clerk of the Assembly, in reading over the sentence declaring the church of *Tongland*

[1] Minister of Tongland.

vacant, twice by mistake called it the church of *Scotland*,
declaring *it* vacant.   There is prophecy in these things.
Yours affectionately,   T. ERSKINE.

77. TO CAPTAIN JAMES STIRLING.

LINLATHEN, *6th March* 1833.

MY DEAR BROTHER,— . . . I enter into much of your
letter, but I feel in it as if you did not give its due pro-
minence to the fact that the great distinction between Christ
the Head and His members is this, that the Father hath
given Him to have life in Himself, whereas the members
of the body have not life in themselves, but have it in Him,
and enjoy it simply and solely by faith in Him (John v.
26-40; 1 John v. 11, 12), that thus men might be taught
to honour the Son even as they honour the Father.   Christ
is given to all men, but the promises are all to Him; and
men participate in them as His spiritual seed, which no
man is except by faith in Him.   The third chapter of the
Epistle to the Galatians, from verse 16th to the end, is
very instructive on this head.   Now, my dear brother, I
believe that you agree with all that I have written; and
yet your statement may lead your hearers to something
different.   Your argument is this, that as God requires
the actions of spiritual life from every man, every man
must have spiritual life in Him, else God would be an
Egyptian taskmaster.   I understand the matter thus: I
see that the personality of each man consists in his will;
and, as man was created not to act of himself, but to be
the image of God, so his will, by its very nature, is constrained always to choose and receive another spirit to act
in it.   The Fall consisted in man's refusing to be God's
image—*i.e.* refusing to yield himself to God's Spirit to act
in him; and thus man thought that he was to escape being
an image, and that he was to be a god himself, showing

forth himself; but he was deceived in this, for his will
could not act alone; it was necessarily an image, and, refusing God, it received the devil's spirit and became his
image; and the consequence was that, as God's Holy
Spirit could no longer come to the unholy creature, man
had no other spirit than the evil spirit to choose as his in-
dweller; and had he been left unredeemed, he could never
have done anything else than evil—just as a man with only
one eye, and that a jaundiced eye, could never possibly see
anything but yellow.   Now, as the redemption of this man
from the necessity of seeing only yellow could be accomplished only by giving him another and a healthy eye, so
that he might have his choice, out of which he would look,
so I understand that the redemption of man from the fall
consists in the life of God having been so given him in
Jesus Christ, that he has his choice at every moment,
whether of the two lives he will live in.

Now, the Spirit of God, which is the life, cannot dwell
with the will which refuses to be acted in by it; if, therefore, each man were a separate individual, whenever he refused to be acted in by this spiritual life he would be
abandoned by it, and have no choice but Satan's spirit;
but each man is a member of a body, of which the Head is
a continual reservoir of life; and when he refuses to be
acted in by this life he is not abandoned by it, for it still
remains in his Head, and is continually coming upon him,
by pulsation after pulsation, seeking entrance.   Now, what
is it that is to constrain his will to choose God's life and
to refuse Satan's?   Is it the knowledge that he has life in
himself that will constrain him to this?   No; it is the
knowledge of Jesus Christ as the gift of the Father's love
and the manifestation of His righteousness—to die and
rise again for every man, so that every man, by faith in
His death and resurrection, might enter into this victory

N

over him who had the power of death, that is, the devil, through a participation in His death and triumphant risen life.   Christ is continually set before us, and we live by having our eye or our faith fixed upon Him as the Head, and not by having it fixed on a life received through Him. My dear brother, I leave this with you, asking your prayers. —Yours affectionately,   T. ERSKINE.

The devil took possession of the flesh, and it is only through the death of the flesh that the devil can be overcome—the voluntary death of the flesh ; and how is this to be ?   Simply through faith in the death of Christ for us. It is thus that we have life.   There is a distinction most important between the Head and the members—as important as their oneness.

78. TO LADY ELGIN.

EDINBURGH, *Saturday.*

DEAR LADY ELGIN,—The distinction which Mr. Bruce draws between a dispensation of principles and a dispensation of statutes is exactly the distinction which I was desirous of pointing out to you as existing between the dispensation of Christ and the dispensation of ἄγγελοι (Hebrews i. and ii.)   The dispensation of Christ embraces in it a oneness with the mind of God—not merely a readiness to do His will when we know it, but a participation in His mind, so that, by a participation in the Divine nature, we enter into the reasons of His will, and do not merely obey the authority of His will.   If I had a person living in the house with me, so gifted by God that, when he was asked whether the will of God were so or so in any case, he always returned an answer of truth in the power of the Spirit, I should in such circumstances have it always in my power to know the will of God, and I might con-

tinually obey it in the spirit of ready submission; and
yet I should be living in the low dispensation of angels
or statutes, and out of the dispensation of the Son
or of principles, if this were my only way of learning
the will of God. And if I were without this apparent
privilege, and though I often mistook the will of God, yet
if my imperfect and defective knowledge and obedience
arose from an inward light, by which I saw the rightness
of a thing as God sees it, then, though my outward manifestation of God would be much less in this case than in
the former, yet my real manifestation of Him would be
much greater, and I should be living in the dispensation
of the Son and of principle, and not of messengers and of
statutes.

There is an expression which I have been in the use
of applying to the Christian religion, which corresponds
exactly to this distinction of principles and statutes, viz.,
that it is a religion of centres, and not of circumferences.
There is a seed of God in the man, which he may cultivate
or neglect. It is manifest that if I were living with such
an oracular person as I have supposed, I should just be in
the condition of the Jews with regard to Moses. Moses
had met God, and they met Moses. I should be living
under a messenger certified by God. I should have my
circumference determined for me, and nothing would be
left for my own perception.

In one of my letters to you, I remember applying this
doctrine of principles and statutes to the two degrees of
conscience. I think perhaps you may now see better what
I meant by it; and by the remarks which I made on the two
first chapters of the Epistle to the Hebrews. The second
degree of conscience is the real freeness of the will; for "if
the Son make you free, you are free indeed."

79. TO LADY ELGIN.

LINLATHEN, 19*th April.*

DEAR LADY ELGIN,— . . . I may here mention what has struck me as to the nature of miraculous works generally. Look into the 4th of Exodus, and read there the account of the two first signs of which there is any record : —Moses' hand becoming leprous and then being cleansed, and his rod becoming a serpent and then returning into the form of a rod. In these two signs we have the history and the prophecy of the world :—1st, human flesh to be sown in corruption, and to be raised in incorruption—that is, the fall and the glorious restoration of man's nature ; and 2d, the serpent gaining a terrible dominion over man, and then being overcome by man's hand. The prophetic part of these facts is that which I believe constitutes the true character of a sign, and that part is the cleansing of the flesh and the paralysing of the serpent. We have here the signs of Christ's kingdom—in the purity of the resurrection-body, and in the binding of Satan. Compare the wondrous works of our Lord whilst on earth with these two. The fulfilment in reality of these two signs will be the realising of the 24th and 8th Psalms. I have misplaced them, for the serpent precedes the leprosy in the history, and it does so, as the cause precedes the effect. These signs were types and prophecies of the kingdom, just as the sacrifices of the law were types and prophecies of the atonement. The miracles, as well as the sacrifices, are never final things ; they do not terminate in themselves ; they are signs of the kingdom. They are signs of that of which righteousness and peace and joy in the Holy Ghost are the reality. The attestation which they gave to God's messengers was that these messengers bore a message relating to the establishment of the kingdom. The raising

of a dead man to life, if that man was to die again, was
nothing at all to our intelligence except as a sign of permanent resurrection; and so the cure of sickness, etc.
We are not to look for permanent cures then, or perfect
cures, or cures in every case where they may be asked;
their very nature as signs is inconsistent with this.   In
this day of grace the power of God's kingdom as manifested
comes forth merely in signs ; the real work of the day of
grace is the spiritual cleansing—the kingdom of God within
us.   The sign refers us always to the coming kingdom, and
thus any resting in the sign is a refusing of its true import.
Holiness and love are no signs ; they are the things themselves ; they are the actual workings of that kingdom of
which healings, etc., are the signs.   The Sabbath was a
prophetic sign of the coming Rest, and most of our Lord's
wondrous works were done on that day to connect them
with the same thing.   His answer to John's disciples in the
7th of Luke, compared with Isaiah xxxv. 5, is very instructive.   The prophecy was not then fulfilled, but there was
a sign of its fulfilment given.   This is an explanation to
my mind of many disappointments in the expectation of
restoration of sick and dying persons.   God would say to
us, "The real miracle does not consist in patching up the
old vessel, but in making it a new vessel; the patching up
of the old vessel is but a sign, a prophetic sign, of the new
creation.   Don't lay such a stress upon the sign ; you shall
have the real everlasting cleansing of the leprosy."   The
dealings of God through Moses with Israel are a wonderful
series of signs ; they are the pattern of the heavenly real
things.   When Moses held the rod over the Red Sea, he
was the sign of man holding up the serpent in triumph to
the view of the creation, and in right of his victory
exercising dominion, long lost but now recovered.   That
is still a prophecy.   The final restoration is the purpose of

Wisdom, and whatever be the means employed by the
wisdom of God, this purpose of His wisdom is recognised
by all her children : Wisdom is justified of her children.
The power by which this is now carrying forward is the
spirit of Christ in man's heart.   This is the true preparation
for the cleansing of the leprosy and the binding of Satan ;
and the signs are prophetic pictures to animate hope, and
to indicate at the same time the actual presence and reality of that power which on the day of manifestation, when
all things are ready, will come forth, not in signs but in
permanent realities.   I am happy you sent that letter to
Lady Matilda.   Any letter I send you, and which you
think would interest her, you may most freely send to her.
I appreciate your scrupulousness on that matter.

It is written, " Whosoever will do the will of God shall
know of the doctrine whether it be of God."   This is the
casting down of man's pride of independence ; it is the
same thing as that word, " I thank Thee, O Father, Lord
of heaven and earth, that Thou hast hid these things from
the wise and prudent, and hast revealed them unto babes."
It is with the heart that man believeth unto righteousness.
Let us remember these things and receive them as the
wisdom and love of God to our souls.   We are to receive
nothing about God at second-hand.   The serpent seduced
man to go out of the limits of God's will in search of knowledge, and God would have us to know that it is only within
those limits that we can have any true knowledge.   We
are creatures, and not independent.

I am happy to hear that your son's indisposition is
removing.   I can easily understand, from a few words which
dropped from you incidentally, as you were mentioning
some conversation which had passed between you and him,
that the relation in which you stand to each other is not
common.   An honest, unfettered, confiding intercourse be-

tween mother and son, on the great interests of man, is a blessing enjoyed by few mothers and few sons.

80. TO LADY ELGIN.

LINLATHEN, 16*th May* 1833.

DEAR LADY ELGIN,—There is a particular application of that subject on which I have written to you, which I wish to draw your attention to. The healing of diseases, whether by the manifest immediate agency of God, or by what we call natural means, is simply a sign of resurrection to come, and it is given not to rest in, but to nourish faith and hope; not to give a satisfaction in the flesh, but to give an encouragement to crucify the flesh now, through confidence in God, who, by this sign, shows His will and power to raise up in incorruptible immortality the flesh which has thus been willingly crucified during the day of grace. We all feel that we need a deliverance, and the flesh calls for it immediately, whilst those who walk in the Spirit wait for the hope of righteousness. Thus the flesh would always convert the sign into the permanent miracle; it cannot receive the truth that the promised deliverance is through blood, that is, through death. Our true deliverance is on the other side of death, and we must pass through death to get it. So our Deliverer is a crucified and risen man, and it is by this way that He leads many sons to glory. He is the way, and those who abide in Him are those who are dying daily to the flesh and present things, in the hope of the future glory, and in the sense of the righteousness of the condemnation which is laid upon the flesh—the idolatrous flesh. Every acting of the flesh is a seeking of gratification to itself on this side of death; it may acknowledge God as the giver of its happiness, or the guard of its happiness, but God is not its happiness Himself; as a man may look to the police of the town in

which he lives as the protector of his happiness, but he has
no happiness in the police; he would be happy to be able
to do without it.   This is idolatry; for that which is our
happiness is really our God.   And this will be the natural
acting of the flesh until it is raised up a spiritual body.
And therefore the life of holiness here is a life of hope of
a future glory, a righteous kingdom to come, detaching us
from the actings of the flesh and the power of seen things,
and thus, by making us partakers of Christ's cross, fitting
us to be partakers of His glory.

Whenever we think that we may innocently and safely
take the natural desires for our guide, whenever we think
that we may without sin and danger make the present
gratification of the flesh our object, we are receiving that
error which is condemned in 2 Timothy ii. 18, " saying
that the resurrection is past already."   Read the whole
chapter carefully, and you will see that this is the spirit
of it : it is not until the resurrection is really past, and
these bodies have ceased to be bodies of sin and death,
that we can safely cease from living by hope of good
things to come, and from crucifying the flesh through that
hope.   The condition of all men is represented by the two
thieves who were crucified with Jesus; for all are upon
the cross in one way or other—pain, anxiety, doubt, etc.
etc.—and all men desire a deliverance ; but some insist
upon it now, others are content to wait : those who live
in the flesh will have it immediately,—" If thou be the
Christ, save thyself and us."   They have little taste for a
crucified Saviour ; for they think as the priests did, " If
thou be the king of Israel, come down from the cross."
They do not wish to be delivered from sin, they wish to
be delivered only from the cross.   But the other thief did
not ask to be taken down from the cross ; he felt the
righteousness of the punishment : " We indeed justly, for

we receive the due reward of our deeds; but this man hath done nothing amiss;" and he was content to wait for deliverance until the coming of Christ's Kingdom,— " Lord, remember me when Thou comest in Thy Kingdom." He made up his mind that he was to continue on the cross whilst he continued in the flesh ; he felt that it was righteous, he knew that it was but for a very little while, and he saw an eternal weight of glory,—"joint heirs with Christ," if in suffering, so also in glory (Luke xxiii. 39-43, Rom. viii. 16-26). Popish penance is the mimicry of a root-truth. Look at the 13th verse of that chapter. It is through the Spirit that the flesh is to be crucified, through love of God and the hope of His Kingdom. . . .

There is another thing which I may mention to you. I think that there is a risk sometimes of losing hold of the great principle and kernel of prophecy, through occupation with its details ; although the opposite evil has certainly been the prevalent one in our days. Is it not the great object of prophecy that, through faith and hope of the glory of God, we should be content to forego present things, and enter into God's plan of condemning and crucifying the flesh? "Heirs of God, joint heirs with Christ, if so be that we suffer with Him, that we may also be glorified together," seems to me the kernel of prophecy, like the object of healings, etc. . . .

The object of prophecy is to draw our view forward out of seen things to the permanent triumph of God's righteous cause. What I meant by the details of prophecy is rather, when the prophecy is more considered than the thing prophesied, as when the sign is more considered than the thing signified. I feel a jealousy of the Morning Watch in this respect.

81. TO LADY ELGIN.

LINLATHEN, 29*th Nov.* 1833.

DEAR LADY ELGIN,—I believe all *notions* of religion, however true, to be absolutely useless, or worse than useless, inasmuch as they have a semblance of good, which may give a lying satisfaction, and so keep us back from taking hold of the substance, which is the living personality of God in our flesh. He is indeed far above all doctrines about Him, however true. He is the truth. A doctrine that can be separated from Himself, and is received separate from Himself, is a vanity and a deception. I enter with my whole heart into what you say on this subject. Only it is the personality of God—a personality whose presence I can recognise in my own heart, and yet know it to be the same personality that is on the right hand of power. When He says, " Come unto me, and learn of me;" we are not to think merely that we have to learn something; but we have to know that if we learn it in any other way than from Jesus, it is a lost learning. We think more of the thing to be learned than of the way in which we are to learn it; and thus our heads are filled with notions instead of our hearts being filled with God. " I will instruct thee and teach thee in the way which thou shalt go, and I will guide thee with mine eye." If we were faithful and patient to wait for His instruction and direction, refusing to act without them, then we should have the mysteries of our God truly taught to us, we should have the life of God taught to us and nourished in us. But we are in such a haste ; we think something must be done immediately ; we think that we cannot go wrong in the ordinary occupations of life, and so we cease to listen for that voice, and we begin to act from ourselves ; and thus our ear gets unused to the Shepherd's voice, and we get used to act without it, and yet not to feel condemned in so doing. What is the

wisdom of a blind man in a strange country? It is simply
holding by his guide (disquisitions about the road and the
plan of the country are vanities to him), and learning always
to know the true guide from every pretender. This last
appears the great difficulty, but I believe that it is impatience, weary of waiting for the satisfying evidence of God's
own voice, which leads us into error as to the true guide.
None need mistake Jesus. If in honest patient waiting we
could mistake a stranger for Him, religion were a vain
thing. The secret of the Lord is with them that fear Him,
and He will show them His covenant. I say this from my
deepest conscious conviction, although in much self-con-
demnation for haste. "Let every man be swift to hear,
slow to speak, slow to impulse; for the impulse of man
worketh not the righteousness of God." I believe that
'wrath' means 'impulse' in this place. Wait, I say, on
the Lord. He will make darkness light before thee, and
crooked things straight. Let us not take God on trust
from any other person. We must each hold by the Head
—individually. . . .

. . . I am perfectly satisfied that the way is " all plain
to him who hath understanding," to him who will trust in
the Lord. What is trust? We have a hundred counsellors,
each prompting us a different way, and offering himself for
a guide; and God says, Blessed is the man that trusteth in
the Lord, I will guide thee with mine eye. But if we look
off from His eye, how can His eye guide us? We are
trusting our own understanding when we look off from
God's eye. The 17th chapter of Jeremiah is full of instruction. Mark the position of the 9th and 10th verses
after the blessing and the curse promised on trusting God
and trusting flesh. God seems therein to warn us that we
may be thinking ourselves trusting in Him, whilst we are
in fact trusting in flesh. Then the 11th verse—riches, got

and held not by right—not in the way of trusting God; knowledge, gifts, held in our own spirit; they are barren eggs, and he that sitteth upon them may be anticipating great things, but the result will be the manifestation of his folly. Then the 12th, 13th, 14th, and then the 15th. Let God be true, and every man a liar. Animal magnetism is indeed a strange thing; but we have to do with the living God, without whom a sparrow falleth not to the ground. It is surely an awful thing for a weak and ignorant sinner to admit any spirit to come between him and God, nay, to court its coming in. Poor woman, I should fear very much that she is throwing herself open to any supernatural power, as if to live amongst spirits were religion. . . .

82. TO MISS RACHEL ERSKINE.

LINLATHEN, *Saturday,* 21*st Dec.* 1833.

BELOVED FRIEND,—My mind has undergone a considerable change since I last interchanged thoughts with you. I have seen reason to disbelieve that it is the Spirit of God which is in Mr. ——, and I do not feel that I have a stronger reason to believe that it is in others. This does not change my mind as to what the endowment of the Church is, if she had faith, but it changes me as to the present estimate that I form of her condition. God is our all, and having God, we have lost nothing. These gifts are but signs and means of grace; they are not grounds of confidence; they are not necessarily intercourse with God; they are not holiness, nor love, nor patience; they are not Jesus. But surely they shall yet appear, when God has prepared men to receive them. Mr. and Mrs. Scott and Mrs. Rich are here. I have much sympathy with much that I meet in them. They fear that the outward forms and magnificent utterances have that in them from which the carnal mind draws nourishment, and that there is a temptation to put these things between God and the soul, and to take them on trust that they are of God, although the hearer himself personally may not be conscious of meeting God in them. The truth and substance of religion is the spirit of Christ manifested in the heart, and consciously recognised in the heart, as the light and life of God communicated to us—the conscious possessing within our hearts that Seed of the woman, who bruises the serpent's head, and to whom all the promises of God are made.

You know that Mr. Scott is entirely separated from Mr. Irving and his church,[1] believing it, as I understand, to be a delusion partly, and partly a spiritual work not of God. He conceives that there is a disposition to yield to spiritual influence, as in animal magnetism, which lays one open to such possession ; but don't say anything in his name, except that he is separate as not believing it. We are in the

---

[1] Mr. Scott had early noticed a tendency in Mr. Irving with which he could not sympathise. "He had from the first," to quote Mr. Scott's own words, " a strength of ecclesiastical, I might say hierarchical, feeling, impossible with my convictions." This feeling was enlarged and deepened by his intercourse with several of the most eminent of the High Church clergy in London, whose sympathy with his prophetical views increased their attraction. It became dominant, and embodied itself in action as the new Church began to be organised. As things progressed in this direction Mr. Scott stood more and more aloof, doubting first, then disapproving, till the divergence between the two friends became extreme. To both this was singularly distressing. Scott's health gave way under it, "to such a degree," Mrs. Scott tells us, "that Mr. Irving sent for me, that I might be the bearer of the earnest expostulation he desired to send to his dear friend, and at the same time save him the greater excitement which their conversation then might occasion. It was the most solemn interview I ever had with any one, and in binding up in my own mind all that he desired me to be the messenger of to my husband I said, ' You believe that organisation produces life ; Mr. Scott believes that life alone can organise : does this then express your great difference ?' He assented. After an hour's audience, in which with awful but affectionate seriousness he stated to me what were my husband's heresies, I said, ' It is very clear to me that the antagonism of the two views is as the north to the south pole,—that they are totally and purely opposite.'. He said, ' It is so. Mr. Scott or I am in dangerous error. The end will show.'"

midst of unexplained things ; but he that dwelleth in the
secret place of the Most High shall abide under the shadow
of the Almighty.   The true connection of man with the
Spirit of God is seeking to know and do His will—" Yea,
rather, blessed are they that know the will of God and do
it."   I cannot believe that there has been no pouring out
of the Spirit at Port-Glasgow and in London ; but I feel
that I have to wait in every case upon the Lord, to receive
in my heart directly from Himself my warrant to acknowledge anything to be of His supernatural acting, and I have
erred in not waiting for this. . . .

83. TO MRS. MACNABB.[1]

January 23, 1834.

MY DEAR FRIEND,—We have had great trial about the
spiritual gifts.   The spirit which has been manifested has
not been a spirit of union, but of discord.   I do not believe
that the introduction of these gifts, whatever they may be,
has been to draw men simply to God.   I think the effect
has rather been to lead men to take God, as it were, on
trust from others ; to be satisfied with God having declared
something to another, and not to expect the true fulfilment
of the promise, "They shall all be taught of the Lord."
Whatever we learn from God by His Spirit's teaching in
our own hearts is true knowledge and eternal life ; but
whenever we go beyond that limit, the measure of our own
faith, we leave life, and our knowledge is only that which
puffeth up.   The regeneration of fallen man consists in his
own inward ear being opened to hear and know the voice
of his God.   "My sheep hear My voice."   It is not what
another man hears and tells me that is life to me, even
though what he hears may be truly from God; I must hear
God Himself, and "they that hear shall live."   I am very

---

[1] The Rev. J. M'Leod Campbell's sister.

much shaken, indeed, as to the whole matter of the gifts. The many definite predictions that have been given and that have entirely failed when tried by Deut. xvi. 22 should lead us to great watchfulness. It is indeed a strange time—a time for keeping close under the Shepherd's shadow. In London the voice appoints ordinances and rules in the Church, and it seems to me that their snare is to trust in their ordinances as their ordained pastors, and prophets, and elders. The 17th chapter of Jeremiah is a word much needed among us.—Yrs., etc.,   T. ERSKINE.

84. TO LADY ELGIN.

LINLATHEN, *18th March* 1834.

DEAR LADY ELGIN,—I know that you will not misinterpret my delay in answering you. I have often wished to do it, but have never been able; and even now, I do not feel that I am sitting down to answer your letter, but rather to thank you for it, and to express to you my sense of the Christian love breathing in it. I cannot answer it, because, as I have not in me a light which confirms it, so neither have I a light which distinctly condemns it altogether—I mean as to its recognition of the church in London to be indeed a church ordered and gifted by the Spirit; although I see much against believing it, which I shall mention. At the same time, my conscience responds fully to all that you say of the domestic order of the families of that church, and I enter into the distinction which you make between the general calls to general holiness and the special calls to the detailed duties of life connected with station and relation, so much pressed in that church; and I do feel that holiness consists in hearing Christ and following Him step by step in the minutest part of the minutest duty, and in acknowledging an ordinance of Christ in all the natural and social relations. And

I recognise such teaching to be according to the mind of
God; and where I see the teachers of such things teaching
by their lives, as well as by their words, I feel that they
possess weighty credentials. And I feel that we need a
church so ordered by the Spirit, and that we have it not.
But even were all the teaching that came out from that
church such as found a witness in my conscience, I require,
besides that witness to the teaching, an equally distinct
witness within me to the power whose utterances they
follow, before I can feel myself warranted (or rather I
should say capable) to receive it as the supernatural power
of the Spirit of God, or to receive its ordering as the ordering of God. When I heard of the second mission of
Messrs. Drummond, Cardale, Armstrong, and Thomson, from
London, I went to Edinburgh. I remained there Thursday
and Friday last week. There were two meetings on
Thursday and one on Friday. Dr. Thomson came down
as the instructor of Mr. Tait and his people as to the
nature of the church. I heard him speak twice in the
chapel, besides meeting him once (unintentionally) in
private. I heard Mr. Armstrong preach once. I heard
also several utterances through Mr. Cardale and Mr.
Drummond, which were very striking, and to which, with
two exceptions, my conscience witnessed fully; but whether
the power by which they spoke was really the power of
God or not, I feel myself perfectly incompetent to say. I
have a witness within me which, I am conscious, tries
truth; but I do not know a witness within me which tries
power. I have once already yielded myself to the acknowledgment of a power, mainly on the credit of the truth
uttered by the power, and I have felt that this was sin,
and that it was laid upon me to take nothing as of God,
except from Himself and in His own light. The utterances
were very sweet and pleasing, even in rebuke, especially

through Mr. Drummond, whose finely modulated English
voice contrasted, even to the natural man, most favourably
with the harsh and distressing sounds which I have heard
in that chapel before; but the shake which I have received
on this matter is, I find, very deep; or rather it would be
a truer expression of my feeling to say, that I am now
convinced that I never did actually believe it. My conviction that the gifts ought to be in the church is not in the
least degree touched; but a faith in any one instance of
manifestation which I have witnessed, like the faith which
I have in the righteousness and faithfulness of God, I am
sure I have not, and never had, as far as I can judge on
looking back—that is, the only true faith, even "the substance of things hoped for." I think that I mentioned to
Lady Matilda at Cadder the circumstances which shook me
with regard to the Macdonalds at Port-Glasgow, that in
two instances when James Macdonald spoke with remarkable power, a power acknowledged by all the other gifted
people there, I discovered the seed of his utterances in the
newspapers. He had read there a foolish rumour about
the time of George IV.'s death, that the Ministers would
probably find it convenient to conceal that event when it
took place, until they had made some arrangements. This
had remained in his mind, and it came forth at last as an
utterance in power, but wrapped in such obscurity of
language as not to expose it to direct confutation; but on
reading the paragraph I recognised such a resemblance that
I could not doubt it, and I put it to him; and although he
had spoken in perfect integrity (of that I have no doubt),
yet he was satisfied that my conjecture as to its origin was
correct. The other instance was a prophetic utterance of
a war in the north of Europe—the language taken much
from the 11th of Daniel; but the seed of it also was a
newspaper paragraph. I thus see how things may come

into the mind and remain there, and then come forth as
supernatural utterances, although their origin be quite
natural.   James Macdonald could not say that he was
conscious of anything in these two utterances distinguishing
them from all the others; he only said that he believed
that these two were of the flesh.   Taplin made a similar
confession on being reproved through Miss Emily Cardale
for having rebuked Mr. Irving in an utterance.   He
acknowledged that he was wrong; and yet he could not
say where the difference lay between that utterance and
any other.   Is there not a great perplexity in all this?
Does the control of a church solve it?

What I heard from Dr. Thomson, both in public and
private, seemed to be at variance with all that I know and
feel of the first elementary principle of true religion.   In
his zeal for a church, he seemed to me to lose sight of the
individual personality of that intercourse with God through
His Spirit within us, which is the basis, and the only basis,
of religion.   He frequently repeated that Christ was only
to be met with in the church, and that the light in man
only answered to the ministrations of the ordained
ministers in the church.   I know that this is not so.   But
if it were so, how could I even be in a condition to discern
the true church?   They say, "Come into the church and
you will see."   The first step, according to this direction,
must be made in the dark.   The first step is a *petitio
principii*, a begging the question; it is taking for granted
the very thing of which I need evidence : that this is the
true church.   I feel the desolateness of being without a
church; I feel the weakness and meagreness, and selfishness
and speculativeness, that arise from our isolated condition ;
but I dare take nothing for granted in this weighty matter,
and I feel very jealous of the urgency with which the
teachers of that church cry down the sovereignty of the

internal witness of the light in every man, and claim submission to themselves on the ground of utterances which
need a further evidence, and which do not carry to my
mind any character distinguishing them in kind from other
utterances which have been manifested to be delusive.
One of the two cases in which my heart gave no response
to the utterance (I don't recollect whether through Mr. D.
or Mr. C.) was, when a seal was given by it to Dr.
Thomson's expression, " Christ is only to be met with in
the church." I cannot know the true church without the
true light, and if the true light does not guide me until I
am in the church, and even then only under its ministrations, where is my guide to the true church? I do not
wish to press their words beyond the meaning which they
themselves attach to them. And they allow regenerating
light before being in the church,—that men may be Christians out of the church. I know in some measure the evil
of being without a church : but I feel that, if this were so in
its full extent, I should be without a God. I cannot express
to you how much I feel of atheism in putting anything, whatever its name may be, above or in place of the witness of God
in my own heart, the true light which lighteth every man.

What you say of William Tait personally I have heard
confirmed by others. He was kind enough to call on me
one day, but I was not at home ; he came in however, and
left a good report behind him. . . .

I feel certain that the individual personality of religion
is not to be lost or diminished, but strengthened and confirmed, by a church ; and that it is by our connection with
Christ that we are to be brought into a church, and not by
our connection with a church that we are to be brought
into Christ.[1] We are commanded to prove all things, but

[1] For Mr. Erskine's idea of what the true Church is, see Appendix,
No. IX. p. 393.

we can only do this in the light of Him who is the true
light enlightening us personally.   And I am sure that we
can escape from the ignorance and darkness which are upon
us, only by keeping close to that light, and receiving instruction from without only as witnessed to by, and in
communion with, that light; for that light is also the True
Life; and no instruction can be life to us, except as it is
witnessed to and received by that life.   Now it seems to
me, that it is against this they teach.   I know, indeed,
that if the question were put to them, whether they would
have a man to disregard the witness within him, they would
say No; and whether a man might not be a Christian out
of their church, they would say, Yes; yet still they would
have him come into their church, though he had no witness
to its being the true one, and after he was in, they would
have him trust the pastor and elders, even in opposition to
the light within himself.   I am sure that I do not wilfully
misunderstand them, but what I have lately heard from
them gives me always the impression that they regard the
ordinances of the church rather as appointments and institutions of Christ, which are to be obeyed and reverenced
and submitted to, and on account of obedience to which a
blessing will be given, than as open channels through which
the Spirit of the Head is to flow into us personally, and as
meeting-places where we are continually to have personal
contact with Him.   I know that they would not allow this;
but I daresay many Papists would not allow a similar
charge against Popery.   I feel as if there were a deep
Popery in their system.   Christ is the true Priest, because
He does not stand between us and God, but we meet God
in Him.   That seems to me the true character of an ordinance.   I see so much good and beauty in their order and
teaching that I am afraid to reject their claims, and yet I
feel also afraid that they are putting men and forms between

God and the people. The charge which God by His prophets brings against His people in the last days is the
taking His ordinances instead of Himself—see Isaiah i. and
all through Jeremiah. They said not, "Where is Jehovah?"
but "The temple of the Lord, the temple of the Lord." I
feel that my part is to wait to be taught of God the meaning of 1 John iv. 2, 3. I cannot believe in its verbal
interpretation, notwithstanding the Probyn children, there
are so many opposite facts. I desire to lie at the feet of
Jesus, and learn of Him to be meek and lowly in heart;
and not to refuse what He gives, and not to snatch at what
His own hand does not give. I hope that I shall not be
led to shut my ear against the true voice because I have
been deceived by a false one; but I am bound to be on
my guard. I believe that an evil spirit, or the flesh even,
may speak of the deep things of God, although in a way
that the true life and light in us might detect it, or at least
guard us from suffering by it. Pray read the tractate in
Penington on "laying the axe to the root," etc., page 184.
There is a remarkable verse, which I once met on a remarkable occasion, that I would also refer you to—
Ezekiel xxvii. 17. Tyrus may buy Judah's finest wheat;
yea, her balm and oil and honey. What is the meaning of
this? You would know what part of the parcel properly
belonged to yourself. Those who are weary are apt to get
impatient, and, in the absence of the sun, to kindle a fire
and to compass themselves about with sparks; and in my
weariness, which has been great, I have done this; but I
am now learning that "all the days of the afflicted are
evil;" but yet, in the midst of that evil, "the merry heart
hath a continual feast" in eating the will of God. I was
happy to meet with Lady Matilda and your son at Cadder.
There is but one wish worth forming for him, or for any
human being, plunged in this horrible pit and miry clay,

and that is, a true oneness with Him who has risen out of it, having overcome death, and him who had the power of death, even the devil. I have sent Lady Matilda a volume of Isaac Penington, and a very curious autobiography of his wife; that copy is all full of pencil-marks for which I am not responsible. Dear Lady Elgin, I have mentioned some of my objections to the London church without fear, although having little light on any part of it, and no light on much, assured that, if you are really taught by God in it, my objections will not hinder you; and that, if you are taking for God's teaching what is not, a pause is useful. I have just heard from Edinburgh; they have had solemn meetings I hear, but I know not the particulars. Old Mrs. Fergusson, Hermand, is dead, and I believe she died a rejoicing Christian. Blessed are the dead that die in the Lord, for they are free; and those who are partakers of Christ's death enter now into that freedom, through Him who hath broken the gates of brass, and cut asunder the bars of iron. My mother and sister desire their kindest regards to yourself and Lady Matilda, and their thanks for your word of kindness. My mother desires also to send her best regards to Lord Elgin, in all which I take part, begging also to be remembered to Mr. Bruce, for whom I sent another letter, in case he goes to Paris. Farewell. The name of the Lord is the strong tower. He is the God of Salvation, working salvation in the midst of the earth. I again return you my thanks for your most interesting letter. I must conclude as I began, by saying that I need more light to enable me to answer it.—Yours very truly,

T. ERSKINE.

85. TO MRS. MACHAR.

LINLATHEN, March 24, 1834.

WE are in great waters at present. The church in London is a wonderful thing. I cannot recognise God in it, yet I cannot distinctly discern an evil spirit in it. The evil that appears to me to be in it is putting the church and its pastors and elders between the people and Christ. It seems to undervalue individual religion. I must beware, however, of condemning what I know not, but I must also beware of yielding to what I know not. All that is done among them is done by what they believe to be the express command of God, disclosed through an utterance. My dear friend, it is comforting to know that God is love, and that if any heart will give itself to God, God will come into it and dwell in it, and manifest Himself to it. " If any man love me he will keep my words, and my Father will love him, and we will come unto him, and take up our abode in him." But the heart is deceitful above all things, and desperately wicked ; and there is a counterfeit of every right thing, so that with a quiet conscience, a man may destroy his soul ; and we may think ourselves hungering and thirsting after righteousness, and we may indeed be filled, but with something else than God's righteousness. Let us watch and pray, and seek meekness and patience. Let us seek the open ear. The deaf adder shutteth her ear, and so do the seed of the serpent. I often repeat, " Blessed are the dead that die in the Lord." It seems to me that this church system is a very outward thing—a coming with observation, although I must admit that there is much truth and holiness in the people as well as the preaching.—Yours, etc.,   T. ERSKINE.

86. TO HIS SISTER MRS. STIRLING.

LINLATHEN, *5th April* 1834.

DEAR CHRISTIAN,—I feel that I owe to you to let you know what I thought and what I think of all that I saw and heard in Edinburgh of the mission from London. I am quite sure that as far as natural disposition, aided by a preparedness from the interpretation of Scripture, could go, I was rather inclined than disinclined to recognise their claims, in spite of all that had been forced upon me, in opposition to such pretensions, in Port-Glasgow, Dumfries, and Edinburgh. All that I am conscious of having carried with me out of these detections, with which to meet this London mission, was a conviction that I ought not to acknowledge anything of a supernatural character to be of God without a distinct testimony within my own spirit to its being indeed of God,—I mean, to the power being of God,—as well as a distinct testimony to the subject-matter announced by the power. I felt the necessity of this from the experience of the bad consequence of being satisfied without it in former cases. All false religion has its origin in taking God at second-hand,—in stopping short of a personal conscious meeting with Him in our spirits—in allowing anything, whether of Divine appointment or human invention, to stand between God and us. Now, however much it may be denied by these dear people, that this is taught by them or allowed by them, I find in their preachings and in their letters continual proofs to me, that this is indeed the tendency of their whole system.

Our neighbours, the Duncans of Parkhill, were here with us lately. He had been invited to Edinburgh when Mr. Irving was there, by command of the power speaking through Mr. Taplin, but as he did not feel it in his conscience to be the call of God, he declined going. He showed us three letters which he had received after declining to go—one from Mr. Tait, one from Mr. Irving, and one from an elder in the London church. In all these letters the argument used towards Duncan is not something to prove that the utterance is of God, but the whole burden of them all is, Obey the pastor. In the London elder's letter there is this expression, "Dear brother, you are not called on to judge the word, but to obey your pastor." This is entirely in unison with what I heard taught, whilst I was in Edinburgh, by Dr. Thomson. They teach that the discerning of spirits is not in the members of the church, but in the pastor, and therefore if the pastor says that the spirit in any one is the spirit of God, the flock are bound to acknowledge and obey it. If the pastor is not sure, there is an appeal to London,—and thus the Papacy appears to be repeated in this machinery. It is evidently understood throughout, that the spirit is taken for granted by a great majority of the worshippers, for that they do not know the spirit by any certain personal knowledge, but on the authority of the officers of the church. Now, read John xiv. 16, 17, and consider that the great majority of the church are by this system placed in the condition of the world, "which seeth Him not, neither knoweth Him," and therefore cannot receive Him. Surely those that receive Him merely on the authority of their pastor do not see Him nor know Him, and therefore cannot receive Him, according to the Scripture sense of the word receive. Look also at the tenth chapter of John. What is the meaning of knowing the Shepherd's voice? Read verses 14 and 15 to see the manner in which the sheep know the Shepherd : "As the Father knoweth me, and I know the Father" (*even as* ought to be translated *and I*) ; it is a comparison, beginning with the 14th and ending in the middle of the 15th verse. It ought to be one verse only. Look also at John vi. 44. In the 26th verse Jesus had charged the Jews with coming to Him for the loaves, as "drawn by the loaves"—but such persons, He says, do not really come to Me ; no one truly comes to Me except he be "drawn by the Father," and the meaning of this is given in verse 45 : "taught of God"—he who has listened to the voice of the Spirit. This is very different from the conclusion of an argument or a conviction of the natural understanding. It seems to me intended and fitted to give people a rest and a confidence without themselves personally coming to God. It seems to me to take away the necessity of personal assurance, for personal assurance does not mean merely an assured confidence of salvation, it is a personal assurance—an assurance from personal conscious knowledge in the light of God. All other assurance is presumption, or taking a thing for granted. William Tait seems to me to have given his *beau-idéal* of the work—for when I came to examine it I find something so different. Whilst I say this against, it is but fair to say that I have got a sight of Drummond's letter to ——, which —— complained of as harsh and unkind. Now, I think —— has misunderstood D., for I like the letter, and think it a kind letter, and I am happy to have seen it, and to have been delivered from a misjudgment.   T. E.

I have been reading Burgh's Lectures on the Second Advent and the Apocalypse with much interest. I agree more with him than with any writer on the subject that I have ever read. This morning (Sunday) I have received two letters, one from the Macdonalds in Port-Glasgow,[1] testifying most strongly against this London mission, and one from dearest Lucy, full of prayer and hope that we shall be brought to receive it. She has certainly not suffered by it. James Macdonald writes that the spirit amongst them declared the London people to be " deceitful workers, transforming themselves into the apostles of Christ." Strange things—spirit against spirit.

87. TO MISS RACHEL ERSKINE.

April 11, 1834.

DEAR FRIEND,—The Israelites were doomed to journey

---

[1] Letters from the Macdonalds to friends in London are given in Dr. Norton's *Memoirs* They are calm, sensible, thoughtful letters—harmonising in their views with those of Mr. Erskine.

through the wilderness until all those who had rebelled against the Lord by refusing to go into the promised land died. That evil generation was just the type of the flesh, which must be worn down and broken and wasted before we are meet for the inheritance of the saints in light. Our carcases must fall in this wilderness, and the life which belongs to these carcases must be shed out either drop by drop or by effusion. This life is in the blood, and without shedding of blood there is no remission—there is none. The life is in the blood, and the will is in the life ; the rebellious, independent will of man must be shed out, for in it the fall consists, and in the shedding out of it redemption consists.

How often things appear to happen for no other end but to provoke and to distress, and, indeed, things do happen to consume and wear out the carcases that must fall in the wilderness. Until they fall we cannot enter into the promised inheritance, and this is the manner of our Father's love therefore—to consume and waste that which hinders our entering in ; and in all that consuming and wasting and wearing out there is a love hidden, and that love, which is God's will in everything, and which is contained in everything that happens, as the kernel is contained in the shell, is the food which God giveth us that our souls may eat and live. This is the manna which is rained round our tents. The people, when they were desired to take it up and eat it, said, What is it ? (for that is the meaning of *manna*) : it did not seem to them to be bread from heaven, yet it was bread from heaven, though only the type of that true bread which our Father giveth us—the meat which Jesus ate, as He says—"My meat is to do the will of Him that sent me." How often when my Father has given me this meat to eat have I said, What is it ? Is this the bread of heaven ? We would eat our own will—that

is, the flesh-pot of Egypt,—and God would have us eat His
will, that we may be of one mind with Him, partaking of
the Divine nature. Beloved friend, how much easier it is
to say this than to do it ! But it is more sweet and more
blessed to do it than to say it. It is an awful judgment—
" Out of thine own mouth will I judge thee, thou wicked
servant." I have often felt this judgment in my own heart;
but I know that it is blessed in this day of grace to yield
the heart to judgment, for thus it is prepared for the day of
judgment, being already purged by the spirit of judgment.
What a wonderful thing it is for poor weak worms of the
dust to be invited to take hold of the will of God, and to
make it their own will, and thus to be united to Omni-
potence. This is the meaning of that word, " Great peace
have they that love thy law, and nothing shall offend
them." . . .

I have since heard from James Macdonald, Port-
Glasgow, that the spirit amongst them had testified against
the London mission, saying that " they were deceitful
workers, transforming themselves into the apostles of
Christ." . . . The blessing of the Lord be upon us all.
The oneness of the opened ear and the prepared body is
very striking : consider it in connection with John x. 14
and 15. We are all well—old and young—thanks to the
Preserver.

88. TO MISS RACHEL ERSKINE AND HER SISTER.

LINLATHEN, 22*d April* 1834.

BELOVED FRIENDS,—I am very thankful for your love,
and I can say that I could scarcely devise any expression
of love more gratifying to me than these pictures.[1] The
most distinct feelings of veneration that I have ever experienced towards human beings are associated with those two

---

[1] Pictures of Mr. Erskine of Cardross and his wife, Lady Christian.

portraits. I never saw anything in either of them that my heart ever ventured to blame; they stand in my memory in perfect purity, surrounded with an admiring love. I remember, when I heard of my uncle's death, I cried the whole day without any intermission. And though she died after my days of weeping were much past, yet she held her purity in the judgment of my heart—after that judgment had begun to venture to act on all, without respect of persons. Their memory is most sweet to me—far sweeter than all the genius of Raphael. And I know what a gift of affection it is from you, and of confidence; for you could not allow them to go anywhere but where you were sure they would find reverence and love. They will find reverence and love from me, you may rest assured. . . .

89. TO MISS RACHEL ERSKINE.

LINLATHEN, 24*th May* 1834.

. . . My dear cousin, I don't think that you fully apprehended what I desired to say to you, when we were together in Edinburgh, on the subject of ordinances, and a sheet is small compass for the subject; nevertheless, let me say a few words by way of re-explanation. It seems to me that many are satisfied with an ordinance, not because they meet God in it, but just because they are convinced that it is of God's appointment. Thus, they will be satisfied to sit under a pastor who, they believe, is ordained of God, and they will receive his instruction and submit themselves to his authority quite in a different way from what they would do with regard to another teacher. They take his instruction for granted; whereas they would only feel themselves justified in submitting to the counsel of the other in so far as they saw God's will and mind in it, that is, in so far as they had the inward testimony that such was His mind and will. And in this way the ordinance of God evidently has the effect, not of drawing them into closer spiritual fellowship with God, but of making them rest satisfied with something short of this; in other words, the ordinance thus received has the effect of dispensing with the necessity of direct contact with God personally, and with the inward witness of His Spirit in their hearts, to everything coming as from Him, before they can admit it. I feel that this is the way of death. It is not the living way, Christ Jesus. I think in my last letter to you I pressed several passages from the 6th of John. Jesus is the true ordinance, because in Him we meet the Father in spirit; and if we don't meet the Father in Him, He says that we have not really come to Him; look at verses 14, 36, 43, 44, 45—the multitude acknowledged Jesus as the Father's ordinance, "that Prophet;" but this acknowledgment of theirs was not the "faith" which Jesus desired. "No man can come to me, except the Father draw him," says Jesus. "It is only seeking and meeting the Father in me, that is really coming to me, and it is only in hearing the Father's voice in your hearts that you really acknowledge me as His ordinance." This is the ear opened and the body prepared which I spoke of to you in comparing Psalm xl. 6 with Heb. x. 5. Ordinances thus misapprehended separate man from God most fatally, because the conscience is lulled by a false peace in submitting to what is believed to be God's ordinance. Dear friend, I believe that this evil exists in the church of London. I have seen it expressed strongly in Mr. Irving's own handwriting, claiming submission to himself as the ordinance, even though there was no inward testimony to the thing which he spoke in the other person. There seems no true knowledge amongst them of the reality of that word, in application to every human individual, "I will instruct thee, and teach thee in the way wherein thou shalt go," etc. I have just been reading a letter of Mr. Campbell's giving an account of a meeting he had with Mr. Drummond, in the course of which Mr. D. strongly and explicitly avows that doctrine of ordinances which I have been bewailing and condemning; he considers them evidently as deputies to the people from God, and not as organs through which they themselves hear God. When Mr. Campbell urged the necessity of the personal hearing the voice of God, for sanctioning everything from God, Mr. D. said that he con sidered it a figure of speech to talk of the voice of God within. And as a proof that Mr. C. did not put on this expression any meaning different from what he intended to convey, I may just copy the last sentences of their conversation. Mr. D. said to Mr. C., "I would venture to say that your hearers, if asked why they listen to you, would just say, 'He is the best preacher we know.'" Mr. C. answered, "William Tait (who was present at their meeting) knew once something of my people, and I would refer to him whether those whom I regarded as indeed receiving my teaching would have so answered; or whether they would not all avow and claim, in all that they had received, that they had been taught of God." On Mr. Tait's assenting, Mr. D. said nothing. Now, Mr. D. did not mean to blame Mr. C.'s people as guilty of any fault, when he supposed that they would give the above account of their receiving Mr. C.'s instruction, but only meant to describe the way that instruction is really conveyed. This agrees exactly with the impression which I received from a letter of Mr. D. to myself. He seems to me to have no conception of the Spirit of the living God being really with every man as his guide and teacher, and thus he is necessarily thrown upon outside things for want of better. W. Tait's account of this work in London may be the account of his own soul, but it is not a true picture of the body.

90. TO MR. W. TAIT, GREENOCK.

LINLATHEN, *16th Oct.* 1834.

MY DEAR BROTHER,—It is one thing for a man to have a light given him by which he may discern all things, and it is another thing for him to use that light. Man's responsibility consists in his having that light, and in his possessing the power of using it or of refusing to use it. For the true light is the light which lighteth every man, "and this is the condemnation, that that light hath come into the world, and men have loved darkness rather than light." This is the condemnation, the only condemnation, and thus he that denies that light in man denies the only condemnation.

I never dreamt of limiting man's responsibility by his actual discernment; on the contrary, I desire, and have desired, to justify God in all the dark wanderings of man, by acknowledging that there is in each " man's hand a price to buy wisdom," and that no man needs to say, " Who shall ascend into heaven, or descend into the deep to bring Christ to him? for that the word is nigh him, in his mouth and in his heart, that he may hear it," Rom. x.; and when I said in my letter to you that men were often very loose in their profession of faith in the Bible, for that they did not truly believe in any truth of God which they had not been taught by the Spirit of God, I was in my mind referring to the 17th verse of that same tenth chapter of the Epistle to the Romans, where it is written, "Faith cometh by hearing, even hearing through the word of God," evidently pointing to that same word which is in the heart (mentioned in the 8th verse), and limiting the true meaning of faith to the witness of that inward word. The natural man understandeth not the things of the Spirit, for no man understandeth the things of the Spirit but by the Spirit, and this is his sin, that he will still live on in the flesh, instead of living in the Spirit which God hath given to him in Jesus Christ. Do I say then that his ignorance of the things of God is his measure of responsibility? No! I justify God in saying that God hath given to him a spiritual light and life in his Son, whereby he may know and do the things of God, and therefore that his ignorance as well as his disobedience has sin in it. He may, however, in the midst of an entire want of spiritual teaching, have arrived at a conviction that the Bible is an inspired book, either by receiving it on the authority of those about him, or by his own historical researches and reasonings thereon, and this he may consider faith, but surely you would consider it a contradiction to say that such a person could exercise faith, for faith "seeth Him who is invisible." He has not received God's witness in it, but man's or reason's; he has not received the witness which "is greater," and so he has not "the witness in himself." Surely his conviction, however conscientious, is not to be confounded with the spiritual faith of a child of God —his conviction is a carnal thing, for it does not see God, which is the true mark of Christian faith. "This is life eternal, when they know thee, the only true God." And how is He known but by faith? He that believeth hath life, just because faith sees and receives God. An unspiritual man cannot have faith in the Bible, just because he does not meet God in it. And in like manner a spiritual man has only true faith in that part of the Bible in which he sees and receives God. To confound these two beliefs is to confound the greater witness with the less. The fact of a man's being without the greater witness is no apology for his being without it, but it proves that he has not divine faith in the thing, for he that believeth hath the witness in himself.

There is a faith which receives God at second-hand, so

to speak, but this is not the faith of the new covenant, for
by it we are no longer servants, but sons.   When Abraham
received God's commandment to leave his own home, and
go to a land which the Lord had appointed for him, he
must have had the witness in himself that this was God's
voice to him, and thus he was in the condition of a son.
When he told the rest of his family and servants, they,
knowing Abraham's character, at once seem to have recognised it as God's commandment, and they were perhaps
eager to obey as unto the Lord, but still they were not in
Abraham's situation; they acted piously and conscientiously
it might be, but they were servants and not sons; they received God at second-hand.   It might have been that there
was high attestation given to Abraham as God's messenger
to them in the way of miracle, but still there was this great
difference between Abraham and them, that God Himself
told Abraham, and Abraham told them.   The charter of
the new covenant is, "They shall be all taught of God,"
that is, they shall all be in the condition of Abraham.
Abraham had met God, the rest had met a man, who, they
knew on the strongest evidence, had met God; the veil of
flesh was between them and God, whereas God had come
within that veil to Abraham; he personally knew God
speaking in him.   So the children of Israel received Moses
as from God; Moses had seen God, and they saw Moses, so
the veil was on their hearts.   In Christ, God came within
the flesh to man, the spirit of Jesus came to each heart
and knocked.   The Jews naturally represented man's relation to God, whilst the first tabernacle, viz. the flesh, was
standing; the relation which may exist without passing
through death.   They received the law by the hand of a
mediator, who heard and saw for them, and then declared
to them what he heard and saw—this was the veil; the
rending of the veil was the opening the channel of personal

communion betwixt every soul and God. There surely has been and is much religion which is acknowledged by God as true, resting largely on a faith of this nature. It is much higher than that of historical evidence. It is a faith that recognises God, but it does not meet Him, for the veil hides Him from it. This outward faith which acknowledged God's appointments and ordinances, but did not meet Himself, is not the faith of the new covenant; it is an easier thing for the flesh, and so the flesh is always disposed to have this instead of the personal meeting with God. A conscientious devout Catholic, believing that if his Church directs him wrong, the responsibility does not lie on his soul, punctually follows the directions of his Church as God's commissioned authorised ordinance to him, and thus he has peace without undergoing the fire of the Divine presence. He is told what to do, and he does it, believing it to be the will of God declared through His regular ordinance. He acknowledges God's authority, and, believing that it resides in this ordinance, he bows to it. But this is not the faith that sees Him who is invisible.

But this seems to me to be the faith which is required by that society with which you are connected, and is held sufficient by them. You seem to ask no more than that men should recognise your Divine ordination, and obey you, and when such statements as that which I have made are objected to you, your reply is that such an objection is opposed to God's revealed plan of blessing man through man. But the man in whom men are to be blessed is Christ Jesus, who standeth at each heart and knocketh, and whatever I may hear from any mouth of flesh, though it were His own, unless I hear it inwardly from Him it profiteth me nothing. " The hour now is when the dead shall hear the voice of the Son of Man, and they who hear shall live," and those only live who hear that voice. They may hear a voice which they believe commissioned by Jesus, but that is not life; they must hear His own voice, knowing it by its own evidence in their hearts. You will say that thus I reject all teaching and all ordinances. Far from it. I have myself much reason to bless God for much that I have learned through the teaching of His servants, but all of their teaching that has been profitable to me has been so by His own Spirit witnessing it to my heart and sealing it. Will you read John x., 14th and 15th verses, not in our English version, but in the original, and not as two separate verses, but as one sentence : "I know my sheep, and am known of mine, *even as* the Father knoweth me, and I know the Father." That is the true meaning of it. Now, think how Jesus knows the Father, whether it be at second-hand or no, and then say this is the way in which the sheep know Jesus. It is not the ordinance of Jesus that they know, but Jesus Himself, as it was not the Father's ordinance that Jesus knew, but the Father Himself, and so the true knowledge of an ordinance in the Church does not consist in discerning and acknowledging it to be of Christ's appointment, but in. meeting Christ in it. This is just the distinction between the old covenant and the new, between the dispensation of messengers and the dispensation of the Son. Your letter to me seems to indicate that you do not much regard this distinction, and that all that you want is an attestation to anything that it is of God's appointment or commandment, as the Jews had an attestation in the building of the tabernacle that it was of God's appointment. But this surely is not according to the mind of Him who says, " Henceforth I call you not servants but friends, for the servant knoweth not what his lord doeth."

What you tell me of Mr. Campbell's principles, and of his conversations with Mr. Drummond, only proves to me that you have entirely misunderstood him, as you have en-

tirely misunderstood me.   You say that Mr. C. held that
the outward thing professing to be of God must catch hold
of the witness for God within me, else I am irresponsible
in rejecting it.   Now I am sure that he meant to say, that
there must be something within, on which the outward
things may take hold, else there can be no responsibility.
There must be the faculty of sight, else there can be no
responsibility for not seeing.

My dear friend, I see that you are much fixed in these
things.   I believe them to be delusions; I see in them a
return to Judaism, and a real throwing away of the spiritual dispensation under the show of maintaining it.   The
true spiritual dispensation does not consist in the outward
voice of God in the Church, for the Jews had that in their
carnal church in the wilderness.   It consists in the indwelling of the Spirit in the heart, in knowing God personally
in the heart.   Not that I at all mean to reject the outward
voice as inconsistent with the spiritual dispensation, but I
must have evidence for its reality much stronger than what
at one time satisfied me.   I have had much evidence against
it since then.   The 4th No. of the Church is strong evidence,
to my mind, that the doctrine there pressed is not of God.
The rules given in Timothy and Titus for the choosing of
office-bearers are completely set aside by the system of your
Church.   These rules show that the office was conferred on
the ground of a recognised manifestation of the spirit of
Christ in a person, qualifying him for the office, and thus
the fellow-members in the body met with the spirit of
Christ in him, and not a mere ordination, however attested.
And thus God manifested in the flesh is no official or con-
ventional thing, but a blessed reality.

My dear friend, let us seek meekness and humility, not
a mere suppression of proud expressions, but meekness and
humility of heart, and let us walk tenderly, working out

our salvation with fear and trembling, knowing the deceitfulness and wickedness of our hearts.   I do not feel hardly
towards you, or those connected with you ; on the contrary,
I love you, and in love let me say that your Church seems
to me both contrary 'to the spirit of Christ and to the
letter of His word, and that the voice on which it is built,
and by which it is attested, seems to me exceedingly to
need attestation.—Farewell.   T. E.

91. TO THE REV. EDWARD IRVING.

MY DEAR BROTHER,—[1] . . . Wherever I find the authority
of God commanding or forbidding, although I may not enter
into the spirit of the ordinance, I am bound to yield my
submission ; but in this case I am, from some carnality,
shutting myself out from the liberty of children.   Even so,
as I recognise the Bible as a whole to be the inspiration of
God, the want of the internal witness and light to any part
of it does not lift me from under its obligation ; but only
I feel that in that part I am untaught and unprofited,
although my Father gave it to me for teaching and pro-
fiting.   I acknowledge its inspiration, but I am not receiving in that faith which is of the operation of the Spirit.
But unless there be an internal witness to the things of
God in man, man can have no responsibility at all. . . .
Is it on your authority that I am to risk my soul ?   You may
speak a thing which I had never conceived, nor imagined,
nor heard before ; nay, it might be opposed to all my pre-
conceived thoughts on the subject, and yet I may find a
witness in me to it contending against all my own
theories on the subject, and showing me a glory to God
in it, which I cannot gainsay, so that I am compelled
to acknowledge the word you have spoken as the word

---

[1] The first paragraph of this letter is the same with that in the letter to
Mr. Tait. It then proceeds as above.

of God, quick and powerful. From whom do I receive this? Certainly not from you, nor on your authority, but through you. If I acknowledge the same word, not from the same inward witness to it, but because I believe you to be an ordained pastor, I get nothing that is quick and powerful; I receive it as a servant, not as a son; I get it not from God through you, but from you, and on your authority, as a recognised pastor of God's ordination. The faith of the Jews in the construction of the tabernacle was a very different faith from that which we are called to exercise, and very different from that which Abraham had in God, and which doubtless many of those who understood not the meaning of the tabernacle had in God. But for that outward second-hand faith they had an outward foundation in the miracles they saw. Now, you require this outward faith, but without any outward foundation. The patterns of the heavenly things could only be understood by those who knew the things of which they were the patterns, and the most absolute and unquestioning submission to these pattern ordinances was a very different thing from that faith which is "the substance of things hoped for, and the evidence of things not seen." This is the faith of the new covenant; it is itself the grain of mustard-seed, the kingdom of heaven within. My dear friend, what I feel in your letter is the entire annihilation by it of all true personal, spiritual religion or conscious communion with God. If man has not that in him by which that which comes from God can be distinguished from that which comes from another quarter, he is incapable of religion, and if men are to be taught not by the Spirit of God, but by a man, what is the use of your pressing on your people that they should not take their pastor as a substitute for Christ, or as a third party bearing a message to them from Him, but that they

should meet Christ in their pastor? I conceive that this
expression of meeting Christ in the pastor is susceptible
only of two different meanings. The one meaning is that
the people should look to their pastor as the Jews looked
to their high priest, whether he was a man of God or not,
yet as an ordinance of God to them, through whom they
were to expect a blessing. This is, however, not properly
meeting Christ, it is only meeting Christ's appointment;
that is, it is meeting Christ's substitute, or a third party
acting for Him, and there is no such thing recognised in
the new covenant. The other meaning is, that the people
should discern Christ's own teaching in the teaching of
their pastor, by the Spirit's witness within them. The
first of these meanings belongs to the patterns of the
heavenly things; the second belongs to the heavenly things
themselves, to that Church in which all are taught of God.
I believe that you would take the first meaning; because
I think that under spiritual names you are returning to
the patterns, although you have none of those outward
signs to show on which the authority of that outward
Church was founded; and although your warning of the
danger of taking the pastor as a substitute for his Lord
appears so contradictory to it, God manifest in the flesh is
no official or conventional thing, it is a blessed reality.

92. TO MISS STUART.

CADDER, *Saturday night, Dec.* 13, 1834.

YOU will have heard of the death of Irving. You cannot enter into my feelings on this event, as you did not
know him or regard him as I did. He has been a remarkable man, in a remarkable age. He was a man of much
child-like feeling to God, and personal dependence on Him,
amidst things which may well appear unintelligible and
strange in his history.—Yours most truly,   T. E.

93. TO MISS RACHEL ERSKINE.

Feb. 6th, 1835.

DEAR FRIEND,—James Macdonald is to be buried this day at one o'clock. This is another very solemn thing. I believe that to the very last he felt assured that the voice which spoke by him was the voice of the Spirit. He was a servant of Jesus Christ, and his trust and joy were in the Lord, and he was a witness for God. He died on Monday. I had a short letter from his brother telling me of it, and telling me that before his death, but when he felt its approach, he spoke to them many things which would be a consolation to them whilst their pilgrimage lasted. This event has recalled many things to my remembrance. I lived in the house with them for six weeks, I believe, and I found them a family united to God and to each other. James especially was an amiable and clean character— perfectly true.[1] And those manifestations which I have so often witnessed in him were indeed most wonderful things and most mighty, and yet—I am thoroughly persuaded— delusive. The partakers in these things are now dropping off, called one after another to give in their account. Dear Christian would have her history recalled vividly to her by the return of the season when the Lord took her husband to Himself, blessing his soul with His own blessed light, and blessing her by showing that He had thus blessed him. " It is all light to me, the dark valley."

---

[1] George Macdonald died in the year following, and like his brother continued to the last in the assurance that the power by which the utterances was given was supernatural and divine. The narrative given by Dr. Norton of the last days of both brothers conveys a deep impression of the simplicity, humility, and fervour of their piety. That they both died so young, of the same disease which carried off Isabella Campbell, may so far account for the peculiarly vivid and ecstatic form which their piety at times assumed.

CHAPTER VIII.

Letters from 1835 till 1837.

AT the opening of the year 1835 the family at Lin-lathen consisted of Mr. Erskine, his mother, Captain and Mrs. Paterson, and their four children. Within the next two years four of these eight were removed by death: Ann Graham Paterson, the eldest of the children, died on the 3d of May 1835, in her thirteenth year; Mr. Erskine's mother on the 10th of March 1836; George Anna Pater-son, the second child of the family, on the 3d of June 1836 in her thirteenth year; and David Charles Paterson, the youngest child, on the 26th of October 1836.

94. TO MISS RACHEL ERSKINE.

LINLATHEN, 30*th April* 1835.

MY DEAR FRIEND,—About the time that I wrote you Ann's symptoms became worse, and have continued very bad, leading us to apprehend that it may be the will of our Father to take her hence. . . . The dear child seems aware of her situation, and further, she seems to hear her Father's voice, and to have some feeling of His nearness. Her affection for her earthly father, and her remarkable con-fidence in him and delight in his presence, seem given her to teach her what is due to the Father of her spirit. She said to her mother the other day, speaking of her father, " It is just life to me to see his face." . . . Lately when I visited the Duncans they took me to see a deaf and dumb

boy who knew Christ; he was dying in much pain and
much peace.   I had a little Psalter in my pocket, in which
I pointed out verses to him which he could read.   He was
much taken with the little book, so that I could not but
give it to him, although it was a present from a friend;
but he took it only for his lifetime, and it was returned to
me the other day, the dear boy having finished his warfare.
I was struck with his righteousness in reference to this
book.   Miss Duncan one day was going to mark a passage
that had refreshed him, but when he saw what she was
going to do he interposed his little hand, letting her know
that the book was only lent to him for his lifetime, and he
had no right to mark it.   He lived in a dirty hovel, but
his spirit was made pure and clean by the pure Spirit of
God, and this purity and cleanness of spirit kept everything clean about him.   The book, although it was always
in his hand, is as unsoiled as when he got it.   There is
something beautiful and touching in this. . . Ever yours,
                                                                T. E.

95. TO THE REV. ALEX. J. SCOTT.

LINLATHEN, *5th May* 1835.

MY DEAR SCOTT,—Our dear child is taken away.   Her
brief history, as far as this step goes, is concluded.   I feel
that Jesus has been doing that to us through her which He
so often did to His disciples.   He took a little child, and
set him in the midst of them.   The continual giving up of
a naturally very strong will was the lesson which he had
been continually giving her to learn, and which she did
learn, and she found it to be the entering in by the door
into the sheepfold.   Her heart was made glad with that
joy which no one taketh from her, and she departed in the
sense of that joy.   All the other children continue very ill
of the same malady, hooping-cough.   You will let Mrs.

Rich know, and Miss Farrer. At the last it seemed as if a ray of the eternal light filled her. She died on Sunday morning the 3d May.

I wish to know particularly about Mrs. Rich's health.— Yours affectionately,   T. ERSKINE.

96. TO MISS RACHEL ERSKINE.

LINLATHEN, *May* 1835.

DEAR COUSIN RACHEL,—I know how much you are all with us at this time. . . When I look at Ann's countenance, still radiant with that light which filled her spirit before she departed, I feel that I can desire nothing higher for the other children than that they should be partakers of the same blessedness. This is the sixth day since her death, and yet the face is most pleasing, as if to remind us where the spirit is. The parents are much supported, but it is a great breaking up. Ann was no common child. Her activity and friendship, and kindliness and zeal, brought her continually into the eye and thought of all the house, and how much more of her parents, who moreover had a constant anxiety about her in consequence of the fervour of her nature as well as of the delicacy of her frame. Yes, Henrietta was right: happy child—happy, happy, happy. Blessed be the God of all grace for His wonderful works to the children of men. But we can only receive the true comfort from the belief of her happiness, whilst we ourselves are living in the spirit of that blessedness. A mere name won't comfort under a real heart-break. Davie and the father must be touching that happiness in their own hearts if they would escape desolateness. My mother is pretty well, and Jane Stirling's presence has been a great blessing. She was a special favourite of Ann's, and Ann's loving heart rejoiced in the sight of her. Farewell.—Ever yours,

                                                T. ERSKINE.

97. TO MISS STUART.

LINLATHEN, *20th May* 1835.

MY DEAR COUSIN,—I am happy to say that all the children seem now decidedly better, but one is not, and the bereavement is perhaps more felt now, when the anxiety about the others is in a measure removed. And yet the remembrance of her is such that it would be most ungrateful not to give thanks to the Good Shepherd who had led and prepared her for Himself in the wilderness, and then when she was prepared took her into his own rest.— Yours affectionately,   T. ERSKINE.

98. TO MISS RACHEL ERSKINE.

LINLATHEN, *11th March* 1836.

DEAREST COUSIN RACHEL,—My beloved mother is dead. What a solemn event—to her, to us, to me! What a history it recalls, of kindness how unrequited, of offences so freely and fully forgiven! There is nothing so like our relation to God as our relation to a mother. There is none who has borne so much from us; there is none whose forgiveness we have looked upon so much as our due. Sweet mother, she is now looking so sweet, so undisturbed, so pure, sleeping in Jesus! I wish you or Cousin Manie would be so good as write a line to Maria, and to dear Lady Matilda, asking her to mention it to Lady Elgin. I hope Mrs. Graham is better. The tenure of life is uncertain. Our only reasonable business is to seek the kingdom of God and His righteousness; everything else is vanity. My best love to you, my beloved friend. Davie seems to me to feel this very sweetly; it has none of that bitterness which she felt in Ann's death, though it was a sweet death. Dear Christian does not yet apprehend any danger, but it is travelling towards her.—Yours affectionately, most affectionately,   T. ERSKINE.

99. TO THE REV. JOHN M'LEOD CAMPBELL.

LINLATHEN, *March* 14, 1836.

MY DEAR BROTHER,—When I parted from you the other day I little thought that the first letter I should write to you would be to tell you that my affectionate and revered parent was gone hence.

I think I had mentioned to you that she had had a slight inflammatory action on her windpipe, but I thought nothing of it, as the Patersons thought nothing of it, and yet it was the Lord's summons to her.

On Wednesday night for the first time they apprehended danger, and on Thursday morning at half-past seven she fell asleep.

My dear brother, I feel very thankful to be without fear concerning her soul. She was of a very nervous, agitated nature, and I had always the thought that the time of death might have been a very trying time to her, but the Lord gave her quietness of spirit, and delivered her from seeking refuge in those about her whom she loved, and taught her to lean upon Himself. My beloved mother has lived very much in the spirit of a little child, meek and lowly in heart, learning, I trust, from Jesus Himself, and most willing to learn from any one.

She has been to us, in her relation of mother, a most instructive type and witness of the love of God.

I feel in looking back that there is no one except God who has had to bear so much from me, or who has borne so much, and I feel that though I have often grieved her affection, I never could quench it. I can now think of her patience and long-suffering, and whilst I feel much self-reproach, I can bless God that He hath shown me so much of His own heart in her. Your dear father will feel this. I hope that he may find a blessing in the call to be ready and to trust in God, who saveth the poor and needy. As I look on her countenance, so pale and still and sweet, the history of my past life is brought much before me—the vanity of all things, the vain show. My sister bears it better than I expected. There is not so much bitterness of heart connected with this bereavement to her as there was in Ann's. It makes an immense change on the world to me. She was the recaller of past histories to me, in which my sisters had no concern even. Mrs. Erskine is with us, and Miss Stirling went to Cadder.

There are many things which, if it be the Lord's will that we again meet, I shall be happy to tell you of her. Farewell. Remember us before God.—Yours affectionately,

T. ERSKINE.

It is a bitter part of this to me that I was still in Edinburgh.

100. TO MRS. MACHAR.

LINLATHEN, *March* 29, 1836.

I KNOW the regard you had for my mother, and that you will feel as one of us at this time, and you will feel for me as being absent at the time, and having been all winter absent at Cadder, so that I had not seen my mother for a long while. I feel as if I had never known her value till now, nor my duty to her. My dear humble-minded affectionate mother! Loving relations are a great gift from God. There is something in the unweariedness of their love, and especially the love of a mother, that beautifully shows forth the heart of God; it is like nothing else. I had a place and possession in my mother's heart which no undeservingness ever put me out of. I never earned that place; God gave it me. I have often sinned against that love, and grieved it, but I never could quench it. My dear mother! The weary pilgrim is at rest in her Father's house. Her end was most peaceful. She saw the love of

God as a joyful rest and portion for ever, and she fell asleep
in Jesus. May the Lord ever comfort you under trial, and
make you to know the blessedness of being chastened by
the Lord. I often return to that word in Leviticus xxvi.
40, 41, 42 (containing the promise of God to those who
accept their punishment), as a very precious word. We are
always under punishment, and as accepting punishment in
love, we become partakers in the covenant of life. Adieu ;
pray for us.—Yours,   T. E.

101. TO MISS RACHEL ERSKINE.

CADDER, 13*th May* 1836.

DEAREST COUSIN RACHEL,—I don't think for many
years I have had so little intercourse with you as for these
few months past—these few months, crowded with so many
things. We have had to-night a note from Davie, dated
Monday last, containing rather better accounts of Georgie.
We don't feel much encouraged by them, however. She is
in her Father's tender hand, dear child, and nothing inconsistent with His fatherly love will ever befall her. That is
our encouragement, but I don't expect her recovery, and
it will be a bitter cup to her poor mother, whose nature
feels those things dreadfully.

I often feel that there is one heart that used to be
anxiously and actively interested in all these concerns that
has now entered into enduring peace. My dear mother is
at rest. I was happy to see dear cousin Manie at Airth.
I feel an increasing value for their loves and friendships,
which I never earned myself, but which were given to me
in my birth. I remember when the self-conceit of my
heart used to make a different estimate, but I have fully
come back to the unearned system.

102. TO MRS. BURNETT.

CADDER, 30*th May* 1836.

MY DEAR COUSIN,—We have had a painful interest continuing and growing here ever since I saw you. Davie's only surviving daughter had never fully recovered the shock that her constitution sustained last from the hooping-cough. They took her to London, not only with the idea of asking other advice, but with the thought of escaping our cold month of May, and being near Devonshire or some other more favourable climate. They consulted Dr. Clark, who very soon after he saw her told them frankly that he considered her case hopeless, and recommended them to bring her home. This is a very heavy stroke. . . .—Yours affectionately, T. E.

103. TO MISS RACHEL ERSKINE.

[LINLATHEN], *Sunday,* 5*th June* 1836.

MY DEAR COUSIN,—On Friday morning little Georgie was removed from the valley of the shadow of death, knowing and trusting her Leader and Shepherd. Her voyage home was less painful than they had expected; but from the time of her return home the progress of her disease was much more rapid than it had been before. She suffered much, both from pain and breathlessness, but she was kept in perfect patience and quietness of spirit; and the Lord showed her much of His fatherly heart, as He had done before to her sister, so that she was very ready and willing to trust herself alone into His hands.

Davie is very delicate, and the uninterrupted watching which she has gone through on this occasion has, I have no doubt, made a breach in her constitution. James (Capt. P.) is better than I expected. He takes his full share in all these things, you know, not only being a very loving father, but also very anxious to save Davie. They were thankful that they were left to themselves to nurse and attend Georgie; for she was so timid, that their two faces were the only faces that gave her no constraint.

Dear Davie is most sweet. I had hoped to have been to see you all by about this time, and I hope yet to see you. I hope to spend an eternity with you in the kingdom of our Father. . . .

104. TO MRS. BURNETT.

LINLATHEN, *5th June* 1836.

MY DEAR COUSIN,—On Tuesday morning the little sufferer ceased to suffer for ever. I believe that the desire of the heart of God toward the child has been largely accomplished. She knew Him, young as she was, and His love, and that shod her feet with the preparedness to walk any way that he called her to walk, though it was unto death. The parents are very down-broken, though comforted with unspeakable comfort. Little Georgie's two passages were Isaiah xli. 10 and xliii. 2. I send them to you. What strengthened her in crossing that mysterious boundary may strengthen you in the way which leads to it. The Lord be very near to you.—Yours most affectionately.

After Georgie's death the youngest child showing symptoms of delicacy, they took him to Clifton. In vain. He died there on the 26th October. Mr. Erskine was living at the time with his sister Mrs. Stirling.

105. TO MISS RACHEL ERSKINE.

CADDER, *Tuesday night, 25th October* 1836.

BELOVED COUSIN,—Our accounts to-day are that our little lamb is yet alive, but apparently very near his end. . . . On Saturday, which was the day they thought that dearest Daidie was dying, they at one time gave up the . . . applications, and told him that he was dying, and that he was going to God, who would make him good and happy;

and he sweetly answered, "Be good boy." Dear people,
they are in the furnace, and there it is where the Lord
purifies His gold. . . .

On hearing of Daidie's death Mr. Erskine and Mrs.
Stirling hastened to join their sister at Clifton. Leaving
Mrs. Stirling there, Mr. E. returned to Cadder, and shut himself up there in almost entire solitude, devoting himself to the
preparation of his work on Election, which was published
in London, and appeared before the end of the year.[1]

106. TO MISS RACHEL ERSKINE.

LONDON, *Thursday night* [*November* 1836].

BELOVED COUSIN RACHEL,—Here we have been safely
brought, through many troubles and difficulties, which, had
I been told of them before they actually happened, would
have appeared to me enough to have put Christian to death.
Our voyage, however, after it commenced, was very favourable, and Christian has suffered so little that she thinks
of setting off to-morrow morning at nine on the way to
Clifton, where we hope, by the mercy of God, to be on
Saturday. What a heart-break the death of that sweet
child is!—that son of consolation, as Davie called him—
given, as it seemed, to fill up so many blanks, himself taken
away. There were some very interesting particulars attending his death, dear lamb. . . .

107. TO MONSIEUR GAUSSEN.

CADDER, GLASGOW, 21*st Dec.* 1836.

DEAR FRIEND AND BROTHER,—I received your very
affectionate letter, relating to my mother's death, and felt
that it came from a brother's heart. I thank you for your
love, and I thank Him who is the fountain of love that He
hath taught you to love. O friend, let us seek to grow in
love by entering deeper into our Father's love towards us.

[1] See Appendix, No. X. p. 400.

That is the source, and we cannot get it otherwise than by receiving it from that Fountain. I answered your letter immediately, that is to say, I wrote an answer to it, but I did not send it. I find it difficult sometimes to write to you and Merle and Adolphe Monod, because I wish to say things to you all which require more explanations than a letter will allow, and more mixing of love with them than ink will express. If I were conscious of being able to stand unwaveringly in the love of Jesus towards you in conversing with you, I think that I should not delay many weeks to be with you in Geneva. I should like once more also to see your mother and Merle's, whose embrace to me, when I came from Hamburg, from the presence of *Le brave Henri*, I shall never forget. And now, since my own dear mother's departure, I feel my heart drawn to all mothers, and an obligation of reverence towards them all laid upon me for her sake, to whom I cannot any longer pay it, in the outward form.

You have heard probably from Mrs. Erskine before now of the death of another child of my sister, Mrs. Paterson, the sweetest and noblest little specimen of human nature that I ever saw. And this day the tidings of Lady Torphichen's death have reached me, without any particulars or detail, but generally in peace. . . .

As for dear ——, he wrote me a very long letter some months ago, which I have answered at considerable length. I would suggest to you that in intercourse with him his friends ought not to assume the impossibility, or even the improbability, of his thoughts. I mean that they ought not to take it for granted that he is mistaken—considering Mark xvi. 17, 18, is still unrevoked—but they should rather lead him to consider that, supposing that he really had supernatural gifts, yet after all they are only signs ($\sigma\eta\mu\epsilon\hat{\iota}\alpha$) of deeper and better and more important things. Dear friend, give my love to all our friends at Geneva. The grace of our Lord be with you. 　　　　　　T. ERSKINE.

108. TO HIS SISTER MRS. STIRLING.

[*Dec.* 1836.]

MY BELOVED CHRISTIAN,—It is wonderful how very little real use we make of Christianity. It would seem that we had agreed together to say that God loves us better than a mother does her sucking child, and that He orders even the minutest circumstance of our lives in accordance with that love; but that in fact we do not believe it, inasmuch as we welcome the events of life, not on the ground of their being all appointed by the wise love of God, but because they are agreeable to our flesh. " Who hath believed our report ?"

When the inmates of a cottage separate in the morning, to go about their different avocations, knowing that it is only by the profits arising from these that they are enabled to meet comfortably in the evening, they do not separate in sorrow, but in the joyful hope of meeting in the evening better provided in what is necessary for their domestic comfort and *ménage* than they are now. They know that the separation and the work must go before the meeting and the enjoyment, and lead to them. My dear sister, let us seek to realise indeed that we are at this moment in God's school, and that the things which are befalling us are the lessons which He is Himself giving us, because He sees that we need them; and let us further realise that if we neglect these lessons, either by despising them or by fainting under them, we are throwing away eternal life for our souls, and we are grieving the fatherly heart of our Teacher, who knows that He has given us the right lesson, but sees that we will not take it nor profit by it. " Blessed is the man who receiveth instruction."

What is the use of all our reading and writing and speaking and thinking about God, and His love, and His care over us, if we are to see in an affliction nothing more than the distress which it brings? There is something else in the affliction besides this distress, and that something is God's love and eternal life. And the only use of all our reading, etc., is to fix our attention on this which is enclosed within the affliction, instead of having it engrossed by the envelope—the outward form in which God sends it.

"Behold, I bring evil upon all flesh, saith the Lord." We must make up our minds to this, and not merely as to a thing which we cannot resist, but as to a thing right and good, and as being the only way into a true enduring spiritual happiness.

Let us not sink in the torpor of grief, because God is doing what He has said, namely, bringing evil upon all flesh ; but take the prey which He gives us, under it all and through it all, namely, our life, our eternal life.

Lady Torphichen.—There have been two persons taken from each of the three generations into which the Airth family is divided, since March—my mother and uncle Tom, William Macdowal and Margaret Stirling, Georgie and Daidie Paterson. And they have gone in peace, all of them. And God it was who measured to each of them the fit and proper duration of life here ; and shall we differ in opinion or feeling from Him? Would Davie like that her Georgie and Daidie should have gone through what Lady Tor and uncle Tom went through? or does she not see that tender love ordered the lot of her darlings?

With all this, I am convinced that creatures composed as we are require (in order to our being in a proper healthy condition) both exercise of our mental and of our bodily faculties, and that a morbid state necessarily results from the disuse of such exercise : Knox's and Jebb's correspondence has often made me feel the truth of this. You ought to have some regular reading aloud, in which you may all associate. I shall send up these books to you by the box; and, in the meantime, you might get Smith's Select Discourses, one of the books much praised by both Knox and Jebb, and I believe edited by the latter. If James could get a Lucas on Happiness in that old shop, he might buy it for me, and you might find some interest in it. I have bought a *St. Augustine,* so I shall not need that now. . .

109. TO JAMES MACKENZIE, ESQ.[1]

CADDER, *2d Jan.* 1837.

SIGNORE GENTILISSIMO,—I often wish your presence here, my dear friend; and I sometimes wonder how two people, so little bound to any one particular spot, as you and I appear to be, by any outward reason, should see so little of each other, when I believe we both wish to see much more. I can at least say for myself that I wish to see much more of you than I do. I am getting into habits of great seclusion, and I feel them growing upon me, so that the *besoin* of human intercourse is becoming very weak, which makes me sometimes wish a friend's face, not merely to gratify an affection, but to break a habit and awaken a torpid faculty.

I found my friends at Clifton very much dejected, and surely it is not to be wondered at, for the Lord has made them very desolate. They were full, and He has made them empty. My mother's death was a great bereavement to my sister; and then her sweet, intelligent, sociable, honest girls; and then that loveliest infant, the most glorious thing I ever saw; his motions and sounds were all perfect beauty and harmony, and joy and liberty; his *parolettes*

---

[1] Son of Henry Mackenzie, author of "The Man of Feeling," etc., and brother of Lord Mackenzie and the Right Honourable Holt Mackenzie.

are always ringing in his mother's ears, for he had his own name for everything.

The voice of one crying in the wilderness, "Prepare the way of the Lord;" and what is the preparation? "All flesh is grass, and all the glory of man as the flower of grass." It is the true practical knowledge of that which prepares the way of the Lord into each individual heart. What has the world to offer us, but grass, which withereth? So let us e'en lay it aside and leave it, and take the Lord as our portion, for He faileth never. On the contrary, the more He is needed, the more helpful is He found to be. When flesh and heart fail, God is the strength of the heart and the portion for ever.

Another year has passed away with those beyond the flood. I begin to feel very old, and very near death. We shall soon see death. Let us have our loins girt, and our lamps burning, and have oil in our vessels with our lamps, that when the Bridegroom cometh we may be ready to go out to meet Him.

Write to me, my dear Mackenzie, and say that you are coming out. I will keep you as warm as a pie here. I know that you have a good cloak to come in. I heard from David Dow the other day; he is thinking of going to America for a year. There is something very strange in our present ecclesiastical condition—such a variety of sects and forms, that I do not wonder at those who feel a Church to be a necessary part of their religion going into some old well-established order of things like Popery, in order to escape from the confusion. I am thankful that, though I believe the inquiry after a Church to be most important, I do not feel it to be vital or essential. The Church of England is a good quiet orderly system. I have been reading lately the correspondence of Jebb, Bishop of Limerick, and a Mr. Knox of Dublin, in which there are many most in-

teresting things. If you happen to fall in with it I am
sure you would like it. I have plenty of books, if you will
come to me; and you will bring your own book; and your
Great Teacher is here, as well as in Edinburgh. . . . Let
me hear from you saying that the cloak is safe, and that
you are going to let me see it soon again cosying its own
proper lord.—Farewell, dear, very dear friend.

T. ERSKINE.

110. TO HIS SISTER MRS. STIRLING.

CADDER, *12th January* 1837.

MY DEAREST CHRISTIAN,— . . . Will James ask Strong if
he could get me a Chrysostom, the Benedictine edition. . . .
You will find Smith most interesting, but your ignorance
of Greek and Latin and Hebrew must interfere very much
with your enjoyment of him. I almost wonder that, considering what is under the lock and key of these languages,
you do not make the attempt. I read the Hebrew Bible
with greater ease now; I am reading Genesis—what a
wonderful history! What an impression it leaves of there
being something under that simplicity of an immense magni-
tude and depth. This is your season of the year. Your
remembrance of life and death and immortality are written
on all the days of the month. . . . Most affectionately
yours,   T. E.

111. TO MRS. BURNETT.

CADDER, *15th February* 1837.

DEAR FRIEND,—During this time of prevalent sickness
and mortality I have often travelled in thought to —— to
inquire how all there were, especially as the last accounts
that I had were that you had been a good deal anxious
about ——. I hope you will not be long of letting me
hear about you. For though I know the Hand that you
are in, yet I wish to know what the lesson is that He is
teaching you at present, that I may sympathise with you

and learn with you. We straiten our own spiritual education within limits which God never intended, when we confine our learning to His dealings with ourselves personally, instead of partaking in the schooling of others, which, if it did nothing else, would exercise and increase the spirit of love. I have often intended to write more to you about accepting our punishment. I shall try a little now. It seems to me clearly the meaning of the Bible that the great things which Jesus Christ has done for us, namely, His coming into our flesh, and suffering and dying for us, are only then properly and fully beneficial to us when they are in a measure wrought and reproduced in our hearts by His Spirit within us. Thus, though He has tasted death by the grace of God for every man, yet those only who are conformed to His death have the full blessing. And although it is the blood of Christ that cleanseth from all sin, it is only when that blood is sprinkled on the conscience of an individual that that individual is purged by it, so that he is fit to serve the living God—Rom. vi. 5-8; Heb. ix. 14-22. There is one passage on the subject that I would particularly direct your attention to at present, Phil. iii. 9, 10, in which the true righteousness is described—the righteousness which is of God by faith. Now, the main point of this righteousness consists in being made conformable to Christ's death. Now, what was Christ's death? It was a willing surrender of Himself into the hands of the Father, knowing at the same time that it was the Father's pleasure to bruise Him. It was a willing pouring out of all the hopes of the flesh founded on the idea of the continuance of present things; it was an acknowledgment of the righteousness of the judgment of sorrow and death, which, on account of transgression, God had laid on the flesh of which He had become a partaker. And at the same time, while it was a surrender of Himself in filial confidence into His

Father's hands, it was also in full assurance that He was to be gloriously rewarded, by being raised triumphantly from the dead as the new Head and Fountain of life to the Race, by taking hold of whom every child of Adam might be saved. . . .

And what is the meaning of all these beatitudes, through the Old and New Testament, on them who receive the Lord's chastening, who receive His reproof, His instruction (taking the word *receive* in the sense of *accept*, which it evidently bears in many places, as in John i. 12), but beatitudes on those in whom the outward work of atonement is wrought inwardly by the spirit of Christ received inwardly? I may refer to the Proverbs from beginning to end, and to the Psalms also, but see especially xciv. 12, the Sermon on the Mount, also Matt. x. 38, 39, etc., Luke vi., and xiv. 26, 27, and all such passages. This is what I mean by accepting punishment. The Paschal Lamb was truly and properly one : Christ our Passover is slain. But yet it was to be slain in each house of Israel : mark that.

Dear friend, you little can understand how often I think of you. You represent to me your father's house and your grandfather's ; and now whilst I am preparing for the press, I never sit down to write without thinking of the most affectionate heart that ever beat. After a small number sacredly related to me, I feel your father's friendship cleave closest to my heart.

I hope you will understand what I have written, but you will need to read it over twice to do so—not that it is difficult, but that it differs from common teaching.

112. TO HIS SISTER MRS. STIRLING.

CADDER, *29th March* 1837.

MY DEAR CHRISTIAN,—You will feel very solitary after the departure of your companions, dear Davie and her husband and Jemmy; and I know that, although you may easily perhaps get another inmate, you will not easily get another heart such as that one, into which you may pour yours, and out of which you may receive into yours. But there is one—little as it is known—which is the loving Fountain, from which all such hearts as hers are supplied, and which, with all its greatness and majesty, is more tender than even the tenderest, and more capable of entering into the untellable things which are known to each as a burden, in which no brother but He can share. . . .—Your affectionate brother,   T. ERSKINE.

113. TO THE REV. ALEX. J. SCOTT.

CADDER, 21*st April* 1837.

MY DEAR FRIEND,—I am much obliged to Mr. Maurice for sending me these letters,[1] which contain much precious matter. I do not think I ever saw an example of so high an appreciation of objective and formal Christianity joined with such a true sense of the value of what is subjective. In fact, no one can value the objective correctly who does not know the value of the subjective; for it is the subjective only that is valuable, and the other is valuable as conducting to it. I ought to have written to you long ago. Your letter to me whilst I was yet at Clifton was very interesting to me, and I am happy to think that the same perception (and sensation too) of the power and life of the argument of the Epistle to the Romans is still continuing with you, as I judge from my sister's account of the Sunday that they passed at Woolwich.

I am getting on very slowly with my work, but I am getting on. I often feel fettered by not feeling myself permitted more plainly and fully to introduce the final purpose of God towards all men, as the explanation of His

---

[1] Forming the volume on *The Kingdom of Christ*.

present dealings with them. For instance, I am at this
moment at the expression, "Shall the thing formed say to
Him that formed it?" etc. Now I believe that this word
is intended as a general reference to the 29th chapter of
Isaiah (which speaks of the punishment of Israel, and the
sin which was the cause of it), where something like it
appears at verse 16, and that there is a twofold meaning
intended. 1st, Wilt thou think of blinding God with thy
vain reasonings, as thou wouldst do to one of thy fellow-
creatures, forgetting that thy Maker sees in thee that which
thou thyself art conscious of, namely, that thou hast been
living in a resistance to His will? Shall the thing formed
speak a lie to him who knows all about it? And secondly,
And now that thou hast corrupted thyself, wilt thou dispute
with thy Creator about the best way of dealing with thee
for purging thee and bringing thee back? The end of
chapter xxviii. belongs to the same subject, indeed the
whole chapter. The Potter in Jeremiah xviii. is to the
same purpose. With what perfect confidence can we look
upon men lying in the hand of God, even whilst He is
acting towards them as an executioner! If we really recognise as true that "all the fruit is to take away sin," and
that finally this fruit shall assuredly appear. The stoppage
of the process for the individual, whilst it is going on only
for the race, is a heart-breaking thought.

I have been living perfectly alone since ever I returned
from Clifton. I took influenza almost immediately, and
have been confined a tolerably close prisoner till the present
time, in a house full of remembrances and shadows, but
inhabited only by myself and two or three servants, with
whom I have the fellowship of great kindness. I have been
reading Plato with immense interest and astonishment. In
Gorgias I find the doctrine of the atonement in its principle
applied to the conscience, better than in any religious book I

ever read. I mean the principle of " accepting punishment," which is the *fond* of the doctrine. I have also been reading Augustine with pleasure, and finding in him not only living water, but also many things in his forms of thought and interpretation, much more real and less conventional than the system of those who have built upon his foundation.

After being so long myself of writing to you, it is scarcely reasonable to press for a letter, but if you knew how much I value your letters, you would not grudge me them, especially in my present loneliness. Will you give my affectionate fraternal regards to your sister and Mrs. Scott, and thank Mr. Maurice for me. From what I heard in a Quaker church which I went to in my way down from Clifton, I could suppose that the seceding or evangelical party amongst them are very truly described by Mr. Maurice, and are in fact conventionalists, to a certain degree at least.—Yours affectionately,   T. ERSKINE.

114. TO HIS SISTER MRS. STIRLING.

CADDER, 2*d May* 1837.

DEAR CHRISTIAN,—How fast the months pass away! Here is May again. To-morrow it will be two years since I led my mother up-stairs to see our dear Ann P. enter into glory; and the following day it will be thirty-three years since our sister Ann had her bonds loosed.

Our fathers—where are they "He hath concluded all under unbelief, that He might have mercy on all." Wonderful words! describing the working of Him whose name is Wonderful, Counsellor. . . .

115. TO THE SAME.

CADDER, *Friday, 23d June* 1837.

. . . I propose, as soon as I have finished my book and received Davie home, to go south. I am writing my con-clusion, and I find it very difficult to say what I wish to say, without giving more offence than is necessary. From the way in which the first half of the book was written—by fits and starts—I am afraid that it will have very great faults as a work. It is also deficient in arrangement and in proportion; which will make it drag in the reading, to all except those who are really interested in the subject. And then it is, throughout, in direct opposition to the received views of Christianity. So that I cannot doubt but that the most truly religious people in the land will be startled, and even shocked, by many things in it. And then there is not a break or a chapter in the whole book; it goes on as if in one sentence, through 550 pages; which of itself would make even the most interesting book heavy and dull. . . .

Did you ever see such delicious weather? It is like the weather of our youth, which seems to me always to have been far superior to anything that I have experienced since. I remember the last vacation that James and I spent at Cardross with our little dog Jemmy. I had not been well, and we came out before the regular time; they were cutting the lawn for hay, and I remember my uncle and aunt walking amongst the hay-makers, looking so kind and so venerable, and so much loved and so much honoured. . . .

116. TO THE SAME.

CADDER, 28th July 1837.

MY DEAREST CHRISTIAN,—. . . Yesterday I read an article in a late Number of the *Quarterly* on Cathedral Establishments. It is written by one who is both a sweet singer and a wise man of Babylon. There is much in it which Burke himself might have written; but it proves that, although the views and intentions of the Church party are most disinterested and patriotic—and religious, I may add,—yet these views are most markedly confined to the

improvement of the flesh, and the building up of the
national character, by the outward operation of institutions.
The Church of England is a beautiful thing, but it is very
unlike the carpenter's Son and the fishermen of Galilee.
In these latter was exhibited the power of spiritual truth,
and of faith, which, in the absence of all outward support,
took hold of God.   In the former there is a wise and well-
proportioned combination of outward supports.   And
accordingly the advocates of the Church of England always
go back to the Jewish theocracy as their model, forgetting
that that was a type of the spirit rising out of the crucified
flesh.   And yet, as a political event, I should regard the
overthrow of the Church of England as the opening of
floodgates to let the universal confusion on the nation.
The Lord is our shepherd, we shall not lack. . . .—Most
affectionately yours,   T. E.

117. TO THE REV. A. J. SCOTT.

CADDER, *3d August* 1837.

MY DEAR FRIEND,—I have received a request from a
friend of mine in Geneva, who is engaged in compiling a
History of the Reformation, to send him some books on the
subject of the Reformation in England and Scotland.   The
man who wants them is Merle, one whom I love much.
Mrs. Rich knows him under the name of " *Mon brave
Henri,*" and I should like well to put something in his
hands which would really help him in this matter. . . .

I have met with a striking passage in a preface to some
treatises of Dr. H. More of Cambridge, relating to "Divine
Sagacity, a principle antecedaneous to successful reason in
contemplations of the highest concernment.   A principle
more noble and inward than reason itself, and without
which reason will falter, or at least reach but to mean and
frivolous things."   "I have a sense of something in me

while I thus speak, which, I must confess, is of so retruse a nature that I want a name for it, unless I adventure to term it Divine Sagacity, which is the first rise of successful reason, and without which a man is, as it were, in a thick wood, and may make infinite promising attempts, but can find no open champaign where one may freely look about him every way τὸ πεδίον τῆς ἀληθείας.

"It is with us as in the universe, for it is the same *numen* in us that moves all things, and the beginning of reason is not reason, but something better." Your quotation from Whewell was recalled to me by this. Give my affectionate regards to your sister. Let me hear how she is. Is she taking hold of that strength which is peace to those who hold it? Is she looking to the end of the way, and through confidence in the wisdom of the Guide, already by anticipation consciously recognising the suitableness of the way to the end? This is the time of the blood-shedding, and salvation is through faith during, and in the purpose of, the blood-shedding. What a wonderful outward diversity there is in our lots!

Farewell, dear friends.—Yours most truly and affectionately,   T. ERSKINE.

CHAPTER IX.

Letters of Sympathy and Consolation.

118. TO MRS. MONTAGU.

LINLATHEN, DUNDEE, 23*d August* 1825.

MAY the Lord Himself be your comforter and your joy, my dear Mrs. Montagu. Spiritual comfort is to be sought and (blessed be His name) is to be found in Him. He is the fountain, and He says Himself: Ho, every one that thirsteth, come to this fountain. But it is not flesh and blood that can show us the way to that fountain. He will for this also be inquired of by us.

Among many causes which intercept or interrupt spiritual joy, I think that there is one which is not generally attended to, and it is this, we sometimes make it too much our object. If we do anything in religion, as well as in worldly pursuits, with the direct purpose of being happy, we are almost sure of disappointment. A general view of happiness connected with the favour of God is what the Scripture holds out to us ; but if the happiness occupies our desires more than the will of God, we shall find our loss in it. We must seek duty rather than happiness ; we must seek to please God rather than to have spiritual enjoyments. This is the safe road. What wilt thou have me to do or suffer ? We are in the wilderness, my dear sister, and our business is to follow the pillar of fire. This is all our business. Let us spare our anxious hearts a needless care. Oh what a quiet peaceful walk it would be were we fully faithful to our pillar! The Lord is my light and my salvation, my pillar of fire that gives me guidance and assures me safety; whom shall I fear? Oh, it is easy to write or say this. May the Lord put His fear in our hearts, that we depart not from Him—His fear, not the fear of Him, but the fear of losing Him, and so losing ourselves.

119. TO MADAME VERNET.

4th June 1825.

MY DEAR FRIEND,—Though I feel that the voice of human consolation is absolutely nothing in a grief like yours, yet I cannot but express to you how deeply I condole with you, and how earnestly I desire for you that He who alone can comfort may comfort you and your mourning family, and sanctify to you this solemn and heartrending event. "Be still and know that I am God." Within a month God has taken from you your father and your son, but it is God—the God of love, the God who so loved the world as to give His only-begotten Son to die for it. Let your wounded spirit rest on this. Here is a balm for the broken heart. Take refuge in God. Abide in Him. Trust in Him and you shall not be disappointed or confounded. He who restored to life the son of the widow at Nain (Luke vii.) was standing by your son at the awful moment, and ordered every circumstance. He loved your son as He loved the son of that widow, and if it were good for him and for you, would restore him as He did the other. He loved your son, for He made him and died for him, and He says to you as He did to that mourning mother, "Weep not." Oh, what a word is that, coming from the heart of omnipotent love! Oh, may He graciously speak to you Himself, and say, "Be of good cheer, it is I; be not afraid. Daughter, be of good cheer, thy sins are forgiven thee."

And may He open the ears of your heart, that you may hear His voice and feel the sweetness and the power of His consolation. Trust your son with unhesitating confidence in the hands of our Lord Jesus Christ; His hands are kind and tender hands. Your affection for your son is only a faint shadow of the fatherly love of God. Leave, then, all your anxieties in regard to him with God, and receive this event as an invitation to yourself and your family to enter into a closer communion with Him. I know that I cannot enter fully into the feelings of a mother, but I am persuaded that there is not a pang the heart can endure which may not, by the blessing of God, become the seed of holiness and happiness. Our way to the heavenly city lies through a wilderness, through a vale of tears, and our Master walked this road before us. He was a man of sorrows and acquainted with grief whilst on earth, and now He reigns in the blessedness of God. This double inheritance He leaves to His people : " If we suffer with Him, we shall also reign with Him."

Oh, my dear friend, my heart bleeds for you, although I know that all things work together for good to those who love God. And your husband—may the Holy Spirit, the Comforter, show to his soul the unspeakable love of Christ, and turn his natural sorrow into spiritual joy. And your other children, may they all seek and find a brother in their Saviour. God's end in afflicting is to draw us to Himself and to make us partakers of His holiness (Heb. xii.), to show us the vanity and insufficiency of created things, and thus to lead us to choose Himself for our portion. Nothing can separate us from His love. Oh, precious words! Let, then, this love be the great desire and perpetual prayer of our souls. Let the language of our heart be, " Whom have we in heaven but Thee? and there is none upon earth that we desire beside Thee."

"Give what Thou canst; without Thee we are poor,
And with Thee rich, take what Thou wilt away."

God is all. We are His. He ought to be the first and the last in our hearts. Let Him then take His great power and reign within us. This alone is peace; this alone is heaven. I beg to be remembered by you all as a friend who is willing to weep with you, though he cannot comfort you.

120. TO MADAME VERNET.

May 1828.

. . . . I have spent my day with mourners of no common kind. I meet many mourners, but I have rarely met with a more touching grief than theirs. Their names are Mr. and Mrs. Boswell.[1] He is one of my earliest acquaintances, though there has been friendship between us only for the last few years. His wife has been long a much-loved friend of my sister-in-law. They were in Edinburgh a few days ago, and spent some time with us to our great satisfaction. They then went into the country. In less than a week after we had seen them, we heard a report that Mrs. B. had fallen from her horse, and had sustained a serious injury. I went immediately to them, and found that the case was as bad as possible : the injury was on the head, she had suffered a concussion of the brain, and from the moment of the fall to that time she had been almost entirely insensible. He had carried her motionless and senseless to the nearest cottage, and there she had lain ever since with scarcely a ray of hope of recovery. When I came in he took me by the hand, and said to me, "Her soul is safe, blessed be God. I am satisfied that death will be to her a great gain, and I feel I need this blow. I have been at a distance from God of

[1] Of Balmuto, near Kirkcaldy.

late, and occupied more with the gifts than the Giver, and
it is thus that He chastens me, to draw me back to Himself, and at the same time calls her ripened spirit to glory."
I felt then the supernatural power of the gospel ; it brings
the strength of God to the support of man.   Mr. B. told
me that he was quite satisfied when the event took place,
that God would enable him to resign himself entirely to
the wisdom and love that orders all things, but that, in the
meantime, he felt very anxious and agitated, whilst it was
yet undetermined.   I went to him again to-day, and I saw
her ; she was a sweet and true and humble follower of the
Lamb.   Oh, how her outward form was changed ! and how
full of consolation did that conviction appear to me that her
soul is safe, she is in the Ark ; the storms may rage, but
nothing can hurt her ; she is a branch of the true vine, she
has rested her soul on the love of God in Christ Jesus.
Yes, there is a reality in the things of religion, and all
other things are shadows.   God is really near to those who
trust in Him, and puts light into their souls even when
everything around them looks dark.   I am persuaded that
God speaks peace within her even now when all the powers
of her mind seem suspended.   She has a calm upon her,
unlike an earthly calm : it is a gift from a Father to a
child.   Oh, how sweet everything is, which is felt to come
from Him !   She knew me when I entered, and stretched
out her hand to me, though she could not articulate any
words.   It was an overwhelming spectacle ; there was
the   husband, and   there   were   brothers   and   sisters
weeping, and there was another there, whom our eyes of
flesh saw not, who partook of the affliction, and who, I trust,
will sanctify it to all our souls.   My dear friend, you are
a mourner.   I tell you this story, as a story of your own
family, for they are your brothers and sisters in Christ,
and in sorrow, and in hope.

Madame writes that she is much alone, and it is perhaps good for her to be alone. The real teacher is the Spirit of God; man darkens counsel by words without knowledge, and the heart that would learn from God must be alone with God. He is the only teacher, as He is the only portion of the soul. And how prone is the poor blind soul to go after other teachers, and other portions; and thus to cast away the only good of which it is capable, —the pearl of great price. Atheism is deeply rooted in the corrupt nature of man. Don't you feel it so? It seems a strange question. Do you believe in a God?—and yet how few do believe this simple truth to any practical effect! No man really believes in God until God reveals Himself to his soul. He says, "Look unto me and be ye saved, all ye ends of the earth." Yet who looks? I wonder at myself, and at my fellow-creatures, that we should in the midst of our sins and sorrows, have heard of the love of God in giving His own Son for us, as a sufficient and almighty deliverer from sins and sorrows, and that, after having heard this, we should have our thoughts occupied by anything else except this condescending goodness, and this great salvation. Surely if we believed it, our hearts would be filled by it,—what else is there for us to care about or think about? We are on the borders of eternity, and everything which is not eternal is unworthy of our occupation. I rejoice in your nearness to God, and in His nearness to you and to your dear daughter; and I desire with my whole soul to bless Him for that precious truth which He has revealed to us in the gospel, even that He hath loved us with an everlasting love—that He hath taken upon Himself our nature and the burden of our transgressions, that we might be cleansed from guilt, and that we might be persuaded to confide in Him, and to cast ourselves and our concerns for time and for eternity on

His fatherly care, that we may walk with Him in peace through this wilderness, and live with Him in eternal glory hereafter. You say that M. suffers in the presence of her God and at the feet of her Saviour. Blessed be His holy name for the grace given unto her, for in His presence darkness becomes light, and crooked things straight. A few hours will level all distinctions, as a poor dying friend of mine said the other day ; they will level all small passing distinctions of earthly joy and earthly sorrow, and they will establish the great distinction between the children of light and the children of darkness ; and even now we in some measure enter into eternity when we feel ourselves in the presence of our God : " Thou art my hiding-place !" Oh what a hiding-place ! There may be loud storms and boisterous waves without, but in that hiding-place there is peace—a peace passing understanding. This is the substantial reality,—my God loves me,—His arms at this moment support me,—His kindness at this moment cheers my heart. . . .

Let us live on the brink of eternity, waiting the coming of our Lord, for He will come and will not delay ; and until He calls us hence, let us learn to know His voice as He speaks to us in His word and in His providence. We make great distinctions amongst events and duties, we call some important and others trifling ; but God is in every one of them, and where He is nothing can be trifling, all is full of deep and solemn interest, because all is full of God : "Open thy mouth wide and I will fill it" (Ps. lxxxi. 11). Lord, open thou the mouths of our hearts and feed us with thine own love,—with Thyself, thou art the bread of life. Dear friend, may the presence of God be your dwelling-place. May He shine on your soul and be to you a sun, and a shield, and a fountain of living waters. I think of you all daily when I look up to my God, and then I think of

the balm that is in Gilead, and of the Physician that is
there, and how He was anointed expressly to bind up the
broken-hearted, and to comfort all who mourn. May He
teach you with a deeper conviction that no created good
can be the portion of the soul. . . It is such a comfort to
me, in thinking of your distresses, to remember that you
know why distresses are sent, and that you can pray and
open your heart to God and stay yourself upon Him. We
all acknowledge and believe that God gives help, and yet
we often remain unhelped. God gives, but man often loses
the benefit of the gift by not knowing how to receive it.
We may have just thoughts and striking thoughts of God's
love to us, and of His will to help us, and yet in the hour
of trial we may find that we had been deluding ourselves
with thoughts instead of faith and principles, amusing our
fancies instead of feeding our souls. We need humility
and meekness, and the spirit of affectionate clinging dependence. This is the spirit in which alone we can receive
God's help. "The scorner seeketh wisdom and findeth it
not,"—it is a solemn word, he seeks wisdom and he seeks it
in vain, because he is not a humble receiver, but would
draw his wisdom from himself, he is a scorner. There is
another also who seeks wisdom, who wishes to be wise and
good, and wishes in vain, " L'âme du paresseux ne fait que
souhaiter et il n'a rien, mais l'âme du diligent sera en-
graissée." These words are to be kept in mind when we
read, "Ask and ye shall receive, seek and ye shall find."
We may ask and seek in a wrong way, proudly or indo-
lently, and then we ask and seek in vain. What a fearful thing it is to exclude ourselves by the sin of our hearts
from that largest promise, "Seek and ye shall find." By
thinking, men in general mean something very like talking
to themselves, whereas the true thinking is listening to
God's voice,—" Écoute, et ton âme vivra." God's desire for

us is, not that we should have thoughts on holiness, but that we should be holy, and so life is God's plan of education to train us in holiness—to train us to have to do with Him in everything, and to see and love and choose His will in everything. *Habite la terre et nourris toi de la vérité,*—there is a will of God revealed to us in everything which is truth, the manna of the wilderness,—*le pain quotidien* which our Lord teaches us to ask, the bread that cometh down from heaven from our Father.

Oh what an unspeakable difference there is often between the practical will and the theoretical will! Every man approves of that which is right, and even chooses it, whilst it is at a distance, and demands no sacrifice from him ; but when it is close to him and demands the sacrifice of his humour or pride or self-will in any form, then is the trial. He whose true desire it is to get free from pride and humour and self-will will welcome the call, *et regardera comme un sujet de joie d'être exposé à une telle épreuve,* whilst the mere speculator will carry his theory with him, but will refuse to take up his cross and follow Jesus. Man is always standing, like the ass which the disciples of Jesus were sent for, at a place where two ways meet, and these ways are the broad way and the narrow way—he is always in the one or the other, but he may always go by a single step out of the one into the other ; they are near each other, separated only by a will. . . .

It comes very near to my frequent experience, the danger of substituting knowing good for being good. . . .

How precious is the love of God! Well may our souls say with David, "Thou art my portion, O Lord!" It is this love that sweetens all other loves, even to those who do not perceive it, nor apprehend its presence ; but whether perceived or not, it is there, giving an idea of something above self, and above perishing flesh,

even to those who seem to be following a mere natural
impulse. The very husks which the swine do eat, and
which the prodigals of the earth devour so greedily, are
yet flavoured by His heavenly presence. Oh, why should
any one be content to take the husk when the love of God,
that food of angels, that meat of Jesus Himself, is given to
us, contained in the husk! But spiritual things are only
spiritually discerned, and if we live not in the spirit, we
must take the husks alone, rejecting that which the husks
contain. How common is this sin, this folly, even in the
children of the kingdom, who have learnt to know their
Father's voice in some measure! Every event of life, every
circumstance of our lot, is a husk containing precious food,
—instruction in righteousness, communion with Jesus,—
and yet how much of life we receive as a mere husk, without
seeking for or receiving the hidden sweetness! Is it not
overwhelming to think how the Father's heart must be
grieved by this stupid and miserable carnality in His children, which shuts them out of so much profit and enjoyment to their souls!

121. TO MISS RACHEL ERSKINE.

2d May 1828, 12 *o'clock.*

MY DEAR, DEAR COUSIN RACHEL,—. . . I have seen
Mrs. Boswell,—a sweet sight. She told me that she could
neither think nor speak much, but "I have had one great
mercy," she said; "when my friends thought that I was
suffering a great deal, I was suffering nothing, but on the
contrary I was enjoying a great deal. The presence of
the Saviour was always with me, and the impression of
the last time I was at the Lord's Supper, when my husband was on one side and my brother on the other."
This was at a time when she seemed perfectly shut
against all impressions except pain, when her mind could

not act at all ; but God was with her, and when no other
voice could reach her He spoke a word of peace into her
heart. Gracious Father ! He had made her, and He could
comfort her. Yea, He did comfort her—He did her no
hurt. I cannot tell you how much this demonstration of
divine tenderness has struck me. Oh that it might strike
deep roots and bear fruits of humble confiding love ! I
don't remember whether or not I mentioned to you another
circumstance with regard to her. When her mind first
began to return, her maid read to her some psalm, and
when some of the family came in afterwards, she said,
"—— has been reading something to me out of some
book. I don't know what it was, but it has been a great
comfort to me." How many people know what they read,
but get no comfort ! She did not know what was read, but
she got comfort. Had she not the better portion ? Oh
this boasted intellect has little to do with God or comfort.
On the contrary, it seems to me a drawback. The principle
by which the creature knows the Creator is not intellect,
it is something much higher and much deeper. It is, I
believe, nothing else than the spirit of God in man that
knows God. It is the gift of God—the free unearned gift
of God. " Open thy mouth wide, and I will fill it." May
the Lord open our hearts and pour in the blessing abundantly !

122. TO MADAME DE STAËL.[1]

January 1828.

WHAT can I say to you but that the Lord hath done it ?
His hand has been heavy on you, but, blessed be His name,
He has revealed His love to you, and has spoken comfortably to your soul. Affliction is a sacred enclosure, where
the soul may meet God alone ; and there I trust He has

---

[1] On the death of her husband.

met with your soul, and told you things which flesh and
blood could not tell you. He has promised His presence at
all times to His people, but in a special manner when they
are passing through the waters of affliction. Let us pray,
"Teach us Thy paths, O Lord, and do Thou lead us in
them." What a wonderful path He has led you this last
year! You had no thought of it as you were entering upon
it fifteen months ago, but God had thought of it and had
planned it. He saw it then. His purpose no doubt was
to draw your soul to Himself—to make you feel the emptiness of the creature, and to teach you that He is Himself
the only satisfying portion of the soul. This is His path;
He gave you the best earthly gift—a faithful friend—a
friend to your soul—and He hath taken him from you, after
your heart had been knit to him. He prepared him for
the inheritance of the saints in light, and then He called
him to enter on his inheritance, and thus delivered him
from an ensnaring and disappointing and polluting world,
by the same blow which made the world a desert to you.

Oh, do you think that He who wept at the grave of Lazarus
looked on your affliction unmoved? No, no; His heart is
a heart of tenderness, and you have heard the voice of His
consolation within your heart, "I have chosen you in the
furnace of affliction." May the good Lord bless you and
comfort you, and sanctify unto you this heavy stroke, and
may He be a Father to your child, and lead you both safe
to the heavenly country, where the whole family of God
shall meet again, never more to part. Oh that the eyes
and ears of our souls were opened that we might see and
hear our God in everything—that we might love Him in
our friends, and hear His voice in every event of providence, and walk in Him, and dwell in Him, and hold sweet
counsel with Him. "Whom have we in heaven but Thee?
and there is none upon earth to be desired beside Thee."

When Daniel's three friends were cast into the furnace, nothing was consumed but their fetters; and the Son of God walked with them in the midst of the fire. Oh may the kind purpose of God in your affliction be fulfilled; may your fetters be consumed,—whatever in you is evil in His sight, whatever hinders your enjoyment of Him, and conformity to Him. Nothing that is truly good can be lost, nothing that has God in it; and so all that was really valuable in that endeared earthly relationship is laid up for you, purified from all taint of sin and corruption. I loved your husband well. I had received from him the kindness of a brother, and I can in some measure conceive your loss. Pour out your heart to your Lord; tell Him of your sorrows; tell him you are but dust and can bear nothing, and ask Him to bear you and your burden too. I had a sweet letter from your dear mother. As far as a human heart can sympathise with you, hers will; and as far as human sympathy can help you, hers will. Give her my most affectionate regards. May your dwelling be in God, and may His peace and His Spirit be in you, conducting you through life unto His eternal joy.

T. ERSKINE.

123. TO MADAME DE STAËL.

LINLATHEN, DUNDEE, 16th June 1828.

MY DEAR FRIEND,—You have gratified and relieved me very much by your letter. I bless God for you that your spirit is now more composed, and that though you can still see nothing in life but sorrow, you can yet look upon it calmly. The great lesson that we have to learn here is that the Creator is the only sanctifying as well as satisfying portion of the creature. And our wise and loving Lord uses many different ways and arguments to teach us this lesson, and to put it into our hearts. A friend of mine gave me the other day an idea of Christianity which struck me and pleased me much. It is this : God is in all that He does and in all that He makes or sustains, and God is Love. Therefore, in truth, every event in providence, and every work of creation, is full of holy love, because they are full of God. The fall of man, the corruption of his nature, consists in his blindness to this element of love which pervades and fills all things. He sees the things, but he does not see love in them, and that love is truly their character and essence, because it is the character and essence of Him who is their cause and their fountain. The great practical difficulty is to believe constantly that God is really love, and that it is with Him that we have to do in everything. But He is the hearer of prayer, and His Spirit can overcome all difficulties, and it is a blessed occupation to pray to Him as to a Father who delights in the lisping of His children, and who rejoices over them to do them good. I trust that you are seeking and longing after the full benefit and blessing of your affliction. According to the severity of the affliction is the greatness of the benefit, if it is received in a right spirit—a spirit of prayer, and hungering and thirsting after righteousness. We have but one thing to do—to have our wills grafted upon the will of God, to die unto self and to live unto Him who hath died for us. Yet a few days and we shall have left present and temporal things, and shall have entered into eternity. This then is our great concern. May the Lord grant to you that it may be your one great concern to know and love Him who inhabiteth eternity, and whose love passeth knowledge. And may it be mine ! I should indeed like well to see you again, and the dear child of my dear friend, whom I hope to meet with again where there is no more death, neither sorrow nor crying, for the former

things shall have passed away. . . . How much dependent
we are upon space; a few miles separate us from those we
love. . . . Yours, with much affection,   T. ERSKINE.

124. TO MADAME DE STAËL.

LINLATHEN, DUNDEE, 25*th Sept.* 1828.

. . . There is one wish above all other wishes that my
heart feels for you, even that it may please God to reveal
His Son to you, that you may know the exceeding greatness
of that love of God in which we live and move and have
our being.   He hath given us His Son, and with Him
He freely giveth us all things.   This is the testimony which
the God of truth testifies concerning His Son to every child
of Adam, whether they will hear or not.   Those who
believe this testimony have peace and assured hope of an
eternal glory, and whilst they are in this world they rejoice
in that hope, and walk in the light of their Father's countenance, knowing that every event which befalls them is
full of His love, and is a necessary part of that process by
which He will accomplish His great purpose of mercy in
the restitution of all things.

I sent a work which I have lately published to you, and
to ——.   Will you tell —— that I wish to know how it
suits her?   I wish to know whether she finds it in accordance with the Bible.   I should like well to be either at
—— or ——, to hold communion with you about these
glad tidings of God's love, and of that sacrifice which
hath expiated all sin, and of that promised Spirit which
is given to those who ask it, and which fills the weak,
empty creature with the strength of the Creator.

I think often of the last hour which I spent with you,
and I remember your calamity in the presence of Him
who wept at the grave of Lazarus, and I trust that you

may be taught the full truth of that word, " These light afflictions, which are but for a moment, work out for us a far more exceeding, even an eternal weight of glory, whilst we are led by them to look, not at the things which are seen, but at the things which are not seen ; for the things which are seen are temporal, but the things which are not seen are eternal."

Oh, my dear friend, that God, who is light, and whose light is love, is now present with you and with me ; and what hinders us from rejoicing in His light but the unbelief of our hearts ?   Lord, open our eyes that we may see Thy Light !   Give my love to your boy ; may the Father of mercies bless him and make him His own child ! . . . Farewell.   The peace of God be with you !

T. ERSKINE.

125. TO MRS. MONTAGU.[1]

BROUGHTY-FERRY, DUNDEE, 7th January 1830.

MY DEAR SISTER IN THE LORD JESUS,—I was much struck by receiving from your own hand the communication of an event so overwhelming to the natural feelings of a mother ; and I felt assured that the capacity of making this communication in the way you did it, indicated a great blessing bestowed upon your soul, through a channel in itself not joyous, but grievous.   The mediatorship of Christ is a precious doctrine.   The Kingdom is in His hands, and we are privileged to receive nothing but what comes from His hands and bears His stamp.   He is Himself the Father's unspeakable gift to us, and now everything that comes to us comes through Him, and in its passage through His hands it becomes impregnated and saturated with that

[1] On the death of a daughter.

very love which first gave Him to us, and constituted Him
a Mediator, and nailed Him to the cross, and with all the
holiness too. So let us call nothing common or unclean.
All is holy, for all comes stamped with the print of the
nail, which is our King's stamp. And thus there is in
everything a sorrow and also a joy, which the world understandeth not,—a sorrow for sin, which dishonours God
and destroys souls, and a joy that God's holy love is in
action to destroy sin, and that His cause must triumph,
and that He will be glorified.

The knowledge of this mediatorial reign of our Lord
seems to me to be in a very sweet and special sense the
secret of the Lord, which is with them that fear Him.
They will feel it to be a right thing, that a world of sin
should be a world of sorrow, and that a race, which had
gone away from God into the far country of unbelief,
should find it an evil and bitter thing to do so. They
will sympathise with God, even whilst their own souls are
torn by the bitter wages of sin, and they will look for
coming glory.

My beloved friend, it was indeed a touching addition to
your former letter. She is taken away from evil to come.
She is in the Lord's bosom, who took such as she into His
arms and blessed them. Where are the hands to which
you would trust your dearest and your tenderest, if you
could not trust them in those hands that were pierced on
the cross for every man ? " Thou art my hiding-place,"
says our great Head (for I read all the Psalms as the
utterances of the great Head), and the members have just
to know where they are. They have just to know who it
is in whom they live, and move, and have their being, in
order to join with their Head, and to say with Him
to His Father and their Father, " Thou art our hiding-
place." . . .

LINLATHEN, *13th July* 1832.

MY DEAR SISTER,—How much reason have we to give thanks to our gracious Father, when we think of each other, for all the loving-kindness which He hath made to pass before us and to rest upon us. Blessed be His holy name for the love which now embraceth you in Christ Jesus—for those everlasting thoughts of love which are now providing for all that you need, and for the accomplishment of the purpose of God's high calling in you, though, if need be, it is through much suffering in the flesh. Christ hath finished a work which delivers all who know it from that bondage which consists in the fear of death, and in Him and in His work is our completeness; for He is the Father's gift to us, and in Him dwelleth all the fulness of the Godhead bodily; therefore are we complete in Him, for in Him we possess all things—life and death and all things—yea, God Himself. Thus we have a goodly heritage. If in praying for all men we are commanded to give thanks for them, seeing that there is in the case of every man so much to give thanks for, what thanks ought we to render for those who have been taught of God to know the only true God, and Jesus Christ whom He hath sent! And therefore, although I know that you have been very delicate and very suffering, yet I cannot but rejoice much in thinking of you, and join with you in giving blessing and praise unto Him who hath done marvellous things for you. He hath made us to know that we are not orphans, to wander through this wilderness, seeking good, where we may find it; but that we are the blood-bought children of the Lord Almighty, whose still small voice is ever speaking to us words of sweetest comfort and of mighty power : " I am the

Lord thy God : Fear not, I am with thee—when thou goest through the waters, I will be with thee." This is the voice which we are to be swift to hear; for the word it speaks is life : Hear and your soul shall live. Speak, Lord, for thy servant heareth. When the soul knows the voice, and who it is that speaks it, then is the Son revealed in that soul; for the Son is the Word made flesh ; it is the spirit of adoption crying, Abba, Father. Our God is the God of salvation, and to God the Lord belong the issues from death—the outlet from death, which is the inlet of eternal life—that life over which death hath no power. Christ is the outlet and the inlet of the life itself. He is the true God and eternal life. Little children, keep yourselves from idols. Now look unto Him and abide in Him, that ye may be saved and that ye may abide in salvation ; let your eyes look right forward unto Him, where He sitteth, having passed through death. Look not to the right hand or the left, but look right forward ; for the things on the right and on the left are idols ; they are the hopes which, being uncertain, make the heart sick ; but Christ is the true God, and He is the assured hope that is not deferred, therefore is He the tree of life. Every hour brings His glorious kingdom of righteousness nearer. Look at His coming : it is getting bigger every moment : it is a tree of life—it maketh not the heart sick, for it is not a hope deferred : it is the desire which cometh, for " He will come and will not tarry." He is our portion and our King now—even now ; and although you may have been taught to sell all and buy Him, yet who hath known His preciousness ? It is naught, saith the buyer—even the true buyer of the heart ; he knows not its value, but when he goeth forth—forth from the darkness of this world— then he will boast, for he will then know the value of the heart. Every thought within us reproving unbelief, and calling to holy and blessed confidence and fellowship with God, is the word of the living God—the Christ of God speaking in us. In this way He asks us to give Him to drink ; and those who know the gift of God, and who it is that thus says " Give me to drink," ask of Him, and He gives them living water. May the Lord give you to realise much of His love and His Spirit within you ; and may He teach a blessed dependence for every thought and every feeling—yea every breath ; so that you may ever rest on the bosom of Jesus, waiting for His glorious appearing.— All here unite in love to you and your husband. Let us hear from him about you. And the very God of peace keep you in perfect peace through Christ Jesus. Amen.— Beloved sister, your brother in Christ,

T. ERSKINE.

127. TO MR. MONTAGU.[1]

LINLATHEN, DUNDEE, 11th Nov. 1832.

MY DEAR BROTHER,—I hear that the Lord has been abundant in mercy and loving-kindness in His dealing with you and yours. As a father pitieth his own children, so the Lord pitieth them that fear Him. The Lord is nigh to them that call upon Him. He giveth songs in the night : this life is all night, but He giveth songs in it ; and surely the sweetest song that He gives is when he pours in upon the soul the glorious light of that coming day, which shall dispel the darkness. Blessed be His name that He put this song into the mouth of His handmaid, before He called her hence ; and now she rests from her labours, amongst the blessed dead who have died in the Lord, waiting for the redemption of the body—free from sin—her Father's yearning heart resting on her ungrieved. How slow we

---

[1] On the death of his wife.

are to learn what the love of God is! We need to be
strengthened with all might by the Spirit in the inner man,
in order to comprehend the depth and height of that love
which would bless us through death, which hath bought us
with blood.

I have been much struck lately with the 18th chapter
of Jeremiah. The prophet went down to the potter's
house, and there he saw the wondrous mystery of God's
dealing with man. The potter made a work on the
wheels, and it was marred in his hands, and he broke it
and made it anew. Adam was the first vessel, and he
marred himself in the hands of his Potter, and the Potter
passed on him the sentence of death; He broke the mould
and made a new one. And the new one is Christ, the
Lord from heaven, the man raised from the dead, incorruptible, with the blessing upon Him, even life for evermore.
Christ became the Head of the new work on the wheels
by dying willingly—"No man taketh my life from Me: I
lay it down of Myself; I lay it down that I may take it
again : this commandment have I received of my Father."
God has sentenced the first vessel, the natural life, to be
broken, because it was polluted ; yet He does not intend to
destroy the clay, but to new-model it under Christ the
second vessel. The curse always rests on the first vessel,
and the blessing always rests on the second ; and both
vessels are in the nature, and every man may live in which
he will, but he cannot enjoy the second without consenting
to the breaking of the first, *i.e.* through willing death.
And now the great controversy between God and man is
this, that man clings to the first vessel, on which the curse
rests, and refuses to live in the second, on which the blessing
rests. He resists the breaking of the first vessel ; he
refuses to give up the natural life in the flesh; he desires
a happiness in it, and labours for it, and expects it, and

murmurs against God as the destroyer of his happiness
when He breaks it. All seeking of happiness in the flesh
is just a denial of God's righteousness in the breaking of
the vessel which was marred, and a refusal to submit to live
in the second vessel. The flesh is the rejected and reprobate
vessel, and those who cling to it cling to the curse, and
along with it are rejected and reprobate. Christ is the
chosen and elect one, and those who abide in Him abide in
the blessing, and are chosen and elect. If we would abide
in Christ, we must crucify the flesh, we must in the spirit
die a willing death. All the hopes and prospects of enjoyment in this life belong to the first vessel, and are under
the condemnation: we must pass through death to get at
the blessing. Through faith in the death of our Head we
pass into the blessing before our own natural death ; but
our wills must pass through death for every drop of the
water of life. Christ's death was a willing death, and thus
redemption through His blood is redemption through a
willing death. Let us then consent to the breaking of the
first vessel. Dear brother, it is not broken to be destroyed,
but to be new-made ; and unless we consent to the breaking
of the first, we cannot be partakers with the second. The
first is marred and polluted by sin, and God is righteous
in condemning it. Let us condemn sin in the flesh as
Jesus did, by submitting to be broken. My dear brother,
I have known many dear children of God, but I never knew
a lamb like her. But all that was really precious of her
belongs to the second vessel, which cannot be broken.
Grudge not the breaking of her first vessel : think of the
glorious new-making in Christ.—Yours affectionately,

T. ERSKINE.

Jeremiah xviii. verse 6. He does not speak of God's
right to make a bad vessel, but to break one that was

marred. He sets a blessing and a curse before them. Heb. xi. xii. xiii. and Psalm xl. ; 1 Cor. xv.

Give my thanks and brotherly love to Miss Long ; it was indeed most kind to write to me on such an occasion. The Lord comfort you, my brother.

128. TO MRS. MACHAR.

LINLATHEN, *March* 23, 1833.

WE have need of patience, and therefore we have need of divers trials, for it is by the trial of faith that patience is wrought ; it is by trial that the sinfulness and bitterness of the flesh are discovered. Let us then learn to count it all joy when we fall into divers trials. The course of God's providence is just a continual answer to the petition, " Show me Thy way." But until we see it in Jesus, the living way, we do not understand it—it is just a parable to us ; when we see Jesus, then we know that God's way is also His glory and His goodness (Exod. xxxiii. 13, 18, 19).

This is that mercy and truth of which He says, Let not mercy and truth forsake thee. Oh let us be submissive to this lesson. God shows us a man, weary and heavy laden, burdened with the sin and misery of the whole world, and then He shows us the same man in glory, at His own right hand, dwelling in the blessedness and glory of God. May we not well ask, we who are sore burdened, Show us how hast Thou made this change upon this man ? Then God shows us that this man at every moment died willingly—that He refused at every moment to make a choice for Himself, but said, " Thy will be done." God hath said, " The blood I give thee to make atonement with it," and this man made no other use of it than for what God gave it ; God shows us this history, and then says, " This is my way." And the man Himself in like manner testified that this willing surrender is the way to

God's rest, for He says, "Take my yoke upon you and learn of Me, and ye shall find rest unto your souls." And now from the seat of glory He says the same thing. While He was in this world He walked among men who were all providing for themselves, and guarding against God's dealings with them as if He had been their enemy. But this man provided not for Himself, nor guarded Himself against God's dealings with Him, but submitted Himself meekly. He was alone in this thing, and why was He alone in it? Hear His own words, "O righteous Father, the world hath not known Thee, but I have known Thee." And they who know Thy name put their trust in it. Oh, what fools we are, and slow of heart to believe in the love of God! I have had much proof since I parted from you of the shallowness of my religion, and the power of seen things, in opposition to what I know of God. Read Psalm cvii. That is just God's way—a lower manifestation of Jesus. But Jesus is the living way; He is not only the way, but He is the God whose way it is. He is the God who walks there, and carries in His bosom all who will trust themselves to Him. We are indeed in a very low state, and we may well pray Jonah's prayer (Jonah ii. 7, 8, 9). The Lord be merciful to you and yours, and lead you in His own way.—Yours, etc., T. ERSKINE.

129. TO LORD ELGIN.

LINLATHEN, 7th Nov. 1833.

MY DEAR LORD ELGIN,—I am very sorry to hear that you continue to suffer so much from the tic. A suffering world is indeed a great mystery, but there is a solution of it. "These light afflictions, which are but for a moment, work out for us a far more exceeding, even an eternal weight of glory, whilst we look not at the things which are seen, but at the things which are not seen ; for the things which are seen are temporal, but the things which are not seen are eternal."

There is in each one of us a seed of eternal life, which lies dormant whilst we are occupied by seen things,—by this passing world, with its joys or sorrows,—but which springs and grows up into God when we look to the unseen things beyond death. This world is broken and bankrupt ; death is through and through it in all its parts ; it is the valley of the shadow of death. Our life is under the sentence of death, and everything about us has death in it, and there is but one untainted, undying life in this wreck, and that is God, and He is as near us as the death is, for His is that seed of eternal life in us which lies unknown and unnoticed, though it contains the riches of eternity. Now this is the purpose of pain, that we should be chased by it into God, forced away from the dying things unto the undying, so that the blessed seed of God within us may spring up to Him whose seed it is. It is still the voice of this seed—this seed who was promised, and who has come into our flesh—" Come unto Me, ye wearied ones, and I will give you rest." This is the voice of Him who is despised and rejected of men, and His voice is not listened to, but yet there is no other rest. And what was His rest ? To seek not His own will, but to do and suffer His Father's will. He found His Father's will in every step of His way, and it was His rest and His meat to do it and suffer it. The will of God is God, and he who receives the will of God in doing and suffering receives God. I have ventured to write this to you, because I know that there is but one remedy for every evil under the sun, and this is that remedy.—I remain, my dear Lord Elgin, yours most faithfully,

T. Erskine.

LINLATHEN, 27*th Nov.* 1833.

MY DEAR ——,—Don't allow your heart to hold or to
utter such a thought as that you do not trust God. Though
you feel weak in faith, don't give way to distrust, don't
permit it in yourself. How often is that call given as a
needful one, " Be of good courage," " Be strong ! " Hold
fast the beginning of your confidence without wavering ;
for He is faithful that hath promised. You know that He
is worthy of being trusted, that His love may be trusted
safely, that there is no safety but in trusting in Him. You
know all this, my dearest ——, and you know that now,
in this life of trial, He is trying our faith. After having
shown us what He is to us, what His heart is toward us,
in the gift of Jesus, He will prove our faith and strengthen
it by sorrow and suffering. In Jesus He has shown us
the way to glory, the only way ; and what is that way ?
Sorrow, and grief, and death, suffered in the spirit of confidence. Jesus suffered all, trusting in the Shepherd who
led Him, and He is now at the right hand of power. And
from that place He says to us, " The same love which led
Me leads you ; the same hope which was set before Me is
set before you ; the same strength that sustained Me is
within your reach, but you must walk the same way. None
can come unto the Father by any other way. I am the
way." And, oh, remember the steps of that way ; remember the temptation in the wilderness ; remember the hour
and power of darkness ; remember, My God, my God, why
hast Thou forsaken me ? Yet from under all this weight,
the weight of a world's sin and sorrow, He trusted in God
and was delivered ; and now He is given to us to dwell in
our hearts by faith, that, in His strength, we also may trust

God in the dark hour of this world. " All the days of the afflicted are evil; but he that hath a merry heart hath a continual feast." Christ was the afflicted one, and we are the afflicted, and all our days here are evil—few and evil; to-day is evil, and to-morrow will be evil, but in the midst of it all our table is furnished with that meat which the world knoweth not—a feast of fat things—the love of God and the hope of glory; and our companion is He who says, Behold, I stand at the door and knock; if any man will open, I will come in to him and sup with him, and he with Me. The will of God is the food—that will which is the kernel of everything which we are called on to do or to suffer; that will is the very life of God, which Jesus delighted to manifest.—Yours ever,   T. ERSKINE.

. . . Read the 78th Psalm, and let " Thou art the man " carry it home to thy heart.

131. TO MRS. MACHAR.[1]

LINLATHEN, *Jan.* 16, 1834.

IT has pleased the Lord to give you a child, and to take him from you. No affliction is for the present joyous but grievous, yet afterward it yieldeth the peaceable fruits of righteousness to them who are exercised thereby; and I trust that you and your husband have been enabled to give yourselves up to God in this thing, looking to Him who giveth the increase, that so you may indeed grow up in all things to God, not seeking your own things, nor seeking your own will, but saying from the heart, " Thy

[1] In the published "Memorials" of Dr. Machar's Life and Ministry, we read that "in the autumn of 1833 the shadow of a deep sorrow overclouded his domestic happiness and darkened his dwelling. He had just rejoiced in the birth of a first-born son, and given thanks for this good gift from the Lord, when he was called to resign it." It was on hearing of that bereavement that this letter was written to Mrs. Machar.

kingdom come, Thy will be done." To Mary it was said, " Blessed art thou among women," and yet it is also said, " Yea, rather, blessed are they who hear the Word of God and keep it." There is something very wonderful in the fact that there is at every moment a special will of God towards each of us individually. This is the secret of the Lord which is with them that fear Him. When Jesus sat on the well wearied with His journey, this will of His Father's was His meat. The will of God is the life of God, as the will of man is the life of man. And thus there is a stream of God's life flowing through the whole course of our existence, and when we receive His will into our hearts we are partakers of His life—the Divine nature. Dear friend, " in everything give thanks, for it is the will of God in Christ Jesus concerning you." When in Dundee I called on ――――. I thought there was a broken-heartedness about both, which is the right state for a sinner. "To this man will I look, even to him that is poor and of a contrite heart, and that trembleth at my word." Oh fear the Lord at all times, and let us seek to live in His fear, and to have this fear continually in our hearts that we depart not from Him. T. ERSKINE.

CHAPTER X.

Doctrinal Letters.

To an unknown correspondent who desired to know Mr. Erskine's views as to the Sacrifice of Christ, the following letter was addressed :—

132. EXTRACT FROM A LETTER.

Jan. 15, 1830.

THE virtue of Christ's sacrifice is intimately connected with His being the root of the humanity. He did not take hold of a branch, He took the very root. He came into the place which Adam had occupied. He came into that place where the sap of the tree was as in its fountain.

He became the heart where all the blood was. And when He offered Himself as a sacrifice, and then entered the heavenly holy place, with His blood in His hands, He presented not the blood of an individual, but the blood of the race—the heart-blood. He said, The penalty pronounced upon the humanity was death ; and here the penalty has its execution, for this is the life-blood of the humanity—the life-blood of the heart drained out—the sap of the root drained out. Well, but what of this? As far as Christ was merely the representative (although a full representative) of the whole humanity, His death as a sacrifice could not be a reason or ground for bestowing a blessing on the humanity. The old corrupted sap was strained out under the penalty, and in fulfilment of the penalty; but this was no more than what was due, it was bare right. And the fulfilment of this penalty contained no reason in it why a new sap should be poured in, to carry life and health through those veins which had been so long the conveyers of poison through all the branches. The great secret is, He was in the world, but He was not of the world. He was in our fallen nature. He took part of the same flesh and blood of which the children partook, but He sinned not. He fulfilled all righteousness. He kept the Law. And as the curse came through the first Adam in token of God's abhorrence of sin, so it behoved that the blessing should come in token of God's love of righteousness.

Well, it was He who entered into the root of the fallen tree of human nature, poured out His life an offering for sin, even the life and heart-blood of the human nature. He Himself as an individual also had fulfilled all righteousness; not being subject to the penalty, but being the Head of the fallen family, He freely subjected Himself to the penalty, and thus acknowledged the justice of the sentence on the family. He put to His seal that God was righteous in His judgment, and that this universal view was no more than sin deserved.

And He did all this and suffered all this, that God's holiness might be fully manifested, and honoured, and vindicated in the exposure and condemnation of the sinfulness of sin in the flesh on the human nature, and that thus the barrier might be removed which dammed up the love of God, and prevented it from flowing freely forth on the sinful race.

In all this doing and suffering Jesus gave such glory to God, He so met and fulfilled the desires of God's heart, the longings of His love, and the purity of His holiness—

He so declared the righteousness of God in condemning sin and in forgiving the sinner,—that it became God, as the God of holy love, to bestow the blessing through Him, that is, to make Him the foundation of a new life to that nature which He had assumed, and for which He had made atonement.

And that life is nothing less than the very life which is in the Father, and was manifested in the Son. That life is the Holy Spirit.

In the summer of 1832 Monsieur Gaussen visited this country and spent most of his time in Scotland with Mr. Erskine at Linlathen and at Cadder. The one was in the full fervour of his zeal for those wider views of the love of God, the holding of which had so lately brought down deposition upon his friend. The other was firmly attached to the old Genevan faith. What to the one were confining, cramping fetters, to the other were the needful links by which a coherent, compact, consistent system of divine truth was bound together. What seemed to the one to be a mere fabric of human thought imposed upon the representations given in Holy Writ, obscuring the direct and full perception of God's love to all men in Christ, the other looked upon as the faithful setting forth of the divinely instituted mode by which the sinner was to be reconciled to God, and brought into His fellowship and likeness. Lively discussions between the two ensued. Soon after Monsieur Gaussen's departure the following letter was despatched to Geneva :—

133. TO MONSIEUR GAUSSEN.

(Postmark, 7th Dec. 1832.)

MY DEAR BROTHER,—Although I have had much enjoyment in meeting you once more in this world, yet I have

also suffered much, chiefly because I am sensible that in
witnessing for God's truth to you, I often sinned against
the law of love and meekness and patience. May the
Lord forgive the sin, and mercifully overrule, so that it
may not act in your mind as a reason against any truth
which you heard from me. May the good Lord give you
the spirit of a little child in waiting upon Him for light
on those things which were the subjects of our conversation. My dear brother, it appears to me clear from Scripture that the blessing which God holds out to man through
the work of redemption is *a real and substantial restoration*
to the image of God, which is to be effected by man
becoming the habitation of God through the Spirit (Eph.
iv. 24, ii. 22, and 2 Cor. vi. 16). This is not a fictitious
righteousness, for then it would be also a fictitious blessedness, but it is a real conformity to the will of God. *This*
is the mercy which God promised from the beginning,
"that He would grant unto us that we, being delivered
from the hand of our enemies, *might serve Him without fear
in holiness and righteousness before Him* all the days of our
life" (Luke i. 72-75). See to the same purpose, Acts iii.
26 ; and amongst innumerable passages in the Old Testament let me specially direct your attention to Jeremiah
xxxi. 33, and to Ezekiel xxxvi. 25, 26, which most
strikingly declare this truth. And there is but one kind
of true righteousness, namely, the character of God, for
"none is good save one, that is, God" (Luke xviii. 19),
and therefore, in order that a man should be righteous or
good, he must have God dwelling in him; and thus Paul
writes, "that the *righteousness of the law* is fulfilled only in
those who walk not after the flesh but after the *Spirit*,"
which is God dwelling in man (Rom. viii. 4). That the
righteousness which God desires to see in us is a real
substantial thing is manifest also from those passages

T

which speak of the judgment to come; thus Rom. ii. 6,
2 Cor. v. 10; read also to the same purpose 1 John ii. 29,
iii. 7, 8, 9, 10. "Christ came not to destroy the law, but
to fulfil" (Matt. v. 17). It is quite manifest that there
can be no true blessedness without this true righteousness,
and that the fulfilment of that word, "Enter into the joy
of thy Lord" (Matt. xxv. 21), requires the fulfilment of
those other words, "partakers of His holiness," and
"partakers of the divine nature" (Heb. xii. 10; 2 Peter
i. 4). And thus we are brought to that mighty thing
which is the great object through all the Bible, namely,
the mystery of godliness, the wonder of ungodly creatures
becoming godly, the manifestation of God in the flesh,
which is the true restoration of the image of God to man.

When man hears of such a perfect righteousness, instead
of rejoicing at the tidings of it, he is quite cast down, saying, How am I ever to arrive at it? Has not God said,
"The carnal mind is enmity against God, and is not subject
to the law of God, neither indeed can be"? This fear and
dejection arise from his ignorance of God's righteousness,
for he thinks that he has to build up this perfect character
for himself before he is entitled to have any confidence in
God; and as he feels his inability to come up to this high
standard, he either endeavours to lower the standard of
duty down to what he believes himself capable of, which is
the antinomianism of the Sadducee, or else he substitutes
a doctrine in its place, or rather the perversion of the doctrine of justification by faith, because he thinks it easier to
believe something than to have the perfect righteousness
in reality, which is the antinomianism of the Pharisee.
The Sadducee supposes that he is to open the door of his
Father's house, which has been shut against him, by doing
certain moral duties; the Pharisee thinks to open it by
certain religious opinions; whereas the blessed truth is,

that God has Himself opened the door by rending the veil
of the flesh of Jesus, and now calls every sinner, not to the
task of opening the door, but to the privilege of entering
by the opened and blood-sprinkled door, and of looking to
God as a Father indeed, and of being a member of His
family, partaking in all the interests and prospects of the
family, namely, the advancement of Christ's kingdom on
earth and the expectation of the coming glory. This is
the right place for a man to be in, *c'est à dire*, in his Father's
family and occupied with his Father's interests; this is
his right place, the place for which he was created and
redeemed; this is his righteousness, and in him is fulfilled
the word spoken in Luke i. 74, 75, and in Acts iii. 26. But
now, is this righteousness to be the foundation of his confidence? So far from it, that this righteousness can only be
produced by a confidence already existing. Confidence is
the root of everything good in man, and as it thus precedes
everything good in man, it cannot be founded on anything
in man, but must be founded on something out of man (*au
dehors de l'homme*). And what is it then that man's confidence is to be founded on? God. God has revealed Himself as the foundation of the sinner's confidence, and now in
Christ He invites and commands all the sinners of the earth
to give Him their confidence, because He is worthy of their
confidence, "having made Him who knew no sin to become
sin for them, that they might become the righteousness of
God in Him" (2 Cor. v. 21). God is the blessedness of
the creature, and the punishment of sin in the creature is
to be shut out or cut off from God, and as the punishment
is pronounced in these words, "DEPART, *ye cursed*," so the
forgiveness of sin is pronounced in the words, "RETURN
unto me, for I have redeemed you." No creature which
had sinned could have any right to come to God, or to
enjoy God, or to trust in God, unless God had put away

that condemnation of "Depart, ye cursed," which is due to every sinner, and had said, "Come unto me all ye that labour," etc.; but God is saying during this day of grace to all sinners, "Come unto me," thus assuring them that they may well put their confidence in Him, because He loves them, and confirming this to them by revealing to them the blood and resurrection of Jesus as the ground on which this invitation is addressed to all men. God laid on Jesus the iniquities of us all, Jesus died under this weight, and God raised Him from the dead, thus declaring sin condemned and punished and the sinner freed. On this ground it is that God says to every sinner, "Trust in God." Trust in Him as your Father, your guide, your guard, your everlasting rest. Take no step without him, take no joy without Him. Let Him be your hope, your only hope, not that by thus hoping in Him you are to make Him what He was not before, but that by knowing what He is to you, you may be blessed in Him. "God hath raised Jesus from the dead and given Him glory, *afin que* our faith and hope may be in God." Those who know what God meant when He raised Jesus from the dead have faith and hope in God, and those who are without faith and hope in God are those who do not know the mind of God declared in the resurrection of Jesus (1 Peter i. 21). "It is life eternal to know God as revealed in Christ," because it is in knowing Him that we enjoy Him and become partakers of His nature (2 Peter i. 2, 3, 4). Every man who knows God truly has eternal life in that knowledge, and every man who has not eternal life is without it, in consequence of his ignorance of God (Eph. iv. 18). Now surely it would be great dishonour to God to suppose that we change Him by our knowledge or ignorance; we must therefore acknowledge that the heart of God towards every man is such, that if the man knew it he could not but rejoice in it; for how else could it be life to him to know God? What then is to make me rejoice in God? A sight of God's heart as loving me, a knowledge of God's goodwill concerning me? And how am I to get this sight and this knowledge? Jesus Christ hath come forth from the bosom of the Father to show us the heart of God. " He by the grace of God tasted death for every man" (Heb. ii. 9); and then He said, " He that hath seen me hath seen the Father." It was this that made Jesus "the light of the world." He declared the Father to the world, to the end that whosoever knoweth the Father through Him might live by that knowledge. He came to seek and to save the lost, by declaring to them the Father's heart, and as soon as they know that heart they are glad, they rejoice in salvation; but whilst they continue ignorant of God's heart, they continue to be without eternal life in them. He came to seek and to save the lost. God raised Him from the dead and gave Him glory, that the lost might be saved by putting their faith and hope in God. These lost souls, that is, all men, are called to put their faith and hope in God; they are called to trust in God, not because they have faith, but because God has raised Christ from the dead. A poor sinner rising from the murder of his brother is desired and invited to trust in God, to see God's forgiveness in that word, " Come unto me," and to put his faith and hope in God, because He hath raised Jesus from the dead. " God is the Saviour of all men, specially of those who believe" (1 Tim. iv. 10). God's heart is a heart of forgiving love to us before we believe, but we cannot enjoy God, which is full salvation, without knowing or be-lieving what His heart is to us.

You seem to me to rest not on what God is, but rather on what God has said as distinct from God. Before the coming of Christ men might have made a distinction between God and His Word; but now such a distinction is Socinianism, for God has declared that the Word is God. When it is not God Himself that we meet and trust in His Word, we are breaking the second commandment. Faith has become to the intellectual Protestant churches what the idols of silver and gold were to the Jewish and Popish churches. Why is a poor sinner to trust in God? Is it because God is good, or because *he* has faith? Am I to trust in God because "God was in Christ reconciling the world unto Himself, not imputing unto them their trespasses," or because I am justified by faith? Read the 78th Psalm, marking specially verses 7, 22, 35. God was always "their Rock and their Redeemer," but whilst they believed it not, they put away His salvation—(as the sun is always our light, but when we shut our eyes we are in darkness). He was always their loving, forgiving Father, even in His punishments; they were like the famine in the far country, sent to bring back the prodigal to his father's house. Do you not believe that the heart of God does indeed grieve and yearn over every sinner that continues at a distance from Him? and is not that grief the grief of love, which desires the holy blessedness of the sinner? Yes, it is the grief of love. God created man to be the image of God, and holiness and blessedness. And God did this, because God is love: not to amuse Himself. And this purpose of God towards man hath not changed, but has followed every individual man through every moment of his life, desiring that he should yet be the image of God. And God hath revealed this purpose fully in Jesus Christ, who by the grace of God tasted death for every man, and was raised from the dead into glory, that every man might have confidence in God's purpose, and might yield himself unto God to have that purpose accomplished in him. This restora-

tion of the image is salvation. Salvation is not forgiveness of sin; it is not the remission of a penalty; it is not
a safety. No, it is the blessed and holy purpose of God's
love accomplished in the poor fallen creature's restoration
to the divine image. And as this could only be effected
by God dwelling in man, so the work of Christ has been
God's taking possession of a part of the fallen nature and
uniting Himself to it, without separating it from the rest of
the mass of the nature, and in that part working perfect
righteousness, and so ordering it that this part of the nature
so possessed by God should become the new root and head
of man, from which the Holy Spirit given to Him without
measure might flow forth seeking entrance into every part
of the nature, wherever it can find an open heart. And to
this end is the news of God's love in this great work declared to men, that they hearing it may have confidence in
Him who hath thus loved them, and so open their hearts
to let in His Spirit. So we have no need now to go out
of our nature to meet God, and to get the eternal life
(which is God's life), for God is in our own flesh, and the
eternal life is in our own flesh, and we have but to know
this loving God and the longings of His heart over us, and
to give Him our confidence in order to receive His Spirit
into us.

And Christ's work of atonement was perfected by His
death, not only testifying the love of God to every man to
be a love which would die for every man, but also testifying
that when God would restore man He would not restore
that natural life in which man had sinned, He would not
remove his condemnation from that life on which He had
pronounced sentence of death, and that he could not look
on man well pleased until man had consented to the
righteousness of this sentence and had willingly given up
that natural life which had rebelled against God. The

man Christ Jesus did this, and thus He manifested the
express image of the Father, and so He was raised to be
the second Adam, the mediator between God and man,
between the God-nature and the man-nature. It is upon
this ground that every man is invited and demanded to
delight in God, and to drink out of the fountain of life
which is in His love. Now, can it be said with propriety
that any creature is a condemned creature, whilst it is
commanded as well as permitted to enjoy such a God as
this, and to drink out of such a fountain as this ? Can any
creature be said to be unforgiven for whose blessedness God
is at this very moment working with a love passing knowledge ? *O fortunati nimium, sua si bona nôrint !* Read the
107th Psalm. The only true condemnation consists in being
shut out from that fountain to which we are all urged and
entreated to come that we may drink abundantly.

And surely when persons can acknowledge that God has
given Christ for men and to men, and yet refuse to
acknowledge that the Spirit has been also given as widely
they forget that Christ is God, and that in Him not one
person only of the Trinity, but the whole Trinity, was
manifested. I feel that to separate between the work of
Christ and the character of God is Socinianism. So also I
feel that to suppose Christ given and not the Spirit is not
less Socinianism. It is denying that the Word is God.
Do you not believe that every man is in a very different
condition now from what he would have been had Christ
not come into the world ? The word to every man, if
Christ had not come, would have been, "Depart, thou
cursed," and now, in consequence of Christ's coming, the
word to every man is,"Come to the waters," "Come unto
me, thou weary one, and I will give thee rest." My brother,
if the condemnation consist in the word "Depart," tell me
what is contained in the word "Come." When Paul

declared this change of address, was it too much to call it the forgiveness of sins? Acts xiii. 38. Compare this verse and the following one with 1 Timothy iv. 10. These two verses are a commentary on the two words in Timothy, " The Saviour of all men, specially of those who believe." No man could approach God through Christ, unless Christ had eternal life or the Holy Spirit for him, for no man can come to God except in the Holy Spirit; thus every man has eternal life in Christ, and he has also the natural life ; the first of these is holy and sinless and without condemnation, and the man who walks in it is righteous ; the second is sinful and under a condemnation, and he who walks in it, whether he has been a believer or not, walks under a condemnation. God does not change His judgment, nor does He call evil good, nor does He call good evil. Abiding in the faith of Jesus is abiding in the eternal life —leaving Him is falling under condemnation. Beloved brother, this is the concluding sentence : May the God of peace fill you with peace in believing, and make you to abound in the knowledge of the love of Jesus.[1]

Read 2 Peter, 1st chapter. Farewell.

T. ERSKINE.

These and other letters in this volume, along with the extracts given in the Appendix from the three volumes, " The Unconditional Freeness of the Gospel," " The Brazen Serpent," and " The Doctrine of Election,"—all published within the same period,—will sufficiently indicate the positions in doctrinal belief occupied by Mr. Erskine during the middle and most momentous period of his life.

[1] For letters from MM. Gaussen and Adolphe Monod see Appendix, No. XI. p. 410.

CHAPTER XI.

MR. ERSKINE left Scotland at the close of the year 1837, with the intention of paying another lengthened visit to the Continent. He lingered for three months in London, passed over in April to Paris, where he remained during May, June, and July, having as his close companion for two of these months the Rev. J. M'Leod Campbell, and for a week the pleasure of acting as escort to Dr. Chalmers. In October he proceeded to Switzerland, making a tour of the Bernese Alps with his friend Mr. Scott, and taking up his abode at Geneva, which he did not leave till midsummer of the following year. The event of this period which overshadowed all others was the death of the Duchess de Broglie, to which several affecting allusions are made in the letters which follow.

134. TO HIS SISTER MRS. PATERSON.

OSBORNE'S CALEDONIAN HOTEL, *Xmas Day* [1837].

MY DARLING DAVIE,—I am so far on my way to see you, but I shall be here for a few days yet. . . . I arrived on Saturday night, and thought of going to Woolwich on Sunday, but I was not quite up to it, so I went to the church in the Temple, and enjoyed the peaceful prayers exceedingly. I really prefer the Church of England service to any that I know, it brings us all so much into one, and it makes the minister so much the mouth and the leader of the people, instead of lifting him out from the people, and making him the only doer of anything in the Church. . . .

135. TO HIS SISTER MRS. STIRLING.

SHANKLIN, 19*th Jan.* [1838].

MY DEAREST CHRISTIAN,—It is wonderful to myself that I have been able to refrain so long from writing to you ; I have had so many reasons for writing to you, so many things to tell you, which I knew would interest you. Soon after I came to London I had a visit from a Mr. Dunn (perhaps I told you of him before), who was a friend of Knox and Jebb ; he had read, I believe, my book on Election, and had sympathised with it a good deal ; he thought that it brought out something which was wanting in their system, namely, the necessity of the cross to be received and borne by every one. He told me that many read Knox's book who did not find it condemn the most worldly life. I think he said that Lord Melbourne had liked it. It seems to me to imply a great defect in any work on religion, that it should be able to be read by those who walk without God, and to be read with pleasure by them. Mr. Dunn agreed with me in what I have remarked to you of Knox's ignorance of the meaning of the Atonement.

At Mr. Dunn's house I met first (along with Scott) with two young men, sons of that Mr. Woodford, an Irish clergyman, who published a letter addressed to Lord Stanley, in which he separated himself from those who were complaining of the loss of their tithes, and declared that he felt it to be a great privilege to be put in circumstances by which he might prove to the people that it was not theirs but them that he sought. These young men gave a most candid and conscientious attention to many striking things which Scott said. Mr. Dunn, himself a clergyman, and in the presence of these two young men, both clergymen, asked Scott to read and expound the Scriptures. Another day I was at Dunn's, but without Scott, who was not quite well, and met the same young men, and Maurice, who is a very metaphysical man; I have not got into him yet; I hope, when I return to London, to know him better. He goes a good deal in with Pusey, and the other Oxford people, though they do not sanction all that he says. It is a strange system which substitutes office for spirit. It seems to me to be a direct denial of God manifest in the flesh. Jesus was the Light of the world not by office, but by having the light of God actually in Him and shining out of Him; and He speaks of His disciples as having this same qualification in them,—"As my Father hath sent me into the world, even so send I them into the world." I heard Scott preach an admirable discourse on James i. 27 —"True religion," etc. He said that in that place the word translated 'religion' meant religious service; if any man had seen the Jews sacrificing victims and burning incense, etc., and had asked them if that was their religion, they would have answered that their religion was an inward thing, but that this was the outward service of their religion. There was a ceremonial appointed for the Jewish service by God Himself; and Christians have appointed a ceremonial for themselves; but Jesus appointed as the religious service, as the outward service of His religion, "to visit the fatherless and widows, and to keep unspotted from the world." It is surely a very important subject.

136. TO HIS SISTER MRS. PATERSON.

CALEDONIAN HOTEL, ADELPHI, *6th Feb.* 1838.

DEAREST DAVIE,—. . . I hope James will read the review of Sir Walter Scott's Life: I think that the reading of it would urge him to the reading of the History of the French Revolution, which, I am afraid, he will not read without some new impulse. I wish very much that he would make conscience of reading them both ; I think that it would be good for him—tell him so, with my love. It is good, in the first place, to be brought in contact with a mind like Carlyle's, so unconventional in all matters ; and I also think that it would be good for him to come in contact with some of his deep elements of political science, which in his hands is one with religious obligation. . . . Farewell.— Yours most lovingly, T. ERSKINE.

137. TO HIS SISTER MRS. STIRLING.

CALEDONIAN HOTEL, ADELPHI, *8th Feb.* 1838.

MY DEAREST CHRISTIAN,—I have been returned from Shanklin about a week, and I have again got implicated with engagements to meet or to dine or to see. I have just now been at the British Museum with Scott, Mrs. Rich, and Lady Inglis. I was much struck with the Elgin Marbles ; expression of countenance you have not—for you have no face but one, Theseus's, and that a mutilated one,— but there is immense expression of form and attitude and movement ; immense dignity and grace. The Egyptian remains are very curious—so ponderous and enduring, and generally so unbeautiful. Scott mentioned that the form of the old Egyptian head resembles the modern European more than the Greek or Roman ; and that, phrenologically, they were superior to them, as we are also. There is a lady's wig, with the hair plaited beautifully, in great pre- servation ; and there is a lady herself in a remarkably entire state. It is wonderful to see these people raised from their graves after three thousand years. We also saw Mrs. Rich's reliques of Babylon and Nineveh there, which re- called to her bypast times, as you may suppose. I like

Lady Inglis very much ; she is a most true and tender-hearted friend to Mrs. Rich, and she seems to have a tender conscience towards God. I have received much kindness from Sir Robert and her.

Good old Mr. Dunn, whom I have mentioned to you before, continues his kindness. I was there dining yesterday. He was offered a bishopric once and declined it, on some conscientious ground. Wedgwood was there, and Maurice, who went home with me at night. . . . Wedgwood is a delightful man, full of truth of heart to God and man, and well endowed intellectually also. However, although there were good materials for general conversation (for Scott was there too), yet there was none. We continued all in separate parties, which I always regret in such cases.

138. TO HIS SISTER MRS. STIRLING.

CALEDONIAN HOTEL, 27*th* *Feb.* 1838.

MY DEAREST CHRISTIAN,—I shall begin with your question about Knox's view of the Atonement. The reason why I think that he took a wrong view of it is, that frequently he repeats in the course of his book that our concern is not with what Christ did once for all for us, but that our concern is with what may promote our personal sanctification. It is evident from this often-repeated maxim of his, that he did not see that in the atonement—that work which Jesus accomplished once for all for men—there is a manifestation of the purpose of God towards us, fitted above all other things to promote our sanctification. In the atonement, we see a man suffering to the full what we are called to suffer, and acknowledging it all to be righteous, and giving his back to the smiter, without resisting, and submitting himself to the whole will of God in thwarting man's will, both in doing and in suffering, and then we see this man rising out from the death so endured,

and ascending up into heaven, and saying, Be not afraid
to follow me; for whoso follows my steps in patient obedience shall ascend up to where I now am.   I don't think
that Knox saw that the atonement of Christ, besides being
a righteous reason with God for bestowing on man the
participation in the divine nature, was also the pattern of
all righteousness in man, and the encouragement to all
righteousness in man.   It seems strange that a thing should
be so frequently introduced in the Bible if we have not
much concern in it.   I have not the book here, so that I
cannot refer to it, as I should like to do; but you will find
the maxim of which I speak at the beginning of some of
his more important letters or essays.

I am new-modelling my book, dividing it into chapters,
and making such alterations as I think may make it more
readable.   I think it better to do this before I leave
England, so that I may not be induced to neglect it altogether by indolence and the feeling of distance when I am
abroad. . . .—Yours ever,   T. ERSKINE.

139. TO THE SAME.

HÔTEL WAGRAM, 28 RUE DE RIVOLI,
26th April [1838].

MY DEAREST CHRISTIAN,—Here I am in this great
Vanity-fair; and my heart turns to you as to a reality of
sympathy and love, from the evident outsideness and show
and meaningless noise which is going on in the Tuileries,
outspread beneath my windows; for I am amongst the
slates in the top-story of a Hôtel Wagram, 28 Rue de
Rivoli, whence I see the kingdoms of the world and the
glory of them.   And I am endeavouring to learn, from this
vantage-ground, more fully the lesson, that he who offers
us these things is not to be worshipped, and that He who
offers us Himself, if we will part with all other things, is
to be worshipped.   My dear sister, there are few people

whose company I could wish just now, or to whom I could
very cordially offer a room in my house amongst my slates,
but you are one, whom I could know sitting by me, without being fatigued by the knowledge, at least for a limited
number of hours.   I say that, in case you should accept—
you understand.

It is long since I have written to you—too long, considering our near bond ; and considering also that our
mother is no more seen amongst us.   Her image recurs often
to me.   I feel anew the blank ; for always, when I was
abroad, I felt that there was one who did not cease to think
of me and to pray for me, as she was enabled.   And at
that time you had your honest-hearted, loving-hearted,
cheerful-hearted husband to occupy you ; and Davie had
her sweet rising nursery of immortal flowers, attracting
her by their mystery of love and hope and fear.   But now
it is all changed—a change has come o'er the spirit of our
dream—that dream which will continue changeable and
troubled, until we awake up in His likeness, and shall be
satisfied with it. . . .   T. ERSKINE.

140. TO HIS SISTER MRS. PATERSON.

[PARIS], 14*th May* [1838].

DEAREST DAVIE,—It could not but be that the sight of
home should re-awaken much sorrow.   "Wherefore hast
thou made all men in vain ?"   It sometimes looks that
way ; but we know that it is not so : God would have us
know that eternity, and not time, is our element, and therefore He breaks the time-form of things, that we may be
constrained to live in their eternal substance.   *C'est une
question du temps,* as Madame de B. often says. . . .

So you arrived on the 3d of May, the day that dear
Ann arrived at her Father's house.   How time goes on !
How many millions since then have passed through that

strange dark passage, which she found so full of light. It remains for us still to pass through it ; and the True Light, who lighted her through it, is waiting to be gracious to us also. I thought you would like Sartor; the chapter on natural supernaturalism, Book iii. chap. viii., is a wonderful thing. . . .

The Broglies have left Paris, which makes Paris a very different place to me. I had the pleasure and the profit of three weeks of her [the Duchess's] society, however, and found her what I never see nor saw anywhere else. Mr. Campbell saw her twice, and was much delighted with her. *He* is certainly better. . . .

17*th May.*—. . . I had F. Monod dining with me yesterday ; a very widowed man he is, and full of sad yet sweet recollections of his wife. He is to send me a memoir of her, containing her own journal, which he says is the most interesting thing, next to the Bible, that ever he read. I doubt not it is so to him. He had imbibed some doctrinal suspicions of me, which to a certain degree kept him in a defensive attitude against me, and made him afraid of agreeing with me, lest he should be caught in some trap. He is a good honest man, labouring faithfully in the Lord's vineyard. . . . His brother Adolphe has more of the Scott and Rutherfurd class of intellect than any person that I know in France. . . .　　　　T. ERSKINE.

141. TO HIS SISTER MRS. STIRLING.

71 RUE GRENELLE, ST. GERMAIN, 22*d May* 1838.

DEAREST CHRISTIAN,—Many thanks for your long-looked-for letter. You know how long the time seems, when one arrives at a new place, among new persons and circumstances. This made me feel apprehensive that your letter had met some mischance. So you are at Cadder, and the Patersons at Linlathen, and I am here ; but He with whom

we have to do is not far from any one of us, and our nearness to Him is our true nearness to each other. The spiritual
life knows neither time nor space; and it is by living in it
that we escape in some measure from the bondage of time
and space. It is not by the exercise of imagination or the
intelligence that we can get this liberty, of which Carlyle
speaks so interestingly in one of the concluding chapters
of Sartor; but only by living in the spiritual life, the life
of the conscience, the life of God. . . . Houstoun has had
relief, but he also, within the last two or three days, has had
dreadful returns, with more suffering than he ever remembers; poor man, he is an example of meekness and patience,
most edifying to behold. He and Ann are very friendly;
and in spite of the delight that I have in my new house,
which is a perfect palace, I am sorry to be separated so far
from them by my removal across the river. I used to go
there in the evening and have a *causer* with them; and
now that Charles is away, I was become of more value to
them. *En revanche*, I . am near the Elgins, and near
Madame de B., who, alas! however, has left town for
Normandy; and near one other of my ancient friends. I
love Lord Elgin very much, and the two girls, who are as
fine creatures as ever I saw in my life; I am not sure that
ever I knew girls of their age that I could so readily make
companions of. Dear Lady Augusta[1] is a perfect angel.
Lady E. is full of knowledge and curiosity and discussion,
and kindness to whomsoever it is needful; she is an upright woman, who speaks the truth. Lord Elgin is much
better, and went to England on Sunday. I have this morning
had a long conversation with the French Protestant pastor
of Bordeaux. I spoke to him about conscience; he was
much struck by different correspondences which I mentioned
to him between the outward recorded history of Christ and

---

[1] Afterwards Lady Augusta Stanley.

the inward conscious history of conscience. . . . Yesterday
I had a most affectionate note from Broglie, another from
Madame Cramer, from Geneva, and another from Guizot,
thanking me for a copy of Carlyle's History of the French
Revolution which I had sent him. All these notes would
interest you, both on account of the writers and for their
substance. . . .—Yours ever,   T. ERSKINE.

142. TO MONSIEUR GAUSSEN.

71 RUE GRENELLE, ST. GERMAIN, *28th May* 1838.

MY DEAR FRIEND,—Thanks for your welcome. They
have been indeed eventful years, the five years that have
passed since we last met ; but what years are not eventful
which any man lives in this wonderful life !—undergoing
a training for eternity, invited to direct personal communion
with God, and with the power given him of resisting God
and grieving the Holy Spirit, or of causing joy in heaven
on account of his repentance. · I shall be most happy to
see you, both here and at Geneva ; of course that formed
a part of my plan in coming to the Continent. I thank
you for your hospitable invitations, which I am sure I
should have much pleasure in accepting, but I have already
received an invitation from my dear hostess, Madame
Cramer, so that if my circumstances allow me to take up
my abode in a private house, I am engaged to her.

Dear F. Monod is indeed a most interesting sufferer.
God has revealed the emptiness of the creature to him—
which is a great revelation—and the sufficiency of God,
which is still a greater far. How many there are who stop
short at that first revelation !

I beg my best regards to all your family circle.

Give my love to Merle ; I was indeed happy to see his
honest face, though but for a few minutes.—Farewell, dear
brother, yours affectionately,   T. ERSKINE.

143. TO MADAME DE BROGLIE.

RUE DE GRENELLE, ST. GERMAIN, PARIS,
4th June 1838.

DEAR FRIEND,—I am very thankful to hear that things
are with you as they are; that Mr. Chateau Vieux is re-
covering, and that his wife is with him. I trust that the
event itself will not be lost on any of the parties concerned.
A lost sorrow is so sad a thing. A sorrow in which God
has spoken to His creature, and called it to feel that there is
no Helper but Himself, and that He is there present to comfort, and sustain, and bless,—such a sorrow to be neglected
and thrown off by the creature, and forgotten as soon
as possible, is it not wonderful, and as sad as wonderful?
And such are all sorrows, and all joys too, and all events,
when we read them right. My dear, dear friend, I feel
that this is the element of religion, there being only one
thing deeper, which one thing is truly implied in this,
namely, our own conscious meeting with God in the secret
of our own hearts, and knowing Him there, our own personal God, loving us, longing over us with fatherly longings, and speaking to us so that we may hear and know
His voice, and distinguish it from all the other voices
within and without us. "The slothful man roasteth not
that which he took in hunting, but the substance of the
diligent man is precious" (Prov. xii. 27). All the circumstances which God appoints for us contain in them the
bread of life, which is the will of God; but we often receive the circumstances, and even acknowledge that this
precious thing is in them, without converting it into nourishment for our souls : "we roast not that which we take
in hunting." And our fault in this respect seems to me
always to be the consequence of our not listening. Listening is connected with patience and waiting. We have

two classes of counsellors within us, the one good, being the voice of the Spirit of Jesus in the conscience, the other evil, being the calls to self-indulgence, self-acting, self-judging, etc. The first is a still small voice, which requires listening and attention if we would hear it at all or get acquainted with the speaker. The others require no attention, and are attended to in the absence of an opposite attention. These two are the spirit and the flesh. Christianity consists in living to the spirit, and subduing or crucifying the flesh, that is, it consists in listening to and following and cleaving to the spirit testifying in the conscience ; and ungodliness consists in going forward without attending to this voice of God. Our Christianity is not out of us, but in us. It is not in a book or in a discourse, it is in us, and the book and the discourse are so far profitable to us, as they awaken up, and train, and nourish this precious seed which the Son of Man has sown in all hearts. In every action of my outward or inward man, God sets before me the choice of right and wrong, of His will and my own selfish will, and my action contains my answer to God's counsel. So it is said in Prov. xv. 28 : " The heart of the righteous studieth to answer,"—that is, considereth the counsel of God before acting,—" but the mouth of the wicked poureth out evil things," that is, instead of listening to God, he acts from his own impulse or wisdom. Then again, Prov. xviii. 13, " He that answereth a matter before he heareth, it is a folly and shame unto him." Our wisdom is to listen to God at each step, so that we may have His wisdom to direct us. See Psalm xxxii. 8 : " I will instruct thee, and teach thee in the way which thou shalt go, and I will guide thee with mine eye. Be not like to horse and mule, which have no understanding." He that answereth before hearing is he who refuses to listen to this instructor, and is like the horse and mule, which have no such voice within them. It is an inward voice, and a personal voice, that is, it comes from God personally,—to me personally, as one person might guide another person by the eye,—which is personal in its fullest intensity. Prov. xx. 5 : "Counsel in the heart of a man is like deep water, but a man of understanding will draw it out." This counsel is evidently the Wisdom that speaks throughout the whole Book of Proverbs, and it is also the Word that was with God, and was God, in St. John i. 1-9, which is also "the true light which lighteth every man." And who is the man of understanding that can draw out this deep water? "To depart from evil is understanding." The man who will cease from his own wisdom is he who draws up God's counsels from the great deep. We are placed above this great deep, with an apparatus, a mental apparatus, for drawing it up. And what is this apparatus? It is the same thing in the spiritual world as in the physical : we must create a vacuum in our pump, we must cease from our own wisdom, then the great deep rises up into us. The verse immediately following agrees with this solution (Prov. xx. 6) : "Most men will proclaim every one his own goodness, but a faithful man who can find?" Most men are so possessed by themselves that they have no vacuum into which God's deep water may rise; the faithful man is he who, knowing that he is a dependent creature belonging to his Creator, refuses to be his own guide, or his own end, and thus he creates the necessary vacuum. These things are very interesting to me. I know not whether you will find them so, but I write them in the hope that you may.

I have seen little of any of your friends and mine, but I have seen them, and what I have seen I have been profited by and pleased with. I have called on Madame de St. Aulaire often, but have only seen her once; she lives near me, so that I can easily go. I have seen dear old Madame Guizot, whom I love exceedingly. I have also met Madlle. Chabaud at Madame Pelet's, and liked her well, also M. Grandpierre.

The more I think of our conversations about the different places, which belong to the subjective and the objective in religion, the more I am persuaded that it is impossible that we can mean different things. I think only that you insist too much on conventional language, which I feel called on to avoid, because I find that it is so often used to stand in the place of the thing itself.

My confidence in my guide is the only thing which makes me a good follower, but my confidence in him is not the object of my confidence,—he himself and his trustworthiness are the objects of my confidence. I should like very well to come to you, but I don't like to say to Mr. Campbell that I am going to Broglie without inviting him to accompany me, and I cannot do that, considering the state of your feelings. I must wait some opportunity of doing it rightly. Scott is large and strong—in point of mind, I mean ; he has the largest and fullest intelligence that I have known in any man. I am reading your husband's book with great interest; I shall write you about it when I have finished it. It is always a great delight to me to hear from you even a few words, though the more the better. I am myself a bad letter-writer, and I have also a good many letters to write, besides having on my hands and my conscience the correcting of my book, in which any word of help from you would be most welcome.—Yours ever. With best regards to Madame de Staël.   T. ERSKINE.

I saw your amiable young man at Madame de St. Aulaire's.

Read the passages which I refer to in the English Bible.

71 RUE GRENELLE, ST. GERMAIN, PARIS,
5th June [1838].

MY DEAREST DAVIE,—What means your silence ? Are
you too much absorbed by memory, aided by the return of
the season, and the sight of places associated with those
dear spirits ? The acacia-trees here are in superb beauty,
if such sweet simplicity can ever be rightly called superb ;
and they recall to me our acacia-tree, and Joseph the cat,
and those who used to delight to carry Joseph about, and
to watch his gambols about the tree. "Blessed are they
that hunger and thirst after righteousness" all the day
long. It is the only business that stands out the burden
and heat of the day, and finds bread that endureth amongst
all the husks of life. We are not our own, but God's ;
and we are under His guidance. If I were alone just now
I should leave Paris and go to Switzerland, or perhaps to
Broglie rather, for a little while first. Paris evidently dis-
agrees with me. . . . We live in a most beautiful lodging,
as quiet as if this great Babylon were a hundred miles off
—serenaded not with fiacre-wheels and drivers, but with
sweetest blackbirds, which have an undisturbed possession
of garden and grove ground to a considerable extent behind us. We have a balcony which hangs over and looks
over this pleasure-ground, on which we can walk at our
ease. The weather has been remarkably backward, cold
and wet. Mr. Campbell sometimes suffers from the heat,
I always from the cold, sometimes wearing my heavy
great-coat in the house to keep me warm.

6th June.—The last letter which I received from you
reached me on the 13th May, and Christian's last was on
the 16th. I have written to you both since ; and some-

times think that something has happened which prevents your writing; or perhaps that you have mistaken my address.

At Lady Olivia's, *Marbœuf*, Lord Mandeville, her son-in-law, has a meeting for conversing on the Scriptures every Friday. I was there last Friday alone; Mr. Campbell was at Hahnemann's. The chapter was the first of First Peter. Mr. L. presides. He began with Election, and carried on some conversation on the subject with Lord M. and the others. At last I felt that I ought to speak on it; so I did. They received it very gently, but as a very strange doctrine. Mr. Campbell's heart longs to say something for God; I believe that he will speak at these meetings. I never heard anything more fearfully Calvinistic than Mr. L. He denied that man was here in a state of probation : this world is merely a school for the elect, and preaching is only intended to call them and train them. How different from Wisdom in the Proverbs, whose voice is to the sons of man—the sons of Adam in the original. I should feel thankful to be used to deliver any soul from the yoke of such a system. There is a man here whom I like very much—the Lutheran minister. He is a great friend of Madame de B.; he is German, and is large and wide and full of heart.—Ever yours, my dear Davie, with love to James,   T. E.

145. TO MADAME DE BROGLIE.

71 RUE DE GRENELLE, ST. GERMAIN,
PARIS, 14*th June* 1838.

DEAR FRIEND,—Dr. Chalmers is desirous to see you—and also to see a little more of the country. He is very much obliged to you for your invitation, and will probably

be with you either the end of next week or the beginning
of the week following.   I shall accompany him.

I was at Taitbout on Sunday, and heard the regular
minister preach on that word of God to Abraham : "Ne
crains point, Je suis ton bouclier et ta grande récompense."
I wish you had been there along with me, as it would have
given us an opportunity of mutual explanation as to the
distinction and connection between confidence in God and
consciousness of what is in one's-self.   The preacher said,
" We ought to consider the character of the man to whom
this address was made, for it does not belong to any but
to those who possess this character.   Abraham was the
type and model of the faithful, a devoted servant and
friend of God, etc. etc.   Unless, then, we can recognise
these qualities in ourselves, we cannot appropriate the
address to ourselves."   Now, this appears to me to be
erroneously stated, for the character of man depends on
that which is his confidence.   The man of covetousness
expects happiness from money : he is covetous, just because
money is his confidence ; so of the man of pleasure and
ambition, etc.   Their confidence in pleasure and in power,
as causes or sources of happiness, is the root of their faults.
If you change their confidence you change their character.
If you can persuade a covetous man that money is not *son
bouclier ni sa grande récompense*, but that God is, you change
him from a covetous man into a pious man.   So it seems
to me that the word spoken to Abraham may well be
spoken to every man, in this sense, " Created things are
not *ton bouclier* and *ton bonheur—mais moi Je les suis."*   The
thing in which I put my confidence for happiness has
necessarily a directing influence over my whole being ; it
communicates its own nature to me in some measure.   Confidence in a guide insures my following that guide, it binds
me to him.   Confidence in God makes me one with God,

in a measure, and in so far it is righteousness.   Confidence in God does not give me confidence in Him.   My
confidence rests upon what I know of God's character, but
my confidence, inasmuch as it binds me to a righteous God,
is itself a righteous thing.   The only righteousness of man
is to receive a righteous Leader, a righteous confidence, a
true Guide.   Man is merely a receiver, it is the consciousness of this which prevents the consciousness of his having
made a right choice from producing self-conceit.

When God says to man, " Well done, good and faithful
servant," He does not mean to flatter him, nor to injure
his spirit, by self-exaltation.   If the consciousness of
righteousness is inconsistent with humility, man must
remain in a false position through eternity.—Yours ever,

T. ERSKINE.

Mr. Campbell continues delicate.   I have not proposed
to him to accompany us.   I don't think that he could stand
it very well at present.

146. TO MISS RACHEL ERSKINE.

71 RUE DE GRENELLE, ST. GERMAIN, PARIS,
16th June 1838.

DEAREST COUSIN R.,—I have been longer of writing
you than I wished, but I don't like to send you such expen-
sive letters too frequently.   I feel anxious about Mrs.
Graham, and should like to know what progress she is
making.   I know that you cannot remain an unbroken
trio always ; and you are all rising up into those years that
give attacks of all kinds a greater hold upon the system.
In Davie's last letter she speaks of Mrs. G.'s invalidship as
still existing.   The readiness, the preparedness, is all ;—
to have the feet shod with the preparedness of the gospel
of peace, so shod that we are ready to set off on any jour-

ney, specially the journey home, to our own Father's house, where there is rest for the weary, bread enough and to spare. I have you all present before my heart's eye, and can discern that Mrs. G. looks very bilious, but smiling through her yellow fog. Dr. Chalmers has come to Paris, and is over head and ears with delight; he has an honest, natural, unsuppressed pleasure in seeing everything and every person. My entire want of curiosity makes me an unfit companion for him; but I see a good deal of him, and cannot but love his honest bigness (a cognate probably of highness). . . . I am sorry to see young women of our land brought up in this country. There is an externalness in all things here, beyond what there is with us, which is an unwholesome element, most difficult to be guarded against. . . . Mr. Campbell is not making much progress, but he is certainly better and stronger on the whole. When I was formerly on the Continent I was always alone. Solitude was my habitual condition, out of which I emerged into society; but Mr. C.'s company changes that state. I believe that it is not wholesome for the mind to be habitually alone; it produces selfishness, or at least nourishes it. Mr. Campbell is a profitable companion; he is occupied with the one thing needful, and his mind is a very thinking and original one. . . .

147. TO MISS RACHEL ERSKINE.

71 RUE DE GRENELLE, ST. GERMAIN,
10th July 1838.

DEAR COUSIN,— . . . Dr. Chalmers is to leave Paris this day, after having had a month of great enjoyment, seeing everything with a freshness of interest and curiosity that astonishes me; he leaves Paris quite delighted with it. I had a week of him, making a tour, going first to Broglie, and from that to Alençon, Tours, Orleans, Fontainebleau, and home, visiting beautiful cathedrals, and passing through rich and varied scenery.   I was very happy to have an opportunity of recalling former relations, which had rather fallen into desuetude.   I found him most amiable, most true and infantine, and quite disposed, I think, to give me back the place which I used to hold with him. . . . The activity of his intelligence is very great, and gives him a continual interest; but it works, not about persons, but about things, which is to me a diminution of the interest. There was a considerable party at Broglie, of very pleasant intelligent people.   They all liked the Doctor very much, his naïveté and benevolence were so striking.   Dear Madame was much pleased with him, and the Duke and he had many a long discussion on political economy, the law of primogeniture, the advantage of having large properties in a country, etc. . . . I went to Père la Chaise to see dear ———'s monument again.   What a comfort it is to think that God is the finder of all lost things ! . . . Beloved cousin, farewell.   Love to all.—Yours most affectionately,

T. ERSKINE.

148. TO THE REV. ALEX. J. SCOTT.

ST. GERMAIN, 11th July 1838.

DEAR FRIEND,— . . . The weather is now taking the character of summer, which it has been very long of doing this year, and I long for a sight and a feeling of the Alps.

We, Campbell and I, have had some gratifying intelligence of your visit to Scotland.   I hope you have experienced something of the blessedness of being a fellow-worker with God, and that you are now experiencing it amongst your people at Woolwich.   I am sorry to hear of the slow progress of dear Mrs. Scott.   I. hope the company of her

sisters will do her good. I beg my brotherly love and
regards to them, also to Mrs. Rich and Miss Farrer, Han-
son and Robinson. When you come, will you bring along
with you, for me, two copies of Keble's Christian Year,
and one of Coleridge's Aids to Reflection. Remember me
lovingly to the Carlyles and Maurice. Farewell.—Yours
ever,   T. ERSKINE.

I thank you for your bad news about my book, which I
regret, but do not wonder at, for other reasons than its
being opposed to the usual way.

Write to me soon again, like a good man, some days before you come, leaving time for an answer from this. Mr.
Campbell sends his love.

149. TO MADAME DE BROGLIE.

HÔTEL CASTELLANE, RUE GRENELLE, ST. GERMAIN,
21st July.

DEAR FRIEND,— . . . I have read the Duke's book
through with much interest, and it has created a strong
desire to see the remaining volume. Is it lithographed
yet? The distinction which he draws between the
religious man and the theologian is exceedingly good,
and beautifully illustrated. I hope you will let me have
the sequel as soon as you can; it relates to what has
occupied my own mind for many years—the connection
between man and Christianity, and the relation of that
which is positive in religion to that which is principle.
When I look at the four Evangelists I see a great difference
between John and the others, and in like manner I see a
great difference between the various Epistles. In some I
see the positive almost passed over altogether, in some
strongly pressed, and I sometimes feel disposed to think
that the one class is more intended for one age, and the
other for another. In my own mind, I don't feel that I at

all lose the positive by identifying it with principle, and that which is matter of general consciousness. I don't lose the personal character and relation of Christ to me by identifying Him with my conscience; on the contrary, I find my apprehension of that personal character and relation increased by it. If the Bible is given to us "for our instruction in righteousness," it is certainly intended to address our moral conscience, as otherwise it could not be for our instruction in righteousness. I cannot too strongly express to you the conviction which I have, that man can do no good thing of himself, and yet I cannot too strongly express my conviction that the Spirit of God is always present to him, and that he may take hold of that strength if he will. I believe that the first step is made by God towards all men, but that they may and do accept or refuse according to something in themselves,—a personal choice which belongs to the very essence of their natures. The frequent recurrence throughout the book to the inward test of truth, moral and intellectual, is most pleasing to me,— the intuitive perception of truth, the glance that one sometimes gets into the truth of a fact or a principle which is followed by sudden darkness, and yet remains as a counterpoise against all the darkness, although it is only a memory. I have perfect sympathy with all such things. I hope I may yet have some real conversation with him upon this subject, which is to me the most interesting of all subjects, except the actual thing itself, the life of God in man's soul.

We paid a very pleasant visit to Broglie; both the Doctor[1] and I enjoyed it very much. I saw Madame de Staël as she passed through. Mr. Duparquet has called for me, and has asked me to see him at Etiolles, which I hope to do. Dear fellow-pilgrim, the Good Shepherd be with you,

[1] Dr. Chalmers.

strengthening and comforting you. Mr. Campbell begs to
be remembered to you.—Yours in much love,

T. ERSKINE.

150. TO THE REV. ALEXANDER J. SCOTT.

67 RUE DE GRENELLE, ST. GERMAIN,
2d August 1838.

MY DEAR FRIEND,—I am ready to go with you to Switzerland on a day's notice, and I think that I could now
safely leave Mr. Campbell, if he chose to be left. So come,
bringing, as aforesaid, Coleridge's Aids to Reflection and
two copies of Keble. . . . Poor ——, I think of his burdened unsatisfied heart often. I am miserable ; thou art
miserable ; he is miserable. *Omnes,* we are all miserable.
Such is the drama of life. To discover and feel a wise and
loving personal Will superintending and ordering this
strange history, is a support and a blessed support certainly,
but it does not put away the misery ; and not only a support, for it enables us not to choose to put away our misery
—that is something. Accept thy punishment, and I will
remember my covenant. Yes, it is something, which reaches
into the heart of God, into the infinite, which is, I suppose,
the peace passing understanding.

Remember me to Mrs. Rich and Miss Farrer. Farewell, dear friends.—Yours affectionately,   T. ERSKINE.

151. TO MADAME DE BROGLIE.

HÔTEL CASTELLANE, RUE DE GRENELLE, ST. GERMAIN,
2d August 1838.

DEAR FRIEND,—I do not expect in this world to be delivered from a heavy weight of sorrow. We are called into
a union and participation with Him who was a man of
sorrows, and who, though a Son, yet learned obedience by
the things which He suffered. Beloved friend, faint not,

neither be weary; take up your cross and follow Him unto
the same place whither He hath gone before. I believe
that it was the experience of what you express in your
letter,—I mean the experience of an insupportable burden
of grief, which I could by no means cast off,—which first
led me to take the view of the atonement which I now
take, and to consider Jesus not as a substitute, but as the
Head and Fountain of Salvation, supplying us with His own
spirit, so that we may use the discipline of life, the sorrow,
the agony of life, as He did, to learn obedience, to learn to
find in the will of God, which appoints our path, a union
with the mind of God. Jesus found that will to be meat
indeed, as He walked His weary, sorrowing pilgrimage; He
felt that it was all tender love, and He would have us feel
it also, for we cannot otherwise be made meet for the rest
and glory of God. And as He puts the cup of sorrow into
our hand, He says, Can ye drink of the cup that I drink of?
And shall we refuse or hold back from this fellowship with
Jesus, in the sorrow which kills sin when it is received in
the spirit of Jesus, in the filial spirit? " These light afflictions, which are but for a moment, work for us a far more
exceeding, even an eternal weight of glory, whilst we look
not at the things which are seen, but at the things which are
not seen." The sorrow is not merely a difficulty which we
are to endeavour to pass through as easily and as quickly as
we can, it is the thing which works out the eternal weight
of glory,—not at all in the way of a price paid for it, but as
the wise education and medicine of God. We are like the
Israelites travelling through that dreary desert, until our
carcases, our fleshly thoughts and desires, fall in the wilderness; but in the meantime we have the manna to feed on,
the will of God in all things, and we have the pillar of
cloud and of fire, the presence of God in our consciences
directing us in the way. And shall we say that we are with-

out comfort? And have we not a hope full of immortality? Dear sister, you have often been a channel of comfort to me. I pray God for you, that you may meet a living will of God in every sorrow that bows down your heart, and that you may find your Father's love in your Father's will. Read the 3d chapter of the Lamentations of Jeremiah in the English Bible. I have often found it a precious word of comfort. Accept your punishment, not the punishment of a Judge, but the chastisement of a most tender Father, who afflicteth not willingly, but for our profit. Will you look at my book, pp. 103-105, if you are not afraid? I was out at Etiolles seeing Madame Duparquet. They had just heard of the death of Mr. Cuvier, which seemed a very sore affliction to Madame Duparquet, whose heart is very tender. The discipline is going on in every house, and in every heart. Let us take part in God's work with us. Let us enter into His plan. Dear friend, I do not say that the inward revelation in conscience makes us independent of the outward revelation, but I say that we never rightly receive or believe the outward revelation until we learn it from the inward, and that the use of the outward is to foster and educate the inward. I believe that they are duplicates by the same hand, with this difference, that the inward, being a living thing, and being mixed and surrounded with things of a nature opposed to it, is liable to be mistaken, and even to remain altogether undeveloped, or choked in the heart, whereas the other remains always the same unmixed pure announcement of truth.

152. TO MADAME DE BROGLIE.

HÔTEL CASTELLANE, RUE GRENELLE, ST. GERMAIN,
13th August.

DEAR FRIEND,—I have heard from Dr. Chalmers. He tells me that he has sent a copy of his works, now reprinting,

for you, and another for Mademoiselle Pomaret. He had not
written to you, because he did not like to do it, until he
had been invited to do so by yourself. If you have received
his books, I doubt not that you have already written to
him, and if you have not received them—that is, if they
have not yet arrived,—you may perhaps write to tell him
so.   I should like to hear how Mademoiselle Pomaret is; I
heard from M. Duparquet that she had been unwell.

When I received your last letter, I was so much occupied
that I entirely overlooked the criticisms which you make
in it on the views which you suppose my book contains.
I often feel discouraged from expressing my thoughts, by
finding that I do it in so imperfect a manner as to give
an entirely false impression of them.   I see that I have
given you an impression perfectly foreign to my meaning.
My object is not in the smallest degree to say what the
conscience might do for man without the Bible, but to
say that all that a man learns from the Bible, without its
awakening within him a living consciousness of its truth,
might as well not be learned,—that is, I believe that there
is a real correspondence between the truths of the Bible
and the spiritual part of man's nature, in the same way as
there is a correspondence between the outward relations
of life (as parent and child, husband and wife, brothers,
sisters, friends, neighbours, etc.) and the feelings of
man's heart; and that as a man could not comprehend
these relations of life, if he had not a consciousness in his
heart corresponding to them, so I believe that a man could
not really believe the truths concerning his higher relations
unless he had a consciousness in his heart corresponding to
them, and that in fact he cannot truly be said to believe
them unless that consciousness be awakened.   I wish to
guard people against supposing that they believe a doctrine
of the Bible, or have faith, merely because they believe

that the Bible is true. I believe also that there are different depths of meaning in the same truth, and that according to the degree of spiritual discernment of the deeper meaning so is the profit from the doctrine.

The revelation of God in flesh means not only the revelation of the history of Jesus Christ, but the revelation of God in His relation to man's understanding and feelings and nature in general.

Jesus Christ was God and man, showing that God could in a measure be comprehended by man, and that man's faculties were fit recipients of God. And ought we not to expect this from the account of man's creation "in the image of God"? The image was and is the inward likeness surely, so that man can be a conscious willing co-operator with God, which the lower animals could not be.

I have never supposed the case of a man possessing a Bible and yet putting it from him, on the ground that conscience was sufficient. I think that a man who did so would be found to be sinning against his conscience. But I never suppose such a case; it does not form any part of my argument. I do not oppose the conscience to the Bible, but I say that the Bible is meant and fitted for the conscience, as a telescope is meant for the eye. The conscience is the eye, the Bible is the telescope, and as the telescope does not change the faculty of sight, but brings more objects within its range, so does the Bible to the conscience.

I believe that God has left no man without the means of salvation, and that a man without a Bible has still a God, and a God whom he can get acquainted with through his conscience, and I believe that salvation means a growing in acquaintanceship with God and in conformity to His will.

Remember me with much regard to Mademoiselle Pomaret and your husband, and Monsieur Doudan, and to

your daughter and her husband, if they are with you.—
Yours ever,　　　　　　　　　　　　　　T. ERSKINE.

I intend to go to Geneva next week, early in the week
—on Wednesday perhaps. Write a word.

153. TO MISS RACHEL ERSKINE.

PARIS, 15*th August* 1838.

MY DEAR COUSIN RACHEL,—I believe that I shall leave
this great Babylon of Paris for the little Babylon of Geneva
(for Babylon is everywhere, and of all sizes) in less than a
week. . . . Mr. Campbell intends to return home, when I
leave this ; he has not received any apparent benefit by his
stay here, and he feels very anxious to see his (eighty years)
old father, from whom he has never been nearly so long
separated in the course of his life. I expect Scott to take
his place with me in my journey to and through Switzerland.
It is to me a weighty and anxious undertaking to revisit
my Swiss friends, and to enter with them on matters on
which I know we differ. . . . I had a letter from Dr.
Chalmers the other day, proving to me that he had completely misunderstood my book. I need not think of
writing another book to explain the book which I have
already written. What are you doing? enjoying lovely
Cardross, fair and noble Cardross, with its grave square
tower, and its trees, under which our fathers' fathers have
played, and its beautiful extent of grass, and its seclusion,
and its simple peasantry—simple, that was, but that is no
longer, for simplicity has left our land? It is possible that
on the whole there may be a higher standard of moral
feeling in Great Britain than in France at this present
moment; but it seems to me that we are going down-hill
and that France is rather ascending. The thought of my
country is a very melancholy thought to me. The whole
social system is sick; there is no brotherhood. I some-

times feel as if I could enter into the feelings of the French
nation, when, conscious of the entire want of brotherhood
amongst them, they raised their frantic cry of Liberty,
Equality, Fraternity, or Death ! They felt they needed these
things, but they did not know how to set about getting
them.   They felt the want of brothers, and the only way
that occurred to them of manufacturing brothers was to
set the guillotine agoing, and cannons and muskets and
bayonets agoing, and saying to all men, Be our brothers, or
die. . . .

154. TO HIS SISTER MRS. STIRLING.

BERN, 14*th Sept.* 1838.

DEAREST CHRISTIAN,—I am often recalled to the remembrance of you and Charles at present, by the sight of
places which we all looked at together; for I am now making
with Mr. Scott the same tour that I made with you in the
'24.   These remembrances now must carry us out of the
visible and the finite, if we would, even in imagination,
follow our companions, as almost all our remembrances must
do ; for what can we remember that is not connected with
some one who has ceased to be a part of our visible circumstances ?   And the chief character of interest which
the lofty peaks (which I am now searching for amongst the
clouds) possess, is just that same quality of carrying us up
out of the visible and the finite.   The meeting of heaven
and earth, of the Creator and the creature, is the true
thing symbolised by the scenes before me, and from which
they derive their intense interest ; as it is also the thing
which is at the root of the interest which we feel in following a departed friend into his unseen habitation. . . . I
met at Lausanne with an old friend of mine, who was
pastor of the Reformed Church at Frankfort when I passed
through that city with Begbie, before Archibald joined me

at Hamburg; he is apparently dying now; he is a man of
very remarkable talents and great amiableness. We had
been great friends at Frankfort, and although we had had
no correspondence of any kind since that time, he met me
with much affection and much emotion; he told me that
he would wish to live, if it were the will of God; he had
been, he thought, a gainer by his illness, in respect of his
qualification to teach others the way of salvation; he also
said he had been so happy at Lausanne; he loved and
admired his country exceedingly, and he felt that the loss
of life would be a great privation. Poor fellow, he does
not look as if he could survive long; he remembered every
word that had passed between us at Frankfort, and went
over it all with an affecting interest.[1] I also made a new
acquaintance at Lausanne—with M. Vinet, the most remarkable man in the French Protestant Church; he seemed
to me large and free, and yet deeply serious. I was
delighted with him; he has not the Calvinism of Gaussen
or Merle—at least he has some other thing which balances
it, which they want. I also saw Scholl, whom you, I think,
saw—an amiable, excellent man. The sight of Vinet, and
the reading of some of his books, gave me a hope for the
Swiss and French Protestants which I scarcely had before.
I am convinced that nothing but infidelity can be the consequence of holding that Calvinistic logic so prevalent
through Scotland, and which is preached also, though in a
more living way, through the French and Swiss Reformed
Church. Men require something now which will commend
itself to the conscience and the reason, and if that is not
given them, they have only superstition and infidelity to
choose between, and I think that they are showing that
infidelity is their choice.

I wish you could get Vinet; he is more of Scott's calibre

---

[1] Monsieur Manuel.

than any person that I know. I shall in a future letter
tell you how you may get it. I met Tom Dundas and his
wife at Geneva; I was happy to be met with so much of
the feeling of relationship by him. . . . We intend to go
to Interlachen to-morrow.   T. E.

155. TO MISS JANE STIRLING.

7th Oct. 1838, GENEVA.

. . . You will by this time have received the news of
the death of Madame de Broglie. To many it is a deso-
lating blow; to her poor husband and children, and to
Madame de Staël, it is a desolation, a withering of life.
You knew her, and you loved her, and she loved you;
and you will feel that there is not another creature in
creation that could fill her place to you. I feel that; but
I know that she has entered into peace, and that this blow,
so severe to others, so drying up of the life of many hearts,
has for herself broken in pieces the gates of brass, and cut
in sunder the bars of iron. She died by a brain fever, as
her brother did, brought on, I doubt not, by the continued
wearing down of the material by the immaterial. She
took a slight cold, as she thought, about the 7th September;
on the 11th it appeared serious; on the 22d, at five in the
morning, her spirit flew away and was at rest. The fever
affected her head very soon, but it had no power over her
heart, over her free spirit; she prayed without ceasing, she
loved without ceasing—beloved spirit. I saw her last on
the 21st August. I left her that day with a solemn feeling,
an indistinct feeling of the uncertainty of time-things; but
little indeed did I realise that she was so near her deliverance. She urged me much to go back to Broglie when she
did, which was two days afterwards; she said she wished
much to commune on the things of eternity, and she said
" Il faut du temps, vous savez, pour parler des choses de

l'éternité." When I paid my visit at Broglie with Dr.
Chalmers, he occupied her entirely, so she required a visit
for myself; she pressed it so much that, if it had not been
that I did not like to trespass on Mr. Scott's time, I should
certainly have gone. As I was going out of the room, she
said, " Am I ever to see you again in this world ?" I hope
to pass eternity with her. It is wonderful to me to think
what a place she has occupied in my life, since I have
become acquainted with her. Her husband has been supported in a wonderful manner. He and Madlle. Pomaret
never left her bedside after the fever decidedly took possession of her. Madame Vernet yesterday read me a letter of
Madlle. Pomaret to Adèle,[1] in which she speaks of him as
of one who has consecrated himself to God ; she says, " Auprès de lui, je me trouve comme dans une église ; il est
saint." The impression that she herself made on all the
servants and doctors that came was remarkable ; they felt
that she was holy. And now she is no more seen of men;
her feet, which here were shod with the preparedness of
the gospel of peace, now stand in the gates of the New
Jerusalem. Her son was absent on a walking expedition,
so that they did not know where he was, or how to reach
him. Louise was at Milan ; since she heard of it her grief
has been violent. The God of blessing give them all a
blessing in this bitter cup. I have seen old Madame
Necker, to whom she was as a daughter, the most affectionate of daughters. . . . At Paris get acquainted with
Monsr. Verny, pasteur of the Lutheran Church there—he
lives at No. 11 Rue de Barbette—a great friend of Madame
de Broglie, and one who could appreciate her. . . . We
are strangers and pilgrims on the earth ; the only right
thing is to pray without ceasing, and to love without
ceasing. . . .

[1] Sister-in-law to Madame de Staël.

156. TO HIS SISTER MRS. STIRLING.

GENÈVE, *Oct.* 10, 1838.

MY DEAR CHRISTIAN,—I have lost a great friend, a dear friend, since I last wrote to you. Madame de Broglie's death has changed the world for me a good deal. Her acquaintance has been a considerable feature in my life, more so, indeed, than that of any person whom I have not known from infancy. There was an activity in her friendship—an activity both of heart and of intelligence—that I never met with except in Dr. Stuart, and an activity which was continually directed upwards. Her character had undergone a great change since I last saw her; she was not more occupied about eternal things, but her occupation with them was much more healthy; she seemed to me to live much in the spirit of prayer, enjoying the love and peace of God to a great degree, and making it her business to learn His righteousness. I wish you had seen her; although I believe you will soon see her, and see her in a form which will still more perfectly utter that spiritual beauty which her Creator intended her to utter than the form in which I have known her; but yet I wish you had seen her, that you might understand what I mean when I say that she and our brother James were the two most perfect symbols, in their persons, of a spiritual being, having a mission to fulfil in this world, and not belonging to it, that I have met with in my pilgrimage. I always thought James most beautiful, and I thought her most beautiful. They were both like what I can suppose glorified humanity will be. There was an unspeakable charm about her; such a truth of heart, which used a most remarkable intelligence only for the purposes of truth. I may have as much intercourse with her still, of the most profitable sort; but I cannot help feeling the earth much emptier for her removal.

Oct. 13*th.*—I received your most affectionate and welcome letter the day before yesterday. Yes, she is blessed, but she has left many mourners; her poor husband seems to have received a great blessing to his soul in this cup of sorrow; he seems to have met God in it. Dear Christian, what a wilderness the world is! and how right it is, and how fitting it is, that it should be so; it is just the proper school for constraining us to cast ourselves upon God as our whole portion, and to look through the visible into the invisible. My birthday. Be the Lord my choice.

Oct. 14.—I have been at church, where I met Madame Vernet, who told me that yesterday she had a letter from M. de Broglie himself, poor man. I intend to go out to Carra (her campagne) to-morrow, to see more of her, and to hear of these mourners. I am now living by myself, which I have not done since I left England, having first had Mr. Campbell and afterwards Mr. Scott for my companion. They are both remarkable men; but Scott is, in point of intellect, one of the first, if not the first, man that I have known. I had an interlude of Dr. Chalmers for some days as a variety. He went with me to Broglie, where he was delighted with her, and she with him; that is, with his honesty, and his naturalness, and his kindliness; dear woman, when we took our leave, she told me that she did not consider that as a visit from me, for that she had been so entirely occupied with Dr. Chalmers; she said, " I know you will not be hurt by it." The last day that I saw her was the 21st of August; there was something in our meeting like a farewell, like a leave-taking; she spoke of the danger of being carried away by particular ideas; she expressed her fear for me in that respect, saying at the same time that, although younger than I was, she felt something like a maternal care for me, as well as a sisterly, and she gave me a lithograph etching of one of Overbeck's little

pieces—Jesus standing at the door and knocking; she wrote
the date under it, 21st August, and "Il n'y a point d'autre
Sauveur que moi." He was indeed knocking at the door for
her, in a sense which neither of us thought of at the time;
though she told me that she often felt a most remarkable
longing for death. All her outward relations were happy,
and yet she had a deep melancholy that perpetually weighed
upon her heart. I had a letter yesterday from cousin
Rachel; I am glad to hear good accounts of her invalids.
The weather has become bitter cold here. *La bize* (I don't
know whether that is the true spelling) actually penetrates
into the marrow; it has made me think of crossing the Alps.
Jura is white before his usual time. My dear Christian, I
hope, if it please God, to be with you before very long, and
to arrange to live with you, that we may do each other
what good we can. . . . Yours ever,   T. E.

157. TO THE REV. JOHN M'LEOD CAMPBELL.

GENEVA, 17 *Oct.* 1838.

DEAR BROTHER,—I heard of your marriage from my
sister, Mrs. Paterson. May the Lord abundantly bless
you and her in your relation to each other, and make you
instruments of righteousness in the church and in the world.
I hope you may both prove in your own hearts that your
union is of the Lord.

Your marriage took place just four days after the death
of Madame de Broglie. I think I showed you that little
engraving which she gave me that last day that I saw her
in Paris, representing Jesus standing at the door and knocking. How little did I realise at the time that Jesus was
so soon to open the door of her clay prison, and give a full
release to her blessed yet wearied spirit from the conflict
of this world! I cannot express to you what a gap her
removal makes to me in this visible order of things. She

was connected in my mind with every subject of thought, and she possessed that idiosyncrasy, that individuality that prevents the possibility of her idea ever being confounded or mixed up with the idea of any other being. No other creature could fill the place which she filled in the minds and lives of those who knew her.

Her husband has received the stroke as from God, and though desolate is supported. I can conceive no resource for a human heart that has lost what he has lost but in an entire surrender of itself to God. In the meantime this seems to be his own feeling; he seems to desire simply to do and to receive the will of God. Her friendship has been to me a great gift. She has been a witness to me for God, a voice crying in the wilderness. She has been a warner and a comforter. I have seen her continually thirsting after a spiritual union with God. I have heard the voice of her heart crying after God out from the midst of all things which make this life pleasant and satisfying. She had a husband whose thoughts were large and high, and whose character was noble, affectionately attached to her. She had amiable, promising children. She had herself all the gifts of mind and character—intelligence, imagination, nobleness, and thoughts that wandered through eternity. She had a heart fitted for friendship, and she had friends who could appreciate her; but her God suffered her not to find rest in these things, her ear was opened to His own paternal voice, and she became His child, in the way that the world is not and knoweth not. I see her before me, her loving spirit uttering itself through every feature of her beautiful and animated countenance.

I am thankful to have known her as I have done, and I am thankful that I cannot forget her. I write this to you because you have seen her.

My dear brother, I think of you with much love. I hope you remember my needs before our Father.

I was glad to hear of the meeting which you had with your flock on the pier at Greenock, and of their sympathy with your marriage. May the Lord give them a blessing through you! Remember me affectionately to them, and give my brotherly love to dear Mrs. Campbell.

I hope you will see my sister at Cadder. Could you give my loving regards to your father, and let me hear from you about people and things?

Remember me most kindly to your brother and his wife, and to the Macnabbs. Farewell.   T. ERSKINE.

158. TO HIS SISTER MRS. PATERSON.

GENEVA, *25th Oct.* 1838.

DEAREST DAVIE,—I am living here in a hotel out of the town, free from the tumult, and yet near enough to walk into it or out of it at any hour. My friends the Cramers are very kind. Madame has married her whole family now; but her anxieties have not ceased, for she really cares for their souls more than for their bodies; she is a single-hearted woman, and full of affection. Madame Vernet holds the same place with me that she always did; she is a most profitable person to be with; she is not the least like Aunt Stirling in any other thing but in her continual thirsting after God.

27th.— . . . I am just going off to see old Madame Necker,[1] with whom I can grieve and rejoice over Madame de Broglie. She has lent me meditations on many chapters of the Bible by Madame de B., in the form of prayers—most interesting. Madame Vernet lent me a short account by her (M. de B.) of Mrs. Fry's visit to Paris; she describes Mrs. Fry in a way which recalled herself to me as strongly as if I had seen her and heard her. She was much struck with the simplicity of the Quaker manner, and the readi-

[1] Madame Necker-de-Saussure, authoress of *L'Éducation Progressive.*

ness to receive good and to acknowledge it, wherever and however mixed she found it. There was a young English-woman in the prison or bridewell to which Mrs. Fry was taken. Mrs. Fry said to her, "How long hast thou been here?" Woman—"Six years." Mrs. F., after a silence—"Thou shouldest not have been here." The poor woman burst into tears. M. de B. remarks that these short words reminded her of our Lord's words on some occasions, such as, "Call thy husband, and come hither."   T. E.

159. TO THE SAME.

GENEVA, 15*th Nov.* [1838].

DEAREST DAVIE,—I have just returned from a visit to Lausanne, where I had much enjoyment. Vinet is a delightful man, simple and natural, with a kindly sense of the ludicrous in him, and most candid. Manuel, the other eye of Lausanne, is dead. He was my first continental friend—in 1822.[1] I made his acquaintance when your dear Ann was four months old. Vinet was very willing to confer with me, but he is so continually besieged with visitors that it is not easy to get him for any length of time alone. I saw others of the Lausanne pastors and professors and young ministers, and I observed Vinet's mark upon them all. There is no narrowness about them, and they are

---

[1] "Le pasteur Manuel était un de ces hommes dont ne cessent de parler tous ceux qui les ont connus, mais dont les générations suivantes savent à peine le nom. . . . La sagesse et la poésie découlaient de son âme, 'comme le miel d'un rayon trop pleine.' Le mot est de Vinet, qui ne peut assez dire le bien que cet homme a fait en causant. 'Le charme de sa conversation était si grand, dit-il, qu'on ne croyait d'abord avoir que du plaisir; mais en revenant par le souvenir sur une heure délicieuse passée auprès de cet incomparable causeur, où étais surpris de se trouver riche d'une vertu de plus, s'il est permis d'appeler ainsi toute puissance qui porte vers le bien et vers la vérité.'"—*Alexandre Vinet, Histoire de sa Vie et de ses Ouvrages*, par E. Rambert. Troisième Edition. Laus-anne, 1876.

more natural, apparently living less by rule than by a living
instinct.   The successful candidate for one of their theological chairs within the last two months, acknowledged his
belief of a universal final restoration, and this to the judges
on whom his election depended.   Vinet drove me out (in
a *char*) to a family in the country, the lady of which had
translated one of my books, but had been prevented from
publishing it by hearing that Madame de Broglie was
engaged in the same thing.   I found her a very interesting
person, full of heart and simplicity.   I promised to send
her the book on Election.   I wish to re-write that book,
to make it more compact and more orderly, and I think
that I could probably do it better in Switzerland than in
Italy.   Madame Cramer, dear, kind woman, is urging me
very much to come to her house. . . .   T. ERSKINE.

160. TO MADAME FOREL.

GENÈVE, 19*th Nov.* 1838.

DEAR MADAME,—I send you my book on the doctrine
of Election, or rather on the doctrine of Conscience, for
that would be the truest description of its contents, and at
the same time I would commend it to your patience, and
indulgence, and candour.   You will often feel surprised
and even shocked in reading it,—you will be sometimes
tempted to think me a mere rationalist, but I know that
I am not so.

The leading idea of the book is that each individual man
is a little world in which that whole history which took
place in Judea 1800 years ago is continually reproduced.
Each of us is, or has been, that world spoken of in St. John
i. 10, "He was in the world, and the world was made by
Him, and the world knew Him not."   I believe that the
light which shines in each man's conscience is the real presence of Jesus, "the Word which was with God, and was

God," and that the egoism and vanity and hypocrisy, and worldly and fleshly desires within us, are represented by the Scribes and Pharisees and Sadducees, Herod and Pilate, etc. I believe that the presence of Jesus in us, with His quickening (vivifiant) spirit, gives to each of us the power, whether we use it or not, of joining and taking part with Him against the evils of our own hearts, and I believe that in as far as we do so we become partakers of His nature and members of His body. I believe that Jesus is the one Elect, and that those who by thus taking part with Jesus become members of his body, become also members of the election, and that those who continue to resist Him shut themselves out from the election. In this way also I believe that, as Christ was really given to men immediately after the Fall, all are elect in Him, He being in them all, and all are reprobate or rejected in the first Adam; but that we can make either our election or our reprobation sure by joining ourselves either to the one party or the other. I believe that God takes the first step to every man, and draws every man by His Spirit, and that man's part is acceptance and yielding.

I am sensible that many readers may be tempted to think, from my dwelling so much on the internal history of Christianity in the individual, that I overlook or under-value the external facts; but my desire was to restore what I conceived the lost equilibrium by drawing the attention to that part which had been generally neglected. I also wished to show that we really do not and cannot under-stand the outward history of Christ until we recognise its correspondence with this inward history. The very same mysteries which appear in the outward history of Christ are to be found in our own hearts; and when we find them there, although we do not comprehend them the more on that account by our understanding, yet we feel that we

Y

get the explanation of them.   I believe also that as each man is a world, and a resemblance of the large world, so the whole mass of individuals constitute another unity, another world, and that as Jesus is in each man, so He is the new and heavenly root of spiritual life to this larger world, and that what He did outwardly for the larger was for the purpose of bringing this life and light inwardly to all the individuals.   But I need not go over these things. After you have read it, if your patience holds out so long, I shall be most happy to converse with you about it.   I feel very much obliged to M. Vinet for having introduced me to the acquaintance of yourself and Mr. F.   Indeed, my visit to Lausanne was altogether most gratifying to me. I met with so much fraternity and so much candour.   Farewell for the present, and I remain, with much respect and regard, your obedient servant,   T. Erskine.

P.S.—There is an operation of God going on internally in every man's conscience, and externally in every man's life ; this twofold operation, felt but not understood by us, is what we need to have explained, and the great purpose of the Bible is to give us this explanation.   The truth of the Bible is proved to us by its agreement with what we ourselves feel and know of this twofold operation.   We could not ourselves have found out the explanation, that is, we could not have produced the Bible, but when it is set before us we can judge whether it agrees with the facts and explains them, in the same way that we can judge of Copernicus's system, whether it agrees or not with the phenomena, and explains them.   But our judgment in this case is not merely or even chiefly an intellectual judgment, for it is mainly founded on the discovery of the same mysteries in our own consciousness, and in the facts of revelation. My object is not to make out an intellectual system, but to show that all the Christian doctrines are already in man's heart, though undeveloped and not understood, and that as all religion, in as far as it is religion, must be supernatural, because it is the revelation between the Creator and the creature, so also, all religion, which is true religion, must be adapted to the nature and constitution of man. I am afraid that I have not explained my meaning distinctly.

161. TO HIS SISTER MRS. STIRLING.

[Dec. 1838.]

DEAREST CHRISTIAN,—I often wish that I were sitting beside you, or that you were sitting beside me, that we might help each other in the business of our being; that we might learn our lessons for eternity together. You will have heard that Sir John Hay is dead. Poor Lady Hay will be very desolate; for he was her sole occupation. I hope it will not be without a blessing to her, poor thing; I hope it will discover to her a Father who is ever nigh and ever loving. He was just my age, and we were at school together in the 1796, forty-two years ago! What a deal of lost time have I to lament and answer for! I have sinned against heaven and before thee, and am most unworthy to be called thy son. A most unprofitable servant have I been, and still continue to be. One thing was great, which God supplied:—He suffered human life, and died, as Gambold says. And as I think of past time and past sins and negligences, I think also of past persons, the friends and guardians and companions of our childhood and youth: our mother, Ann, James; our grandmother; Uncle Cardross, Lady C.; the Lauriston venerable pair, and their children; Uncle James, long-looked-for, then returning home to die; Uncle Tom, his young wife; the Kippenross history; the Walkinshaw history; the St. Andrew Square couple; your history; Davie's history.

If ye will accept your punishment, then will I remember
my covenant of life to you. It is the same thing everywhere. I escaped from home, and went to the Continent,
made friends, and I have found death working here also.
If ye die with Him, ye shall live with Him : if ye suffer
with Him, ye shall reign with Him. I had a most affecting
letter a few days ago from M. de Broglie, in answer to one
that I had written him. " Jamais perte ne fut plus grande,
plus profonde, plus irréparable," he says, " jamais la
main de Dieu ne s'est appésantie plus rigoureusement sur
une famille désolée." He concludes his mourning letter
thus :—" On est honteux de l'impuissance des paroles,
et l'on est blessé de les employer tant elles rendent
peu ce qui se passe au fond de l'âme." Poor widowed
heart ! The last tidings that I had of him from Madame
Vernet was that he and his two grown children had returned to Broglie for twenty-four hours, to look again on
the places consecrated by the life and death of their departed saint.

What you say about my book, and about her warning
voice to me, I receive as a warning ; at the same time, I
may say to you that I think that it is from misunderstand-
ing it, that some persons have thought that it detracted
from the work of the Saviour. My object was to call the attention to a view of the doctrine which has been neglected ;
and not at all to deny or exclude that which has not
been neglected. I intend, however, if I can, to write the
book over again, more shortly, and more orderly, and more
distinctly. I feel convinced that the principle contained
in my book is the principle which must be followed out
and developed, if we would preach Christianity with effi-
ciency to the men of this generation. The connection between the gospel and the conscience, including the inward
feelings and consciousness of each man's heart, is the true

starting-point in all religious instruction and argument. That this connection has been much overlooked, and even denied, is unquestionable; and we must retrace our steps in this respect, if we would see an efficient preaching of the gospel. . . .—Yours ever, T. Erskine.

162. TO THE REV. ALEX. J. SCOTT.

Geneva, *2d December* 1838.

My dear Friend,—I ought before now to have acknowledged your letter. You see that I am still here. I am still, however, in the expectation of spending at least a part of the winter at Rome. I have a wish to see that world's grave again, and to listen to the voice which comes out of it. You will have heard that Sir John Hay died there a month ago; poor Lady Hay will be a very desolate widow. Manuel also is dead. Both of these men had a great enjoyment of life, though in very different ways.

I passed a week lately at Lausanne, and saw a good deal of Vinet and of some of the others, pastors and professors. Vinet is very amiable, very natural, and has that basis of thought in him on which thoughts from all quarters can find a footing or a rooting. I like him so much that I could be tempted to spend the winter at Lausanne, if I did not see that he is in such continual request as would prevent much quiet personal intercourse. His sermons, *Discours sur quelques sujets religieux*, are very interesting. He is always aiming at the *terrain commun*, though I do not find that he hits it. It is obvious that the pastoral and professorial society there is much influenced by him. Some of the young clergy I liked very much; they are simple-hearted and free, and undogmatical. There has never been any distinctly avowed heterodoxy at Lausanne, so that they have had no call to define their faith, like our Genevese friends. I was present at a public disputation, at which a dissertation by a candidate for the philosophical chair in the Academy was attacked and defended. The title of the dissertation was *Science et Foi,* and its avowed object was to show that philosophy rightly pursued would reproduce the truths of Christianity, so that the objects of faith would be verified by the intelligence. The disputation was not interesting, but I have read the discourse with considerable interest; and if I return to Lausanne I think I shall try to see the writer. His discourse contains a history of philosophy, which he considers as the history of the development of the human mind. Schelling and Hegel are, according to him, the men who have put the top-stone on the building commenced by Descartes on the subjective side and by Bacon on the objective, for he commences his historical sketch with these moderns. I shall quote for your behoof one of his theses which he undertakes to defend: " La justice est composée de deux élémens, la justice qui punit et la justice qui pardonne. La miséricorde est un devoir de la justice, comme la sévérité et la peine ; ou plutôt la peine n'a pour but que l'absolution."

Dear Mme. Cramer is full of kindness, and her whole family, so also is Mme. Vernet ; but I have little intercourse with Gaussen and Merle, etc.; they are occupied with their academy. I must copy another thesis of this philosophical candidate : " C'est aller contre l'esprit du protestantisme que d'envisager la Bible comme la base et le principe unique de notre foi."

I see something more of Diodati,[1] but he also is very busy, having engaged to give a course on the revival of philosophy. I heard his opening lecture, which was very good. Give my affectionate regards to your people, your own household, Wedgwood, etc.   T. ERSKINE.

[1] Married to one of the Vernets.

163. TO HIS SISTER MRS. STIRLING.

GENÈVE, 3*d Jan.* 1839.

DEAREST CHRISTIAN,— . . . I have just returned from a visit to Lausanne, where I have spent a week very pleasantly in the society of some very estimable people, who have shown me much friendship. If Davie has sent you Vinet's book, you will be able in some degree to judge of his interesting mind ; but his humble and gentle and sensitive character gives his personal intercourse a charm which cannot be communicated by any book containing merely expositions of trains of thought. When I was there, he and many more whom I saw were much occupied with the project of a law for new-modelling in some respects their ecclesiastical constitution ; his reputation for wisdom and conscientiousness forces him into situations of trust and responsibility, which he would thankfully keep out of, and he is at present at the head of an ecclesiastical commission, which is charged with the appointment of ministers and assistants through the Canton, which makes great demands on his time and on his peace. His wife is a very pleasant, intelligent, unpretending person ; they lost a daughter last year, grown up, and their only child now is a son of nineteen, who has been deaf since he was nine or ten, and whose development, in consequence, has been much stopped. I see this is a great trial to them ; and she seems to desire to find the broken body of Jesus meat indeed, and His blood drink indeed. The question of the eternity of punishments has been stirred at Lausanne, by the circumstance that a candidate for one of the theological chairs refused to subscribe to the common doctrine ; notwithstanding this refusal, he was elected. Vinet only says, " La lumière me manque."

There is a very singularly interesting young man whose acquaintance I also made, of a profoundly mystical character, as well as understanding, a disciple of Jacob Boehme,

who gave me a sketch of a work to which he has devoted
his life; he spoke to me for I daresay three hours without
intermission, opening up to me a fine heart and a rich
understanding.   I found him agonised in his spirit about
the destiny of the fallen angels; there is something very
interesting in this for the heart, and his love for these
beings does not interfere with his love for his own kind.
He considers this world and the constitution of TIME as a
remedial dispensation, arising out of the fall of an angelic
race—a parenthesis in the midst of eternity—and his work
is to be a history of TIME. . . .

164. TO LORD RUTHERFURD.

POSTE RESTANTE, GENÈVE, 21*st Jan.* 1839.

MY DEAR RUTHERFURD,— . . . I hope Mrs. R. is well
and all friends.   I desire my most affectionate remembrance to them all.   I think often of you and of them as partakers in a common shipwreck; as sharers in many things.
I look forward to some quiet hours with you, my dear friend,
whom I value highly.   But when are your hours to be quiet,
or indeed any person's hours, on this side of death?   Does
your active spirit retain all its spring, or do you sometimes feel weary?   My friend, we are but cisterns, and we
need a Fountain.   The creature is essentially insufficient
for itself, and this, so far from being a misery, is intended
to conduct us to our greatest happiness—the filial relation
to the Creator.   Christianity is just the history and the
process of this filial relation—this sonship.—Yours most
affectionately,   T. ERSKINE.

165. TO THE SAME.

GENEVA, 24*th Jan.* 1839.

. . . The death of Madame de Broglie has made a great
blank to me.   She was a most singularly gifted person, not

so showy as her mother, but of a far deeper nature. She
had a hunger and thirst after the infinite, in all things, and
all her thoughts seemed to rise out of the infinite. She
had, besides, what is still more uncommon in a French-
woman,—a truth and simplicity of character, which one
rarely finds even in the highest order of men. I know
nobody like her now. She is now with God, after whom
her whole heart longed whilst she was here. She was only
forty-one.

My dear friend, one of us may be speaking of the other's
death before long. I am now fifty, and I feel that I have
not long to live, and I really wish to live for eternity and
for God's purpose in calling me into being.

Farewell. I cannot tell you how well I love you, Rutherfurd, and how much I have prized your steady kindness
and friendship. I think I could die to turn you to God,
your true centre and rest. You will be forced to come
to that centre some day, but it is losing much not to come
immediately. I do not speak this as one superior, for I
feel how much reason I have to be ashamed of what I am.
You have been more faithful to your light than I have been
to mine.—Ever yours most affectionately, T. ERSKINE.

166. TO HIS SISTER MRS. PATERSON.

GENEVA, *5th Feb.* 1839.

DEAREST DAVIE,—What stupidity it is not to be living
in the purpose of God, in a sympathy with the love which
would lead us into holiness and eternal blessedness, by the
only possible way! I am a mystery to myself; for I see,
and sometimes experience, that there is no rest, no happiness, except in a life of prayer and faith, and yet I live
much out of that true and right state. I feel the great
reasonableness of Paul making it his first petition to God
for the Ephesians, that they might be strengthened with

all might by the Spirit in the inner man, that so Christ might dwell in their hearts by faith; I feel how much I need to be taught to cleave to and hold by this strengthening Spirit. I believe that the way is to watch the beginnings of our thoughts, and to nourish our souls by ever looking to the love of God contained in the eternal purpose which He purposed in Christ Jesus—namely, that we should arrive at a conformity in Christ's blessedness by a conformity to His cross. It is an eternal purpose—a purpose that God has had from eternity, and will follow out to eternity. He will not abandon it; He will never allow us to stop short; He will continue the application of His various and wise Providence towards us, making us feel that sin is bitterness, and separation from Him is sin. Yesterday I met for the first time with a daughter-in-law of Madame ——'s, who interested me very much. . . . She told me that she felt that she could not get herself to love God, and yet, for many years, she has done nothing else than try to love Him. I spoke to her of God's love to us as the only thing that could lead us to love Him; she then spoke of the condition of men after death, and of the numbers who died at a distance from God, and asked me what I thought of this as regarding the love of God to man. I then told her frankly what I hoped for all men. She told me that she herself sometimes entertained that hope, but that she could not find it in the Bible, yet she thought there could be no real gospel without it. I think so too—the unending love of God. . . . —Yours ever,   T. ERSKINE.

167. TO MADAME VINET.

GENÈVE, 6 *Feb.* 1839.

M. BOST has brought me the little brochure, and the very welcome letter which accompanied it. I have been entering into the feelings which, I knew, the late proceedings

in your Canton on the subject of religion would excite in
you. It is a call to humiliation and prayer, not to dis-
couragement; for the results are in God's hands, and He
maketh all things work together for good to those that love
Him. The present condition of things at Zürich is a remarkable instance of good coming out of apparent evil.
What I fear most, in Switzerland as well as elsewhere, is
that the contest should become a contest of opinions, a contest between orthodoxy and heterodoxy, instead of a contest between the spirit and the flesh, between spiritual life
and spiritual death. Our business is to give utterance to
that voice which the Spirit of God speaks in our consciences,
and this utterance is to come not out of our mouths only
but out of our lives. Each man is called to be a member
of the Incarnate Word; that is, to have the will of God
expressed in his flesh, and so written in his flesh as to be
seen and read of all men. What a fearful difference between what we ought to be and what we are! Our calling is to be like Christ; filled with the spirit of Christ;
uttering in our words and actions the mind of God; and
what are we? Alas! I know for myself how little of all
that is accomplished in me; and how little the witness
which my mouth gives for God's truth is supported by
living holiness in my inward and outward history. We
are then true witnesses for Christ, and then only, when we
are ourselves experiencing and showing forth in our persons His death and resurrection; the dying unto man's
will, the living unto God's will. The comfort is, that the
cause of true religion in man's heart, and in the world, is
the cause of God. God's heart yearns over it, and God's
power sustains it. We forget where our great strength
lies, when we look to any human strength for the support
of the church. Our strength is in our Head, in Him who
said, "I have overcome the world," and faith is really a

confidence in the unseen strength of God, supporting us in opposition to all appearance of outward strength against us.

I like very well what you say on the subject of my book, although I don't agree with the application of it. The question is, What is the meaning of election in the Bible? You say, "We had better leave the matter as it is left in the Bible—the two extreme points stated—without attempting to reconcile them." My answer is, I think that I have followed the Bible; for it seems to me that the Bible is at special pains to deny the doctrine of personal election in its ordinary acceptation, and to make us understand that the true doctrine is, that those who live in the Spirit are the children of God, and that those who live in their own independent will cannot have fellowship with God, and that all have to choose between these two conditions. The difficulty in the intellect is nothing; but the difficulty in the moral conscience is not nothing. I believe that all the fundamental spiritual truths are out of the sphere of the reasoning faculty, but that they are in the sphere of conscience, and that we do not apprehend them at all, unless we apprehend them in our consciences. When Jesus says to us, "Without me ye can do nothing," He means to persuade us to depend upon Him for our spiritual life; that is, He means to dissuade us from making the wrong choice of depending on ourselves, for surely He does not mean to say, You have no power to choose between dependence on me, and dependence on yourselves. My conviction of the importance of the subject is a very deep conviction.

I am very happy that you like the article on Sir Walter Scott. I agree with you in thinking that the views in it are admirable. You are the first foreigner (as we call all but ourselves) whom I have found capable of admiring it. The name of the author is Carlyle, a man of most original mind. I hope to profit by M. de Breule's obliging offer to be acquainted with me, when I return to Lausanne. Dear friend, I hope that this is not the last letter that I shall receive from you. I feel much obliged to you for your kindness. I feel the blessing of having Christian friends, friends who have communion with God, and who, when they think of me, will pray for me. I beg my respectful and affectionate regards to your husband. Farewell.— Yours most truly, T. ERSKINE.

168. TO MRS. SCOTT.

GENEVA, *20th February* 1839.

DEAR MRS. SCOTT,—I shall say nothing about being ashamed of not having sooner answered your kind and acceptable letter, it being quite clear that if I am not ashamed, I at least ought to be ashamed,—but I shall say, that I hope you will not be provoked by my remissness, to give up all thoughts of continuing your kindness. I never felt a greater need of letters and intelligence from home, or from any friend who will be good enough to send it to me. I have been glad to hear from my sister that Mr. Scott has been well and strong since he left me, and that his heart seems to go with his preaching. I never read of any of the great meetings of operatives in the manufacturing districts without thinking of him and his proposed visit to Paisley. I wish we saw some more men, rightly qualified, who could go through these disturbed masses, and explain to them, that they need something else than a repeal of the corn laws, and universal suffrage, to make them happy. It would be a great thing to let them understand that they are treated with indignity when they are addressed as if they had only temporal interests, and as if they were necessarily dependent on second causes. "To

open the blind eyes" is a high vocation, and I trust that
Mr. S. will be strengthened to fulfil it, profitably for many.

We have all been much scandalised and shocked here by
the election of Strauss (the author of that strange and much-
talked-of book," The Life of Jesus") to fill one of the chairs in
the Theological School of Zürich.   This is the most bare-
faced profession of infidelity that has yet been made in
Switzerland.   At Lausanne also some very unpleasant
demonstrations against piety and religion in general have
been made in the Council of State and amongst the people,
on the occasion of proposing a change in the ecclesiastical
law, of which the giving up of the old Helvetic Confession
of Faith was to form a part.   And here at Geneva, in
an appointment to one of the Theological chairs, my
friend Diodati, son-in-law of Madame Vernet, has been de-
feated by a man who is acknowledged to be in all respects
his inferior, simply because he holds the Divinity of
Christ and the doctrine of the atonement, which the other
rejects. . . .   I have made the acquaintance of Mr. Hare,
the English clergyman, whom I like exceedingly.   He is a
simple-hearted man, very quiet and yet zealous.   He has
been brought up in the evangelical school, but he does not
refuse to go into the meanings of the words.   He is no
connection of the Hares that we thought he belonged to.
I was delighted to see Wedgwood appointed to the office
which replaces my friend.   I hope it is something comfortable in point of salary, and unperplexed, at least morally,
in its administration.

Mr. Pilet, the pastor of the Reformed Geneva Protestant
Church, gave me the other day a very curious history of a
case of animal magnetism, which an intimate friend of his,
in whom he has the most perfect confidence, communicated
to him.   Mr. Pfeiffer (the friend of Mr. Pilet) is a pastor
in some place near Frankfort.   His servant-maid was

subject to violent nervous pains in the head. He one day made the experiment of drawing his hands over her face and head, as he had seen or heard of magnetists doing. The woman, to his horror, fell into a state of *extase*, out of which he could not draw her. She continued in this state six weeks, during which time she seemed to possess a sort of omniscience. One day she said, " I am tormented by my mistress seeking that key; tell her it is in such a place " (her mistress had never told her that she was seeking a key). Another day she said to her master, " There are two people, a man and his wife, at the door, coming to ask my advice on a particular matter, but I cannot burden my conscience with it." He went to the door, and told the people what his servant had said, and they went away blushing. One day a man, who had lately published a book, called, and she spoke to him as if perfectly acquainted with his book and also with his character, for she played off his vanity with the most remarkable skill and poignancy of wit. One day (a more important day in its results) a professor of rather an enthusiastic character came. She spoke to him eloquently and profoundly on all subjects, so that the man was perfectly enchanted. He remained some days, and before going away he told Mr. Pfeiffer that he must do him the favour of asking his servant's hand for him. Pfeiffer endeavoured to reason with him, but in vain. So he consented, and asked the lady, who was quite agreeable. The professor went away. In the meantime the period of enchantment was drawing to a close. One day she said, " In four days I shall be as I used to be," and in fact, on the fourth day, she got up in the morning and set to her work in the kitchen as usual, which had been intermitted during all that period of six weeks. Soon after the professor returned, and found his bride a perfectly different being from what he had left her. He attempted to get off, but she remembered the matter quite well, and held him to it, and she is at this moment his wife, without having had any return of talent or *extase* from that time. One day during the *extase* she desired to take a drive in a *char*. Her master took her out. It was a bright sun, and she kept her eyes steadily and intently fixed on the sun the whole time, without seeming to suffer the least from it. This recalls to me another story that a Lausanne minister told me. We were walking, and his dog met us. He said to me, "That has been my companion for several years. Before I came here I lived in an old château of the same date as Chillon. There were said to be ghosts in the château, and the fact is that that dog, the whole time he was there, never slept. He always sat in a watchful attitude, with his eyes fixed upon something. As soon as we left the castle, he took to sleeping like other dogs. Farewell, dear Mrs. Scott. Give my affectionate regards to your husband and your sisters. The thought of rest is sweet to the weary.—Yours, etc.   T. ERSKINE.

Letters are thankfully received, whether they are answered or not.

169. TO CAPTAIN PATERSON.

GENEVA, 21st *March* 1839.

MY DEAR JAMES,—Davie's short letter is a large record of the goodness of God. I have the conviction, which I have just been expressing to Mr. Hare, the worthy English clergyman here, that there is no such thing as a sudden death, in the strict meaning of the word; I believe that God always, in some way or other, warns the spirit of death before He sends it. We know not what had passed in ——'s heart before he passed into eternity; but we see that His Father's care was following him, and that the loving message which He sent him through his mother was accompanied with an inward voice, which had been received into his conscience. My belief in the continuation of the process of spiritual education beyond this life relieves me at all events from the agonising thought that twenty-six years of negligence are to fix the eternal condition of the soul for good or evil. I cannot read the passage contained in the 11th chapter of the Epistle to the Romans, verses 30-33, without wondering that any should think that the Bible decidedly teaches that doctrine. . . Farewell.—Your affectionate brother,   T. ERSKINE.

170. TO HIS SISTER MRS. PATERSON.

GENEVA, *27th March* 1839.

"Mais lors même qu'une pauvre mère croit, et ne murmure point, elle souffre ; les jours passent, les nuits reviennent, le soleil se lève tous les matins. Quelquefois, il semble qu'il vient nous dire, que ce n'est pas grande chose, que la souffrance d'un petit être d'un jour, tel que nous ; d'autre fois, il semble nous dire de la part du Très Haut, *Je suis toujours le même ;* rien ne pourra diminuer mon pouvoir, ma compassion, ma tendresse pour les enfans des hommes ; courage, ma fille, *ton fils n'est pas mort, mais il dort ;* et à ce langage, si réel quoique silencieux, notre âme se relève, elle est soutenue, elle se ranime : elle sent que le Seigneur est là."

DEAREST DAVIE,—The sentence which I put at the head of my letter is an extract from a letter which Madame Vernet has given me to send to Mrs. Patrick [Stirling].[1] You know that Madame Vernet lost a son fifteen years ago, in a most distressing way. There was a fire in the neighbourhood, and young Henri Vernet, about twenty years of age, along with several of his companions, went to give their assistance. Madame V. saw her son enter the burning house, but

---

[1] Whose son had been killed in an accident.

she never saw him come out; he and most of his companions were crushed by a falling beam. Mrs. Patrick's story awakened all her sympathy, you may suppose, and she has written her a letter, from which I have transcribed this sentence, which appears to me to contain a very touching and beautiful thought. . . . There was something exceedingly tender in the appointment that Mrs. Patrick should have written to her son as she did, and that he should have answered her as he did. There is a continually watchful care over us, ordering all our lot, every step. O ye of little faith! How my conscience answers to that word! How reasonable it is to trust ourselves to the keeping of infinite love, and infinite wisdom, and infinite power! We feel that we cannot choose rightly for ourselves, and that He cannot choose wrongly; and do we not know that all the end is to take away sin? Blessed end! O for its accomplishment! Farewell.

171. TO MISS RACHEL ERSKINE.

GENEVA, 26*th April* 1839.

DEAREST COUSIN,— . . . Dear friends, I feel with you all on the state of Mrs. Graham's health. There is something very solemn in the thought of her life being near its close, and that the days still given are leave-taking days, preparatory to that separation which, though only temporary, is so awful, from the thought of the scenes to be passed through before you meet again. I am sure she is peaceful herself in the prospect of what is before her; humility is always peaceful, it trusts in God and has no pretensions of its own. God resisteth the proud, and giveth grace unto the humble. "Lord, be merciful to me a sinner," seems the language of one who has more fear than hope; but it is not so; the soul that really appeals to the mercy of God, giving up all other claim, has strong confidence.

I have much pleasant intercourse with Madame Vernet, who overflows with love to God and man. I like this country exceedingly; I like the simplicity of their way of life. Very few people here have a man-servant, except their gardener, who is also their *char*-driver. You see no fine furniture, no show in any department; and you often find great friendships between their highest people and their lowest. There is a much deeper civilisation here than with us, which makes the minds of all ranks more capable of comprehending each other. But it is a civilisation which carries simplicity along with it, because it is a more mental thing than it is with us.   T. E.

172. TO HIS SISTER MRS. STIRLING.

GENÈVE, 22d *May* 1839.

MY DEAR CHRISTIAN,— . . . I think that I shall go to the other end of the lake very soon, that I may see a little more of Vinet before I leave the country.[1] I have just read a most exquisite piece of criticism by him, on Lamartine's last published work, in the *Semeur*, a periodical which often receives contributions from him. There is to be published immediately an important work of his, on the connection between the Church and State; that is not the title, but it is the subject. Madame de Staël has come to Geneva since I last wrote you; she is to me a recaller of many things. She feels herself a remnant, for she had completely adopted her husband's family; and she feels herself alone, although her own most amiable family open their hearts to her. She has brought little Paul de Broglie with her, who has been committed to her by the Duke; he is a beautiful boy, liker his mother than any of the rest in the form of his face and

---

[1] For some notices of Vinet, and his intercourse with Mr. Erskine, see Appendix, No. XII. p. 412.

in the colour of his eyes, but he is full of gaiety, which she never was, from the beginning. . . . Paul not only recalls his mother to Madame de Staël, but also her own Auguste, who was born after his father's death, and who lived till he was nearly two years old—a magnificent, matured child, she says. She has also brought with her a most striking portrait of Madame de B., taken from memory, with the assistance of a very poor portrait, by a lady who knew her, and who, I should judge from the expression, must have appreciated her. There is an expression of sadness in it, such as I scarcely ever saw in a picture, and at the same time she seems to have hold of a strength which sustains her under it, and seems to draw her up from it. It is a holy-looking thing, and yet there is a most agonising interest in it, which would seem incompatible with its holiness. It makes one understand the worship of saints and relics. I have written to M. de B. to ask him if he will allow me to get it copied here by a lady who does these things remarkably well, and he has answered me in the very kindest manner, giving me the permission. . . .—Yours ever,

T. E.

173. TO HIS SISTER MRS. STIRLING.

Genève, 10th June [1839].

My dearest Christian,—I have been very long of answering your last letter, containing cousin R.'s most interesting account of dear Mrs. Graham. I wrote to cousin R. herself. It may be all over by this time, and it will soon be all over for us all, as far as this world is concerned. As to dear Mrs. G., I feel persuaded that she will lie in her Father's hand without fear, trusting in the love which gave Jesus for her, and that to her the dark valley will be, as it was to your husband, all light. O Christian, how death destroys the importance of all hopes and fears connected

with passing events, and brings out the importance of
everything connected with eternity ! Life is the education-
time, the seed-time for eternity; there lies its whole importance. The mere misery arising from the political over-
turn of the whole earth is not so much to be feared or de-
plored as a single unconscientious movement of the spirit
of one individual. Opposition to the Spirit of God is the
only real evil, and conformity to Him is the only real good.
The first Adam refused to die to himself, and he fell into
judicial death; the second Adam consented to die to Himself, and He was raised into glorious immortality. Our
three cousins have a place to themselves in my mind, quite
apart from all other people; they are connected with my
early remembrance of their father and mother, and of Cardross, which is the purest remembrance that I have. But
there is a hope purer than any memory; there is a future
better than any past; the accomplished purpose of God
will be a glorious thing—man become the habitation of
God through the Spirit; that will be a thing which will
bear looking into. It will not be dependent for its charm
on a youthful imagination. The two surviving sisters will
feel very widowed, but their time also is near. Her cheerful equality of temper, her daylight, her enjoyment of all
things, made her a delightful inmate and companion, and
the house will be very dull without her. But they will
follow her spirit in its ascent to Him who gave it, and
they will be comforted. . . . Farewell.—Yours most affectionately,   T. E.

174. TO THE SAME.

. . . The little manuscript volume which accompanies this
note contains short sketches of some of Foster's sermons,
taken by one of his hearers. Dr. Stuart had showed them

to me during his life.   I was forcibly struck by many things
in them; and after his death, when Miss Stuart kindly
asked me to name some memorial that I should wish to
possess of my much-loved and highly revered friend, I asked
for these notes.   I have read them over again with increased
satisfaction and impression.   He brings the invisible world
and eternity to bear with much force upon the mind, as
the regulator of our feelings here in time.   Whilst I read
them, I felt the solemnity of having pressed the dead hand
of my friend, after the interview between his disembodied
spirit and God had taken place.

From what I have felt of your mind, I think that you
will like them; and I am sure that you will not be sorry
to have a memorial of Dr. Stuart, lately a stranger and
pilgrim, now joined to that great multitude that no man
can number, who have come out of great tribulation.   I
hope, too, that you will forgive me for wishing to stand
associated in your recollections with things which shall
never pass away, and with that world where I hope to pass
an eternity with you. . . .

175. TO HIS SISTER MRS. STIRLING.

. . . My present wish and endeavour is to turn my whole
mind and strength to do God's will—not to look forward
or behind, but giving myself up, practically up, to Him
whom my soul loveth.

There are many parts of the Bible from which I have
too often revolted, when setting my heart on things below
—those parts which tell that tribulation awaits us here,
and bid us raise our souls to heaven.   Now, they are my
delight, and my comforters, and my prayers.   I have not
yet that spirit—the spirit of a pilgrim, yet a willing servant
—but I aim at it, and I feel confident God will give it, for
Jesus' sake.   I wish to be very busy in the duties God has

given me to do, I would make it my meat to do His will, and pray earnestly that I may so be brought to abide in Christ that His character of holy separatedness, yet continued exertion, may be given to me. When I can fix my mind on this object of my existence, I feel it fills it; I feel happy and refreshed.

There is a young man dying in L—— whom I go to see when I want peace. His is a singular instance, so all agree. Seldom does that peace which Jesus left us reign so purely in the spirit. His life has been short, but important. For some time the conviction of sin, and an unutterable sense of the holiness of his divine Judge, drove him to such despair as to unhinge his mind. But a sight of a crucified Saviour dispelled the gloom. One cannot look on him without recognising whose he is and whom he serves. The image of the Lamb of God is stamped on his spirit, and shines through the very expression of his countenance. To see him is to see verified the promise, " Peace I leave with you." He says little, but that little emanates from deep feeling, and is as opposed to a wordy profession as light to darkness. He assents to nothing that he has not felt and been influenced by. He is not well enough to read to himself, but his mind dwells on the promises which are hid in his heart. I bid him repeat to me what comforted him; he repeated the last verses of Ps. lxxiii., and then the two last of Rom. viii. He does not suffer; his peace never varies. Every thought, every hope, hinges on the Saviour. He abides in Him, and oh, how richly does Christ abide in this dying saint! I but once heard him sigh; it was when I asked him if he would be satisfied yet to live a long life here below. He sighed and paused, and hesitatingly said, " Christ would give me grace to be resigned to His will, but oh, to be with Him would be far better." . . . Yet blessed be God, I think that I feel more that my only hope and my satisfying portion is in heaven. I think I in some degree close with that covenant which says, " In the world ye shall have tribulation ;" because in Christ I find peace. Yet oh, how dependent at each moment am I ; and I am willing to be so. I cast myself on Jesus ; Lord save me. . .

. . . The very Rev. old Ebenezer Brown[1] I have twice heard preach, and a most interesting exhibition it is ; he is a specimen of old Presbyterian eloquence and style. There is something very dignified in his energetic yet subdued manner ; his old broad Scotch, his deep sonorous voice, rendered very inarticulate now from old age, but famed in his youth for reaching a mile at tent preachings ; and oh how fain would he that it reached many and many a mile, if he could but bring poor sinners to his loved Saviour ! Somehow, every word he utters melts me to tears ; Christ crucified is all his theme, all his salvation, and all his desire. Humility, simplicity, serene peace, and that single repose in the Saviour which has brought the spirit of Jesus so eminently and so purely into his heart and life, are what characterise this aged saint. The pathos, the spirit, the unction of his preaching, surpasses all eloquence, and is overcoming to an unutterable degree ; none could imitate it, none could ever equal it, unless imbued with the same spirit from on high. . . .

176. TO CRAMER MALLET.

VEYTAUX, 22*d June* 1839.

DEAR FRIEND,— . . . This place is surpassingly beautiful ; it speaks of " Him who in His strength setteth fast the mountains, who is girded about with power." The lake, which is so sweet and gentle, and so full of light, adds its

---

[1] Of Inverkeithing. See the exquisite sketch of him by his grand-nephew, Dr. John Brown, in a letter to John Cairns, D.D., in the *Horæ Subsecivæ*, Second Series, pp. 270-276.

testimony that the Mighty One is also the Loving One.   You know the villages that are scattered so beautifully along the foot of the mountains, detached from each other, and surrounded each by its own forest, and yet united together by their simple footpaths and by their common connection with one church, which calls out their peaceful families by its well-known bell, and collects them for one common purpose.

I am at Veytaux in the parish of Montreux, in the Maison Masson.   Excellent quiet people.   Under me lives the suffragan of the minister of Montreux, of whom my landlord's son (who was my guide in a beautiful walk this morning) gave me a very pleasing account.   Write me a note like a good man, and tell me about dear Merle and his wife.   Give them my most affectionate regards and fullest sympathy.   I like to think of them and to grieve with them, hoping that all their sorrows will one day be turned into joys.   Farewell, dear friend, and with best regards to your own good family, mother, sister, daughter,—I remain, yours ever,   T. ERSKINE.

APPENDIX.

No. I.—Page 1.

HENRY, THE THIRD LORD CARDROSS.

HENRY ERSKINE, the first Lord Cardross, was the second son of the great Earl of Mar. David, the second Lord Cardross, Henry's eldest son, took part with the Covenanters on the breaking out of the great civil war. Such, however, was his high sense of honour that he was one of the seven Barons who protested against the giving up of the King to the English army at Newcastle in 1646; and such was his abiding loyalty, that he suffered severely afterwards under Cromwell's government of Scotland. His son Henry, the third Lord Cardross, succeeded to the title in 1671. True to his father's principles, he joined in vigorous opposition to the Lauderdale administration, and came in for his full share in the profuse persecution of that period. Heavily fined for allowing worship to be performed in his house by one of the ejected clergymen; thrown into prison, where he was forced to linger for years; another heavy fine imposed because his lady had a child, born when he was in prison, baptised by an outed minister; his pleasant home invaded and garrisoned for eight years by a rude soldiery; outlawed at last, his estate escheated and bestowed upon one of Lauderdale's nephews, every appeal to the Crown for justice and mercy pitilessly rejected, hopeless for himself and despairing of his country, he fled to America, where he established a plantation on Charlestown head in South Carolina.[1]

A few years afterwards he and his people were driven from their new and hopeful home by the Spaniards. Returning to Europe, he repaired to Holland. He and his younger brother John had both commands given them in the army of the Prince of Orange, accompanied the Prince on his expedition to England, and shared in its success. In Scotland Lord Cardross raised a regiment of dragoons, and under General Mackay did effective service in establishing the Revolution Settlement. His estates were restored, he was sworn in a Privy Councillor, and made Master of the Mint. Enjoying much of the confidence of King William, he promised to be one of the most useful servants of the Crown. But his health had been undermined by the hardships of former years, and he died at Edinburgh on the 21st of May 1693, in the forty-fourth year of his life.

On the death of the eighth Earl of Buchan, David, the fourth Lord Cardross, succeeded to that title. The late Earl of Buchan, and his distinguished brothers Henry and Thomas Erskine, were his grandchildren.

No. II.—Page 29.

TESTIMONIES TO THE EFFECT OF THE WORK ON "THE INTERNAL EVIDENCE OF REVEALED RELIGION."

Professor Noah Porter, of Yale College in the United States, when in Scotland in 1866, addressed a note to Mr. Erskine, from which the following is an extract:—

---

[1] *Wodrow's History*, etc., vol. ii. pp. 248, 288, 294, 357, and vol. iii. pp. 192, 194.

" DEAR SIR,—Excuse the liberty taken by an entire stranger, of whom you have never heard, and who is from a distant land. I have been in Scotland twice, once in 1853, and once about a week since. In both instances I have inquired respecting yourself and your writings, but have not been able to learn those particulars which something more than curiosity excited me to wish to know. If it had been possible I would have sought to see you, but I was prevented from so doing by circumstances which I could not control.

" I wished to say to you that your little work on the Internal Evidence of the Christian Religion has been in America a work highly esteemed and of potent theological influence. My father, who has been the pastor of one flock for nearly sixty years, once said to me that that book had done more than any single book of his time to give character to the new phase of theology in New England, which began about 1820, and in which Dr. N. W. Taylor, Dr. L. Beecher, and Dr. Moses Stuart, and many others, were prominently concerned.

" This new theology pervaded the Presbyterian Church, and eventually led to its disruption into two bodies, the so-called Old and New school bodies, in 1836 or 1837. The volume still is esteemed very highly for its argument and its just discrimination between the theology of the schools and the theology of the Scriptures. Your later writings were not received with such general favour, but candid and friendly critics understood how you were led to adopt the views asserted in them, by the extreme and cast-iron rigidness of the Scotch theology."

M. Vinet, in a letter to his friend M. Leresche, of date 19th December 1823, referring to the work on the " Internal Evidence," says :—

" J'ai lu en entier, avec un plaisir bien pur, le livre d'Erskine ; je compte bien le relire. Tu as raison, la méthode y manque. Mais quelle simplicité ! quelle conviction ! quelle vraie chaleur ! quels aperçus nouveaux et intéressants ! La qualité de laïque de l'auteur a singulièrement contribué au plaisir que m'a fait ce livre ; elle lui donne même un mérite et un caractère particuliers. Si je ne haïssais par principe ces expressions : ' Je suis d'Apollos et de Céphas,' je me laisserais aller volontiers à dire : Je suis d'Erskine. Il n'enveloppe pas l'Évangile de ténèbres ; il nous fait bien sentir que si l'on ne peut concevoir le *comment* des mystères de la religion, le *pourquoi* est parfaitement accessible à notre raison, qu'il doit l'être et qu'il n'y a point de vraie foi sans cela. L'œuvre de la rédemption est bien développée d'après ce principe ; l'opération du Saint-Esprit également bien présentée, non pas toutefois d'une manière qui puisse plaire à tout le monde, mais ce n'est pas un défaut. En un mot, ce livre me paraît singulièrement propre à ouvrir les yeux à ces malheureux hommes du monde, qui méprisent ou repoussent l'Évangile parce qu'ils ne le connaissent point du tout. Dieu veuille que cet ouvrage produise les bons effets qu'a désirés son auteur ! . . . ." [1]

This work was translated into French by the Duchess de Broglie, and was published at Paris in 1822 under the title, " Réflexions sur l'évidence intrinsèque de la vérité du Christianisme."

These testimonies to the impression made at the time, and the influence exerted afterwards, by " The Remarks on the Internal Evidence for the Truth of Revealed Religion," receive a curious confirmation from Dr. Newman. No. 73 of

---

[1] *Alexandre Vinet, Histoire de sa Vie et ses Ouvrages,* par E. Rambert (troisième édition ; Lausanne, 1876), tome première, p. 47.

"Tracts for the Times," which is occupied with the introduction of Rationalistic principles into religion, begins thus :—

" It is not intended in the following pages to enter into any general view of so large a subject as rationalism ; nor to attempt any philosophical account of it ; but, after defining it sufficiently for the purpose in hand, to direct attention to a very peculiar and subtle form of it existing covertly in the popular religion of this day. With this view, two writers, not of our own Church, though of British origin, shall pass under review, Mr. Erskine, and Mr. Jacob Abbott.

" This is the first time that a discussion of (what may be called) a personal nature has appeared in these tracts, which have been confined to the delineation and enforcement of principles and doctrines. However, in this case, while it was important to protest against certain views of the day, it was found that this could not be intelligibly done without referring to the individuals who have inculcated them. Of these, the two authors above mentioned seemed at once the most influential and the most original."

A certain form of the internal evidence for Christianity having been stated in order to be repudiated, it is added :—

"This is in fact pretty nearly Mr. Erskine's argument in his Internal Evidence ; an author concerning whom personally I have no wish to use one harsh word, not doubting that he is better than his own doctrine, and is only the organ, eloquent and ingenious, of unfolding a theory which it has been his unhappiness to mistake for the Catholic faith revealed in the Gospel."

The following extracts, from the ninth edition of the book, will confirm what has been said about it in the text :—

" Many persons, in their speculations on Christianity, never get farther than the miracles which were wrought in confirmation of its divine authority. Those who reject them are called infidels, and those who admit them are called believers; and yet, after all, there may be very little difference between them.   A belief of the miracles narrated in the New Testament does not constitute the faith of a Christian.   These miracles merely attest the authority of the messenger,—they are not themselves the message. They are like the patentee's name on a patent medicine, which only attests its genuineness, and refers to the character of its inventor, but does not add to its virtue."— Pp. 183-4.

"The Monarch of the Universe has proclaimed a general amnesty of rebellion, whether we give or withhold our belief or our attention; and if an amnesty were all that we needed, our belief or our attention would probably never have been required.   Our notions of pardon and punishment are taken from our experience of human laws.   We are in the habit of considering punishment and transgression as two distinct and separate things, which have been joined together by authority, and pardon as nothing more than the dissolution of this arbitrary connection.   And so it is amongst men; but so it is not in the world of spirits. Sin and punishment there are one thing.   Sin is a disease of the mind which necessarily occasions misery; and, therefore, the pardon of sin, unless it be accompanied with some remedy for this disease, cannot relieve from misery." —Pp. 196-7.

"When we speak of benefits freely bestowed, we say of them, 'You may have them by asking for them,'—distinguishing them by this mode of expression as gifts, from those things for which we must give a price.   Precisely the same idea is conveyed by the Gospel declaration, 'Believe and ye shall be saved.'   When it is asked, How am I to obtain God's mercy? the Gospel answers, that 'God has already declared himself reconciled through Jesus Christ; so you may have it by believing it.' Faith, therefore, according to the Gospel scheme, both marks the freeness of God's mercy, and is the channel through which that mercy operates on the character.

"It has been my object, throughout this Essay, to draw the attention of the reader to the internal structure of the religion of the Bible,—first, because I am convinced that no man, in the unfettered exercise of his understanding, can fully and cordially acquiesce in its pretensions to Divine inspiration, until he sees in its substance that which accords both with the character of God and with the wants of man ; and, secondly, because any admission of its Divine original, if unaccompanied with a knowledge of its principles, is absolutely useless."—Pp. 199-200.

No. III.—Page 45.

EXTRACTS FROM THE "ESSAY ON FAITH."

THE following extracts, from the fifth edition of the Essay on Faith, will have a special interest for those who desire to trace the progress of Mr. Erskine's opinions :—

"I do not set human reason above divine revelation, but I consider that divine revelation is intelligibly and practically addressed to human reason and human feeling; and that man is therefore bound, as a matter of duty, and even of respect, to bring his reason and feelings into contact with it. I believe that revelation was given for the purpose of exhibiting the character of God, and of thus influencing the character of man ; and when I see a distinct connection between this object and the doctrines of revelation, I conceive that I understand them as they were intended to be understood, although I may be unable to account for all the facts and principles which are assumed in them.

" Thus, when I say that I understand the doctrine of the atonement, I do not at all mean that I can explain how God and man were united in Christ, nor even that I can account for the necessity of an expiation. I mean merely, that I can see that this fact and this principle, when admitted, exhibit in a wonderful manner the infinite compassion and the infinite holiness of God, and have a most powerful natural tendency to humble, and purify, and elevate the human heart. If I did not discern this moral meaning in the atonement—if I did not see that it threw light on the character of God, and tended to sanctify the character of man—if I perceived nothing in it but the fact of the divine and human natures being united in one person, and this person suffering death, as the victim of a justice which he had never offended—if this were all that I could discover in it, I should say, I have good reason, from other circumstances, to believe that this book is the word of God, which He has graciously given me for my instruction ; and therefore I believe that there is some instructive meaning, and some important truth, contained in this extraordinary fact, but what that meaning is I cannot say ; when I know it I am prepared to believe it."
—Pp. 30-2.

" We are not commanded to believe merely for the sake of believing, or to show our ready submission to the will of God ; but because the objects which are revealed to us for our belief have a natural tendency to produce a most important and blessed change on our happiness and our characters. Every object which is believed by us operates on our characters according to its own nature. If, therefore, we have taken a wrong view of revelation, that wrong view will operate upon us, and produce a bad effect on our characters. This shows the importance of a correct knowledge of the truth contained in revelation." —P. 94.

"As soon, however, as we open our eyes, we know that it is light; and as soon as we understand and believe the Gospel we know that we are pardoned."—P. 110.

"The pardon has been proclaimed simply, in order that the power and influence of sin may be overcome; we are therefore falsifying the record, and undoing its purpose, if we teach men to cast off their sins as a preparatory work previous to believing, and in order that they may accept of the pardon."—P. 117.

"The object presented to our faith in the Gospel is the character of God manifested in Jesus Christ, as the just God and yet the Saviour. It is the remission of sins through the blood of atonement shed for us by love unutterable. It is God in our nature standing on our behalf as our elder brother and representative, bearing the punishment which we had deserved, satisfying the law which we had broken, and, on the ground of this finished work, proclaiming sin forgiven, and inviting the chief and the most wretched of sinners to become a happy child of God for ever and ever."—Pp. 127-8.

"My object in this Essay has not been to represent faith as a difficult or perplexed operation, but to withdraw the attention from the act of believing, and to fix it on the object of belief, by showing that we cannot believe any moral fact without entering into its spirit, and meaning, and importance."—P. 142.

No. IV.—Page 63.

THE SWISS ARTIST, M. BAILLOD.

In 1826 a small volume was published, entitled "Arvendel; or Sketches in Italy and Switzerland." The author did not give his name, but he is now known to have been the Hon. and Rev. Gerard Noel. In this volume he tells of his first meeting this Swiss artist at Rome "sitting with a book in hand upon the fragments of a Corinthian column;" of the close and affectionate Christian intercourse which followed; of their almost daily walks together from the Forum to the Coliseum; and their final parting when Mr. Noel left Rome for Naples. "Arvendel," the name assumed by the author, "returned when the spring had clothed with fresh leaves the overshading walk from the Forum to the Coliseum. But the friend who had consecrated this pathway moved along it no more. The simple, firm, patient, elevated heart of Albert (the name given to the Swiss) had ceased to beat. He had breathed his last sigh amidst the consolations which another Christian friend had been permitted to afford." That other friend was Mr. Erskine, who appears in the book prominently afterwards under the name of St. Clair. Mr. Noel and he met daily at St. Peter's to walk together through the ruins and out upon the hills surrounding Rome. Afterwards at Geneva they met again, to "walk often together by the tranquil shores of the lake." The conversations between Arvendel and St. Clair, given many of them at length, evidence this at least,—how very strong the tie was that then bound the two friends together.

The following extracts are taken from the journals of Rothe, the well-known German divine :—

"*Rome,* 18*th June* 1824.—Early this morning Mr. Erskine brought me tidings of the death of M. Charles Baillod, a painter from Neuchatel, belonging to the French Reformed Church. I visited M. Baillod daily for more than a month, to my great edification and refreshment. In the previous summer he had been seized by a very dangerous affection of the lungs, from which, however, he seemed to have almost recovered. The doctors at Geneva (probably in order to get him out of their hands) had recommended him to pass the winter in Rome as a sure means of complete restoration. But, soon after his arrival at Rome, the malady returned, and unmistakable symptoms of consumption appeared. He was in poor circumstances; but a wealthy Scotch advocate, by name Thomas Erskine, who was then in Rome, at once undertook to provide for his needs, placed him under the treatment of Dr. Clarke, the English physician, and afterwards, when he went for a few months to Naples, left him under the care of his servants, defrayed the expense of his funeral, and on his account considerably prolonged his stay here. This Mr. Erskine (who, by the way, knows and loves our Heubner) is a man of amiable character and spirit, in fellowship with whom I have passed many happy and instructive hours. In the literary world he is known as the author of several very deeply thought-out treatises (*sehr tief gedachten Schriften*) upon Christianity.

"The sickness of our common friend was a manifest triumph of Divine grace, and its power over human nature. For more than four months, through terrible pain and distress, he had never closed an eye,—he had to change his posture almost every five minutes in order to be able to breathe,—but there never passed from his lips a cry of impatience, and he was always filled with Divine comfort and love. Almost the last words which, in extreme distress, he spoke to Mr. Erskine were, 'J'ai eu des moments tout à fait surprenants dans lesquels l'amour de Dieu s'est manifesté à moi d'une manière dont vous autres, qui vous restez encore dans la pleine vie, ne pouvez pas avoir d'idée.' A few hours afterwards he will have had quite other surprisals. One could see in everything that he had lived for several years faithfully and devoutly in the presence of God.

" 19th *June.*—With Mr. Erskine and two French Swiss I attended the funeral of Baillod. The funeral service was performed, under the escort of four Grenadiers, according to the very beautiful English liturgy in the French translation. It was an impressive moment. We stood upon the heights of the new cemetery, which overlooks the Tiber and a great part of the city. The sun had just risen ; beneath lay the city, wrapped in thick mist,—the highest domes alone stood out clearly. Around us and the graves alone it was bright and clear day. We silently shook hands, addressed to the departed a 'Farewell till we meet again' (*ein Lebewohl auf Wiedersehen*), and descended to the bustle below."—RICHARD ROTHE, *Ein Christliches Lebensbild*, von F. Nippold (Wittenberg, 1873), pp. 371-2.

No. V.—Page 127.

EXTRACTS FROM "THE UNCONDITIONAL FREENESS OF THE GOSPEL."

THE leading ideas in the " Unconditional Freeness" are sufficiently indicated in the following extracts, taken from the fourth edition :—

" Christianity may be considered as a divinely revealed system of medical treatment for diseased spirits. Heaven is the name for health in the soul, and hell is the name for disease ; and the design of Christianity is to produce heaven, and to destroy hell. The idea therefore, of having heaven, without holiness, is like the idea of having health without being well,—it is a contradiction in terms."—P. 9.

" Pardon, then, is not heaven—any more than a medicine is health."—P. 11.

"What is the misery of man? His mind is diseased. He was made to regard and enjoy God, as his chief object; and his faculties will not work healthfully in the absence of this object. But he has left God, and he wearies himself in seeking good from created things. The sentiment of the love of God is to his mind what the key-stone is to the arch; when it falls from its place, ruin is the consequence."—P. 13.

"The great cause of the disorder and misery that distract the human mind, is averseness or indifference to God."—P. 14.

"The only medicine which can cure this dreadful and wide-spreading disorder, must be something which will replace the key-stone in the arch,—something which will rekindle love towards God, which will do away fear, and inspire confidence."—P. 15.

"The medicinal virtue of the Gospel lies in the manifestation of that holy love with which God so loved the world as to give His only begotten Son as an atonement for its sins. Holy love is the great principle developed in the Gospel. It is the union of an infinite abhorrence towards sin, and an infinite love towards the sinner. This mysterious history is the mighty instrument with which the Spirit of God breaks the power of sin in the heart, and establishes holy gratitude and filial dependence. The belief that the Deity took upon himself the nature and the penal obligations of the sinner, that he might, consistently with justice, restore his forfeited life and remove the barrier which the offended law had placed between him and the Throne of Grace, the belief of this must give a new view of the malignity of sin, and a most touching and overpowering view of the compassion of God."—Pp. 16, 17.

"The use of faith then is not to remove the penalty or

make the pardon better,—for the penalty is removed and
the pardon is proclaimed whether we believe it or not,—
but to give the pardon a moral influence, by which it may
heal the spiritual diseases of the heart, which influence it
cannot have unless it is believed."—P. 22.

"Men are not, according to the gospel system, pardoned
on account of their belief of the pardon, but they are
sanctified by a belief of that pardon, and unless the belief of
. it produces this effect, neither the pardon nor the belief are
of any use. The pardon of the Gospel is a spiritual medicine;
faith is nothing more than the taking of that medicine; and
if the spiritual health or sanctification is not produced, neither
the spiritual medicine nor the taking of the medicine are
of any avail; they have failed of their object."—P. 23.

"The gratuitousness of the Gospel, then, consists in the
unrestricted freeness of the pardon which it proclaims.
Its terms are without condition and without exception.
It proceeded from that love with which God so loved the
world as to give His only begotten Son for it. . . . It is
God in Christ reconciling the world unto Himself. This
pardon then is an unchangeable thing like God Himself.
Man neither makes it nor merits it. God reveals it, or
rather reveals Himself in it. God manifest in the flesh
becomes the representative of sinners. His sufferings and
death gave the solemn and appalling measure of the divine
condemnation of sin, and of the divine compassion for the
sinner."—Pp. 26, 27.

"The Gospel reveals to us the existence of a fund of
divine love containing in it a propitiation for all sins, and
this fund is general to the whole race, every individual has
a property in it, of the same kind that he has in the common light and air of the world which he appropriates and
uses simply by opening his mouth or his eyes. Is it not
clear that as soon as any one really knows that such a

fund exists, and that it is indeed the gift of God to the world and the common property of all the individuals in the world, just as the natural air and light is, he will immediately infer his own particular interest in it, and enter into the enjoyment of it, and he will make the blessed discovery which no tongue can rightly describe, and no mere intelligence can rightly conceive, even that he himself has a possession, an unalienable, an everlasting possession in the heart of God."—P. 88.

"And as the giving of the vine to the branch includes all that the vine has to give, so the giving of the Immanuel to the world includes all that God has to give. *When we know this, we are justified by faith,*—that is to say, we assume our God's forgiveness as included in the gift of himself. He neither loves nor pardons us on account of our belief in his testimony, for it was whilst we were yet enemies and unbelievers that Christ died for us; but the belief of his love, and of the gift which his love has bestowed, will give a confidence that we are dearly welcome to him,—that we are his accepted ones,—his adopted children. And whilst we do not know this, or remain insensible to it, we are not justified,—that is, we do not and cannot look to the holy God without distrust or terror,—we have nothing but his condemnation, for condemnation consists in the absence of his pardoning love, and that love is allowed to lie at our unopened door.

"I know that justification is generally considered to mean pardon, or the imputation of Christ's righteousness, and I believe that sometimes it may have this meaning in the Bible. But yet I am persuaded, by reasons which I shall afterwards explain, that it chiefly bears the meaning which I am now attributing to it, namely, *a sense of pardon, or of acceptance, or having the conscience purged of guilt,*—and that *justification by faith* always means *a sense of acceptance and safety arising from a belief of that accepted propitiation which has been made for the sins of the whole world.*"—Pp. 89-91.

"Now, if a man really looks to his faith in anything as the ground of his pardon or hope before God, he is as much nourishing the spirit of independence, and as much walking in that spirit, as if he trusted in his obedience. Self is in the one case, as well as in the other, the axis on which the man turns, and the root out of which he grows. And he can scarcely avoid falling into this error in some measure, if he thinks there is no pardon for him until he believes. For if the pardon does not exist until he believes, and immediately exists when he believes, surely his belief has something to do in making it. It is in vain to tell him, that faith does not make it, but only receives it. For he may ask, Where is it then before faith receives it? If my faith only receives it, it must have been in existence before my faith. The only idea that I can attach to the expression, *receiving the pardon by faith*, is that of *believing in the pardon;* but in order to this, the pardon must have been a real pardon before. If the gospel, as it stands in the Bible, actually includes my pardon, then it is clear, that when I believe the gospel, I shall also believe my pardon as a part of it, and thus my faith will receive the pardon. But if the gospel does not in itself contain my pardon, how can my belief of the gospel be a receiving of pardon?" —Pp. 95-7.

"If the gospel were, that God only loved those who should believe in Christ, and that Christ died only for those who should believe in his sacrifice, it is clear that such a gospel does not embrace my pardon, nor the assurance of God's love to me, unless I am a believer; and, therefore, that my belief in such a gospel can give me no comfort, nor peace, until I first ascertain that I believe in Christ.

And thus my belief in Christ is made something distinct from a belief in the gospel, and is only a prerequisite condition in order to my drawing comfort from the gospel; and thus also pardon and the love of God are made rewards of faith in Christ. But this is not the gospel of the Bible, nor the view of faith contained in the Bible, as every attentive reader of that blessed book must know."—P. 99.

" A very common idea of the object of the gospel is, that it is to show how men *may obtain pardon;* whereas, in truth, its object is to show how *pardon for men has been obtained*, or rather to show how God has taken occasion, by the entrance of sin into the world, to manifest the unsearchable riches of holy compassion. And it is to present this most important truth (as I cannot but consider it) to some who may not have thought of it before, that I have published this book,—and it is for this same reason that I have chosen to depart from the common phraseology on the subject,—because I have found the common phraseology liable to misinterpretation. Thus I have observed, that even the phrase *free offer of pardon* is so interpreted, that the very existence of the pardon is made to depend on the acceptance of the offer. The benefit of the pardon does most assuredly depend on its being accepted, but the pardon itself is laid up in Christ Jesus, and depends on nothing but the unchangeable character of God."—Pp. 102-3.

" When I consider this important feature of the first promise (its universality), I cannot help thinking that the modern commentators on prophecy have reason, when they say that the expectation of the restitution of all things occupies a much less space in the common announcements of the gospel, or in the thoughts of Christians, than it ought to do. It is the chief feature of that gospel which was preached to Adam, and it is bequeathed to the church in the last words of inspiration as an enduring consolation and expectation,

—" Behold, I come quickly." The general statements of
the gospel in our days relate too exclusively to what is
already past, and to the individual salvation of each believer. Of course, it is impossible altogether to separate
the doctrine of Christ's sacrifice from its general and future
results ; but these results seem to me not brought forward
by preachers as they are in the Bible. I do not speak of
the detail of these results, nor of the particular fulfilment
of the prophecies which relate to the last times, because
I do not feel myself qualified to speak on these subjects;
but I speak of a fixed and longing expectation, of the sure
and fast approaching accomplishment of those promises
which announce the final triumph of the Messiah, the
establishment of his reign upon earth, the manifestation of
the sons of God, and the full development of all those
high privileges which arise out of their union with their
divine Head. This doctrine appears to me now in a very
different light from what it once did. If the selfishness
of individuality be really one of the chief elements in the
fall of man, it might be expected that the divinely bestowed
medicine for sick souls should contain an ingredient specially fitted to counteract and remove it. And such an ingredient I find in the universality of the declaration and
purpose of the gospel, which must necessarily impress its
own character on the hope of every one who rests upon it,
—for the first hope which any man can arrive at with
regard to his own personal acceptance with God, must be
drawn from the great general manifestation of Divine love
directed to the destruction of evil, and the restoration of
the ruined race. The individual drops are thus merged in
the ocean, and self is lost in the 'liberty, the universality,
the impartiality of heaven.' "—Pp. 82-4.

" The terms in which the Gospel has all along been proclaimed seem to me to involve necessarily a universal and

unconditional forgiveness of sin. . . In short, I am led to regard the pardon of the gospel as another name for holy compassion, that divine attribute for the manifestation of which I believe this world was created, and thus a part of the unchangeable character of God, rather than a particular act."—P. 92.

No. VI.—Page 163.

MR. ERSKINE'S EVANGELISTIC LABOURS.

MR. ERSKINE was brought up as an Episcopalian, and may be said to have continued so all his life. He was ready, however, to join any Church in which he received spiritual benefit. When his sister married Captain Paterson, and came to reside at Linlathen, he attended with them the ministrations of the Rev. Mr. Russell at Dundee, and partook of the Communion in the Independent chapel there. In Broughty-Ferry, which lay much nearer to Linlathen, there was a chapel, built originally by the Haldanes as one of their missionary stations. It was then the only place of worship in the village, and the services in it, conducted generally by laymen, had been irregular, and growing more infrequent. Mr. Erskine bought this chapel, and invited ministers of different Churches to occupy its pulpit. Occasionally on Sunday evenings he delivered an address in it himself. At first it had been chiefly, if not exclusively, in the morning and evening domestic religious services, to which all were invited, and which many from the neighbourhood attended, that he had addressed a wider circle than his own household. "The first time I saw and heard him," Mrs. Machar tells us in a letter dated February 2, 1877, "was, I think, in the summer

of 1822, when he was living for some time at Westhaven
or Carnoustie. Several friends from a distance were with
him, to whom his instructions had been blessed. He held
morning meetings in the hall of the hotel in which he was
living, to which all were welcome. I remember hearing
him several times there, and was much struck with the
simplicity and earnestness with which he set forth the
truth. I remember well the chapel at Broughty-Ferry
before it was in Mr. Erskine's possession. Dr. Dick the
philosopher preached in it for some time. I remember
hearing a striking sermon from Dr. Chalmers there, and
several other ministers besides. I give an extract from a
letter of my own, written in November 1825, soon after
we came to the neighbourhood of Linlathen. 'Mina and
I have been two nights at Linlathen to hear Mr. Erskine,
who lectures every Thursday night to a considerable
audience. Although a lay preacher, we were much
delighted with his teaching, which I think cannot fail to
make a deep impression. I intend to go as often as I can.'
He continued these lectures in the old and new hall at
Linlathen, which were much appreciated by the people of
the neighbourhood, some coming from a distance of several
miles.' He visited also in the families around. Where
there was sickness, or sorrow, or spiritual distress, he was
always ready to impart spiritual light, to comfort the
sorrowful, to sympathise with them in their afflictions, and
to extend temporal aid wherever it was required. Many
were the appeals to him on this account, and none were
ever made in vain. In the summer of 1826 he went to
the Continent, which was a great grief to many. I do not
remember him at Linlathen again till September 1828,
after he had met with the Rev. Mr. Campbell of Row and
Alexander Scott, with both of whom he was much delighted.
He was accompanied by the latter, who remained some

time at Linlathen, and preached in Dundee, and several
times in the hall at Linlathen.   In the summer of 1829
he went with all the family to Row, where he held meetings
for Scripture-reading and prayer every morning in his
own house.   A number of the residents and strangers
attended daily.   In 1830 he with the family and party
spent the summer at Row, or in the vicinity."

During these eventful summers Mr. Erskine and his
family attended the service and partook of the Communion
in the Established Church.   His personal efforts in the
way of co-operating with Mr. Campbell were multiplied
and unceasing.   Morning and evening at family prayers
he gave a short exposition, listened to by as many as
could obtain entrance.   At the same time, as he tells
Madame de Staël, he was preaching three times a day, and
often more.   His hopes were quenched and his efforts
modified by Mr. Campbell's deposition.   On his return to
Linlathen after that event, excluded from the communion
of the Independent church at Dundee, and often preached
against from the pulpits of many of the Established
churches, he took upon himself the teaching of his own
household, conducting a forenoon and evening service
every Sunday in the hall at Linlathen, open to all disposed
to attend.   "I remember," says Mrs. Machar, "being
there two or three times in the summer of 1832.   As I
then left for Canada, I do not know how long he continued
them."   They were continued till he left for the Continent
in 1840, and discontinued after his return.   In truth, such
methods of publicly addressing others as a quickened zeal
and a kindling hope led him for a season to adopt, were
not congenial to his shrinking and sensitive nature.

He had a friend to whom he was tenderly attached, and
with whom he had much in common, who in this respect
was otherwise constituted.   Henry Wight was like himself a

gentleman by birth, and had been an advocate by profession, who had thrown up all secular pursuits to devote himself to the service of the Cross. Like Mr. Erskine, he too had been deeply affected by the Row teaching, and had for a time believed in the spiritual gifts. His robuster build and firmer fibre had carried him safely and prosperously into the most forward kinds of Christian activity, till he became "the best, indeed the only good, street preacher we have ever heard."[1] Largely and successfully engaged in evangelistic labours, Mr. Wight invited Mr. Erskine's co-operation. It was to this invitation that the following reply was given :—

"LINLATHEN, 14*th May* 1833.

"MY DEAR BROTHER,—I was thankful for the love of your letter. I believe, as you say, that active labour is profitable to the soul, and yet I am sure that there is a great danger on that side also. Whilst we labour, having constant communion with God in our labour, so that it is not we that work, but the Spirit in us, our labour is profitable indeed and blessed indeed ; but when we do things *for* God instead of doing them *by* the Spirit of God, it is a different matter. There is a risk of substituting activity in working for the life of faith ; there is the risk of seething the kid in its mother's milk—that is, of offering up the sacrifice of the flesh, not in water nor in fire, the two emblems of the Spirit, but in the mother's milk, another form of the very flesh which is offered up. I am much struck with the number of conversions that I hear of under your preaching, my dear brother. Surely there is a great blessing accompanying you. I should be very

---

[1] See the preface to the Memoir of Henry Wight, by Dr. John Brown, in which that fine delineator of character has sketched the leading features of one of the kindliest, manliest, most devoted evangelists of his day.

much obliged to you, when you have leisure, if you could write me an account of any marked cases. I need much to be stirred up; I have great deadness in myself, and the deadness all around is most fearful. The Lord is laying sickness at present upon many, and some seem to be opening their ears to the voice; but in general they can hear of the great things of God's love and of God's judgment with the most awful unconcern. A sister of Theophilus Methven died here in the Lord a few days ago. 'The sacrifices of God are a broken spirit; a broken and a contrite heart, O God, thou wilt not despise.' The way in which we are called to walk is Christ crucified, a blood-sprinkled way, and they who walk in it drop out their own blood, drop by drop, for the joy set before them. Give my affectionate regards to your wife; all here who know you both send their love.—Yours affectionately,   T. ERSKINE."

No. VII.—Page 183.

EXTRACTS FROM "THE BRAZEN SERPENT," WITH OPINION OF M. VINET.

IN a letter written by Monsieur Vinet to Mr. Erskine in 1844, he says:—"Laissez-moi vous dire combien je dois à un livre qui vient de vous, quoique vous ne me l'ayez pas envoyé: 'The Brazen Serpent. (Le serpent d'airain.)' Que de choses qu'il me semble avoir toujours pensées. Oh! s'il m'était donné de sentir avec vous comme il m'a été donné de penser avec vous!"

The following extracts, from the second edition, are given as illustrative of the testimonies of Mr. Maurice and M. Vinet:—

2 D

" But why was this suffering of our nature in the person
of Jesus needful? It was a fallen nature; a nature which
had fallen by sin, and which, in consequence of this, lay
under condemnation. He came into it as a new head, that
He might take it out of the fall, and redeem it from sin,
and lift it up to God; and this could be effected only by
His bearing the condemnation, and thus manifesting, through
sorrow and death, the character of God, and the character
of man's rebellion; manifesting God's abhorrence of sin,
and the full sympathy of the new Head of the nature in
that abhorrence, and thus eating out the taint of the fall,
and making honourable way for the inpouring of the new
life into the rebellious body. . . .

" When we ask, What is the meaning of the sufferings of
Christ; or in what way did those sufferings tend to accomplish the purposes for which he had left the bosom of the
Father, and came to this world? we ask a question which, in
its bearings, involves the whole character and purposes of
God, and the whole character and prospects of man. If this
question were put to many persons, we should probably get
various answers. One answer that would be pretty generally given to this question is, ' that He came to save sinners,
and that He could accomplish this only by suffering in their
stead the punishment due to their sin, because thus only
their salvation could be reconciled with divine justice, and
thus only could it become a righteous thing with God to
remit the punishment of the real offenders. In this way
both the justice of God and His love were magnified. His
justice, in demanding the full penalty of the law; and his
love, in providing a substitute to stand in the place of the
real offenders, and bear that for them which would have
overwhelmed them in everlasting perdition, if they had been
obliged to bear it themselves.' I believe that the Spirit of
God has made this view of the atonement spirit and life to

many souls—and yet I believe that, with some truth in it, it is a very defective view, to say the least of it.

"This view of the atonement, which is generally known by the name of the doctrine of Christ's substitution, has, I know, been held by many living members of His body— and yet I believe that, with some truth in it, it contains much dangerous error. In the first place, I may observe, that it would not be considered justice in an earthly judge, were he to accept the offered sufferings of an innocent person as a satisfaction for the lawful punishment of a guilty person. And as the work of Christ was wrought to declare and make manifest the righteousness of God, not only to powers and principalities in heavenly places, but to men, to the minds and consciences of men—it is not credible that that work should contain a manifestation really opposed to their minds and consciences. Let me here entreat of my reader to be patient and not to misunderstand me, nor to suppose that, by using this language, I do at all mean to deny or bring into doubt the blessed truth, that Christ tasted death for every man,—for verily and indeed I believe that Christ did taste death for every man, and that, too, in a far deeper and truer sense than is taught by the doctrine of substitution in its ordinary acceptation. The humanly devised doctrine of substitution has come in place of, and has cast out the true doctrine of the headship of Christ, which is the large, and glorious, and true explanation of those passages of Scripture which are commonly interpreted as teaching substitution. Christ died for every man, as the head of every man—not by any fiction of law, not in a conventional way,—but in reality as the head of the whole mass of the human nature, which, although composed of many members, is one thing,—one body,—in every part of which the head is truly present.

"If my right hand had committed murder, and my left

hand had committed theft, and my feet had been swift to shed blood,—were I to suffer beheading for these offences, no one would say that my head had been the substitute for my hands and my feet. And although, in this case, it be true, that the planning head is the real offender, and therefore is the proper sufferer, yet the force of the comparison is not thereby destroyed, for even if these members were capable of independent action, they would be punished in the punishment of the head, because they are all really contained in the head, in virtue of its being the root of that system of nerves which, by pervading them all, does in fact sustain them all. . . .

" And *secondly,* he did not suffer the punishment of sin, as the doctrine of substitution supposes, to dispense with our suffering it, but to change the character of our suffering, from an unsanctified and unsanctifying suffering, into a sanctified and sanctifying suffering. And thus, when our Lord himself speaks to the disciples about His cross and sufferings, He uniformly calls upon them to take up their cross and follow Him, by the same road of suffering. This connection is marked through all the Evangelists, and must therefore be a designed connection.—See Matt. xvi. 21-25; Mark viii. 31-35 ; Luke ix. 22-24; John xii. 23-26. And Paul desires fellowship in Christ's sufferings, and conformity with His death. The substance of all these passages proves that the substitution of Christ did not consist in this, that He did or suffered something instead of men, so as to save them from doing or suffering it for themselves. And this agrees with the obvious fact, that Christ's death does not save the believer from dying a natural death, nor does His sorrow save the believer from sorrowing. On the contrary, the believer dies ; and moreover, dies daily, in consequence of and in proportion to his faith. What Christ did for us, was done for us in a sense and with a view very different from that of saving us from doing it ourselves. He fulfilled the law, for instance, certainly not with the view of saving us from fulfilling it, but, on the contrary, with the very view of enabling us to fulfil it. For the salvation of Christ consists mainly in ' writing the law upon our hearts,'—and He made Himself a sin-offering, ' that the righteousness of the law might be fulfilled in us, who walk not after the flesh, but after the Spirit.'

" When, therefore, it is said that Christ did or does things for us, it is not meant that He did or does them as our substitute, but as our head. He does them for us, as a root does things for the branches,—or as a head or heart does things for the body. . . .

" But if Jesus did not suffer punishment to dispense with our suffering it, what has He accomplished for us by suffering for us ? Take this answer in the meantime. Sin can only be burned out of our nature, by our sense of its misery, and by our acquiescence in the righteousness of that misery —which acquiescence we can never truly give, until we see the holy love of God resting upon us, and manifesting itself in the law against which we have sinned, and in the misery which is inflicted upon us through our sin, and on account of our sin. But holy love is a thing which our natural life is incapable of seeing ; for our natural life is consciously under the condemnation of sin, and is bearing its punishment, and it cannot draw near to God, or look on God ; for its condemnation implies and contains a separation from God—it therefore cannot know love, or see love, because God is love—the natural life, in truth, is the carnal mind, which is enmity against God. And thus, while we continue to live in this natural life, and to see things in its light, we can see nothing in the punishment of sin but what increases our fear, and enmity, and opposedness to God. And thus punishment acts as a poison until we see it by

the light of another life—an uncondemned life—which has
freedom of access to God, and which can see His love.
Now, this is the great thing which Christ has accomplished
by suffering for us; He has become a head of new and uncondemned life to every man, in the light of which we may
see God's love in the law and in the punishment, and may
thus suffer to the glory of God, and draw out from the suffering that blessing which is contained in it. . . .

"The work of Christ is thus the source of life. It was
a work which no creature could have done—a work which
none but He could have done—a work without which no
man could have been saved—a work, to attempt to do which,
or to add to which, is to crucify the Son of God afresh, and
without which no man ever did or ever could have done
any of those things which his leader and head and God
calls on him to do, or indeed ever could reasonably have
been called on to do them. It was the great work of
atonement, on the credit of which, before it was accomplished, and through the channel of which, since it has
been accomplished, the love of God, in the form of favour
and forgiveness and the gift of the Spirit enabling man to
glorify God, has been given to every human being."—
Pp. 34-58.

"With reference to what is written in the 2d chapter of
this book on the subject of substitution, let me beg the
reader's attention to a few lines more. In the first place,
substitution is not a Bible word, but I do not wish to contend either for or against words; I wish to contend for the
truth of God,—and if ever I have unnecessarily jarred
against the feelings of any child of God, by my use of words,
I grieve for it as a sin. But I am satisfied that I have not
been guilty of this sin, in objecting to the word substitution
as characterising the relation in which Christ stood to us
in His sufferings, because I am satisfied that there is a dan-

gerous error connected with the word. Substitution always supposes that the person suffering in the place of another is quite distinct from that other, and quite free from all righteous liability to the doom under which that other is sentenced to suffer. This is, I believe, the idea generally associated with substitution,—and it is as conveying this idea, that I object to the word, for this idea really controverts the true humanity of our Lord Jesus Christ. For though, whilst He was yet in the bosom of the Father, before He took our nature, He was free from all liability of suffering, and was under no call to suffer for men, except the importunate call of His own everlasting love, yet after He took our nature, and became the man Jesus Christ—He actually stood Himself within the righteous liability of suffering, not indeed on account of any flaw in His spotless holiness, but as a participator of that flesh which lay under the sentence of sorrow and death, and being now engulfed in the horrible pit along with all the others, He could only deliver them, by being first delivered Himself, and thus opening a passage for them to follow him by; as a man who casts himself into an enclosed dungeon which has no outlet in order to save a number of others whom he sees immured there, and when he is in, forces a passage through the wall, by dashing himself against it, to the great injury of his person. His coming into the dungeon is a voluntary act, but after he is there, he is liable to the discomforts of the dungeon by necessity, until he breaks through. This is one man suffering for others, but it is not substitution."— P. 263.

No. VIII.—Page 185.

THE SPEAKING WITH TONGUES.

THE speaking with tongues appears to have impressed Mr. Erskine and Edward Irving in the same manner and to the same effect. "The languages," says Mr. Erskine, reporting their effect upon his ear, "are distinct, well-inflected, well-compacted languages; they are not random collections of sounds; they are composed of words of various length, with the natural variety, and yet possessing that commonness of character which marks them to be one distinct language. I have heard many people speak gibberish, but this is not gibberish, it is decidedly well-compacted language." "The whole utterance," says Mr. Irving, "from the beginning to the ending of it, is with a power and strength and fulness, and sometimes rapidity of voice, altogether different from that of the person's ordinary utterance in any mood; and I would say, both in its form and in its effects upon a simple mind quite supernatural. There is a power in the voice to thrill the heart and overawe the spirit, after a manner which I have never felt. There is a march, and a majesty, and a sustained grandeur in the voice, especially of those who prophesy, which I have never heard even a resemblance to, except now and then in the sublimest and most impassioned moods of Mrs. Siddons and Miss O'Neil. It is a mere abandonment of all truth to call it screaming or crying; it is the most majestic and divine utterance which I have ever heard, some parts of which I never heard equalled, and no part of it surpassed, by the finest execution of genius and art exhibited at the oratorios in the concerts of ancient music." A third witness, who tells us that he had many opportunities of seeing the gift exercised, says, "The exhibition of the gift transcends all power of description; no description can convey an idea of the reality. . . . . A previous silence and an extraordinary change of countenance will generally intimate to others its approach, and it will then occur that they will clutch the nearest friend by the hand with an iron grasp, and speak out in the tongue, part of the time perhaps with the eyes closed, and then opened with the most intensely searching and fixed look. . . . The deportment of the speaker is extraordinary in the last degree; the countenance receives a dignity and a ravishment of expression superhuman; all traces of a self-agent are fled from the features; the tone of voice is quite unearthly. You stand in the immediate presence of God."[1] Mr. M'Kerrell wrote down some of the utterances, of which the following are specimens :—" O Pinitos, Elelastino Halimangotos Dantita, Hampooteni, Farimi, Aristos Ekampros."

Mr. Robertson has also given us some specimens, one of which, being an unbeliever, he somewhat irreverently turned into a stanza running thus :—

> " Hey amei hassan alla do
> Hoc alors leore
> Has heo massan amor ho
> Ti prov his aso me.
>   *Chorus*—Hey ho, ammei ammei."

At the close of Mr. Robertson's volume, " A Vindication of the Religion of the Land," will also be found a facsimile of the characters written "like lightning " by Mary Campbell.

No. IX.—Page 211.

IDEA OF THE CHURCH.

"A church is 'God manifest in flesh' of man,—the *mind of God* shown forth in the willing, conscious acquies-

---

[1] *An Apology for the Gift of Tongues*, by Archibald M'Kerrell, Esq. (Greenock, 1831), pp. 10, 11.

cence and co-operation of men,—a body of men of whom
may be said that which John testified of Jesus, 'The only
begotten Son which is in the bosom of the Father, He hath
declared him.'

"God is light; Jesus, God manifested in flesh, was the
light of the world; because He showed or declared God's
light to the world; and the very essence of the church is
the continuation of the same showing forth of light by the
indwelling of Jesus in His members. If there were *only
one man* in the world who knew God, or who had God's
light in him, *that man* would be the church of the living
God on earth, joined by the one Spirit to the church above,
and his business and delight would be in everything to
show God's light,—in every thought, word, and deed,—to
God Himself, to men, angels, devils; and therefore to be
watchful, to be continually receiving out from the fountain,
and guarding against everything which would hinder that
continual receiving, and so prevent the giving out of light.
If there were two men who knew God, and had this light
in their hearts, they would be the church, and they would
mutually aid each other in their common office of 'showing
forth God;' they would learn to watch for each other's
souls; and where the one was weak and the other strong,
where the one was ignorant and the other instructed, so
to order matters that he who had much should have nothing over, and he who had little should have no lack, to
the end that God might be declared in their relation to
each other, and to the world around them. The Spirit of
Christ is one Spirit, but it was only in its fulness in Jesus,
in the members it appears in parts, and yet parts of the
same Spirit; as the number of the persons in whom it
dwells increases, the variety of the parts or gifts will be
more apparent, and the exercise of spiritual discernment
and love in recognising the gift of each, and yielding its

right place to each gift, will be proportionally increased. He that has the gift of teaching (of course I don't mean human talent) in the Spirit will be recognised as a teacher, and he whose heart is filled most with the Shepherd's love and authority will be recognised as the one to whom Jesus says, 'Feed my sheep; feed my lambs.' Thus the church will grow from the inside, and not from the out. The actual presence of the gift will be recognised as the ordinance, and thus Christ Himself, and not merely His appointment, will be met in the ordinance. The Spirit of Christ manifested in a particular gift, and derived by the spiritual understanding, seems to constitute the ordinances of the Christian church, and so there are rules given for the choice of fit persons to fill the different offices (James iii. 1, 2; 1 Tim. iii.; Titus i. 5-9), which rules commend themselves to the conscience. Matt. xx. 20-23 seems to belong to this same principle.

" According to the law of Moses, which was the dispensation of angels or messengers, the lineal descendant of Aaron was the high priest, and the other priests were likewise determined by the rule of *blood*, and the people were called on to recognise them as such, whether they recognised the Spirit of God in them or not, for it was not God's Spirit in them, but God's authority appointing them, which constituted their ordination, and it was the duty of the Jews to acknowledge this ordination, and the blessing of God doubtless rewarded obedience. This system of ordination formed a part of the *patterns of the heavenly things* as much as the nailing together the curtains. It was all made *from the outside ;* it was like a tree made by a carpenter. But this was only the *pattern* of the Christian church, the true heavenly thing. In Christianity the outward form is to grow *from the inside.* The one Spirit in the body is that out of which the order of the body proceeds, and that one

Spirit acts through the renewed will and understanding of
men, so that the order proceeds according to light and discernment consciously felt through the body, which is composed of the children of light. The ordination in the
Christian church is one with the ordination of Christ
Himself, who was raised to the lordship of men and the
lordship of the universe, not in virtue of an arbitrary
appointment like Aaron, but because He was *essentially*
qualified for them. He was *in fact* so much better than
the angels (the ordinances of the Mosaic dispensation), as
He hath by inheritance obtained a more excellent name
than they. This dignity was not conventional, neither
were His priesthood or sacrifice; they were all verities and
realities in the eternal nature of things, and the ordination
of the various members of His body is as much a verity and
reality, being the varied manifestation of his Spirit actually
in the members, and recognised by the other members in
the divine light of which they are partakers.

"The appointment of a man to an office in the church,
by an utterance of the Spirit, and not by a discernment
of his gift, seems to me to be a departure from the principle of the Scripture quoted above, and also from the
whole meaning of the dispensation of God manifested in
the flesh, which calls man to be a partaker of God's light,
and not merely to be obedient to a voice, though attested
as His. The true oneness of the Body arises from and
consists in the oneness of the Spirit, that is in each member
having the Spirit of Christ consciously, and thus being
bound to all the rest in the oneness of life, as well as of
love. It cannot consist in any *putting together of parts.*
And the one life which circulates through the body from
Jesus the head and heart, carries light and strength to
each member, which will be consciously recognised as the
light and strength of Jesus although passing through other

members to them.   As in the natural body, it is not that
the eye sees a thing and tells it to the other members, but
light is consciously let into the body through the eye ; the
other members use the eye for this end, and the ordinance
of the eye in like manner consists in its *real gift* and not
in *an office.*

"God manifested in flesh is the definition of the church,
and *in this* the ordinances of the church differ from the
ordinances of the world.   I may have had a bad father
and a bad magistrate, but still they are God's ordinances
to me, though He is not manifested in them, and I shall
find His righteousness in their unrighteousness.   But I
cannot admit the ordinance of a teacher *in the church*
when God is not manifested *in him,* when I do not consciously meet God *in him* teaching me.   It is not enough
that I know him to be of God's appointment to tell me
things from God,—that is returning to the dispensation of
angels ; the dispensation of the Son has this in its character,
'they shall be all taught of God,' not taught by one commissioned by God, but *by God.*   'My sheep know me, *as* I
know the Father,'—*in the same way of knowledge,* by mutual
understanding, ' I count you no more servants, but friends,
for the servant knoweth not what his lord doeth,' he only
receiveth his orders.

" I feel the sin and the misery of Individuality, and I
have received the truth of Christ in our flesh as the gift of
the one heart of God to the whole human race, which would
bless men by uniting them all in God.   I feel also the
blessing of mutual dependence in exercising true love and
humility, whilst we receive out of God through the channel
of the brethren.   But when we see and feel selfish individuality and want of love and humility, where is the
remedy? Surely in the Spirit, and not in the putting together
of things without the Spirit.   Surely the way to invite back

the grieved Spirit of our God is to take no step without Him, and to cease our resistance of Him. When the Holy Spirit first fell on the Gentiles in the house of Cornelius, Peter simply declared Jesus to them. He did not speak a single word about framework. The same in the history of the pouring out of the Spirit on the Ephesian disciples (Acts xix.) Their receiving Jesus as *their* Lord was their preparation for the baptism of the Holy Ghost. In fact, what is the true receiving of Jesus but the receiving of the baptism of the Holy Ghost? I feel that what I have written here about a church is substantially true according to the Scriptures, and according to the spirit of the dispensation of Christ, and inasmuch as I find Mr. Irving and the church in London going on directly opposite principles, I cannot but consider them as going in opposition to the revealed will of God. The whole ceremony of their church is founded on utterances in the Spirit. The office-bearers and movements of the church, and their interpretation of Scripture, have all this same authority, are all delivered in this way. This is not according to the dispensation of God manifest in the flesh, as far as I can understand it. The utterances might as well come out of a cloud as out of human lips. God manifest in flesh is God's mind consciously and willingly received into the soul of a man, and so making the man partaker of God's nature, and the confidant of God's plans. Faith cometh by hearing, even hearing *that word which is nigh* us, in our mouth and hearts (Rom. x. 17, 18). It doth not come by hearing an outward voice, without that attestation. But they also deny that a man can know the mind of God out of *their* church, or that he can meet with Jesus or know His light out of their church. I know that is not true, and if it were true, no man could enter their church in God's light; he would be obliged to take that step at a venture.

"Their ordinances are all from the outside, not from the inside, and they (the ordained persons) are considered to receive the word from God, and to deliver it to the people on the credit and ground of their ordination, so that the people are not taught by God, but by God's commissioned and attested agent. This does indeed appear to me an establishing of the dispensation of angels and a fixing of the veil on the heart when Jesus is read. I cannot understand a oneness such as this is, consisting in *submission* to ordinances, and not in standing in the common light of God concerning all things, compared to the oneness between the Father and the Son.

"I do not like to speak about the baptism of the Holy Ghost, but I believe it to be much connected with the superiority of the dispensation of God manifest in the flesh over the dispensation of angels.

"It may be asked, How can an individual Christian constitute a church ? can a single stone constitute a temple ? But an individual Christian stands in a different position to a church from that in which a single stone stands to a temple. The single stone contains nothing of the architectural harmony and beauty of the temple, whilst the individual Christian contains in a *measure* all that is in the church. An individual Christian is to a church that which the first shoot of an acorn is to a full-grown oak. He has in him, in a measure, the love and the knowledge, and the watchfulness and the zeal of the pastor and elder, and prophet and evangelist. In this respect the comparison of natural and dead things, spiritual and living things, falls short of a true resemblance."

EXTRACTS FROM "THE DOCTRINE OF ELECTION," ETC.

"My object in this treatise is to set forth, as distinctly and simply as I can, the grounds on which I have come to the conclusion, that the doctrine of God's Election, as taught in the Bible, is altogether different from, and opposed to that which has passed under the name of the Doctrine of Election, and been received as such, by a great part of the professing church, through many ages."—P. 1.

" I held this doctrine for many years, modified, however inconsistently, by the belief of God's love to all, and of Christ having died for all—and yet, when I look back on the state of my mind during that period, I feel that it would be truer to say, I submitted to it, than that I believed it. I submitted to it, because I did not see how the language of the 9th chapter of the Epistle to the Romans, and of a few similar passages, could bear any other interpretation ; and yet I could not help feeling, that, on account of what appeared to be the meaning of these few difficult passages, I was giving up the plain and obvious meaning of all the rest of the Bible, which seems continually, in the most unequivocal language and in every page, to say to every man, 'See, I have set before thee this day life and good, death and evil, therefore choose life that thou mayest live.' I could not help feeling, that if the above representation were true, then that on which a real and righteous responsibility in man can alone be founded, was wanting, and the slothful servant had reason when, in vindication of his unprofitableness, he said, 'I knew thee, that thou art an hard man, reaping where thou hast not sown, and gathering where thou hast not strawed.' Above all, I could not help feeling that if God were such as that doctrine

described Him, then the Creator of every man was not the
friend of every man, nor the righteous object of confidence
to every man ; and that when Christ was preached to sinners, the whole truth of God was not preached to them, for
that there was something behind Christ in the mind of God,
giving Him to one, and withholding Him from another, so
that the ministry of reconciliation was only an appendix
to a deeper and more dominant ministry, in which God
appeared simply as a Sovereign without any moral attribute,
and man was dealt with as a mere creature of necessity
without any real responsibility."—Pp. 3-5.

" Thus, besides his own individual personality, we see two
powers in every man—the one, the power of this world
and of its prince ; and the other, the power of the world to
come, and of its Prince.   These are the flesh and the spirit,
the seeds or principles of the first and second vessels.   The
man is not either the flesh or the spirit, he is separate from
both, but they are seeds sown in him, and his capacity of
acting is merely his capacity of choosing to which of these
two active principles he will yield himself up.   They are,
as it were, two cords attached to every heart, the one held
by the hand of Satan, the other held by the hand of God.
And they are continually drawing the heart in opposite
directions, the one towards the things of self, the other towards the things of God—the one being the reprobation,
and the other the election.   Thus man, in all his actings,
never has to originate anything ; he has only to follow
something already commenced within him ; he has only to
choose to which of these two powers he will join himself.
Here, then, I found that which I had approved in Calvinism, and which I required as an element of every explanation of the doctrine which should be set up in opposition
to Calvinism, namely, a recognition that there is no self-
quickening power in man, and that there is no good in man

but what is of the direct acting of the Spirit of God."
—Pp. 58-9.

" When we see the two natures, of flesh and spirit, so in
every man that he may join himself to either of them, and
thus become either reprobate or elect, we see the root of
the doctrine of election. And when we see rightly the gift
of Christ, we shall see that as He is the true light which
lighteth every man, so also there is in Him a communication of life to every man. For 'in him was life, and the
life was the light of men;' and thus the light which lighteth every man is a living light—a light whereby he may
live. And thus by the entrance of the word into our flesh,
not only has God been brought near to us, as an object of
trust and love, but also His living Spirit, the divine nature,
has been communicated to us subjectively as a capacity of
embracing God, whether we exercise it or not. . . . The
whole responsibility of man consists in his power to recognise and follow this inward drawing of God, or to reject it,
according to his own personal choosing."—P. 61.

" Let me not be misunderstood, as if I said either that
man can, in his own strength, turn to God, or of his own
origination would ever desire to do so,—but man, since the
gift of Christ, need not do anything in his own strength.
The strength of God is communicated to him, in the seed
of the word sown in his heart, so that he may take hold of
it, and walk with God; and it is only by his own wilful
refusal to use that strength that he is without it. Conversion is, indeed, man's first step in the spiritual life, but he
never could have taken this step, nor could he ever rightly
have been commanded to take it, unless God had first taken
a step towards him. The Word who was with God, and
was God, and in whom there is life, hath come into man's
nature—into the whole mass of the nature,—as a fountain
of life, to quicken every man, and as a living cord, to draw

man up to God. And shall we now speak and reason about man, as if he were yet in the condition into which Adam's fall brought him, before the Word was given ; though now in Him, ' God is the Saviour of all men, specially of those who believe,' and in Him also ' the grace of God which bringeth salvation to all men hath appeared,' and ' where sin abounded, there hath grace much more abounded ' ? Most assuredly there is in Jesus Christ a *general* salvation for the whole race, inasmuch as in Him they are lifted again into that state of probation from which in Adam they had fallen, and are provided with spiritual strength to go through their probation, whether they use that strength or not : but none becomes *personally* a partaker of salvation, except by personally turning to God. And, in like manner, there is in Jesus Christ a general election for the whole race—inasmuch as, in Him, they are lifted out of that state of reprobation into which, in Adam, they had fallen ; but no one becomes personally elect except by his personally receiving Christ into his heart." —Pp. 141·3.

" With regard to the second head, namely, the importance of the outward Word, I am sensible that I have exposed myself to misapprehension, especially in those parts of the work where I have asserted the unprofitableness of the outward Word, in the case of persons who were not listening to the inward word. But the reader will understand me, if he carries along with him, that by this expression I mean to describe persons contenting themselves, and pacifying their consciences, either with the formal reading of the Bible, or with the mere understanding of its theology, but without seeking or finding spiritual communion with God in it. Whilst they continue thus to read it or study it, no one surely who knows what religion is, would consider it profitable to them. Yet even in their case, I could not

wish that they should give up the reading of the Bible.
They are at present without faith, but the Bible has an
intrinsic aptitude to produce faith. It contains, in the
largeness of its inspiration, a tally corresponding to everything in the hearts of all men, and a key to every variety
of their outward circumstances; and God is continually
preparing a way for it into their consciences, by the events
with which he is meeting them in His providence, making
them, through the discipline of these events, feel the truth
of what it testifies of the wickedness and desolateness of
the heart which is away from God, as well as the suitableness of its counsels and threatenings and consolations, to
their experience and condition. And as the Spirit of God
is ever bearing the same witness within them, although it
may be generally disregarded, the coincidence of these two
solemn voices, from within and from without, will sometimes strike like a knell upon them, and bring home to
them the feeling that the Searcher of hearts is dealing with
them, and that they are entangled in his net, and that there
can be no true deliverance for them, and no true abiding
rest for them, but in knowing Him, and in being of one
mind with Him. It is in the hope of such a result as this,
that I feel thankful to know that even those who are without faith are reading the Bible; for those who are in the
practice of reading it are more in the way of this operation
than those who read it not.

"And for this same reason, it appears desirable that there
should be books, proving the inspiration and authority of
the Bible, by all sorts of argument, notwithstanding the
danger there is of men mistaking their assent to a demonstration for that faith which saves the soul; because a man
who is really convinced that the Bible is a supernatural
book, is more likely to seek God in it, than one who regards
it as of at least doubtful origin."—Pp. 157-9.

"Thus every man has, in his present state of trial, three distinct wills within him, of which he is himself conscious, —first, the will of God striving with his conscience; second, the will of Satan or self ruling in his members; and third, the elective will, in his own personality, which determines with which of the other two wills he shall side. This last will, though it has this peculiar prerogative, is yet never itself the dominant will, it only chooses which of the other two shall be dominant."—P. 281.

"The conscience which God has given to every man is a much higher gift than either an outward or an inward oracle, such as we have been supposing. It is a capacity of entering into the reasons of God's actions and commandments, it is a capacity of a true spiritual union with Him; and thus when we meet the will of God in our consciences, we receive it in the way of participation, or as an infusion, so to speak,—whereas, when we meet it in an oracle simply, we receive it as an impulsion. That which does not enter by the conscience, but is merely put upon us, or conferred on us, can never really affect our nature,—it may elevate us as instruments in the hands of God, but it cannot elevate us into fellowship with God. And therefore the smallest conscious and sympathetic conformity to the will of God is a much higher thing than the being made the instrument of raising the dead, or declaring things to come. In the one case the nature is really elevated: in the other, it is only used for an elevated purpose."—Pp. 513-14.

"The Protestant does the same thing with regard to the doctrines of religion that the Papist does with regard to religion throughout. He relieves himself from the personal obligation of apprehending their truth in the light of his own conscience; he looks to the Bible as the Papist looks to the church, and he adopts whatever doctrines he thinks that he finds there, without feeling the obligation of personally seeing their truth in the light of his own conscience, before he is really entitled to call himself a believer of them. He thus substitutes outward authority, in the place of the light which is Life, although he condemns the Papist for doing that very thing."—Pp. 515-16.

"But when I say that we are not left to lean on any outward authority for our knowledge of God, and of His ways towards us, let no one think that I am putting aside the Bible as an authority; for my meaning is simply this, that although many most important truths are set before us in the Bible, which never would have entered our hearts, had they not been thus set before us; yet that being thus set before us, they are then only profitable to us, and even truly believed by us, when they awaken within us a corresponding form of our inward spiritual consciousness, so that we recognise them henceforth, as truths which we ourselves know to be truths, by conscious experience, and not merely on the outward authority of the Book.

"There are many facts in our intellectual experience quite analogous to this, which might be used to illustrate it. Thus, a man may be perfectly incapable of making any advance in mathematical science by his own original and unassisted efforts,—and yet if Euclid be put into his hands, he may find himself quite able to follow and appreciate the reasoning, and thus to gain a very considerable acquaintance with the subject. His mind in consequence is filled with a new class of ideas, which he has acquired entirely from the reading of this book. And yet it is not on the authority of the book that he rests his conviction of the truth of any of the propositions contained in it, but on his own personal discernment of their truth. Indeed, we could not consider him to have entered in the slightest degree into their meaning, if we found him resting his belief of them on the authority of the book, or on any outward authority whatever. Nor indeed would we call such a belief a mathematical belief at all. And yet had not the book presented the truths outwardly to him, the inward intellec- tual types might have lain for ever dormant within him.

"In this case, we do not feel that we detract from the importance of the book, when we say that it is subordinate to the inward intellectual authority; that is, when we say that it is to be judged by that authority, and that no man can believe it rightly except by discerning its agreement with that authority within him; and that any other kind of belief is not a belief which suits the subject, because it is not a belief which discerns truth in the subject.

"And in the same way we do not detract from the import- ance or from the authority of the Bible, when we say that then only can its authority be rightly acknowledged by us, when we discern its agreement with the testimony of the spiritual witness within us, and that its great importance consists in awakening our consciousness to the presence and the instructions of that spiritual witness."—Pp. 523-26.

"Metaphysicians have disputed whether conscience is a simple faculty, or whether the impressions which we ascribe to it are produced by a combination of faculties. And if there be no higher nature in it than man's nature, it is of little consequence which of these opinions we adopt; because, on this hypothesis, our power of obeying its intimation, which is certainly the important point, could not be affected by the correctness or incorrectness of our opinion. But if the voice in our conscience is the indication of the actual presence of God within us, a knowledge that it is so is of immense importance to us; for thus we enter into the secret of God's love towards us, and of His purpose concern- ing us, that our hearts should be His temples, and that we should be one with Him, through Jesus Christ; and thus also we discover, that though in ourselves we are only ignorance and weakness, yet we have within our reach, and within the limits of our own nature, the infinite wisdom and infinite strength of God, to which we may unite ourselves, and we are thus encouraged to run with confidence the race that is set before us.

"Some of my readers may think that I have given too great a place throughout the whole book to·the subject of conscience; but in this I have acted from the conviction that neither the doctrine of Election, nor any other doctrine, can be rightly understood except through the doctrine of conscience."—P. 544-46.

The following Note is appended to the Treatise on Election :—

" In two former publications of mine, the one entitled, a Tract on the Gifts of the Spirit,—the other, the Brazen Serpent,—I have expressed my conviction, that the remarkable manifestations which I witnessed in certain individuals in the West of Scotland, about eight years ago, were the miraculous gifts of the Spirit, of the same character as those of which we read in the New Testament. Since then, however, I have come to think differently, and I do not now believe that they were so.

" But I still continue to think, that to any one whose expectations are formed by, and founded on, the declarations of the New Testament, the disappearance of those gifts from the church must be a greater difficulty than their re-appearance could possibly be.

"I think it but just to add, that though I no longer believe that those manifestations were the gifts of the Spirit, my doubts as to their nature have not at all arisen from any discovery, or even suspicion, of imposture in the individuals in whom they have appeared. On the contrary, I can bear

testimony that I have not often in the course of my life
met with men more marked by native simplicity and truth
of character, as well as by godliness, than James and George
M'Donald, the two first in whom I witnessed those
manifestations.

"Both these men are now dead, and they continued, I
know, to their dying hour, in the confident belief that the
work in them was of the Holy Ghost. I mention this for
the information of the reader, who may feel interested in
their history, although it is a fact which does not influence
my own conviction on the subject.

"To some it may appear as if I were assuming an importance to myself, by publishing my change of opinion; but I
am in truth only clearing my conscience, which requires
me thus publicly to withdraw a testimony which I had
publicly given, when I no longer believe it myself."

With reference to this Note, Mr. Duncan of Parkhill,
Arbroath—who was a chosen associate and friend of
Mr. Erskine all through the period to which it refers—in
a letter dated December 30th, 1876, says, "Looking into
the Memorial of the Macdonalds brings many things
vividly before me. Norton says they were gentlemanly
men, which is most true; and what he says of George's
face shining as you can believe Stephen's did, I once saw,
when he was speaking in that power, when we were quite
alone on the hill above Port-Glasgow, when I had made a
remark on the beauty of the sun setting on the Clyde, and
he broke out about the new heavens and the new earth.
I could never agree with what Mr. Erskine said in his
note, although I doubt not that their own spirits came in
at times. From conversations with Mr. Erskine I am
satisfied that he would have been glad that he had not
said so much as he did say."

Letters from MM. Gaussen and Adolphe Monod.

The two following letters are on the same sheet of paper :—

"Les Grottes, *Mercredi*, 1 *Oct.* 1834.

"Mon cher Frère,—Ayant eu la douceur de posséder quelques jours Adolphe Monod sous mon toit, j'ai désiré que deux amis qui aiment tant à reporter sur vous leurs conversations ne séparassent pas sans s'être eux-mêmes rappelés à vos prières et aux souvenirs de votre amitié chrétienne. (Il part demain matin.) Quant à moi, je puis vous dire combien souvent mes pensées me ramènent aux momens que j'ai passés avec vous depuis notre première prière à Royal Circus jusqu'à celle de notre séparation le 17 de Novembre dans l'hôtel de Glasgow. Je désire que tous ces souvenirs aussi se résolvent en prières et en actions de grâces devant Celui qui a prié pour nous le front contre terre. Je ne saurais vous exprimer, cher ami, avec quelle joie fraternelle j'ai ouï dire que votre foi était devenue plus simple, et que votre conversation, toujours pleine de sentiment, se reportait sur l'ensemble des vérités et des espérances de la foi, sans vous laisser aller à des présomptions qui en isolent quelques unes. Vous pourrez faire beaucoup de bien quand, avec les dons qui vous ont été confiés, vous vous attacherez humblement à développer l'une après l'autre les sentences du Saint Esprit, telles qu'elles se présenteront sous vos mains dans la Sainte Écriture, et sans vous embarrasser d'y établir ou d'y confirmer des systêmes.

"Cher frère, je me sens uni à vous par des liens indestructibles, parceque je les sens rattachés à Celui qui est la tête toujours vivante de son Corps, à Celui qui était, qui est, et

qui sera.   Votre nom revient souvent sur mes lèvres
devant Dieu et devant les hommes, et cette saison rappelle
plus souvent mes pensées sur les souvenirs de l'automne
1832.   J'aime à penser avec reconnaissance à votre accueil,
non pas même tant à cause de ce qu'il eut d'affectueux,
qu'en memoire de ce que j'y trouvai d'édifiant.   Que le
Seigneur vous multiplie ses consolations, et vous gouverne
toujours plus par son Esprit !   Adieu en Lui.   Quand je
prie pour vous, j'y joins votre mère.   Vous apprendrez
avec intérêt que la mienne est en bonne santé, et que son
âme est bénie.   Merle est malade de la poitrine ; priez
pour lui et pour nous.   Je lui ai fait lire les deux lettres
que j'ai reçues de vous et ou vous parlez des doctrines :
j'aurais voulu qu'il vous écrivît.   Marc Vernet part demain
pour l'Italie avec son père et Anna.   Madame de Staël et
sa belle sœur sont à Coppet.   Nous avons plus d'une fois
élevé notre voix en prière dans cette famille pour Madame
Erskine et pour vous dans le tems de la maladie de ——
Elisabeth.   Recommandez-moi au souvenir chrétien de
Scott, de Madame Rich, de Capitaine Stirling, et de vos
parents à Glentyan.   Adieu encore.   Demandez pour moi
la sanctification.—V. affectionné,   L. GAUSSEN."

"AUX GROTTES, 1er *Octobre* 1834.

"BIEN CHER FRÈRE,—Il m'est doux de me joindre à un
frère aussi aimé que Gaussen pour écrire à un frère aussi
aimé que vous.   C'est par vous et par lui, plus que par
aucun autre homme, je crois, que sous la bénédiction d'en
haut j'ai été amené des ténèbres à la lumière, et de
l'angoisse à la paix.   Que le seigneur vous rende au double
le bien que vous m'avez fait de sa part !   J'ai reçu dans le
temps la lettre que vous avez eu la bonté de m'écrire en
réponse à la mienne.   Je recommande encore à vous, et
par vous à vos amis, l'œuvre que le Seigneur a commencée

à Lyon, et qui s'y continue avec un succès, non éclatant, mais solide et croissant, autant que j'en puis juger—plus spécialement en ce qui concerne les catholiques ; et s'ils ne peuvent l'aider par leurs dons, qu'ils l'aident par leurs prières, et combattent le bon combat avec les pauvres de Lyon. Que le Seigneur vous bénisse dans vos voies, bien aimé frère, qu'il se glorifie en vous ! qu'il vous garde de toute erreur, qu'il vous en retire pour sa gloire en vous et par vous. Je fais pour vous du fond du cœur, et vous prie de faire pour moi, la prière de Paul, 1 Thess. v. 23, 24. Saluez pour moi, dans le Seigneur, toute votre maison. Ma famille, ma femme, mes trois enfans, dont le dernier, né le 29 Août dernier, est un fils, sont bien. Gaussen vous aura peutêtre entretenu de l'objet de mon voyage à Genève. Priez le Seigneur de me conduire, en sa lumière et en sa paix. Que la paix soit avec vous.—Votre tendrement affectionné et reconnaissant frère,

"ADOLPHE MONOD.

"*P.S.*—Je ne puis trouver, en particulier, votre doctrine du pardon universel dans l'Écriture *lue avec l'esprit du petit enfant*, Jean iii. 36. Mais que le Seigneur nous éclaire les uns et les autres lui seul ; et nous donner de ne pas juger, mais de nous aimer !"

No. XII.—Page 355.

VINET AND SAINTE-BEUVE.

"IL n'était point rare que des étrangers de distinction, en séjour ou en passage à Lausanne, souvent attirés par la renommée de Vinet, vinssent ajouter à l'éclat modeste et au charme de ces réunions cordiales. Un de ceux qu'on y vit le plus souvent fut l'Écossais Erskine, qui avait une

manière si originale et en même temps si profonde de
comprendre le christianisme. 'Il est grandement héré-
tique, dit-on, écrivait Vinet ; mais c'est un bien bon
chrétien.'[1] Il n'avait rien dans l'esprit d'agressif, rien
qui appellât la discussion ; sa conversation était sérieuse
sans raideur, nourrie de faits et d'aperçus, et il était rare
qu'on le quittât sans être riche de quelque idée nouvelle.
Quand il reprit le chemin de l'Écosse, en 1839, après un
séjour de plusieurs mois à Lausanne, Vinet et lui étaient
amis pour la vie."—*Alexandre Vinet, Histoire de sa Vie et
ses Ouvrages*, par E. Rambert (Troisième Edition ; Lausanne, 1876), tome second, p. 45.

Speaking of Bourdaloue and Vinet, Sainte-Beuve
says :—

"'Je lui ai dû, pour mon compte, une des plus vives et
des plus sérieuses impressions que j'aie éprouvées, et que
ce nom de Bourdaloue réveille en moi. Il y a neuf ans
(juin 1839), je revenais de Rome,—de Rome qui était
encore ce qu'elle aurait dû toujours être pour rester dans
nos imaginations la ville éternelle, la ville du monde catho-
lique et des tombeaux. J'avais vu dans une splendeur
inusitée cette reine superbe : Saint-Pierre m'avait apparu
avec un surcroît de baldaquins et d'or, avec de magnifiques
tentures et des tableaux où figuraient les miracles d'un
certain nombre de nouveaux saints qu'on venait de
canoniser. J'avais admiré surtout, d'un des balcons du
Vatican, les horizons lointains d'Albano, vers quatre heures
du soir. En présence de l'Apollon du Belvédère, j'avais vu
notre guide, l'excellent sculpteur Fogelberg, qui le visitait
presque chaque jour depuis vingt ans, laisser échapper une
larme ; et cette larme de l'artiste m'avait paru, à moi, plus
belle que l'Apollon lui-même. Un bateau à vapeur me

[1] Lettre à Mdlle. Elise Vinet, du 10 novembre 1839.

transporta en deux jours de Civita-Vecchia à Marseille, et
de là je courus à Lausanne, où j'étais six jours après avoir
quitté Rome. Le lendemain de mon arrivée, au matin,
j'allai à la classe de M. Vinet pour l'entendre,—une pauvre
classe de collége, toute nue, avec de simples murs blanchis
et des pupitres de bois.—Il y parlait de Bourdaloue et de
La Bruyère. L'Ecossais Erskine (le même qu'a traduit la
duchesse de Broglie) était présent comme moi. J'entendis
là une leçon pénétrante, élevée, une éloquence de réflexion
et de conscience. Dans un langage fin et serré, grave à la
fois et intérieurement ému, l'âme morale ouvrait ses trésors.
Quelle impression profonde, intime, toute chrétienne, d'un
christianisme tout réel et spirituel ! Quel contraste au
sortir des pompes du Vatican, à moins de huit jours de
distance ! Jamais je n'ai goûté autant la sobre et pure
jouissance de l'esprit, et je n'ai eu plus vif le sentiment
moral de la pensée.'—*Derniers Portraits*, pag. 495."—*Ibid.*
pp. 208, 209.

Writings of Mr. Erskine published during his Lifetime, with Dates of Publication.

I. REMARKS ON THE INTERNAL EVIDENCE FOR THE TRUTH OF REVEALED RELIGION.

Edinburgh, Waugh and Innes, 1820.
Fourth Edition, 1821.
Ninth Edition, 1829.

Translated into French by the Duchess de Broglie, and published in Paris, 1822, under the title "Réflexions sur l'Évidence Intrinsèque de la Vérité du Christianisme."

Translated into German, and published at Leipzig, 1825, under the title "Bemerkungen über die Inneren Gründe der Wahrheit der Geoffenbarten Religion."

II. AN ESSAY ON FAITH.

Edinburgh, Waugh and Innes, 1822.
Fifth Edition, 1829.

Translated into French, 1826, and published at Paris under the title "Essai sur La Foi."

III. THE UNCONDITIONAL FREENESS OF THE GOSPEL.

Edinburgh, Waugh and Innes, 1828.
Fourth Edition, 1831.
New Edition, 1873.

Translated into French under the title "La Pleine Gratuité du Pardon," and published at Lausanne, 1874.

IV. THE BRAZEN SERPENT, OR LIFE COMING THROUGH DEATH.

Edinburgh, 1831.
London, Whittaker, 1846.

V. THE DOCTRINE OF ELECTION, AND ITS CONNECTION WITH THE GENERAL THEORY OF CHRISTIANITY, ILLUSTRATED FROM MANY PARTS OF SCRIPTURE, AND ESPECIALLY FROM THE EPISTLE TO THE ROMANS.

London, James Duncan, 1837.

VI. THE GIFTS OF THE HOLY SPIRIT.

Greenock, R. B. Lusk, 1830.

VII. INTRODUCTORY ESSAY TO EXTRACTS OF LETTERS TO A CHRISTIAN FRIEND.

Greenock, R. B. Lusk, 1830.

VIII. INTRODUCTORY ESSAY TO THE WORKS OF THE REV. JOHN GAMBOLD, A.M.

Collins' Select Christian Authors; Glasgow, 1822.

IX. INTRODUCTORY ESSAY TO THE SAINTS' EVERLASTING REST.

Collins' Select Christian Authors; Glasgow, 1824.

X. INTRODUCTORY ESSAY TO THE LETTERS OF SAMUEL RUTHERFORD.

Collins' Select Christian Authors; Glasgow, 1825.

Edinburgh University Press:

T. AND A. CONSTABLE, PRINTERS TO HER MAJESTY.